The Lovers and the Dustman

by
Lynn Bushell

Copyright © 2021 by Lynn Bushell
All rights reserved.

Lynn Bushell studied Art History and Philosophy at Edinburgh University and Fine Art at Edinburgh College of Art. She divides her time between her home in Suffolk and the west coast of the Normandy Peninsula, which is the source for most of her paintings.

'The Lovers and the Dustman' is her fourth novel.

Website: www.lynnbushellart.co.uk.

Also by Lynn Bushell

Remember Me
Schopenhauer's Porcupines
Painted Ladies

For Pippa

Table of Contents

Prologue 1

Part One 7

Part Two 117

Part Three 191

Part Four 271

Part Five 367

Part Six 467

Part Seven 551

Part Eight 577

Part Nine 621

Epilogue 667

Prologue
Cookham 1935

'It's no good. Please stop, Stanley, I can't bear it.'

There's a pause before his head appears over the blanket. He looks like a schoolboy who's been told he hasn't done well in a test he thought he'd sail through. 'Hilda liked me touching her. She told me it was wonderful.'

'Well I don't think it's wonderful. It makes me want to gag. The whole thing is revolting.'

'Don't say that, Patricia. You don't mean it.' He shifts his weight, hoiking himself up onto his elbow. His head's level with my knees now. 'It was your suggestion,' he says, with a hint of petulance.

'Don't give me that. You've been on at me endlessly to go to bed with you. You've worn me down. All I said was that I would be prepared to try it. Ouch, you're leaning on my foot.'

'You're so beautiful. I want to stroke you.'

His hand creeps towards my leg. There's paint under his nails and I can feel the hard skin on his finger-tips. I wish he wouldn't keep his vest on when he takes his trousers off. The dark hairs on his chest curl over it. The vest reminds me of those sheets that market gardeners put over their gooseberry bushes to keep off the greenfly.

'Please don't do that, Stanley. I've just told you I don't like it.' He pulls back his fingers in a claw. 'Why is it so important that we do this anyway?'

'It's what God wants.'

I snort. 'I've never heard that argument before.'

He sits up cross-legged and the bed-springs sag. It's one of those wrought-iron affairs that Stanley brought back from a scrapyard. Judging by the state of it, the mattress was still on it. Stanley's studio is not a place you'd want to spend much time in. It's a corrugated iron shed with a clapped-out stove releasing dust and toxic fumes into the air, a naked light bulb hanging from the ceiling and a rug that covers half the floor but is so worn there is no longer any pattern on it. By the easel is a trestle table with a palette, screwed up balls of paper, jam jars - one of which appears to still have jam in it - and a stale loaf of bread which has been hacked at with a blunt knife, spewing crumbs onto the floor-boards. And this is a man who owns a house on three floors with a tennis court.

'Why don't we try the other way around? Or I could come up to the top end.'

'Will you listen to me, Stanley. Changing ends is not what it's about.' I edge my way across the mattress till my back comes up against the rail.

He reaches for his glasses, carefully unfolding one arm then the other and adjusting them across his nose. His eyes are magnified and look as if they're too big for his face. They're Stanley's most endearing feature but there's nothing at this moment that I find endearing about Stanley.

'But you do believe we're meant to be together?' The eyes flicker back and forth across my face.

'You're married, Stanley. You have children. Don't you think all this is rather tasteless in the circumstances?'

'Hilda understands. We're soul-mates.' He starts playing with his toes, the way that babies do when they're not sure if they belong to them or not. 'I hadn't even kissed another woman when I married her.'

'But you were over thirty!'

'I did think about it. Actually, I thought about it all the time.' The look in Stanley's eyes suggests the memory has lost none of its rich store of questionable detail. 'But I was afraid lust would contaminate my vision. Then I found it was my vision. I was up in heaven. But things haven't been so good between us lately. She won't let me come inside her.'

'I don't think you should be telling me this, Stanley.'

'She's not prudish. I don't want you thinking that. But she's so caught up with these Christian Scientists. They're joyless. They don't think sex is important, but it is. It's vital to our spiritual transformation.'

'You think when cows mate it turns them into something else? They're still cows, Stanley.'

'If you've watched dogs rutting, you can tell they're tapping into something more themselves. I've seen it on their faces.'

'God above.' I nudge my feet across the mattress and reach for my underwear. 'I need to get back. Dorothy's expecting me.' I pull the nylon shift on. 'I don't want you telling anyone what's happened here this afternoon, is that clear?'

Stanley's looking at my legs again. I used to like it when men told me I had good legs, but somehow whatever Stanley does has a forensic quality about it.

'Nice,' he says. His fingers hover in the air. 'We'll still be joyful, won't we?'

He is sitting with his penis overlapping one thigh. It's the same pose he adopted for his painting of the two of us. It's propped against the wall as if it's there to mock us. I've forbidden Stanley to exhibit it. It's bad enough to listen to the gossip without adding evidence to back it up. This isn't how I had imagined myself going down in history.

'Joyful?' I say. 'Yes, why not?'

***

Part One
1929
Temptation

I

I'd met Stanley for the first time on a January afternoon in 1929 when he and Hilda came into 'The Copper Kettle'. I'd been filling in for Ida Buckpitt. There was no one in the café and I'd gone into the kitchen for a cigarette. The door onto the street blew open and there was a belch as it was sucked back. It was one of those bleak winter days when there's a constant drizzle in the air and anybody caught outside is desperate for a place to shelter and get warm.

I saw them making for a corner table. Hilda looked exhausted. As she took her coat off, I could see a dark stain on her dress over her right breast. Stanley had a baby tucked under his arm. He had been talking nineteen to the dozen in a curiously high-pitched voice, the baby bouncing up and down against his hip. He paused, then reached across and curled his hand around her breast and rubbed his thumb across the nipple.

I barged through the door into the café, letting it slam after me. I'm capable of throwing people out, though Ida has a crisis every time I do. I say she doesn't need these people and she tells me that she does. How sad is that, if you're dependent for your livelihood on somebody who fondles women's breasts in public.

'What can I get you?'

Neither of them seemed embarrassed that I might have seen them. If I hadn't been there when he did it, I'd have put him at no more than sixteen. The brown suit he had on could have come from that cut-price department store in Maidenhead and although he was not bad-looking, what you noticed was the pudding basin haircut which had never been in fashion even in this God-forsaken outpost of the Empire.

He pulled out a chair and plonked the baby on it like a bag of shopping.

'We'll have steak pie, please.' He hadn't asked me for the menu which meant they'd been in before and Ida knew them.

'Yes sir. What about the baby?'

'What about the baby, Hilda?' he said, and she shrugged.

'No steak pie for the baby, thank you.' He gave me the sort of smile that seems to let you in on something, but you're not sure what. I took my notebook out.

'Steak pie for two, then.' I said.

Later, when I got home and told Dorothy about them, I left out the bit about him fondling Hilda's breasts.

I watched them from behind the door into the kitchen whilst they ate. He took one of the paper serviettes I'd given them and started drawing on it with his free hand, waving it in front of Hilda every now and then for her approval. Suddenly it struck me where I'd seen his face before. He had been featured in the local paper some months earlier, with pictures of a chapel he was decorating for a woman who had lost her brother in The Great War.

'I've seen your work in the papers,' I said when they'd finished and I'd gone in to collect the plates. He turned to look at me. I had already clocked that this was somebody who liked to talk about themselves.

It turned out Hilda was an artist too, so I explained that Dorothy and I had both been to the 'Slade', like them. He mentioned several painters, none of whom I knew, but as they left he said 'You'll have to come and see the chapel I've been working on.'

When Stanley said *You have to*, that is what he meant. There was no *Would you care to...* or *One day you might...* His work took precedence over whatever anybody else was doing and it was assumed that anyone allowed to see it would feel privileged. 'Why don't you come on Sunday,' he'd said, gaily, as they left.

I watched them making their way back along the High Street in the rain. They made an odd pair. Hilda, several inches taller, walked ahead with long, slow strides, whilst Stanley trotted after her, side-stepping to avoid pedestrians, his arms still flailing in the air. I went on looking until they were out of sight.

II

'Have we got anything arranged for Sunday?' I had said to Dorothy. It's rare for either of us to be doing anything, whatever day it is, so I'd decided it would be a good way in.

When she discovered what I had in mind, she came up with the usual objections. She prefers to make it look as if she's giving things some thought, but in the end she usually says no. Dorothy hates meeting people.

'I don't think so, darling. Burghclere is a long way.'

'It's not that far. I thought you'd be interested to see the paintings. He's spent four years working on them.'

'He's invited both of us?'

'Of course. I wouldn't go without you.'

'What have you told him?'

'I said we'd been students at the Slade, like them, and that we'd lived in Paris.'

'Dear me, are you sure you haven't made us sound impossibly glamorous?'

'They're not the sort of people who would be impressed. They aren't at all stuck up.'

'Well, after all, he's not that well-known.' Dorothy was wishing that she hadn't been so quick to recognise the name. She'd heard of him, of course. We'd seen his father wandering through the churchyard in a bowler hat and dressing gown, the sort of thing you'd be locked up for in a city but which you could get away with in a village where the residents were nearly all related one way or another.

She went over to the window and pretended to be busy scooping up the fallen petals from the fuchsia on the sill. The kitchen window at 'Moor Thatch' looked out onto the garden with a grassy slope behind it leading up to Cockmarsh Hill. The hill, which was an ancient barrow mound, curved down towards the river on the other side. Because we liked to look at it, we spent our daylight hours in the kitchen unless Dorothy was working in her studio. The table was piled high with books.

She tipped the handful of dried petals in the bin we kept for compost. The lid gave an irritating little click as it came down. She gave her hands a brisk shake to suggest the end of her participation in the conversation.

'I called at the library on my way home to see what they had on him,' I said, determined not to back down till I'd had my say. 'He's got a painting in The Tate of Cookham churchyard. There are people from the village rising from their graves to look at what's been written on their headstones.' I paused and then went on as if I had just remembered. 'Stanley's painted himself lying on a tombstone in the same suit he was wearing when he came into The Copper Kettle. It's like seeing someone in a film and finding yourself sitting on the bus beside them on the way home.'

Dorothy laughed grudgingly. 'You're star-struck, sweetheart. Get a grip.'

I started picking at a loose thread in my stocking. If I wore it on the other leg the next day, I might get away with it, although I'd noticed ladders always worked their way round to the front.

'This place is so dull. I'm stagnating, Dorothy. I sometimes feel as if I'm waiting for my life to start.'

'At your age isn't that a trifle optimistic?'

'England's such a dreary country to be poor in. Wouldn't it be nice to meet some interesting people?'

She began to speak and then thought better of it. She was wondering whether this was one of those occasions when she ought to give in gracefully. She came back to the table and picked up the plates and cups left there from tea.

'Whatever you say, sweetie.'

III

Burghclere turned out to be farther than I'd thought and although Stanley hadn't specified a time, it was already after midday when we got there. From outside, the chapel - a rectangular brick building with three long glass windows dropping down onto a solid, heavy oak door - seemed to have been purposely designed to put off visitors.

'It's like a crematorium,' said Dorothy, dismissively. A glint of sunshine on the red brick and the apple trees that flanked the path went some way to dispelling the unsympathetic first impression.

Other than a woman's bicycle propped up against the wall, there was no sign of anybody else's presence, but the door was open. I will usually only go to exhibitions if I get an invitation to the private view where I can get a drink, but Dorothy prefers to go when no one else is there.

She gaped when she saw what was on the walls. Inside, the building was a cross between a gallery and a cathedral. On the end wall, partly hidden by three rows of scaffolding with steps between them, was a floor to ceiling painting of dead soldiers rising from their graves, uprooting dozens of white crosses as they clawed their way up through the mud. I was amazed that somebody as small as Stanley could conceive of anything on such a monumental scale.

Along the side walls, painted in the muted reds and browns that seemed to have been borrowed from the wooden ceiling, men were lugging tea urns, scrubbing floors and sorting laundry into piles. A soldier suffering from frostbite had his feet scraped by an orderly. Another kept his foot warm over a hot water bottle.

A Bach Cello suite was playing in the background. As the record faded out, a needle skittered on the vinyl.

'What ho!' came a voice from overhead. We looked up and saw Stanley waving to us from behind the wire on the top-most level of the scaffolding. He started to climb down the ladder, his hands not quite in co-ordination with his feet so that occasionally he missed a rung. There was a sharp intake of breath from Dorothy.

Once on the ground, he smiled at me and turned to her. 'Is this your sister?'

Dorothy sighed imperceptibly. I sometimes tell people we're sisters in the hope of staving off inevitable gossip, though I can't pretend it's worked well so far. When we lived in Paris almost everyone we knew was queer; there wasn't any need to be discreet. We've been at pains to keep our heads down since we came to Cookham, though as Dorothy remarked it's odd that villages where incest is accepted as a necessary means of furthering the population should take issue with a pair of harmless lesbians.

'Your paintings are remarkable,' she said, to fend off further questions. 'What a privilege to see the work in progress. Thank you.'

Stanley rubbed his hands together and then crooked his elbows out, inviting us to take an arm each. 'Let me show you round.'

We took up our positions either side of him. He walked with little jerky movements, like a puppet when the strings have snagged. I'd once heard Dorothy described as being 'like a barn door'. I am tall and willowy and Stanley was at least four inches shorter than me, so there must have been a hint of the burlesque about the three of us as we stepped out.

One of the paintings in the arches showed a lorry load of wounded soldiers pulling up outside a pair of iron gates. 'That was Beaufort Hospital,' said Stanley. 'There weren't any gates. I added those because I wanted to suggest the soldiers were arriving at the Gates of Heaven. I took the Scrovegni Chapel as a model', he said, and then added as an afterthought, in case we hadn't paid our lecturers enough attention at the Slade, 'Giotto.'

Dorothy looked sideways at me and I pressed my lips together. Dorothy and I have been to the Scrovegni Chapel. I was waiting for her usual barbed comment - Dorothy is always on the look-out for pretentiousness - but then she turned towards the nearest painting, pointing to an orderly who lay flat out, a mop in one hand. 'That's not how I'd scrub a floor,' she said.

'He was a mental patient,' Stanley said. 'He used to drop the mop and make slow circles with it on the floor.' He mimicked the hypnotic sweeps. 'The awful thing about the Army was that everything was so quick. There was never any opportunity for contemplation. That was how he managed to get something out of it, you see?'

'And do you see the sacking that he's kneeling on as like a prayer-mat?'

Stanley peered at Dorothy as if she'd just said something so profound he needed more time to digest it. 'That's exactly how I see it,' he said.

He'd already stopped addressing his remarks to me, although I'd noticed that he acted as if there were several hundred people hanging on his every word. I'm used to artists and their egos - after all, I am one - but it was already clear that Stanley's ego fell into a category of its own.

He stretched his hand out to the figure in the painting, as if saying *There, what did I tell you* and gave a disarming little giggle. He turned. 'I remember one man in the hospital who never spoke unless he heard a dog bark and then he would tell us someone had just thrown themselves off Clifton Bridge.'

He gave his arm to Dorothy and they moved on. I trailed along behind like one of those pathetic tourists you see in Italian churches, following a guide. I felt put out that Stanley, who was my discovery, appeared to have been taken up by Dorothy, lock, stock and barrel.

As I watched him making those quick little gestures with his hands, I could still see the fingers curled round

Hilda's right breast and I wondered what it would be like to feel that thumb against my nipple.

It took us an hour to come back to where we started. There was one chair in the chapel, piled with rags and sketches. I saw Dorothy glance longingly towards it. On the few occasions when she meets somebody she finds interesting, Dorothy is like a car that normally won't go above a certain speed but suddenly accelerates in order to keep level with another car that's threatening to overtake her. She was running out of fuel.

'I don't suppose there's somewhere we can get a cup of tea?' she interrupted. Stanley held a finger up as if admonishing her for the interruption and then reached under a pile of rags next to the chair and found a flask. Another search revealed two cups that hadn't been washed since the last time they were used. I watched as Dorothy scooped out a speck of something that was definitely not a tea leaf from the surface.

Stanley carried on obliviously. 'What I'd really like to do,' he said, 'is paint a *Church of Me* in Cookham.' Dorothy's expression faltered. 'Well, it would be more of a cathedral really. Once I've finished this job for the Behrends I'll be looking for another patron.'

'Isn't Cookham rather small for a cathedral?' Dorothy suggested. There's not much to Cookham other than the High Street flanked by fields and since it's bordered by the Thames on three sides there's not much room for expansion.

'That's why I would need a patron. I'd be basing the cathedral on the lay-out of the village, so the nave would be the High Street and the houses on each side the transepts. There'll be three main altarpieces, each one twenty foot high, and a frieze of paintings with predellas that go all the way around.'

'And how long will that take?' Dorothy leant one hand on the chair back.

'Fifteen, maybe twenty years.'

'That's quite an undertaking?'

'I see Church House as my life's work,' he said, blithely.

'I imagine it would have to be,' said Dorothy.

'It will be dedicated to the people I have loved – my sister Flongy, Hilda, Elsie – she's our maid. They'll all be in there. Some of them, like Hilda, will have smaller chapels of their own .'

'They'll all be women, then?' I said.

He stared up at the ceiling. 'Yes. I want the church to be a celebration of my up-in-heaven moments.'

I glanced sideways. Dorothy was giving me one of her *time we went* looks.

'So it won't be a religious chapel,' I said.

'Oh yes, it'll be a hymn to love.' He threw his head back, spreading out his hands and gazing at the ceiling with a beatific smile. 'What could be more divine than that?'

He was still staring up into the ceiling as we left, the women he had chosen to immortalise in his imaginary *Church of Me* already up there, vying for a prime position in the apse.

'He's mad,' said Dorothy, as we stepped out onto the path.

IV

I thought that was the end of it, but when we'd got home and she'd had time to recover, Dorothy declared that Stanley's chapel was a work of genius and Stanley was a fascinating personality, although you'd only want him in small doses.

As we soon discovered, Stanley didn't *do* small doses. It was all or nothing. In the weeks that followed, although he and Hilda were still lodged in Burghclere to facilitate work on the chapel, he spent quite a lot of time in Cookham and he'd started calling in at Moor Thatch each time he was there. For Dorothy, who had no company for months on end apart from me and the occasional stray cat, he was a revelation.

There was nothing Stanley didn't have an attitude towards or an opinion on. After a morning in the studio, he'd wander down from Malt House Cottages, the terraced house he'd rented near the school and if we happened to be in the kitchen, we would see him cross the stile and take the path across the common and know he was heading our way. It was often dark before he left.

Through him we learnt about the group of intellectuals and artists Stanley called the *Bloomsberries* and their leader, Roger Fry, who was dictating everything that happened in the art world at that moment. Politics, which interested Dorothy and which she didn't often talk about with me because she thought that I was ill-informed, turned out to be another of their shared enthusiasms.

I wished I'd been able to contribute more towards their conversations. I would have liked Stanley to think I'd received at least a basic education, though it turned out that he hadn't been to school at all until he was sixteen. He and his brother Gilbert had been home-schooled by his father and his sister.

Sometimes as I sat and listened to them, I would let my dress ride up a little and I saw his eyelids flicker. I had found a way of catching his attention. Sadly, I soon realised Stanley was incapable of doing anything discreetly, so it wasn't long before it captured Dorothy's attention, too. She wasn't going to demean herself by turning round but she inclined her head to let me know she'd worked out what was going on behind her back.

Occasionally, when he was talking, Stanley would stop in the middle of a sentence or there'd be a long pause and I knew his eyes were on me. There was something disconcerting in his stare. It was the way you might look at a painting or the objects in a still life waiting to be rearranged into a composition.

When he left one evening after a particularly lengthy visit, Stanley kissed me on both cheeks, then turned to Dorothy and shook her by the hand. Until then all we'd got out of him was a wave. I worried about Dorothy's interpretation of this new development, but she just looked up at the clock and grunted.

'Five more minutes and he'd have outstayed his welcome.'

'I thought you enjoyed his company.'

'When you can get him talking about something other than himself, yes.'

When we first knew Stanley, Dorothy had grudgingly admitted that she found his energy and his unlimited self-confidence engaging. In the end, it was the fact that they seemed to be inexhaustible, that made you question whether they were qualities at all.

'Would you like me to put more water in the pot?'

'No thank you, dear. I'm full up to the gills with tea.'

'A whisky, maybe?'

'Now you're talking.'

V

It was after Stanley started turning up with presents for me and when I was not there to ask whether I would join them, that it finally became apparent which of us he'd come to see. The things he brought weren't what you would expect from someone you had only known a few weeks: nylon stockings, for example. Dorothy and I had phased out most of those things from our lives that could be seen as luxuries. I smoked and she drank whisky but less often than we would have liked and nylon stockings had been absent from the wish-list for the past six months. I was delighted to be given presents, but it bothered Dorothy that by accepting them we'd put ourselves in thrall to him.

At her behest we cut back on the invitations, although Stanley seemed to take his welcome at Moor Thatch for granted. It was rare for a weekend to pass without a visit from him and occasionally we went to church on Sunday, followed by a long walk, simply so that we could tell him we weren't going to be in.

Although she'd have no truck with organised religion, Dorothy enjoyed the rituals attached to it. Nine hundred years ago, there was a Lady Chapel on the site, built as a tribute to a female anchorite who'd lived in Cookham and been paid a halfpenny a day by Henry II. Dorothy insisted that it was the anchorite she came to worship.

I'd decided to attend the service on my own one day when she was laid up with a chesty cough. She'd had rheumatic fever as a child and it had left her with weak lungs, exacerbated by the English climate and the years we'd spent in Paris. I imagined many of the women we'd known then were dead now.

It was one of those warm, unexpectedly delightful days you sometimes got in early spring. The church was just a few yards from the river and the shouts of people on the tow-path and the joyful barking of dogs frequently drowned out the sermon.

I left through the old part of the graveyard. Stanley's grandparents were buried there, although the cemetery was now so overgrown with brambles that you couldn't tell one tombstone from another. Underneath a chestnut tree I passed a cherub with his head bent and a blackbird singing on his shoulder.

As I was unravelling the twine wrapped round the gate post, I saw what looked like a heap of clothes abandoned on a stone sarcophagus. I hesitated. 'Stanley, is that you?'

He paused and whipped away the handkerchief that had been covering his face. 'What ho!' He squinted at the sky.

I had remarked to Dorothy how Stanley treated certain parts of Cookham - notably the churchyard and its occupants - as if he owned them. He was constantly seen loitering amongst the concrete Angels with their crumbling coronets, or squatting down infront of head-stones, scratching at the algae to see what was written there.

He rubbed his eyes and sat up, shuffling across the slab and dropping down into the thicket growing up around it. As he looped his leg over the railings, thorns snagged on his trousers and I had an eerie sense of forces reaching from within to keep him there. I held my hand out and he dragged his leg free, leaving a thin shred of cloth behind him.

'Do you often do this?'

Stanley gave the concrete slab a pat. 'I feel at home amongst the dead,' he said. 'I like to lie here wondering what thoughts are going through their heads.'

I'd heard that in his painting of *The Resurrection*, many of the dead weren't dead at all, but friends of Stanley's. The dividing line between the living and the dead was of no more significance to him than that between reality and his imagination.

There was a thin spattering of lichen on the shoulders of his jacket. I reached out to brush it off and stopped, remembering the couple in *The Resurrection* climbing up out of their graves, the wife, unable to resist the habits of a life-time, brushing damp earth off her husband's jacket.

We walked down the path together, Stanley side-stepping a colony of ants that scurried out from underneath a stone as we went past.

'Just listen to that silence,' he said, pausing at the gate and gazing upwards at the sky. It was a strange remark for somebody who'd hardly drawn breath since I met him.

I'd expected Stanley to turn off towards his own home when we got to Odney Lane but he kept pace with me until we reached the War Memorial. A group of small boys squatted in the dust next to the railings, playing 'Whip and Top' with what looked like a turnip.

As we paused to watch them, one boy whipped the turnip top particularly hard and it shot out across the gravel, ricocheting off my leg. I gave a little shriek, more from surprise than pain.

There was red mark on my leg above the ankle. Stanley dropped onto his knees beside me, dabbing at the spot. I'd never seen the top of Stanley's head. His hair was coarse, like rope, with highlights where the sun had bleached it. It did not look as if it had seen a comb in months.

'You're hurt.' He jerked his head up, narrowing his eyes against the sun.

The boy who'd sent the missile rocked from one foot to the other, his cheeks crimson. His companions drew back in a huddle, putting space between the culprit and themselves.

'No, not at all. It just surprised me, coming at me like that.'

Stanley traced his finger round the outline of the bruise and let it rest a moment at the centre of it. As the finger grazed my skin, it felt as if someone had pulled a drawstring in my stomach. He looked back over his shoulder at the boy.

'He didn't mean it, Stanley. Please don't make a fuss.' I looked over his shoulder at the boys and nodded. They dived for the turnip top and scattered. Stanley scrambled to his feet.

'I'll see you home.'

'There's no need. Really, I'm all right.'

He hesitated. 'I was going to call round today in any case,' he said. 'I have some news. I wanted to tell both of you together.'

For a moment after he'd made his announcement, neither of us spoke.

'You said you had another two years work to do at Burghclere,' Dorothy said. She looked quickly at me and I shook my head to indicate that it was news to me, too.

'I don't have to paint the pictures there,' insisted Stanley. 'I can paint them here and then install them afterwards.'

'I thought the Behrends had provided you and Hilda with a cottage on site for as long as you were working on the chapel?'

'They have but I'd rather be in Cookham. Everything I need is here.'

He looked at me and gave a coy smile. I sensed Dorothy was struggling to accommodate these new developments and wondering if they had anything to do with me.

'So we'll be seeing more of you?'

'Yes,' he said. 'I've decided I shall buy a house here. I've already got my eye on one.'

'Well, maybe once you've got your own home Hilda and your daughter – *Shirin,* isn't it - will also want to spend more time here.'

'I don't think so,' he said in the same voice you might use to say it's raining outside. 'Hilda doesn't like to travel whilst she's pregnant.'

I stared. 'Hilda's pregnant?'

'Yes,' he said. 'She found out last month.'

There was a brief pause whilst we absorbed the news. That's it then, I thought, and I felt the sort of flatness that comes when you have been building up to something and it doesn't happen.

Dorothy recovered first. 'Congratulations, Stanley.' She stopped short of adding 'Well done.'

VI

Three months later, Stanley was in Cookham full-time. He had bought a large house in the middle of the village, 'Lindworth'*,* which, although dilapidated, was much grander than 'Fernlea'*,* the house where he grew up and where his father and his sister Annie lived until his father's death.

Presumably, this was to show the village that he was returning to it a successful artist, though it was a mystery to most of them that someone could get paid for doing what he did. There had been talk about the state of Fernlea. Old Pa Spencer had been highly thought of in the village in his time. The fact that he and Annie lived a hand-to-mouth existence in a house devoid of creature comforts whereas Lindworth could accommodate a family of half-a-dozen without overcrowding, fuelled the gossip.

It seemed money was no object. In the grounds there was a pergola that Stanley was converting to a studio. He had installed a Bechstein in the downstairs parlour of the house and sometimes in the middle of the night if he was still awake, we would hear strains of Bach or Chopin drifting on the air across the common and imagine Stanley sitting in pyjamas and an overcoat at the piano. He had also had a telephone connected and had bought a car from Remington's, a garage in the High Street, for £200. He hated driving and had never fully mastered the technique so for long periods the car remained parked on the back lawn.

Hilda's pregnancy appeared to have made little difference to the way they carried on their lives. Although whenever they appeared together they seemed to be totally absorbed by one another, Hilda still spent part of every week in Burghclere or in London at her family home whilst Stanley spent his time in Cookham.

Dorothy and I had sensed for some months that the marriage was in trouble. We were at a picnic by the river organised by Hilda and her brother Richard Carline, when we'd first heard Stanley arguing with Hilda.

Since the picnic was on Bell Rope Meadow only half a mile from Moor Thatch, whereas other members of the party had to motor down from London, even Dorothy accepted that it would be churlish to turn down the invitation.

It was not until we got there that we found the party didn't just consist of Stanley and the Carlines but a number of their arty friends: the painter Henry Lamb, his new wife Pansy and a friend of Stanley's, Jas Wood, who was older than the others by a decade and seemed rather out of place.

I heard him telling Dorothy he was a specialist in Persian art, but recognising that the subject wasn't one that we were likely to know much about, he turned the conversation round to us. There was a crumpled look about him which I liked. He was the sort of man you feel it's safe to flirt with, courteous and friendly and with nothing predatory about him. He was very big with huge hands and he seemed to make a point of being clumsy as if this were part of the performance. He'd known Stanley since the War.

Whereas at Burghclere we'd had Stanley's sole attention, here it was as if he was on loan from Hilda when he spoke to anybody else. His eyes would constantly return to her, like metal filings drawn towards a magnet. He had swapped the old brown suit and tie that seemed to have been melded to his skin, for a white shirt and trousers and a navy blazer. 'Quite the young blade,' Dorothy remarked.

Whilst Richard was manoeuvring the car into position, Stanley wandered over to the river, staring downstream to Turks boatyard and Lock Island where a skiff was slicing through the water. He stood with his hands dug deep into his pockets, a dark silhouette against the cloudless sky. We'd had an early morning shower but the rain had cleared. Several hours of sunshine had dried out the grass and gossamer was drifting on the air, an indication of the heat to come.

Jas stood beside me: 'This is the exact spot on the bank where Stanley painted his *Swan Upping,*' he said. 'Do you know the picture?'

'I remember looking at a reproduction of it in a magazine.'

'He started it before the War and went back to it afterwards. He told me he felt bound to finish it but that the War had turned it into history. That four years changed the face of England.' He bent down to pat the grass. 'We're standing on a patch of ground that's been immortalised.'

'Do you think Stanley's an important painter?'

'Yes, I do. I think he's probably the most important painter we've got.' It was not clear if by *we* he was referring just to Stanley's friends or England.

Richard called out: 'Come on, Stanley. Give a hand here.' For a moment it was as if Stanley hadn't heard him; then he turned around and stared at us as if he wanted to commit the scene to memory before anybody moved.

We found a stretch of grass next to the bank that was already beaten down. The men unloaded picnic hampers, hauling them across the grass and Hilda followed with the rugs for us to sit on.

She looked younger than she had that day when she and Stanley came into The Copper Kettle, with the bloom which pregnancy confers on certain women. She had on a white dress, open at the neck with her hair tied back loosely in a scarf. She gazed across the river, smiling every now and then, but with the air of someone who was not entirely *there*. I saw why Stanley might have fallen for her. When she caught my eye, she held it for a moment and then looked away.

Her brother helped to spread the rugs out and then came and sat down next to me. Though he was some years younger, Richard's likeness to his sister was unnerving. He was tall and had a long face with the same full mouth and heavy-lidded, brown eyes. He'd have been considered handsome in a bloke-ish way; the sort who would look good in uniform.

When I first met her, Dorothy told me I had a gift for making people fall in love with me. Until then I'd not recognised it as a gift. Flirtation was like football. Every now and then I'd score a goal. I realised straight away that I'd scored one with Richard.

'Stanley tells me you lived just across the road from him in Cookham when you were a girl,' he'd said when we were introduced. The way he said it: '*gal*', not 'girl', and with a slight smirk, I knew he was flirting with me and that, unlike Jas, he meant it.

'Yes, my father had a posting here for three years.'

I had seen him glancing at my left hand. 'You're not married then?' he said.

'I was engaged. Before the War.' I looked away as if the memory was too painful for me to go into detail. 'He was lost.'

'I'm sorry,' Richard said. 'There must have been a lot of girls like that.'

'Yes,' I said. 'I suppose there were.'

He'd looked over his shoulder. 'Your friend isn't taking much part in the jolly, is she?'

'Dorothy? She's not that keen on parties. She's my sister, actually.'

'Your sister?'

'Preece, née Hepworth. Preece was my fiancé's name.'

'Ah. I thought….'

'What?'

'I thought you had been students at the Slade together?'

'That's right. Both of us went into art.'

'Our home in Hampstead is a meeting place for artists. You must come.'

'I'd like that.' He had gone all soft around the gills. I may be thirty-five and passing myself off as twenty-nine, but I decided in that moment that I was a match for Hilda's brother.

Lunch turned out to be a very grand affair with patés, pheasant and champagne kept chilled with ice packed in around it. When Jas took it out, the melted ice ran down his leg and everybody laughed. I'd have been mortified but Jas laughed, too. He said he was so wet he might as well jump in the river and have done with it.

I noticed Stanley taking sips from Hilda's glass and offering her titbits off his plate. Whilst Dorothy avoided overt gestures of affection, Stanley seemed to act entirely as he felt, with no regard for social etiquette. He had been whispering to Hilda and he suddenly threw back his head and laughed. She reached across and swept the hair back from his forehead and the gesture was so full of tenderness, I had to look away.

'You know at one point it was Stanley's brother that my sister planned to marry,' Richard murmured.

'No, I didn't.'

'She chose Stanley in the end. I think it was the right decision... for him, anyway.' He laughed.

When lunch was over, everybody stretched out on the grass and read or went to sleep. Except for Stanley. He and Hilda moved a short way off from where the rest of us were sitting and that's when I heard him say it.

'What I hate about you, Hilda,' he threw out, 'is that you're sad. I'm bursting with ideas and wanting you to share them and it's as if you've caught hold of me and swung me round into the dark.'

It shocked me that his mood could change so rapidly, but what I heard next shocked me even more. 'What I find wonderful about Patricia is the feeling that she's up for anything. It's liberating.'

'Yes, it must be,' Hilda had said bitterly.

'It isn't like you to be jealous, Hilda.'

'All right. You can have her if you want.'

'Oh Hilda!'

I'd looked round to see if Dorothy had heard them. She sat with her back against a hamper and her eyes closed. Stanley had his fists bunched up against his temples. Hilda looked as if she wished the ground would swallow her:

'I'm worn out, Stanley. I can't argue with you. Sometimes when I'm listening to you going on about how we can use sex as a way to God, I think you make up these ideas in order to excuse things in you that you can't do anything about. You know they're not right, so you feel you have to justify them.'

'I thought we were of one mind about it, Hilda. When you're not whole-heartedly behind me, I feel let down, as if we've set off together on a journey and you're always looking back over your shoulder.'

Hilda got up and began to slot their plates and glasses back into the hamper. Stanley stood up, kicking the grass sullenly. The others were now on the move, too, and there was a general shift in the direction of the cars. As Hilda went to follow, she glanced back over her shoulder.

'You're the one who's having second thoughts about our marriage, Stanley, not me.'

Dorothy swore afterwards that she would never be persuaded to accept another invitation. It was not just the embarrassment of listening to the Spencers arguing with one another.

'Did you know the Slade's ex-students would be there mob-handed?' she demanded.

'No, of course I didn't. I had no idea that anybody else had been invited.'

'Next time maybe you would make a point of checking.'

I was still not sure how much she'd overheard. 'Don't be a kill-joy, Dorothy. It's been weeks since we even put our heads outside the door.'

'I'm sorry if your life with me is boring.'

'It's not boring. It's just… lacking texture.'

'Texture? Are we talking rugs or tapestries?

'It made a change to see some other people, that's all.'

'I'm not keen on other people, as you know.'

I crossed to the settee and slipped my arms around her neck: 'Stop sulking, Dodo. When you're wearing that loose cardigan it pulls the corners of your mouth down.'

'I'm not sulking.'

'Yes, you are.' I rubbed my cheek against hers. Dorothy has dry skin faintly perfumed by the soap she uses. When I said I liked it she insisted that it didn't have a scent. 'It must be you, then,' I said. 'Just think, perfume companies have gone to all that trouble to produce a scent they could have got for free from you.'

'Except that you're the only person who can smell it.'

'Good.' I nuzzled up to her. 'I want to be the only person who can smell it. If we're sisters, I suppose that would explain it.'

'Sisters.' Dorothy guffawed. 'You really think that anybody would buy into that? I know the folks in Cookham are a bit slow, but they're not blind. We can probably rely on them to work it out.'

Still, Stanley hasn't worked it out yet so it can't be all that obvious.

VII

When the Carlines asked us to an 'At Home' some weeks later, I knew, after the debâcle at the picnic, that it wasn't something Dorothy would want to go to and because the invitation was addressed to me, I wasn't sure she'd been included anyway.

'It's you they will be after,' Dorothy said when I showed the invitation to her.

'Don't be silly. They know we're a couple.'

'Do they?' She looked sideways at me. 'I thought you'd told everybody we were sisters.'

'Well whatever we are, they're inviting both of us.' I suddenly remembered a remark I'd overheard when we were at the picnic. Richard had been telling Henry Lamb that I was someone Stanley had met in The Copper Kettle and found *interesting*. 'Rumour is she drowned one man and tried to drown another,' he'd laughed. 'This time it could well be Stanley who goes under.'

'You've not talked to anyone about our life before we came here, have you, Dorothy?'

'I haven't talked to anyone full-stop. Except for Stanley and it's usually him who does the talking.'

'It's just that the Carlines seemed to know about that incident at Grim's Dyke. I heard Richard telling Henry Lamb about it.'

'When you drowned poor old man Gilbert in the lake.'

'He didn't drown; he had a heart attack.'

'Whilst rescuing you from the water.'

'How would anybody know about that?'

'The old man was a National treasure. He was famous for his operettas. It was bound to cause a fuss.'

'It's horrible to think that something you do when you're seventeen will keep on coming back to haunt you.'

'Dare I say the lesson one might learn from it is not to act unless you've thoroughly considered what the consequences of your actions might be.' She's reminding me what happened on the last occasion that I acted without thinking of the consequences. Dorothy won't hesitate to use whatever weapons she has in her arsenal, however blunt with over-use they are.

'You talk as if I killed him. No one asked him to come in and rescue me that day.'

'You're right. He could have stood there on the lake-side and just watched you drown. I would have.'

'No, you wouldn't.'

'Want to bet?'

'Why don't you come? I would enjoy it more if you were there.'

'I doubt if the *'At Home'* would be improved by my attendance. Don't go on about it, sweetheart. I've said go.'

VIII

The Carline's London home was typically bohemian with paintings crammed together on the walls and throws and tye-dyes flung across the sofas to disguise the wear and tear. The pictures were hung side by side and one above the other all along the passage with so little space between them they reminded me of summer exhibitions at The Royal Academy. Amongst them I glimpsed photographs of Hilda and her brothers, one of which - a boy with long curls and a look of saintly innocence - I recognised as Richard.

Tall arched windows on the side wall let in what light could be garnered from outside. The house was on a tree-lined avenue which in spring would have been awash with blossom. It was in that gracious part of London overlooking Hampstead Heath and, though the sky was grey and sullen, the sharp criss-cross pattern of the branches etched against the sky and the loud cawing of the rooks were more suggestive of the countryside. The distant sound of traffic was the only clue that we were just a few miles from the city centre. I could understand why Hilda might prefer to spend her time here rather than in Cookham which, though beautiful in summer, could be bleak and comfortless in winter and did not have the same lively company to compensate.

The house was square and solid, painted white with wrought-iron balconies and window boxes overflowing with geraniums. There was a smell of lavender and incense in the hall, combined with something damp and slightly clinical that turned out to be half-a-dozen nappies on a makeshift washing-line in one room off the passage. A coal fire was smouldering in the grate and they were steaming gently.

Hilda came into the hall with Shirin underneath her arm and handed her to Stanley.

He laughed as he scooped her up into his arms. 'How are you, duckie?' I was not sure if he was addressing Hilda or the baby.

She and Stanley kissed each other lingeringly on the mouth. She nodded. 'We're all right.' She wore a loose shift, with her hair down, as if she had only just got out of bed.

'This is Patricia,' Stanley turned to me. 'You met her at the picnic. You remember?'

When I'd told him Dorothy would not be coming with me to the Carline's party, Stanley beamed. 'We'll go together,' he'd said. 'I can drive us to the station.'

I'd persuaded him to meet me at the end of School Lane rather than outside Moor Thatch. As far as Dorothy knew, I was going up to London on my own and meeting Stanley there. I wasn't sure how she'd react if I'd said we were going up together.

He had chattered non-stop from the moment we got on the train in Maidenhead until the taxi dropped us outside Downshire Hill. If Hilda was surprised to see me there alone with him, she hid it well. 'Yes, I remember,' she said, giving me a passing glance as she reached out to take her daughter back.

I thought she wasn't going to acknowledge me beyond a nod, but then she held her free hand out. She didn't ask me if I'd like to hold the baby. I thought women always did this, either out of pity for the women who did not have babies, or because it was the only way that they could get a rest from them. I had the feeling Shirin would immediately start to bawl as soon as Hilda handed her across to me. I've never managed to ingratiate myself with animals or children. If they showed the slightest inclination to be friends I'd be delighted, but they don't.

'Will you be coming up?' said Stanley.

'In a minute, when I've finished down here.' Hilda turned back to the room and shut the door.

'Is that the room you paint in when you're up in town?' I asked him as we climbed the stairs up to the next floor.

'Yes. I have to look between the nappies if I want to see the fire. The paint won't dry because the air's too moist.'

'You couldn't find another room to paint in?'

'I could have the attic if I wanted.'

'Wouldn't you prefer that?'

'I like being in the same room Hilda's in,' he said. 'And having Shirin there is nice.'

'They don't disturb you then?'

'Oh no. I put bits of them in the paintings. Nothing's wasted.'

'Dorothy would go mad if she had to do her painting in the same room I'm in. We did share a studio at the beginning but then Dorothy decided that she needed to be on her own.'

He turned and looked at me intently. 'You're not necessary to her vision then?'

I scoffed. 'No, Stanley, I'm not necessary to her vision.'

'Only, you see I've decided that you are to mine.'

'I am to your what?' I said and he frowned. 'What is it you've decided I am, Stanley?'

'You're my Cookham muse,' he said.

There was a buzz of conversation and the clink of glasses coming from a large room off the landing, which suggested that the party had been going on for some time. A dishevelled-looking young man carrying his jacket and a woman with a silver fox fur cape around her shoulders and her shoes tucked underneath her arm, spilled out onto the landing and we stood aside to let them pass.

Inside the room I caught the scent of Turkish cigarettes which I'd not come across since we came back from Paris. Men and women sat in small groups drinking cups of tea or holding tumblers of white wine.

I caught a glimpse of Richard Carline and he waved. His mother had been talking to a young man whose white shirt and red cravat looked inappropriately casual beside her evening dress. She touched his arm to bring their conversation to a close and she and Richard edged their way towards us in a pincer movement.

Richard kissed me on the cheek whilst Mrs Carline gave her son-in-law a chaste hug. I had the impression that she tolerated Stanley for her daughter's sake, but that he wouldn't necessarily have been invited to her soirée on his own behalf.

I wore a gown that night which had been put together from a pattern in *Peg's Paper* headed 'Dresses that will fit in everywhere.' I try to keep up with the fashion, but I don't think Dorothy would notice if I wore a coal sack. She was quick to point out that those who attempt to *fit in everywhere* invariably fail to fit in anywhere, but still a quick look round the room had reassured me that there were a lot of people here who weren't concerned to fit in.

My dress was made out of satin, calf-length and decolleté. I will say one thing for myself, my breasts may sag a little but they have been trained to do what is required of them. They won't pop out if I bend down, though to be on the safe side I make do with leaning forward slightly so that anyone I'm talking to can get a glimpse of what is in there but will not risk being swamped.

The Carlines were an odd lot. They talked all the time about art in the way that Dorothy and I discussed the price of beef or where we'd go on holiday, assuming that we could afford one. But you sensed that whilst they chattered they were sizing you up, even Hilda, though she might have been forgiven if that was the case.

That's how it was with Mrs Carline: whilst her gimlet eye was questioning what I was doing in her drawing room, her son-in-law on one side of me, Richard on the other, she was talking about a Mantegna exhibition at The National Gallery which I claimed rashly to have been to. She asked how I thought his work compared with that of his contemporary, Bellini.

Seeing I was struggling, Richard said he loved the rabbits in Bellini's paintings. 'When you look at *Christ's Betrayal,* you might almost think it was a landscape. There are rabbits everywhere. The story's almost incidental. It's pure pantheism. Wouldn't you agree, Patricia?'

I could only nod. I felt humiliated, knowing that from then on I would be consigned in his mind to the *pretty face but no brain* category.

'You're an artist too, dear, I believe,' said Mrs Carline, thinking no doubt that I wouldn't be there if I wasn't.

I smiled weakly. For some reason I have always felt a fraud whenever I'm referred to as an 'artist'.

Hilda joined us with the baby under one arm. She was carrying a potty in the other hand and plonked the one onto the other in a corner of the room.

Next to the table with the drinks, the young man in the white shirt had begun to argue with a man whose waistcoat and black tie seemed to annoy him.

'Do excuse me,' Mrs Carline said. 'I'd better intervene. I don't want Charles and Freddy challenging each other to a duel.'

The young man turned to her. 'What do you think about this latest jaunt of Beatrice and Sidney's, Mrs Carline? Aren't they marvellous?'

'They're very staunch,' said Mrs Carline, diplomatically. 'Especially Beatrice.' She gave a little laugh to indicate that there was such a thing as being too staunch. 'Though I can't help thinking they're a bit long in the tooth to join the revolution. Lord knows what the Soviets will make of them.'

'They're icons over there. I heard that Lenin had translated their book on Trade Unionism into Russian.'

'Yes, it was a case of boredom twice blessed,' said the other man.

There was a smattering of laughter from the others. The young man turned furiously to a very thin girl with a page boy hair-cut, who had laughed along with everybody else. She wore a spangled knee-length dress and as she moved, the tiny mirrors sewn onto her bodice caught the light from an enormous three-tiered chandelier above her head and made her look a little like a sparkler. She tipped back her head and took a long draw on her cigarette.

I reached for Stanley's arm: 'Who are those people?'

'His name's Freddy Ashworth. And the girl's called Fleur.'

'Not them...the people they're discussing.'

Stanley looked at me a moment. 'Beatrice and Sidney Webb. They're Fabians.'

I wasn't much the wiser.

'I thought you were a devoted Communist,' the woman in the spangled dress said, turning languidly towards the man who wore the waistcoat and black tie. She had a voice that matched her outfit perfectly.

'I was.' The man turned his attention to her, slightly altering the angle of his body to exclude his rival. 'I sold all my bourgeois trappings before going out there: dinner jacket, books that in a worker's state would be superfluous; I even closed my bank accounts.' He shrugged. 'What use was money in a country where the bankers had all been eliminated?'

There was an embarrassed titter. 'And what happened?' said the woman.

'As my wife remarked, we might as well have stayed in Didsbury. Revolutions, as the word implies, tend to end up where they began.'

'With bloodshed, do you mean?' said Mrs Carline, sceptically. She touched the elbow of the young man, anxious that her soirée wouldn't end the same way.

'Go there as a visitor,' the man continued, and you'll see the usual collective farms, schools, factories. But what is going on in the remotest villages? I'll tell you what; they're starving. Not just undernourished as they are here. What those happy, smiling peasants on the posters are concealing is despair and deprivation on a level people like us can't imagine.'

'Mr Shaw, the writer, said there were no shortages of food there,' said a matron in a flowered dress and tight curls.

'Mr Shaw, the writer, is a fool then,' said the man.

At least I've got that to take back to Dorothy, I thought. She'd never rated Shaw's plays highly.

This time even Mrs Carline seemed unable to negotiate the silence. And then suddenly a fluted voice piped up from somewhere on the far side of the room: 'Saint George for Merrie England / No Soviets for Me / I quite enjoyed the Sibier / But thank the Lord I'm free.'

There was a ripple of applause and he responded with a low bow. Mrs Carline turned to Richard: 'We'll have no more talk of politics, this evening. Richard, dear, perhaps you'd top up everybody's glass. And put some music on the gramophone. '

'Thank God for that. I thought they'd never stop.' The thin girl in the spangled dress was standing next to me. Her face was powdered white and emphasised the pillar-box red lipstick she was wearing. 'All this talk of politics just makes me want to curl up on the floor and go to sleep.'

'There is one thing the Soviets deserve some credit for,' the woman next to her replied. 'Theirs is the only country where abortion's legal.'

I felt colour rising in my cheeks. 'True,' said the girl. 'I wouldn't recommend it, though. The operations are performed without an anaesthetic.'

Her companion sighed. 'We women always end up paying one way or another.' She moved off. The woman in the spangled dress inclined her head towards me and held out her hand. 'Fleur Laycock. You are?'

When I said my name she drew her top lip in, as if she wasn't certain if it rang a bell.

'You won't have heard of me.'

She raised an eyebrow. 'Really? Is there nothing wicked you can boast of having done, then?'

'Not in present company.'

'No?' She inclined her head. 'I don't know where you'd go to find a more forgiving audience. At least in England we still have the freedom to be naughty.'

'Have you been to Russia?'

'I went last year for the celebrations in November. Somebody I knew had been invited. Incidentally it's not called 'Russia' any more, although I don't suppose it matters unless you're addressing someone in the *Politburo*.'

'Did you have a good time?'

'Grief, no. I was bored to death. The place is so drab and their celebrations are like funeral processions – rows of grey men watching column after marching column - you can't tell the men from the machines. Then in the middle of it, Kirov, one of Stalin's top men, was assassinated: on his orders it was said. That livened things up no end.'

'Is that true.....that Stalin ordered it?'

'Oh, absolutely.' She glanced sideways at me, held my eye a moment and then winked. I realised she was flirting with me. 'Did you come with someone?'

'Stanley brought me.'

'Ah.' She nodded and looked over to where Stanley stood next to the window talking to an august-looking man with grey hair and a cardigan that could have come out of the factory owned by Dodo's father.

'That man Stanley's talking to is Otto Spengler. He's a lecturer on Russian literature.' Their voices drifted over to us. Fleur smiled. 'It sounds as if Stanley's managing to hold his own.'

'Oh yes, he won't have any difficulty there.' On one of his first visits to Moor Thatch we'd learnt that Stanley and his siblings had been in the habit of discussing works by Flaubert, Dickens, Saint Augustine and Hans Christian Anderson around the dinner table. It was nothing like the home-life I'd had.

Fleur took out a cigarette pack from the tiny bag tucked underneath her arm. I recognised the blue pack with the gold surround. She held it out to me. It was a cheaper brand than I would have expected somebody like her to smoke. The foil was crumpled.

'I picked these up from a bar we called at on the way here,' she said. 'They were lying on the counter.'

'If you look, you'll find a card inside.'

She flipped the packet open and took out the card. There was a section of a face on it. She turned it in her fingers.

'That's the left eye of *The Laughing Cavalier*.'

'You don't say?' She up-ended it and squinted at the image. 'Who would want the left eye of a cavalier?'

'The picture is by Frans Hals. Once you've managed to get all the bits that make the face, you send them to the manufacturers and they send back a reproduction in a frame.'

She pursed her lips: 'What are you meant to do with that?'

I laughed: 'You hang it on the wall, if you're that way inclined.'

She looked at me and tilted her head. 'And are you that way inclined?'

I gave an awkward laugh. 'Apparently, it's what they do in all the new suburban semis.'

She continued staring at me for a moment and then went to put the card back in the packet, hesitated and reached in her handbag for an eyebrow pencil. She wrote something on the card and gave it to me.

'What's this?'

'It's the number of the telephone where you can reach me.'

'This is where you live?'

'No, darling. It's where Freddy lives. I'm camping out with him just now.'

'You're camping out in Park Lane?'

'Would you have me camping out in Dalston?'

'Park Lane's not exactly where you would expect to find a socialist.'

'I'm not a socialist. Between ourselves, I find the working classes rather dismal.'

'I thought Freddy...'

'Oh God, Freddy. You can't take his word for anything. He has this massive guilt thing where the workers are concerned. He feels he should be doing something, but he just gets in the way. He hands out wads of notes to homeless people and then watches them go straight into the pub.'

'Don't you think unemployment is a problem?'

'Oh yes, it's a problem. But I don't think Freddy is the answer to it. Rousseau had the right idea when he said we should cultivate our own front lawns.'

'Is that what Rousseau said?'

'Well, something like that.' She stubbed out her cigarette and looked round vaguely. Stanley was still arguing with the professor.

'Dostoevsky's more about sin and redemption,' he insisted. 'Chekov's plays are tragi-comedies.' He pushed his glasses further up his nose. 'They're not the same at all.'

'Well there you are,' Fleur murmured. 'Now you know.' She peered into her empty glass. 'Have you read Chekov?' she said, vaguely.

'*Crime and Punishment*?'

'No, poppet, that was Dostoevsky. Chekov wrote *The Cherry Orchard,* though *The Seagull*'s probably more famous.'

She went through the bottles on the table and selected one that was still half full, pouring what was left into my glass. 'A shame you're not here on your own. Still, next time, maybe.' She leaned over and her lips brushed mine. She held the glass out. 'Down the hatch.'

I left the Carlines that night feeling that I needed to spend two days in a decompression chamber before going out into the world again.

IX

The version of the 'At Home' I was planning to give Dorothy had been severely edited. She'd spent the evening listening to a concert on the wireless with

Tiddles, Stanley's tabby, on her knees. Initially he'd asked if we could look in on the cat when no one was at home. He'd bought it from a litter born at Ovey's Farm and given it to Shirin as a birthday present. Although Shirin and her mother now spent almost all their time in London, they did not think Tiddles would adapt to living in a city.

When the cat decided unilaterally that it would prefer to live at Moor Thatch, Dorothy said that at least the cat would get rid of the mice, although since she insisted that we feed it three meals every day, there wasn't much incentive for it to go out and hunt.

An early dispute over territory had left it with the tip of one ear missing and a long, serrated scar over its left eye which had darkened to look like an eyebrow. The result was that it seemed to wear a permanent expression of surprised disdain. It jumped down as I edged my bottom onto the settee where Dorothy was sitting with her feet up.

'Was it fun?'

'The Carlines certainly know how to party.'

'So what did you talk about?'

'We covered Socialism, Russia – though apparently they call it something else now - rabbits in Bellini's paintings, and a play by Dostoevsky.'

'Dostoevsky didn't write plays.'

'Chekov, then. I can't remember what the play was.'

'Try *The Seagull*'.

'How did you know that?'

'Unlike you, I was reasonably well educated.'

'I'm the one who went to boarding school.'

'Precisely.'

The cat jumped back onto the settee and I got up. The room felt warm and I unlatched the window, leaning out across the sill. The air was heavy with the scent of stocks. The garden – wild, but not unmanageably so - was possibly the most attractive feature of Moor Thatch. The house was poky with faux Tudor beams that Dorothy detested and small, leaded windows that kept out the light but weren't much use as insulation. Any heat came from the red brick fireplace so in winter it was cold and smoky and in summer you could hardly breathe in there. With Dodo's weak lungs it was not an ideal place to live. At least the privy was indoors although the upright cupboard on the landing where it had been housed was so small that when you were sitting on the throne your knees pressed up against the door.

I leant both elbows on the window sill a moment, took a deep breath and then shut the window, fixed the latch and drew the curtains. Dorothy was waiting:

'Nothing interesting happened then, apart from you discovering a few things that you should have known already?'

I'd decided it was not the moment to tell Dorothy about Fleur Laycock, or that I was Stanley's muse, especially as I was about to ask her for a favour I knew she would be reluctant to agree to.

'Richard Carline's asked me to go dancing at the Palais.' I said lightly. He'd approached me as I waited in the hall for Stanley to flag down a taxi. Richard's cheeks were flushed and I could tell he was a little drunk. He said how much he had enjoyed our chat and then asked casually if I liked dancing. Would I care to join them at the Palais later that month?

Dorothy was looking at me shrewdly. I'd run out of cigarettes and feeling suddenly in need of one I pulled a drawer out and began to rummage through it.

'What did you say?'

'That I'd let him know. You don't mind, do you?' Yes, of course she minded. She knew I'd be out to have a good time and that when I put my mind to it, I usually succeeded.

I had been surprised to be invited. Richard made it seem as if a group of them were going and he thought that I might care to tag along. It sounded fun. Perhaps Fleur Laycock would be there. In Paris, Dorothy and I went to the sort of places where we'd dance together. We had found a queer bar called *Le Monocle* where women wore tuxedos, smoked cigars and sported white carnations in their button-holes. You'd never get away with anything like that in England.

'I thought it was Stanley you were interested in, not Richard Carline.'

'I'm not interested in either of them, other than as passports to a new life. Richard is a member of The London Group. He shows work at The Goupil. If we're nice to him he might be able to arrange an exhibition for us.'

Dorothy was tapping out a tune with one hand on the chair arm. 'How nice do you think you'd need to be?'

'His family are all artists, Dorothy. We can't afford to be so isolated. What's the point of all these pictures if we've nowhere to exhibit?' I took out a half-smoked pack of cigarettes. She rolled her eyes. I bent to light a taper from the fire and drew the smoke in, giving it a chance to circulate before I breathed out. 'Please say yes. You know how I love dancing. And you won't believe how grateful I'll be afterwards.' I sat down on the chair arm and leant forward, nibbling at her ear-lobe. When she turned her head. I kissed her on the mouth. 'Please.'

X

For a woman who'd got used to being more or less invisible, it made a pleasant change to be the object of so much attention. Dorothy was loving in her own way; she would sometimes comment if I'd bought a new blouse or done something to my hair, but she would not prostrate herself in front of anybody. She thought it was dangerous for people to be worshipped.

Although she was usually the driving force when it came down to what we did, I was invariably the one who worked out how we did it. Dorothy did not know how to change the channels on the wireless, mend a plug, or read a map and I'd begun to realise Stanley was, if anything, less practical than she was.

Coming back to Cookham on the train that evening in the darkness, he'd been bursting with ideas for future paintings, leaning forward in his seat, gesticulating with those impish fingers that were never still. I watched their shadowy reflections in the window. Every now and then he grasped my hands and gave a little tug on them as if to pull me off my seat and onto his.

Most men will not declare themselves unless they're confident they'll get a favourable response but Stanley seemed to think that anything he wanted would be granted automatically. It was like having someone turn a spotlight on you. In the glare you couldn't see who was behind the spotlight and you couldn't make out anything on the periphery. The only thing you were aware of was a blinding light that you suspected might end up by giving you a headache. At the same time, it was thrilling to feel part of that necessity.

As we stepped down onto the platform in the gloom, the engine shot a plume of steam into the air that sounded like a burst of raucous laughter. The train shuffled off into the darkness. Through the lighted windows of the station-master's office I could see the station-master sitting by his coal fire.

On the way out, we had come as far as Maidenhead in Stanley's car, since trains to Cookham didn't run into the evening. There had been a cold snap after weeks of weather that had been unseasonably warm and when we came back to the car, there was a thin layer of ice on the windscreen which he wiped off with his sleeve.

As soon as we were in the car, he started chattering again. I must have dozed because the next thing I heard was the crunch of gravel as we pulled up outside Moor Thatch. Stanley turned the engine off. He leaned across and brought my hands up to his lips.

'You will sit for me, won't you?' he insisted, putting his face so close up to mine that I thought he might be about to kiss me. I was not sure if it was a statement or a question. 'Please, Patricia, say you will.'

'Yes, if you want me to.'

His face broke out into that blissful smile. One thing I liked about him, I'd decided was that when he smiled, his whole face lit up. There was nothing Stanley did by halves. He radiated happiness and, in that moment, he looked beautiful.

'It's going to be wonderful,' he murmured. 'I'm so happy. I've not been this happy since....' he searched his memory. 'Not since Hilda said she'd sit for me.'

It was a little disappointing to discover, just as he'd decided I would be his muse, that I'd joined Hilda rather than replacing her. I hoped I wouldn't be compared with Hilda when I took my clothes off. I supposed that at some point I would be posing in the nude for him. He kissed my hands again before releasing them.

'You don't know what this means to me,' said Stanley.

XI

We'd agreed that I would go to Lindworth for a sitting on the Tuesday following the 'At Home'. I had picked a day when I knew Dorothy was going into Maidenhead to stock up on her art supplies. I'd mentioned casually that Stanley had asked whether he could make some sketches for a figure painting he was working on. I made it sound as if I'd be there for an hour at the most. I'd barely have the time to take my coat off, let alone the rest of my clothes.

As I walked down School Lane, past the War Memorial and up the High Street, I felt like a schoolgirl on a first date. I'd dressed up for the occasion in a yellow dress with high heels and a little handbag swinging from my wrist. You couldn't pass unnoticed in a village so I reckoned I might just as well be bold about it. Dressing to undress might seem a waste of time, but knowing I looked pretty added to the frisson of excitement I felt as I crossed the lawn at Lindworth to the shed which was now Stanley's studio.

The backyard of The King's Arms lay beyond the garden and a couple of hod carriers unloading barrels from the brewer's drays glanced up and whistled as they rolled the beer barrels across the cobbles to the cellars.

When he saw me, Stanley's eyelids flickered in surprise. He clearly hadn't felt the same need to present himself in an attractive light. He wore the old brown suit which seemed to be his uniform for almost all occasions and his hair looked as if somebody had tied a knot in it.

He seemed confused, as if he'd been expecting to see someone else there, and then he gave one of his disarming smiles. 'Patricia.'

He stepped back and I walked past him. The first thing that struck me was the atmosphere inside the shed, a heavy, dark smell that reminded me of compost when it's broken down into a rich mulch. Looking round I couldn't see where it had come from unless Stanley was the source. An aspidistra in the corner was long-dead.

The studio was not much bigger than the scullery at Moor Thatch. Every inch of surface had been commandeered by jars of brushes, paint tubes, books and magazines. One book, which he'd left open on the work bench, had a blob of red paint on it. *'Boethius'* was written on the spine. It was in Latin.

We stood looking at each other awkwardly. 'You look nice,' he said, finally. His eyes took in the yellow frock under the coat. I felt ridiculously over-dressed.

'What shall I do then?'

He glanced at the bed. 'Why don't you take your things off and sit over there?'

Did he mean everything? I hesitated. I'd expected him to offer me a cup of tea first or at least to spend five minutes talking to me.

I toyed with the buttons on my coat. This wouldn't be the first time I'd posed in the nude. In Paris we were slipping in and out of one another's studios the whole time. I would not have thought twice about taking off my clothes if I'd not gone to so much trouble to dress up first.

Stanley turned back to the work bench and began to squeeze paint out onto the palette. I took off my coat and draped it carefully across the chair back, lining up my shoes beside it. There was no screen in the studio and Stanley hadn't given me a wrap to put on, so I hurried through the awkward bits. Having insisted that his future lay in my hands, I'd thought taking off my clothes in Stanley's presence would be more of an event. What I had not expected was that he would stand there with his back to me.

I waited, thinking that at any moment he would glance over his shoulder and then, overwhelmed, drop down onto his knees. The minutes passed. I heard him whistling quietly to himself - a snatch from one of Handel's Oratorios. His head swayed back and forth in time with an imaginary chorus. Up till now I'd thought that I had something Stanley wanted; I could barter with it. But his attitude suggested he'd already taken what he needed and the only question now was what to do with it.

I crept up to the mattress. When he heard the springs squeak Stanley turned. I scrunched myself up at the top end with my knees under my chin.

'How do you want me?' I said.

He stood with his hands clasped, staring at me with his head on one side. He seemed perfectly relaxed now that I'd taken off my clothes. I could remember being in the Life Room at the Slade where there was always that brief tension when the model cast the wrap aside and stepped up on the podium. In France, the men were naked, too; you soon got used to it. It wasn't till the model stepped down from the platform that the atmosphere was charged again. I realised I had no more power naked than I had when dressed. Less, possibly.

'Could you stretch out across the mattress,' Stanley said, 'and put your arms behind your head. Like this.' He demonstrated. If I followed his instructions I'd be totally exposed, although the bed was set against the wall and on the same side as the window so that anybody passing, if they looked inside, might get a brief glimpse of a leg but not much else.

He stared at me for several minutes before turning back to face the canvas. I watched as he mixed the paint and then applied it to the surface in small dabs. He sat hunched over like a schoolboy at his desk, his concentration absolute, his tongue occasionally poking out between his lips.

He'd shaved that morning but so carelessly that he'd left little tufts of hair around his chin. There was a criss-cross patch of threads on one arm of his jacket where the sleeve had parted from the shoulder and been stitched inexpertly, presumably by Hilda though it was a task I could imagine Stanley taking on himself. He'd told me that when Shirin was a tiny baby he had often changed her nappies.

Every now and then he threw quick little glances my way that did not engage with me but seemed to be confirming something, like a writer going back over his notes. He didn't, unlike Dorothy, insist on silence in the studio, but I suspected, if I did speak, that he might not hear me.

My eyes scanned the room. There was a poster advertising one of Stanley's exhibitions, postcards on the pin-board of Renaissance paintings, letters from his dealers and propped up against the wall a painting with dogs running riot in a graveyard. One had cocked its leg against a tombstone.

'When is Hilda coming down?' I said at last.

'Tomorrow.'

'Does she know I'm sitting for you?'

With a rag he carefully removed a patch of colour he had just applied. He sat back. 'Yes, I told her.'

'Did she mind?'

He looked surprised. 'No. I explained I had to have you for my work.'

I didn't like the thought of Hilda grudgingly condoning my association with her husband, letting Stanley out but on a leash and with the understanding that at any moment she could reel him in. But then I wondered how I'd feel if Dorothy had wanted to bring sitters to her studio to draw.

'Do you paint Hilda?'

'All the time.'

'I meant like this.'

He pursed his lips. 'No.'

'Why not?'

He stopped painting and sat with the brushes resting in his hands. He ran his thumb along the shaft of one of them. 'They aren't the sort of pictures that I see her in.'

'You see me naked whereas you see Hilda dressed?'

He thought about it. 'That's right,' he said. I was not sure whether to be flattered or put out. I had expected Stanley to be deferential, grateful, anxious to impress me; in short, to behave the way he had when we were coming back to Cookham on the train. I had forgotten that an artist in his studio has all the same advantages that an opposing army has when it's on home ground.

As the afternoon wore on, the sun moved round. We hadn't spoken since our previous exchange. The light was shining at an angle through the window, falling on my ankle. I became aware that Stanley had stopped painting and was gazing at it. We watched as it edged its way across my foot. The patch of sunlight lingered in the hollow underneath my ankle and then crept onto the arch and down towards the toes.

'I'd like to creep across you like that,' Stanley murmured, almost to himself. He went on staring at it till the sunlight moved on and the foot was plunged back into shadow. For that moment, I had had his full attention but it wasn't me he had been captivated by, or even part of me. He wasn't worshipping my ankle, he was worshipping the way light had transformed it for an instant.

I was getting pins and needles in my legs. 'What time is it?'

'I don't know.'

'Only I told Dorothy I'd only be an hour. I've been here all afternoon. It'll be dark soon.'

'You're not going?'

'Yes, I think I'd better.'

As I edged my way across the mattress, he made little clawing movements at the air in front of him. Whilst I was rolling up my stockings, he was following my every move. It was as if the moment I stepped off the podium, I'd come to life. I glanced up as I fastened my suspenders.

Stanley reached out suddenly. I jerked back, thinking that he was about to grab me, but his fingers traced a path around my head and shoulders before hovering in mid-air.

'You'll come back tomorrow?'

'Not tomorrow. Next week maybe.'

'Next week?' His face fell.

'I'm filling in for Ida in The Copper Kettle at the weekend.' I did not tell Stanley I was meeting up with Richard on the Saturday. I didn't want him telling Hilda.

'But I need you,' Stanley said.

I gave a quick smile. 'So does Ida. Sorry, Stanley. I might manage Tuesday.'

Stanley stood there like a schoolboy who's just had his pocket money frozen. Twice he went to speak and then thought better of it.

'All right. Tuesday,' he said, sulkily.

XII

The evening I was due to spend with Richard at the Palais, he'd agreed to meet me off the train. I saw him waiting at the barrier as we pulled into Paddington. He wore a suit and looked much older now that he was dressed up, although by my reckoning he was at least six years my junior. Still, when I glanced at my reflection in the window of the cab, I wasn't disappointed.

I knew he was looking at me but I kept my head turned, gazing from the window at the shabby, run-down streets of Shepherds Bush, an area you'd think twice before walking through alone. I had been taken to the Palais just after it opened in the last year of the war. It was *the* place to go then, with its lacquered Chinese columns and pagoda roof. The dance floor was made out of maple and you had the feeling when you danced on it that it was moving with you. It was ten years since I'd been there and I wondered whether it would still seem as romantic as it had then.

On the way there, Richard sat so close to me that when I glanced at him I saw the faint nick on his chin where he had cut himself that morning with a razor. He had pale, sad eyes. Jas told me he had flown planes in the War; I'd seen that look on almost everybody who survived.

Once on the floor my body automatically remembered all the steps. We spent an hour racketing around the floor and then went over to the bar. I sat down on a high stool with my legs crossed. Stanley's latest present of a pair of nylons meant I hadn't had to draw a pencil line down each leg at the back.

I noticed Richard glancing at my knees. He gave a shy laugh and pretended to be looking at the lanterns hanging in the roof. I turned the conversation to the Spencers. When I asked him what he thought of Stanley, he said that his sister had her work cut out.

'They called him 'Cookham' at the Slade. Before he started there, he'd written down his thoughts on scraps of paper which he put in tins and buried, so the village would remember him. He sees his paintings as a kind of Baedeker: the path to God is down the High Street and across the common. Just keep walking and you'll get there.'

'Dorothy says England is the only place you'd find a painter like him.'

'I agree. Stan is so English, it's embarrassing, but lots of people want that, ordinary people devastated by the War. A resurrection in a country graveyard thirty miles from London, three miles outside Maidenhead, is what they need.'

'You like his work then?'

'Stanley's bonkers, but he is a genius. You just have to put up with all the other stuff.'

It wasn't until we were in the taxi going to the station that I got the bill for what had up till then been a diverting evening. When he leant across to tell the driver where to drop us, Richard put his hand on my knee, gently pressing on the flesh. I felt his nail snag on my stocking, which annoyed me. I tried shifting sideways but he moved my knee back and then slid his hand a little higher up my leg and let it rest there.

I decided it was easier to act as if I hadn't noticed. We weren't far from Paddington by this time. I looked out the window of the cab. It had begun to rain and people scurried for the shelter of shop doorways, struggling to unfurl umbrellas and turn up the collars of their coats. The pavements glistened in the dark.

The cab pulled up at traffic lights and as the lights changed, Richard launched himself at me. Our foreheads cracked. His mouth was slobbering its way across my cheek. I saw the driver looking at us in his rear-view mirror.

'Stop it,' I hissed, pushing him away. He hesitated.

'What's the matter? Don't you like it?'

'No, I don't.' I thrust his hand aside.

'We've had fun. Don't you think a girl ought to say thank you when she has been treated to a night out?'

'Not in that way.'

'Kissing in the back of taxis is beneath you, is it?'

'I don't like men mauling me. You know the driver's watching us.'

'Good luck to him. I'm sure he's seen a lot worse.'

He wrapped one hand round my wrist and pressed it to my side. His breath was coming in short bursts.

'Will you get off!' My free hand slipped and caught him on the jaw.

He sat back, red-faced, his hair plastered thinly to his forehead. His eyes narrowed. 'There's a rumour going round that you don't like men.'

'I don't like men who behave like you.'

'I thought you'd been engaged. You must know what they're like.'

He made another lunge. I grabbed a fistful of his hair. He looked bemused as if it were a game and I was guilty of not playing by the rules. 'It's true then. They say that freak you cohabit with is not your sister, after all.' He laughed unpleasantly.

'You think because I won't let you take liberties with me, I don't like men? It's easier for you to think that, I suppose.'

He muttered something underneath his breath. I caught the driver's eye. He stared at me a moment and then slid the window back and pulled into the kerb. 'St Pancras,' he said. We were three or four streets from the station, but I didn't care.

As he was on the pavement side, I had to wait for Richard to get out. He stood there at the kerb. I stepped onto the pavement, smoothed my dress down and walked past him. It was raining now in earnest and I felt it trickling underneath my collar.

'Thank you for a pleasant evening,' I said, stiffly. 'I can find my own way to the platform.'

He got back into the cab without a word and slammed the door.

XIII

I'd hoped that Dorothy would be in bed when I got back, but as I let myself in through the front gate, I could see her through the window sitting by the fire. I paused a moment in the scullery and leant against the wall. I'd spent an hour walking back and forth across the common in the drizzle, summoning the courage to come in. I didn't want to own up that on this occasion, as on others in the past when I had acted in defiance of her wishes, Dorothy had been proved right.

I'd once gone out in Paris on my own. It was our first year in the city and I wanted to see more of it. I took the Metro to a place I'd chosen on the map for its exotic name - *Les Lilas*. It turned out to be a wasteland of slum tenements and bombed-out buildings with grass growing through the rubble; not a lilac bush in sight.

Unwilling to abort the outing without some reward, I went on walking. By this time it was late afternoon and getting dark. A man approached me in the twilight whispering something in a low, insinuating voice. I started walking in the opposite direction, thinking I was going back the way I'd come, but now the streets looked unfamiliar. I went past a café that I wasn't sure had been there on the way out. Inside, men were playing mahjong. I could hear their throaty laughter and the clack of counters on the marble table tops. The air inside was thick with cigarette smoke.

The men sitting at the tables turned and looked at me with guarded interest, as you might look at an animal at auction before putting money down on it. A man behind the counter, washing glasses, looked up and I asked him for directions to the underground. He looped his cloth over the rack and stood with his arms folded as if he'd been asked a knotty question and was struggling to find an answer. One man made a comment and the others laughed.

'It doesn't matter,' I said, backing out. 'I'll find my own way.'

As I passed a row of boarded-up shops, I heard something on the inside being dragged along the floor. A rat ran out into the road with what looked like the torn pelt of an animal snagged onto one of its hind claws. It hesitated, its front paws suspended in the air as it picked up my scent, and then it darted back into the building.

It was dark now and the streets were empty. I shrank back into the shelter of the doorway. I was lost. The minutes passed and then I heard a low whine in the distance, like an animal in pain except that it was spaced out and accompanied by something heavy bumping over cobbles. It drew closer and a woman with a thick scarf covering her head and half her face, came into sight. She had a small boy at her side and pushed a cart on metal wheels ahead of her. One skewed wheel screeched each time it did a revolution. Seeing that I was about to speak to her, the woman murmured to the boy and wrenched the cart towards the kerb.

I ran towards them. 'S'il vous plaît', I said. She shook her head. 'Le Metro,' I insisted. She stared at me for a second and then gave a quick glance back over her shoulder, nodding. 'Merci,' I said. 'Merci.'

Turning down another street, I saw it: the art-nouveau fretwork at the entrance and the name, so much more beautiful than anything else that *Les Lilas* had to offer.

When I finally got back to our apartment in *rue Lamarck,* Dorothy was darning. She put down the shirt.

'Did you enjoy your walk?'

'I got lost.'

'Did you find a friendly gendarme to escort you on your way?'

'No.'

She looked at me for a moment in the same way she was looking at me now and then she sighed and crossed the room. She took my hand and led me to the alcove where the bed was, laid me down and took my shoes and stockings off. She pushed me gently underneath the eiderdown and slid in next to me.

'Don't ever leave me, Dorothy,' I'd whispered.

She glanced up now as I came into the room and studied me.

'Not quite as much fun as you'd hoped?' she said. She always knew.

I started to take off my coat but I was wet and I'd begun to shiver. I sat down and wrapped the two flaps of the mackintosh around my knees. 'The dancing was all right.'

'Well, that was what you went for, after all.'

'Yes, it was nice to go back to the Palais. Must be fifteen years since I was last there.'

'If the dancing lived up to your expectations, am I right in thinking Hilda's brother was the problem?'

Underneath the raincoat I felt clammy. 'I'm not sure he's very…nice.'

'Did you imagine that he would be?'

'Some men must be all right.'

'If you say so.'

'They would never have behaved like that before the War.'

'If you've spent four years killing people, you're less bothered with the courtesies, I dare say.' She got up. 'I'll make us both a hot drink. Get yourself to bed. I'll bring it up.'

She lumbered over to the door and suddenly it was as if a rubber band had snapped inside me. Tears were streaming down my face.

'I'm sorry, Dorothy.'

She came back to where I was standing.

'It was awful in the cab. He was all over me. I couldn't stand it.'

She encircled me with both arms, rubbing one hand up and down my back.

'He said things that were horrible. And now he'll go round telling everybody else.'

'I doubt it. After all it won't reflect that well on him. In any case they'll find another source of gossip soon enough.'

'Don't you care what they say about us?'

'After all this time, I'm used to it.

'We might as well be living in a ghetto,' I said, hotly.

'We are living in a ghetto. That's what a ghetto is, a group of people bound by race or creed or sexuality imprisoned with their own kind in a small space. Here, the difference is that only you and I are in it and it's called *home*. Why do you think I'm reluctant to go out into society? Sometimes it simply isn't worth the risk.'

'It wasn't like that when we lived in France.' Of course, now that we were no longer living there, France had become a symbol of democracy and freedom. At the Slade it was considered *chic* to flirt with members of one's own sex, but you weren't supposed to take it seriously. If you did, you were dubbed 'sad' and frozen out. I'd endlessly complained to Dorothy that if we lived in Paris we could please ourselves and nobody would care, till one day Dorothy had said, 'Well, why don't we just go there?'

'Go to Paris?' I had suddenly felt shaky. Dorothy was adamant that, if we did, it had to be a new start. She'd insisted we should only take one suitcase each.

I gloried in her courage and wished I could share it. But instead I cheated; I took little keepsakes with me, secretly – reminders of a home-life I had hated - and I made sure I had the addresses of acquaintances who I could call on in a crisis. Why, I wondered, didn't I accept that in a crisis Dorothy would be the one I called on. Was I thinking, even then, that maybe when the crisis came it would be Dorothy who left me?

For the first year we were there, I'd revelled in the freedom Paris gave us. Being in a place where nobody was taken seriously, where you could be anything you liked, was liberating till I realised that I needed rules precisely so that I could break them. Dorothy was not like that. She stayed the same no matter where she was. In Paris she could merge anonymously amongst people who were just like her. I didn't want to merge; I wanted to stand out and Paris was the place where I thought I could do it. It was also where I learned that those who stand out pay a price for it.

Most of the arguments we had there weren't, as they were now, in consequence of being poor. At that time Dorothy was still receiving an allowance from her father. There were lots of rich Americans in Paris but the gap between the rich and poor was not as obvious as it was in England. Most of what we needed was affordable.

The rows we had were usually in consequence of other people. Dodo didn't flirt; she didn't need to. I discovered that what had attracted me to her, appealed to certain other women. At a party given in *rue Jacob*, I had noticed a fey-looking girl who couldn't have been more than twenty, paying Dorothy particular attention. She had a ridiculously girlie hair-cut and a look of innocence which in that company could only have been counterfeit. Her cupid bow lips had been painted scarlet and stood out against her pale skin like a wound. She had gone over to where Dorothy was sitting and sat on the floor beside her, gazing up, her little elfin face and pointy chin inclined at a seductive angle. I could not believe that Dorothy was unaware of what was happening.

Then I realised she was perfectly aware. She knew that she was being targeted and she was quietly revelling in the attention.

I had never wondered whether Dorothy might be upset by my coquettishness. I knew it was a game and I assumed she knew it, too. This was the first time she had paid me back in kind.

I'd gone to get myself a drink. When I came back they were still sitting there but now the girl had put her hand on Dodo's knee and Dorothy was leaning forward so that no one else could overhear their conversation.

Earlier that evening, when she realised Dorothy and I were English, the girl told us that her ancestors had come from Aberdeen; their surname 'Mathurin' was on a census taken by the early kings of Scotland. There had even been a Saint named after them. When I had snidely said to Dorothy that she seemed over-anxious to impress us, Dorothy replied that it was hard to think of anybody claiming to have come from Aberdeen unless it was the truth.

I tapped her on the shoulder: 'It's eleven, Dodo,' I'd said casually.

She glanced up: 'Is it really?'

'If we don't go now, we'll miss the last train.'

'We can always walk. It's not far.'

'You hate walking,' I said, tightly.

'After all the food and wine we've had, I think a walk would be an excellent idea.'

'Where are you off to?' said the girl. Her accent with its long 'o's and its tendency to add a 'w' where none existed, put her in the 'Boston' camp like many of her countrymen who'd made a home in Paris. She would be the pampered daughter (daw-tah) of a banker or *Old Boston money*, sent to Paris to complete her education. She was doing that, all right, but maybe not quite in the way her parents had imagined.

Her eyes kept on flickering towards me as if checking my response. I kept my face blank.

'That's the way I'm going,' she'd said when she heard where we were living. 'My apartment's in *rue Lécuyer.*'

Her French was execrable. 'I've never heard of it,' I said.

My scorn was wasted on her. 'Just around the corner from the *Square Marcel*. Why don't you come for tea?'

'Tea?' I laughed. 'That's kind, but we don't *do* tea.' In fact, this was at Dorothy's insistence. She did not like anything that cut into the working day. In any case, the salons where you drank tea weren't the ones we were invited to. Ours served drinks from eleven in the morning onwards. After six the alcohol was often laced with drugs. I had heard rumours that a number of the *invertis* who pitched up at *Le Monocle* were on cocaine or heroin. The pupils of their eyes were pin-points. It was hardly worth the effort of becoming friends with them. One week you'd see them flaunting themselves, living as if there was no tomorrow, and the next week they were gone. You needed to be grounded in that crazy world if you were going to survive and Dodo was my anchor.

'So what did you think of her?' I said, when we got back to our apartment.

'Who?'

'The girl who tagged along this evening – Gretha Mathurin. The one who claimed to be descended from a Saint.' I fumbled in the drawer for matches. There was no light on the stairs and once inside we had to feel our way round the apartment till the lamp was lit. Sometimes we just fell into bed and didn't bother.

Dodo grunted: 'She seemed rather taken with us.'

'It was you who she was taken with.'

'I didn't notice.'

Yes you did, I thought, but I did not pursue it. We had gone to bed and made love. She went through the motions but she wasn't as enthusiastic as I thought she should be.

'You're not concentrating,' I'd said, grumpily.

'I didn't know one had to concentrate.'

'You might as well just go to sleep.'

'Perhaps I will. I do feel rather tired.' She yawned and gave my arm a pat. 'Goodnight, dear. Sleep well.'

Dorothy knew that I never slept well when we'd had an argument, although at that point we had not yet had it.

'Are you tired of me? Is that it?'

She had turned onto her side, away from me. She'd told me once that sleep was her escape from situations that she didn't want to have to deal with. 'Normal people can't sleep when they're anxious,' I'd said. She gave one of those infuriating smiles. 'I'm fortunate in that respect,' she said. 'For me it works the other way.'

She'd hesitated and then turned to face me. 'Why would you think that?'

'It's usually the reason when you start to flirt with other people.'

'You flirt all the time.'

'It's different.'

'Is it? In what way?'

'For me it's just a game.'

She'd looked at me and nodded. 'Is that so?'

'Whereas when you do it, it's to punish me for something.'

'And what do you think you've done that warrants punishment.'

'I didn't know that I'd done anything. That's why I'm asking.'

'It was Gretha who attached herself to me. She has an interest in painting.'

'Everyone in Paris has an interest in painting.'

'She spent time in Colarossi's studio last year. She wanted to know what I thought of him.'

'She's an admirer, then?' I smiled sarcastically.

'Of Colarossi?'

'No. Of you.'

I saw another yawn rise up in Dorothy. When it erupted it had gained conviction en route.

'Are we going to be seeing her again?'

'She said she might call in.'

'She might call in! You swore when we first came here that our home would never be a place where people called in uninvited.'

'She's not uninvited. I invited her.'

'You didn't think to ask me first?'

'No, dear, I didn't. You invited Gladys Esteritch and Clayton Morris to call in on us without consulting me first.'

'They're a couple.'

'What's that got to do with it?'

'I wasn't trying to get off with Gladys Esteritch or Clayton Morris.'

'No one said you were. I wasn't trying to get off with Gretha.'

'No? You could have fooled me.'

Dodo sighed: 'You're being very childish. I don't have the slightest interest in that little strumpet. Actually, I found her mother far more fascinating.'

My jaw dropped: 'Her mother!' I was not aware her mother had been there. 'But she'd be in her forties!'

'Older women have their uses. You can have a proper conversation with them for a start.'

'I didn't see you talking to her mother.'

'I took care to be discreet.'

'Why?'

'I was anxious to avoid the sort of tenth degree we're having now.'

'Why bother telling me at all, then?'

'I am simply pointing out that if I wanted to betray you, I'd make sure you didn't know about it. Go to sleep. If Gretha does call, you can deal with her. I'll stay out of the way.'

She'd turned her back on me. I lay awake for some time trying to remember Gretha's mother and re-play whatever conversation we had had with her. I put my hand out, resting it on Dodo's thigh and pressed my lips against her shoulder. 'Dorothy?'

'Mmm?'

'You won't leave me and go off with Gretha's mother, will you.'

Dorothy let out a snort. 'For heaven's sake, as you just pointed out, she must be in her forties.'

'But you said...'

She put her own hand over mine and held it. 'Silly girl,' she whispered. 'Gretha's mother wasn't there. I've never met her. I doubt either of her parents have set foot in Paris. If they had, they'd never have sent her here.'

I growled. 'Sometimes, Dorothy, I hate you.'

After every argument there'd be a truce and during that time Dorothy would be magnanimous. Though not demonstrative she would occasionally tell me that she loved me. I knew better than to ask for more.

The night I came back from my evening out with Richard Carline, I slept with her arms around me and each time I woke up, they were there. I am a restless sleeper but that night I didn't stir. I knew, no matter how uncomfortable she was, that Dorothy would stay like that until the morning.

For the next week, I remained at home. Had Dorothy been less obsessed with work I might have been content to carry on like that, but every morning after breakfast she would disappear into the studio and having washed up, read the papers and worked out which bills had to be paid and which ones could be put off, I was at a loose end. I was also out of stockings, thanks to Richard Carline, so before long I was wondering how I could engineer another trip to Maidenhead Department Store without the need to sit for Stanley and without another head-to-head with Dodo.

XIV

Stanley turned up at Moor Thatch the afternoon I had agreed to sit for him, to find out why I hadn't come. I heard him remonstrate with Dorothy who'd said I wasn't well. He called again the next day and the next, till Dorothy, exasperated, told him that he didn't need to keep on calling round; when I was better I would let him know.

'The way he carries on, you'd think he was infatuated,' Dorothy said tartly.

I had started getting letters from him; not the usual *sorry you're not well, I hope you'll soon feel better* sort that didn't tell you anything you didn't know already. Stanley wrote the way he talked. The letters rambled on, a passionate reiteration of his need for me. The word 'love' cropped up several times. He even mentioned 'sex'. But it was all about the pictures he had in his head. My worry that he might declare himself in writing and I'd somehow have to stop the letters falling into Dorothy's hands turned out not to be a problem. I soon gave up reading past the first page.

By the third week I was ready to go out into the world again. We'd had a run of days when it felt sinful to be indoors. It was warm, the bees were foraging amongst the flowers, cuckoo pint and thistles grew wild in the hedgerows and the grass was knee-high in the ditches. The air resonated with excess.

I shouted through the door of Dodo's studio to ask her if she'd like a cup of coffee and she shouted back that I could 'leave it outside'.

I don't like closed doors especially when it's Dorothy who's on the other side of them, and I particularly hate it when she can't be bothered coming to the door to tell me that she doesn't want to be disturbed.

I left her coffee on the stairs, put on the sort of hat that gets you noticed, with a big, wide, floppy brim that simultaneously hides and broadcasts the identity of anybody wearing it, picked up the wicker shopping basket and stepped out into the sunshine.

Having got the bulk of what we needed from the General Stores, I called in at the baker's for a loaf and one of their jam tarts. What I'd loved most about our time in Paris had been the patisseries. In England, do'nuts and vanilla slices were the only cakes on offer in the years after the War. In Paris the arrays of pastries were a feast not only for the stomach but the eyes – the colours and the textures and the little flourishes of icing – pink and green and yellow. *Chouquettes*, puffs of pastry so light that they melted on the tongue and left behind the sugar crystals sprinkled on them, were my favourite. I could eat them by the dozen.

Living in Montmartre was like being at a birthday party where the treats kept coming. Dorothy, who'd hated birthday parties as a child and always had to give up her balloon to somebody less fortunate, did not share my delight in its excesses.

There's a little annexe tucked behind the counter in the baker's where they serve tea and I toyed with the idea of treating myself to a scone. I'd get one half price in The Copper Kettle but because I work there, every time their doorbell pings I feel I ought to leap up and put on a pinafore. I once asked Ida if she ever fancied going out to tea and she said no; the treat for her was Monday when the shop was closed and she could have a gin and tonic for her lunch.

I saw that all three tables in the bakery were taken. Summer brings an in-flux of day-trippers to the village, drawn by the river with its rowing boats and sailing dinghies and that balmy atmosphere that in reality does not exist outside of memory.

I walked back past Ovey's Farm and Pyke, the cowman nodded to me. He was clearing pig swill from the courtyard. Pyke was one of the few people I remembered from my first time in the village. At thirteen I had conceived a passion for a boy who worked on Ovey's Farm. He couldn't have been more than eighteen.

When he passed me on the road outside the farm he raised his cap to me. Men had occasionally done this in the past but I was always with my parents and it was a gesture of politeness to my mother rather than to me. But here I was, my satchel swinging on my shoulder, walking down the High Street and this handsome boy with fair hair and the bluest eyes I'd ever seen had doffed his cap to me and made a little bow. As he walked off, he'd turned around once, giving me a wave. That did it. I had never been in love before, but I'd be carrying this passion with me in the abstract all my life.

When I returned to Cookham seventeen years later, Ovey's Farm was still there, but there was no sign of William. I knew William was his name because I'd heard another of the farm-hands call him 'Billy'. I eventually tracked him to the War Memorial. There were three 'William's' on the bronze plaque. I supposed *my* William must be one of them.

As I was walking back across the common, I glimpsed someone in a brown suit flitting in and out between the trees. I waited.

'Stanley?'

Several seconds passed and then he stepped out from behind a tree and sidled over to me.

'Are you following me?'

He considered: 'Not exactly.'

'What does that mean... not exactly?'

'Dorothy said you were ill. You weren't receiving visitors. I wrote you letters but you didn't write back.'

'It seemed silly, writing letters when we live just round the corner from each other.'

'I had hoped you might be well enough to come today, you see. Or yesterday.' He smiled.

A fortnight earlier I might have been seduced by his desire to lure me back into the studio, but I'd learned one thing during that first session: it was not me Stanley was concerned for. I was necessary, yes, but rather in the way that lungs are necessary to a man who wants to go on breathing. They're of no use whatsoever on their own. I'd had enough of being used.

'I don't think sitting for you is a good idea,' I said, as if I'd given it some thought and reached a difficult conclusion.

He looked baffled. 'Are you saying you don't want to be my muse?' He ran his fingers through his hair and let his hand rest on his head a moment as if he was not sure what to do with it next. 'Hilda loved to sit for me. She told me it gave meaning to her life.'

'But that's the whole point, Stanley. You can't suddenly decide that you're replacing Hilda. It's not fair to her.'

'I'm not replacing Hilda. It's not like that. You're my Cookham muse.'

'How many muses are there?' I threw out, sarcastically. 'A *Cookham Muse* implied there might be one for Downshire Hill or Burghclere – anywhere that Stanley had *hung out*. The question had been meant rhetorically, but Stanley pursed his lips.

'Well there was Elsie, obviously…'

I stared. 'What's obvious about Elsie?'

'She's our maid,' said Stanley. 'She's divine. You have to meet her. You would understand. She's…'

'Yes, all right, I know who Elsie is. I've seen her in the village.'

'Elsie…'

'Stop it, Stanley, I'm not interested in Elsie. Who else….?'

'There's my sister Flongy….'

'So it isn't sexual, this feeling?'

'Oh yes, almost all of it takes place down there.' He pointed at his groin. I followed the direction of his gaze. I'd thought I had one rival, Hilda, two if I included Stanley's painting. I was either dealing with an innocent or someone unbelievably promiscuous.

'Does Elsie know about this?'

'I've explained it to her and she always listens but I'm not sure how much Elsie understands.'

Let's hope it's not too much, I thought. 'You know that when you talk about these things, you run the risk of women thinking you mean something else.'

'What else?'

I sighed. 'They might think that you want to sleep with them.'

'I do,' said Stanley.

'But you just said one of them's your sister!'

He shrugged: 'I'm just saying that the feeling is the same. It's how I know it's not specific. It applies to everything.'

I'd known for some time that you couldn't count on Stanley in a rational argument. How could a man who knew so much be so naive about the world he lived in.

There were times when Stanley's lack of *savoir-faire* seemed almost suicidal.

'If you're looking to keep Elsie as your maid, I wouldn't say too much to her about whatever's going on *down there*. You don't want her to get the wrong end of the stick.' I had an afterthought. 'And let me make it clear now, Stanley, that - especially if the list's that long - I won't play second fiddle to your wife or anybody else.'

'You wouldn't have to. There would be no question of you playing second fiddle. Please, Patricia, say you'll come back to the studio.' He put his hand out and his fingers brushed my sleeve.

I hadn't set out to play hard to get, but by resisting Stanley's overtures, I realised that I'd upped the stakes. If I were to agree to sit for him again, I stood to gain more than a pair of nylons. I paused.

'I'm not only worried about compromising Hilda, Stanley. I'd be giving up a lot of time. I do have other things to do, you know.'

'You mean your waitressing?'

'No, Stanley, I don't mean *my waitressing*. You've obviously forgotten Dorothy and I are painters, too. The difference is that, unlike you, at present we can't make a living from our art. We do sell some of what we do, but not enough. We're struggling to keep up the mortgage payments on Moor Thatch.'

'I'll pay you for the sittings,' he insisted.

Would it be indelicate, I wondered, to inquire how much? At least the principal had been established. 'That would help, of course, but I doubt whether it would be enough. The way things are we'll probably be forced to give up Moor Thatch and move out of Cookham altogether.'

'You can't leave!'

'We may have no alternative.'

What he said next was so bizarre, I thought I must have misheard.

'You could always come and live at Lindworth?'

'What!'

'There's no-one on the top floor. It's where Hilda puts her Christian Scientists when they come down. She says the top floor of the house is there for friends.'

'I doubt that Hilda would put me and Dorothy into the category of friends.'

'Of course she would. She's always liked the idea of an artist's colony. There'd be no rent and you would be on hand for when I needed you.'

The idea that I'd be *on hand* for Stanley was just one of many things the proposition had against it, though the thought of living rent-free in a house the size of Lindworth certainly had its attractions.

'It's a kind thought, Stanley, but I can't see Dorothy agreeing to it.'

'Can't you ask her?'

'There'd be no point.'

'I can't paint the pictures I've got in my head unless you're there, Patricia.' Stanley grasped my arm.

I glanced over my shoulder and saw someone coming down the path towards us. 'Stanley. I must go.'

'Say that you'll sit for me. Please.'

'I don't know. Perhaps. I'll have a word with Dorothy.'

'You'll mention Lindworth?'

'Yes. I'll let you know.'

He stood there scuffing his feet on the dirt path like a horse and then he bent towards me. I turned sideways and the kiss, which wasn't well-directed in the first place, landed on my ear. He stepped back and then turned and walked across the common, flapping one hand at the earth as if saluting insects in the grass.

XV

'You'll never guess what Stanley has come up with.' I looped my coat on the peg inside the door. 'He reckons it's the answer to our money problems.'

Dorothy was spooning cat food out into a bowl. She stopped with the spoon halfway from the tin. The cat was yowling at her ankles. Now that I had almost had to give up smoking altogether, I resented what we spent on cat food and I didn't like the way the cat stretched out its claws each time it saw me. Dorothy had barely had a chance to put the bowl down on the floor before the cat had sunk its face in it.

'You told him we had money problems! Oh, for goodness sake, Patricia, have you no shame?'

She bent down and rapped the spoon against the bowl to dislodge the remaining gobbets of a substance that looked nothing like the picture on the tin.

'I told him we were struggling to keep up the mortgage payments on Moor Thatch. He's offered us the top floor of his house rent-free.'

She gaped: 'Are you mad?'

'Think about it, Dorothy. To say we're struggling is an understatement. You might not have noticed, living in your ivory tower, but we're in trouble. It was generous of your father to afford us Moor Thatch, but the business died when he did. No one's buying woollens anymore. The only person who still wears a cardigan is you.'

'I've known you wear a cardigan,' said Dorothy. 'And Mrs Arkwright in the General Store, she often wears one.'

'Maybe she could take another one in lieu of what we owe her.'

'Do we owe her?'

'Yes, of course we do. The only money we have coming in is from my work.'

'You mean your waitressing?'

'I was referring to my art-work.' I can see her lip curl even though she's turned her face away. 'Your art-work, then, but I'm the one who has to sell it. If you weren't so anti-social, we could market you under your own name.'

'If you had a bit more talent, we could market you under yours.'

There was the sort of silence that you got before an earthquake, then a faint plop as a single drop of water dripped into the sink. She turned the tap off with a wrench. 'How could you tell that man about our private business.'

'If we end up being thrown out, Dorothy, the village will soon know about it. Stanley tells us all about his private life in any case. He's never been much good at keeping secrets.'

'Hasn't it occurred to you that he might not be any good at keeping ours?'

'I just said that I couldn't spare the time to sit for him; I had to work so we could pay the mortgage. He's agreed to reimburse me for the sittings so at least if I go back I won't be doing it for nothing.'

'I thought the agreement was that you'd sit once or twice for him.'

'He says it's not enough.'

'There's a surprise,' said Dorothy.

'I'll get more out of him than Ida Buckpitt has been paying me. I think he genuinely wants to help us, Dorothy. The house is far too big for them. They don't need three floors.'

'It's a shame they didn't think it through before they bought it.'

'It seems criminal that they've got all that space and we're cramped into what is basically a two-up, two-down. You could house three families comfortably in Lindworth.'

'I was not aware you'd been inside it.'

'He described it to me. I suggested he should rent the top floor out. He said that Hilda wanted it kept free for friends. She's keen on the idea of artists living there.'

'Is that right?' Dorothy said sceptically. She picked the empty bowl up from the floor and put it in the sink. 'It's a ridiculous idea.'

'I said you wouldn't like it. But it would be a solution, Dorothy. I have to think twice before buying cigarettes. I wake up in the night and I feel ill.'

'You might feel better if you didn't smoke so much. In fact we both might. Has he mentioned this to Hilda?'

'He says she agrees to everything he wants.'

'Well, you can tell him that I'd rather crawl to Rome in sackcloth on my knees.'

'You don't think that's a tad ungrateful? You would like to be with other artists, wouldn't you? Especially artists who have galleries that show their work and lists of people rich enough to buy it. Isn't that what we've been aiming for?'

'Don't you learn anything from past experience?'

'If you mean Richard Carline, the two things are not the same.'

'You thought that if you cosied up to him enough he might get you an exhibition at The Goupil. You came back from that excursion with your pride in tatters and two laddered stockings.'

'Stockings Stanley had donated in the first place. We're beholden to him anyway.'

'I'm not beholden to him and I don't intend to be.'

'If it was left to you, we'd end up on the streets.'

'A place where you'd feel thoroughly at home,' said Dorothy, unwisely.

We were on our usual collision course. The point at which the argument imploded differed every time. Sometimes I put an end to it and sometimes she did. I had never heard her shout. As I got louder, she got quieter. I'd start ranting; she'd remain calm. In the end I'd storm out of the house and stay out long enough for her to miss me, or I'd break down and she'd feel obliged to comfort me.

On this occasion, I decided I would bring the confrontation to a close. I held my hand out. Several seconds passed while Dorothy took stock and then she laid her own hand in my palm. I turned it slowly and unfurled the fingers so the hand was lying flat. I stroked each finger tenderly towards the tip and curled my index finger in a circle at the end before I moved on to the next one. When I'd finished stroking every finger, my hand moved up to her wrist. I wrapped my fist around it, paused a second so that she could brace herself and twisted hard.

She winced but gave no other indication that she'd been affected. She turned, making her way back along the hall and upstairs to the landing, clumping down the corridor and disappearing finally into her studio. She closed the door behind her quietly.

Part Two
Lust

I

'She won't budge now. I know Dorothy and once she's made her mind up, that's it.'

My left leg was folded at an angle and was numb. Since Stanley had begun the picture on the easel, he'd made certain not-entirely-welcome changes to the composition. I was lying naked on the mattress with my arms behind my neck as I had been before, but now he had inserted his own figure in the background. He was staring down at me with his habitual expression of surprised bewilderment and he had got his glasses on so he looked even more like a voyeur.

The atmosphere inside the studio was heavy, almost airless, with the window permanently misted. Stanley dipped the brush in oil and wiped it on a paint rag. He was only half attending to the conversation. 'Hilda wasn't keen on the idea in any case. She's worried that you're taking me away from her.' He sat back to examine what he'd done.

I wondered how the residents of Cookham would respond to seeing me in one of Stanley's paintings. Although several of them had been given walk-on parts in pictures like the *Resurrection*, unlike me they'd been *transfigured*, to use Stanley's term. 'Transfigured' meant they'd been distorted until they were barely recognisable as human beings - having orgies in the cemetery or rummaging through dustbins with their willies out.

He'd been a source of gossip all his life, but in a situation where the village felt obliged to take sides, they would feel a bond of loyalty to Stanley which they wouldn't feel towards me. That's what bothered Dorothy. We were outsiders and we would remain outsiders. Even our position on the outskirts of the village seemed to count against us. Everything in Cookham happened on or near the High Street: Ovey's Farm, with outbuildings accommodating cows as well as horses, was halfway along the street and next door to the bakery there was a blacksmith's forge. With all that open land surrounding it you would have thought the village might have spread its boundaries a bit but no, its gaze turned inwards rather than towards the outside world.

I reached across the mattress for my wrap. This time I'd brought a shawl in with me so that I'd have something to put on when I got off the mattress. Although there were two cups in the studio and water could be heated on the stove, the sink was permanently clogged with paint. When Stanley offered to make tea, I had refused.

I went around the back of him and glanced over his shoulder. I'd persuaded Dorothy to let me sit for Stanley on the understanding that it would be temporary and that I would be discreet. I could imagine her reaction if and when she caught a glimpse of this. My breasts sagged and the flesh was pock-marked. I looked bored and disagreeable. As Stanley's muse, I might have hoped for something more inspiring. His depiction of himself was even more unflattering.

I'd heard him telling Dorothy that love was the defining factor of his work. He loved the figures in his paintings from the inside out and their outside appearance was an accurate reflection of that love. I didn't like the thought that Stanley loved me *warts and all*. Nobody wants their warts recorded for posterity.

He'd put a leg of mutton in the foreground of the picture.

'Why the leg of mutton?'

'There's a *Leg of Mutton Pond* in Hampstead. Maybe that's it. It's where Hilda and I did our courting. Things like that just pop up when I'm painting. Everything that happens now is the result of what has happened in the past.'

'It looks as if you're telling everybody I'm a piece of meat.'

'The leg of mutton isn't just a leg of mutton. It's a metaphor.'

'Whoever looks at it will see a leg of mutton, Stanley, not a metaphor. And when they look at my thigh next to it, they'll make the obvious connection. And you could have taken off your glasses. It looks odd when I've got nothing on.'

'I want to look at every wrinkle, every hair. I want to crawl across you like an ant.' His eyes passed down my body, stopping to refuel at key points on the way. I'd realised by observing him when he was painting that it was the nature, not the depth, of Stanley's concentration that changed when he had a paint-brush in his hand.

Whilst I was stretched out on the mattress, I was like an object in a still life, but the instant I moved, his appraisal relocated from his head to somewhere lower down. The change was so immediate that I was tempted just for fun to put the wrap on and then take it off again, but as I let the shawl slip off my shoulder I heard Dorothy's voice like the distant tolling of a bell, insisting it would *end in tears*. I tucked the shawl in round me.

'Aren't you worried people might misunderstand your work?'

'Misunderstand it?' He looked at the painting. 'How?'

'They might think it's obscene?'

He looked bemused. I gave him time to think about it. He spread out his hands and carefully picked out a bit of paint from underneath his nails. He glanced up. When he spoke, it was deliberately, like a missionary attempting to impart the Christian message to a savage who has never heard of God.

'My paintings celebrate Man's nature.'

I glanced round the studio. The painting of dogs running riot in the churchyard was still propped against the wall.

'That's not the point, though, is it?'

'Isn't it?' He stood back from the easel, toying with the brush and gazing at me with those sad calf-eyes of his. 'The feelings I'm expressing are the ones God's given us, Patricia, so he must have wanted us to have them. Hilda thought so, too. She said she never doubted it. She opened me to such a world of longing that I couldn't bring myself to think of it as bad.'

It seemed to me that Hilda had a lot to answer for.

II

One worrying development was that the presents Stanley bought for me when we went shopping were becoming more outlandish. Although we'd discussed the question of him paying me and every now and then when he remembered or I brought the subject up, he'd hand a roll of notes across to me, I felt that being paid diminished me not just in his eyes but my own. It meant the only perks I got from sitting for him at the moment were the presents and I felt I'd earned them.

Since he saw his urges as a gift from the Almighty, Stanley never bothered to disguise them. On arriving at the store, he made straight for the 'Lingerie' department, picked the items for me – black and frilly which was not what I'd have chosen for myself, and then insisted that I try them on and let him see me wearing them. He'd bought a pair of very high-heeled shoes which he brought with him in a bag for me to wear as an accompaniment. The sales girls thought it hugely entertaining. You could see them tittering behind their hands.

I got home after one such outing, tired and needing tea and sympathy, to find that Dorothy was not inclined to give me either.

'Where have you been all this time?' She kept her voice low, but I'd registered the signs: the empty glass of whisky on the windowsill, a pile of books left open on the sofa, picked up and abandoned. Dorothy was far more capable of living on her own than I would be, but her imagination had had time to fester and the sight of me disgorging myself from a taxi, laden down with parcels was the last straw.

'Maidenhead Department Store.' I threw the parcels down onto the sofa. 'And before you ask, I haven't had a pleasant afternoon.'

She eyed the packages. 'You seem to have come back with more than you set out with.'

'If you mean the parcels, they contain three negligees, six pairs of stockings with clocks running up the shins, a packet of three different coloured lacy ribbons for my hair, a pair of shoes with heels so high that I can barely walk in them and chenille knickers that are so sheer, frankly I might just as well be in the nude.' I rubbed my ankle where the heel had chafed it.

'How exciting. I'm assuming someone else picked up the tab?'

'You don't think I'd buy chenille knickers for myself.'

'The taxi must have put you back a bit. Or did he pay for that as well?'

'Yes, actually. I said I couldn't manage with the parcels.' I leaned back and closed my eyes. I'd often get a foot massage from Dorothy when I came home after a stint of waitressing but there was not much chance of that this afternoon.

'Perhaps we should be grateful that he didn't feel obliged to help you carry them.'

'He offered. I said no. He would have stayed to tea and then you would have had to listen to him. Anyway, I'd had enough by then. I had to try on every item in the store whilst Stanley sat and slavered. It was utterly humiliating.'

'But you managed to put up with it. Well done.'

She elbowed her way past me and went through into the kitchen. I saw that the plates from lunch were still there on the draining-board. She took a tea-towel with a picture of Canarvon Castle on it from the dresser, shook it out and made a face before replacing it and taking out another.

I reached for the pinafore hung on a hook behind the kitchen door. 'I'll wash, you wipe.' I filled the bowl with water and scooped washing soda into it. At least if I was washing up I'd have my back to her.

'I thought we had agreed that Stanley's place was with his wife.' She held the tea towel at arm's length. 'Why isn't she here with him?'

'She's insisting that her gynaecologist must be a Christian Scientist. There aren't a lot of those in Cookham.'

'Her reluctance to spend time here hasn't anything to do with you, then?'

'Oh for heavens' sake! Why are you so possessive?'

'I know how susceptible to flattery you are, Patricia. I'm familiar with the courtship ritual. I may not know the gestures, but I recognise the scent.'

I slam the cup I'm washing on the draining board. The handle drops off. Dorothy retrieves the handle and picks up the cup. She throws the two halves in the bin. 'Remind me why you're doing this.'

'If we don't wash up every now and then we won't have any plates to eat off.'

'We may not have any cups to drink out of if you continue to wash up.' She takes another plate out of the rack. 'Why have you gone on seeing him; that's what I'm asking. And do please go easy with the china.'

'Stanley's useful to us. He knows everybody in the art world.'

'So far he's not been in any rush to pass his contacts on to us.'

'It takes time. I can hardly ask him outright. You try hawking your work round the galleries and being nice to the directors. Let's see how far you get. I know cultivating people for our own ends is a concept you find disagreeable, but at the moment Stanley is our only hope. I'm doing this for both of us.'

'I promise you it isn't me he's buying frilly knickers for.' Her voice was scathing. It had been the knickers that she really took exception to.

'Perhaps I can persuade him to buy jewellery instead. At least it's something we can sell on.'

'You don't think he might expect to see you wearing it a few times first.'

'It isn't just the underwear….' I hadn't meant to bring this up in front of Dorothy. I knew exactly what she'd say.

'Well…?'

'I think he likes wearing women's clothes. He's got a thing about them.'

I'd arrived at Lindworth for a sitting ten days earlier and there was no one in the studio. I'd wondered what the house was like and now I had a reason to go in and find out. I'd discovered Stanley in the bedroom trying on a skirt of Hilda's and saw he had a chemise on underneath it. When I asked what he was doing he said he was curious to see if putting on her clothes brought Hilda closer to him.

'Does it?' I'd asked.

He had looked at his reflection in the mirror with his head on one side. 'No, but they feel nice against my skin,' he said.

By telling Dorothy that Stanley liked to dress in women's underwear, I might, I thought, distract her from the idea of me wearing it.

She tossed her head. In Paris we'd had friends whose tastes were more bizarre than that and we accommodated them without a fuss. But Cookham wasn't Paris and what passed for risqué there, would not be tolerated here.

'He isn't secretive about it. He sees nothing wrong in any of it. It's another kind of love. It doesn't cut him off from God. It *is* God.'

Dorothy harrumphed. 'If we were living in the sixteen hundreds they would have set fire to him by now. I take it you're not in a rush to join him on the pyre.'

'No thank you.'

'Give him up then. Let him find another focus for his fantasies. I hate to say *I told you so*, but it was obvious from the start that Stanley didn't only want you as a sitter, just as Richard Carline didn't only want to take you dancing.'

From now on she would be using Richard Carline like those chokers you can put on dogs to pull them up short every time they make a wrong move.

I knew that if Stanley went on turning up at Moor Thatch uninvited, Dorothy would finally lose patience. In the hope of phasing out some of his late-night visits, I had given him a diary similar to one that Dorothy and I used. If we'd done something the other wouldn't like, or wanted to suggest something and were uncertain how the other would respond, we wrote it down in order to avoid a head-on confrontation. I did not add, when I gave it to him, that I hoped it was how we'd avoid one.

He had turned it over in his hands: 'I can write anything I want to?'

'Within reason.' He was fingering the cover. *Within reason* was a limitation Stanley didn't find it easy to adapt to. 'All right, you can write down anything. It's only you who will be reading it.'

He frowned. 'I thought you meant that you and Dorothy would read it.'

'Stanley we're not a *ménage à trois*. If you've got something to communicate why don't you write to Hilda?'

'I do write to Hilda. Every day.' He ran his finger-nail along the bristles of the paint-brush he was holding. Every gesture Stanley made these days seemed to be laden with erotic overtones.

'There must be some thoughts you have that you'd rather people didn't know about. Why don't you put those in the diary?' He'd looked up at me ingenuously.

There was nothing Stanley would find reprehensible enough to warrant keeping it a secret.

I ought to have turned round then and walked away without a backward glance. I should have. But I didn't.

III

So far Dorothy was not aware that I was posing in the nude for Stanley, so when he suggested he and Hilda ought to paint a portrait of me, my first thought was that it would at least suggest to Dorothy that everything between us was above board. It would also make a change for Stanley to be looking at my face, although it was more difficult to see what Hilda would be getting out of it.

'I want you to be friends,' said Stanley. 'You and Hilda have to love each other. It's important to me.'

'Well I'm sorry but I can't love Hilda and I'm sure that if you asked her she would tell you that she doesn't love me either.'

'She admires you though. And you've said that you like her painting.'

Actually I liked it more than Stanley's. That was not the issue though. 'You know how I hate being looked at.'

'But if Hilda wants to, couldn't you say yes?'

'You must have bullied her into agreeing.'

'I don't need to bully Hilda. She says there is always something in my wants that justifies them. Hilda understands me.'

'Why don't you just carry on with her, then?' I said, irritably. I invariably started off defending Hilda, only to find Stanley was her number one supporter. Still, my portrait on show at a London gallery might offer us another way into the art world. At least it would prove I knew the artist (and his wife, of course).

A fortnight earlier we'd heard that Stanley had been made a member of The Royal Academy. I was delighted and not just for him. It meant a huge leap forward in career terms. Being an Academician would enhance his reputation and increase the value of his paintings and the better-known he was, the easier it would be to make capital of our acquaintance with him.

I had hoped to bring our conversations round to a discussion of what he might do for us now that the offer to move into Lindworth had been shelved, but it was soon apparent that there was no subtle way of dropping hints where Stanley was concerned.

'What would you do with them... the portraits?'

'I give everything to Dudley. He's my dealer.'

'How did you get taken on by him?'

'He asked me if I'd like to show at 'Tooth's' whilst I was still a student.'

'Lucky you.'

'The dealers came to the Diploma Shows. They must have come when you were there.'

At least it seemed to have sunk in that Dorothy and I were also painters. She had been approached by dealers in her final year. I hadn't. She gave up the chance to sign up with a gallery because we had already made our minds up that we'd go to France.

'They did. We had our offers. But we moved to Paris. It seemed more exciting at the time.'

He nodded. Faced with choosing Cookham or the international centre of the art world, Cookham would have won hands down with Stanley.

'Now that we've moved back here, it would obviously be useful to have somewhere to exhibit,' I said, slyly.

'You could speak to Hilda's brother.'

'You mean Richard Carline?' It was as if somebody had pulled out an elastic band inside me and released it. 'Why would I do that?'

'He shows his paintings at The Goupil.'

'Wouldn't Tooth's be just as good?'

'Oh no,' said Stanley, as if the idea of us exhibiting alongside him was unimaginable. 'I don't think so.'

'I would rather not ask Hilda's brother for an introduction.'

He shrugged. 'You could try Lefevre's. They show living artists.'

'So do Tooth's!' I felt like yelling. But I smiled demurely and took off my wrap. 'Perhaps I will.'

IV

I'd not planned to run into Elsie, but when I saw her emerging from the pharmacy, I sidled up to her as if I'd happened to be going in the same direction. She knew who I was, although we'd not been introduced.

'It's Elsie isn't it?'

'Miss Preece?' She stopped and hooked the basket she was carrying onto her other arm. She had an open, friendly face and I could understand why Stanley found her so engaging.

'That's right. I live near the common. You work for the Spencers, don't you?'

'Yes, I've been with them since I left school. I thought I'd have to go outside the village to find work so I was lucky to be taken on by them.'

It struck me that this girl with her outgoing and obliging nature and her love of Cookham would be far more suitable as Stanley's *Cookham Muse* than me. She genuinely liked the place.

'What is he like to work for… Mr Spencer?'

'He's a lovely man,' said Elsie. 'He explains his pictures to me. He says he wants me to understand what they're about.'

'And do you?'

Elsie glanced over her shoulder as if to make sure that Stanley wasn't within ear-shot and then giggled: 'Actually, I've no idea. It's all beyond me.'

'Has he asked you if you'll sit for him?'

'He often draws me when I'm working. He likes watching as I shred the green beans or put sheets out on the line. When she was tiny, I put Shirin in a drawer so she could see me working. Mr Spencer loved that.'

'You don't mind him looking at you?'

'No, of course not. Why would I mind?' She laughed.

'You have a fiancé in the village, I believe?'

'Ken. Yes. We're saving to get married.' Elsie bunched her shoulders and the colour rose up in her cheeks. It wasn't Stanley's prurient attention, but the fact of having a fiancé, that had made her blush.

'So you'll be leaving Lindworth?'

'Not yet.' She sighed. 'It'll be years before we can afford a wedding.'

I knew if I went on questioning her, she'd become suspicious. We'd already stood there gossiping for quarter of an hour. As if to confirm the fact, the church clock struck the hour.

'I must get on.' Elsie patted the loaf of bread she'd bought. 'Nice to have met you.'

'Good luck, Elsie,' I said, genuinely. 'And congratulations.'

'You mean my engagement,' she said, beaming.

Actually that wasn't what I'd meant but I smiled anyway.

V

The bathroom with its monstrous water tank, supported by iron brackets built into the wall, was not Moor Thatch's most attractive feature. The iron bath had rusty drip stains underneath the taps which no amount of scouring could shift; the lino on the floor was cracked and beetles squeezed out of the gaps. A rug with loose threads that your toes became entangled in and which would skid across the floor when you stepped onto it with wet feet, was the only luxury, but we felt fortunate to have a bathroom and the presence of the boiler meant that it was always warm in there.

Bath night was usually on Fridays, just in case we happened to be doing something at the weekend. Although there was barely room for any other furniture beyond the wash hand basin and a towel horse, on a Friday we traditionally took a chair up from the kitchen so that we could occupy the room together.

We took turns to be the first one in the tub. I loathed the water being second-hand and lukewarm, but it didn't bother Dorothy. That night it was her turn to go first. I was sitting on the rim and giving her a back scrub.

'Dorothy, have you been cutting your own hair again?'

'You weren't here.'

'Oh for goodness' sake you could have waited till I got back, surely.' I looked at the zig-zag of the hair-line just above the topmost vertebrae. 'Hair only grows a quarter of an inch a month, you know. It wasn't likely to become a problem in the next ten minutes.'

'I'd already cut the front. I thought I might as well go all the way round.'

'Carry on like this and you and Stanley will be indistinguishable from each other.'

'Stanley's hair-cut's in a category of its own.'

'So's yours now.' I raked through the bathroom cabinet for scissors. Perching myself on the ledge behind her, I attempted to make good the desecration. Dorothy had what a portraitist would call *a good head*; well-formed with distinct planes and a curve below the skull that gave it an authority. I didn't like heads that descended in a straight line, as if nature had decided it could not be bothered finishing the job off properly.

'You've got a lovely head,' I told her, 'especially where it curves into your collar at the back.' I ran my hand along it. I'd discovered long ago how vulnerable Dodo was to touch. Sometimes in public, just to gee things up a bit, I'd lean across her, putting one hand lightly on her wrist as if to emphasize a point. I'd feel the tremour underneath the skin, although she never let on how it was affecting her unless we were alone.

I tidied up the line of hair. Although she parted it the way a man would, she would never pass for one. Men's hair grew differently. I wished she'd take more trouble over her appearance but whenever I suggested something, she'd say she could not be bothered. I occasionally bought a pair of shoes for her and once I came home with a blazer that I'd seen in Maidenhead. She tried it on but it was too smart altogether. Dorothy liked to pretend she didn't care what people thought but she would go to any lengths in order not to stand out in a crowd.

'How can you cut your hair behind when you can't see what's happening? You're fortunate you didn't puncture the carotid artery.'

'I promise if I did that, it would be deliberate and I would make a better job of it.'

'The hair-cut or the other?'

Dodo snorted. 'You would hardly cut your hair first and then top yourself.'

'Good. That's all right, then.' Still, I wished I hadn't said it. I was terrified that one day Dorothy would unilaterally decide she didn't like her life and she would simply end it. She could do that. I'd be too scared. They would have to drag me off-stage, screaming, clinging to the sets. It wouldn't matter how old and decrepit I was, how incapable of functioning. I might be on a respirator or incontinent, or gaga; I would never have the guts to top myself. But she would.

'Stanley wants me to let Hilda paint my portrait,' I said in the same tone.

Dorothy's head jerked towards me, barely giving me the time to whip the scissors clear. 'You must be joking. You think Hilda, with a young child and another on the way will want to do a portrait of her husband's floozy.'

'That's unfair.'

'All right. What is your title, just in case I'm tempted to address you?'

I'd anticipated that when I eventually told Dorothy I'd started posing in the nude for Stanley, we would have a row about it but if this was her reaction to a portrait painted by his wife I came to the decision that I wouldn't bother telling her at all.

'I thought you'd be relieved to know that it was all out in the open.'

'If you put two females in a cage when they're competing for the same male, the most likely outcome is that they will tear each other into shreds.'

'We're not competing for the same male. Stanley wants his wife to get back into painting. He says she's done hardly anything since Shirin came along. I can't see Hilda ripping anyone apart in any case. She seems to spend most of her day asleep.'

'Perhaps her husband is a vampire. Have you thought of that?'

'Or maybe Hilda is and she can't get enough blood to sustain her. That's why she's so sleepy.'

'I'd watch out if I were you.'

'If I come home with bite-marks on my neck, you'll know why.'

I made an impression with the sharp point of the scissors, pressing lightly on the skin below her neck where there were little groups of freckles. I thought of the vessels underneath the skin criss-crossing one another and, beneath the veins and arteries, the bones. I had an image in my head of Dorothy as she would be a hundred years from now, a skeleton sat upright in the bath, her knees bent slightly, her wrists overlapping them, her head a grinning mask of teeth and empty sockets where those mesmerising blue eyes currently resided.

I once asked her whether I could have her blue eyes in the next life. She'd said 'Yes, if I can have your legs.'

'You want my legs!' I laughed. 'They'd look ridiculous on you. And since you normally wear trousers, what's the point?'

'Would you say that about a Ming vase – *what's the point?* You don't just covet things because they're useful. It's enough to contemplate them.'

'There you are, then.' I'd pulled up my skirt and crossed my legs. I swung the top leg back and forth a few times like a hypnotist with a pocket watch and then uncrossed them and sat back, my knees not quite together.

She'd regarded me a minute with her head on one side. 'Very nice,' she said and then got on with what she had been doing at the time.

The skin under the scissors went white and then colour flowed back into it again. I pressed the point down, slightly harder and a tiny spot of blood appeared. I stared at it. It was like looking into a volcano, waiting for it to erupt and send its molten rocks and lava crashing down the mountain side. I'd only need to press the point a little farther in and that would be the end of Dorothy.

She'd barely moved. She might sense something going on behind her back but she would not do anything to save herself. The water in the bath was lapping gently at her ankles. Both her arms were resting lightly on her knees. Outside, I heard a sparrow chirping in the undergrowth.

'Whatever are you doing?' Dorothy said, calmly.

VI

I had not seen Hilda since the evening of the 'At Home'. I was worried Richard might have told his sister what had happened that night at the Palais. He'd have put a rather different slant on it, of course. I would have been presented as a cross between an ice-queen and a vamp, the sort of girl (*gal*) who gives men the *come on* and then slams the brakes on once they're up and running.

Almost more distressing was the thought that Richard might confide in Jas Wood, though I wasn't sure why Jas' good opinion mattered so much to me.

The Saloon was parked outside the gates at Lindworth so I knew that Hilda had arrived. She had insisted that we have the portrait sittings there and I was glad she had. I didn't want her coming to Moor Thatch and seeing us together, me and Dorothy. Men miss things; they see what's infront of them or what is in their heads already, whereas women tend to notice what is in the background first.

So far, the only bit of Lindworth I'd seen was the corrugated iron shed in the garden and the bedroom on the first floor of the house which still gave me a shudder when I thought about it.

Stanley went into the house to eat and sleep but since he didn't always bother to do either, days passed when he wasn't in the house at all.

I rang the bell and Hilda let me in. Though obviously pregnant, she had not put on as much weight as I'd have expected. Her condition was more obvious when she was walking: sashaying from side to side instead of moving in a straight line, though she managed to glide elegantly nonetheless. The hall was full of crates as yet unpacked. On one of them there was a gramophone and next to it a pile of records.

Hilda led me down the passage, past the door into the scullery. I caught a glimpse of Elsie kneeling on a square of cloth and scouring the pavers with a donkey stone. There was a mangle with a washboard leaning up against it just inside the door and on the draining board a packet of blue dollies and a square of starch.

I followed Hilda down the corridor and upstairs to a large room on the second floor. There was no carpet in the room or on the stairs. It was completely bare except for Hilda's easel, a brass bed which had a chamber pot tucked underneath it and a wash-stand with a marble top. Books had been piled up in a corner and there was one open on the bed. In Paris, Dorothy and I read anything we could lay hands on. I'd heard *Ulysses* described by one of our friends as the filthiest book she'd ever read so naturally we wanted to get hold of it.

It seemed that Hilda's tastes were fairly narrow. When I asked what she was reading, she told me it was a book by Mary Baker Eddy and asked if I'd like to read it. I said I'd got several books already on the go and I'd get back to her.

Downstairs the front door slammed shut and there was a crunch of footsteps on the gravel. I assumed that this was Elsie going out.

I sat deliberately at an angle so I could watch Hilda watching me. That way I felt less at a disadvantage. My eyes kept on wandering towards her right breast. Even now I felt a flicker in my stomach when I pictured Stanley's thumb against the nipple.

She was certainly a handsome woman, although in that melancholy, introspective way beloved by the Pre-Raphaelites. An aura of mute suffering surrounded her. I wondered if she was aware how much I knew about her. But then it occurred to me that maybe she knew more about me than I would have liked, not necessarily from Richard but in consequence of Stanley's irritating aptitude for honesty.

She stared at me a moment and then mixed some paint and tried it out in small strokes on the palette before she applied it to the canvas. Once we'd started there was no attempt at conversation. She was totally absorbed. I wondered what would happen when she had to paint my eyes and there was nowhere she could go to get away from me.

I was relieved in retrospect that Stanley's offer for us to move into Lindworth hadn't come to anything. The rooms were elegant and well-proportioned with large windows and high ceilings, but the house reeked of neglect and was pervaded with a musty scent. I would have liked to throw the windows open and let in some air.

Originally, Stanley was intending to set up his easel next to Hilda and paint with her, but then he'd decided it would give us more chance to discuss him if he wasn't there. I doubted we would take advantage of the opportunity, however. Hilda was the silent type. It seemed the two of them wrote letters to each other even when they were at home together.

Since I'd started seeing Stanley, I'd been writing in the diary quite a lot and so had Dorothy. If we continued in the same vein, I would have to buy another one. We'd not yet reached the stage of writing ten or fifteen pages to each other every day, however. I discovered that this was the norm for Hilda when I saw a cardboard box of letters in the studio. They'd need a second home soon, just to store the letters.

On the wall there was a portrait which did not resemble anything I'd seen of Stanley's and which I assumed therefore was one of Hilda's. Although, since they married, Stanley said her time was taken up with trivialities like gardening and housework, I saw little evidence of either.

Stanley's sister, Annie, who still lived in Fernlea spent the daylight hours at an upstairs window staring down into the street. The last time Stanley visited, he'd had to take a spade with him to clear a pathway through the rubbish in the hall. In spite of Elsie's efforts, Stanley's own home was a rubbish heap by normal standards so I baulked at thinking what Fernlea must be like. I could see the house from where I sat, its crumbling brick facade held up by ivy. It was one of two 3-storey villas, separated from the road by cast-iron railings and a privet hedge. In buying Lindworth Stanley might have thought that he could keep an eye on Annie, but it was apparent that inside Fernlea things were becoming desperate.

I sat for an hour and a half without a break. Like Stanley, Hilda seemed indifferent to comfort, whether it was hers or other people's. I was starting to feel stiff but wasn't looking forward to the moment when we stopped and had no option but to talk to one another.

Painting me was her chance, if she cared to take it, to exact revenge and my chance to discover what she really thought of me. It was a risk. As Dorothy was quick to point out: 'You are letting someone who has every reason not to like you, paint a portrait that could outlive both of you.' Like many painters, Dorothy had one eye on posterity whenever she picked up a brush. It was enough for me if what I'd done was recognisable.

'I gather you've been spending most of your time recently in London,' I said when the silence had begun to grate on me.

'Yes, George, my brother, isn't well.'

'I'm sorry.'

'I've been helping Mother to look after him. My older brother Sydney died five years ago so Mother's naturally concerned.'

There was a fluttering in the window and a brimstone butterfly flew in and settled on the sill. It bent its wings to Hilda as if genuflecting. Both of us had turned to look at it. I had the feeling it was watching us, too, its antennae trembling slightly from the breeze or possibly from apprehension.

Although we were well into September, there had not yet been a frost. There was a warmth and ripeness in the air. I loved the fulsomeness and slow decay of Autumn and I sensed that this might be a favourite month for Hilda, too.

I glanced at her. She had leant slightly forward, her head tilted, an expression of such rapt attention on her face, that it was clear she had forgotten everything except the butterfly. I could imagine her in front of one of Stanley's pictures, not like me immediately on the look-out for some impropriety, but willingly accepting what she saw. With Hilda it was all or nothing. When she threw in her lot with the Spencers, she signed on forever. Possibly the only person more obsessed with Stanley than the man himself, was Hilda.

Her apparent weariness was not a sign of lack of energy, though looking after Stanley full-time could bring anybody to their knees. With Stanley, everything was concentrated in his head. Although his body was expressive and his hands particularly so, he never wasted energy and it was this ability that Hilda had perfected. When she focused her attention on an object, it was as if she had skewered it. The butterfly remained transfixed. It wasn't till she took her eyes off it that it felt free to fly away.

My thoughts had drifted. I was suddenly aware that Hilda had stopped looking at the butterfly and turned to stare at me, as if she had just realised who I was.

'Why did you come here?' she said.

'Stanley said you wanted me to sit for you.'

She frowned: 'I meant to Cookham.'

'Ah. My father had an Army posting here in 1907, so I knew the village.'

She had turned back to her painting. 'Are you staying?'

'I've no plans to leave at present.'

She seemed to consider. 'You know Stanley won't leave. He belongs here.'

'Why would either of us need to leave?'

'He thinks that he's in love with you.'

'Perhaps he is.'

'But you don't love him.' I had the impression that she would prefer it if I did.

'I don't want Stanley, Hilda. Not in that way.'

'Then you ought to let him go.'

'He's free to go.'

'He isn't; you've bewitched him.' For the first time I could hear an echo of resentment in her voice.

'That's not my fault.'

'When I met Stanley, he thought lust was something to be feared.'

'He seemed to have got over all that by the time he met me.'

Hilda's look implied that she held me responsible if that was so. 'He broke off our engagement six times, not because he didn't love me. He was fearful that sex might get in the way of his creative vision.'

'I expect he was relieved when he discovered that it didn't.'

Any irony was lost on Hilda. 'She took several steps back from her painting, frowning so that I was not sure whether she was frowning at the painting or at what I'd just said.

'I wish you would go away,' she murmured, but she went on looking at the picture. It was as if she had said it to herself. I didn't answer.

I passed Fernlea on my way back to the cottage. The small garden at the front was overgrown with brambles creeping out onto the pavement. The gate had subsided on its hinges and hung open. The house looked abandoned. I glanced up and caught a glimpse of Annie at the window.

Twenty years before, I'd passed Fernlea one evening on my way home from the station to the house in Odney Lane which we had leased for the duration of my father's posting. It was early in September and already dusk. Inside, a paraffin lamp hanging from the ceiling threw a pool of light onto a table around which sat seven or eight children, eating, chattering and laughing. I could hear their voices from the pavement outside.

There had been eleven children in the Spencer family, nine of whom survived, the youngest being Stanley and his brother Gilbert. In my head I went around the table ticking off the names beginning with the eldest: Percy, Sydney, Gilbert, Flongy, Annie, Horace... Stanley.

I had never sat down to a family meal like this. At weekends when my older sister and my brother were at home, we ate in silence with our parents. No one spoke unless they were invited to. I would have given anything to sit around that table, talking freely, laughing, able to be anything I wanted, rather than the opposite of what my father wanted.

Our domestic life was run on military lines which may have been why I felt an aversion to the former Sergeant-Major who ran Arkwright's Stores, although it wouldn't have explained why Dorothy detested him. My father had one weakness – me. Through him, I learnt the currency of charm and how to barter with it. If my siblings wanted something, I would be the one tasked with the job of asking. I could *get round* Daddy. I delighted in my power until I began to realise I no longer had complete control of it.

As a young child I had liked sitting on my father's knee. At thirteen it was not a place where I felt comfortable. I didn't like the smell of pipe tobacco that clung to his jacket and the sticky, tar-like substance that clogged up the ends of his moustache. That scent which was peculiarly male no longer reassured me. I sensed something threatening in the way my father curled his hand around my leg to stop me sliding off his lap. When I was little I had loved to ride his knee as if it were a horse and when it bucked or dived I shrieked with laughter. This delighted terror was what Daddy wanted from me. His needs hadn't changed but mine had.

A way out presented itself one weekend when, chafing at the silence round the dinner table which was broken only by the slurping noise my father made as he spooned soup into his mouth, I said something amusing and my brother laughed. The sound broke off abruptly as my father's hand came down across my cheek. The slap felt like a wet towel. Seconds later came the pain.

I didn't know if what I'd said had made him angry or the fact that I'd addressed my comment to my brother, not to him.

I stared at him and as I went on staring, his expression wavered. I got up and left the table. I would never sit on Daddy's lap again. I knew the power of withholding my affection. Two could play at that game.

'It's because he loves you,' Mother had insisted later. Neither of them had much of a gift for words.

From then on I would flirt with any man who crossed my path, especially if my father happened to be watching.

I'd gone to the Slade because I knew it would annoy him. He had wanted me to be a secretary or a book-keeper. My talents certainly lay more in that direction but I wasn't doing anything to please my father.

He'd reluctantly agreed to foot the bill as long as I agreed to live at home. I wouldn't. In the end he paid for me to go in any case. He was still trying to win back my love. Each time he gave in, I despised him more. It was a pity that he died before I had an opportunity to dandle Dorothy in front of him.

VII

'You managed to get through the day then?' Dorothy was lying on the sofa with a book in one hand. She was stroking Tiddles with the other. They looked as if they'd been grafted onto one another. Every time I looked at Dorothy's left hand, the cat was on the end of it, the way that Hilda's breast was always on the end of Stanley's right arm when I thought about it.

I pulled down the collar of my shirt. 'No bite marks on the neck as far as I'm aware.'

'How's Hilda?' Dorothy scooped up the cat and put it on the floor. It wasn't pleased. It walked round in a circle, its tail bristling. Dorothy picked two stray cat hairs off her skirt and put them in the ash-tray.

'Just the same. Unfathomable. She must have been beautiful when she was young. There's still a bit of that there.' Dorothy liked to pretend she wasn't influenced by anything as trivial as beauty, but her whole career was given over to it, so of course she was. And in an odd way I felt I owed something to that woman who saw what I thought I saw in Stanley when we first met. Where we differed was that she still saw it, whereas I was not sure what my feelings were for Stanley any more.

'I understand how Stanley's ideas have a way of getting out of hand when Hilda is involved,' I said. 'She never questions them.'

'I wish I had a partner like that.' Dorothy bent down and scoured the carpet for the pencil that had fallen off her lap when she picked up the cat. She's one of those infuriating people who don't read unless they've got a pencil in their hands. She could be reading *War and*

Peace and she would still be looking for an opportunity to annotate it with improvements.

'I say when I think a picture's good.'

'You only get to see the good ones.'

'You don't need my backing then?' I said.

'I don't, but Stanley does. It's vital to him to have someone who believes in him wholeheartedly.'

'But that's the whole point, Dorothy. I wasn't looking to take over as the family muse.'

'You're not the teeniest bit flattered by the idea that you could end up as midwife to a masterpiece?'

'Put that way, it sounds horribly organic.'

Dorothy had gone down on her knees and found the pencil underneath the sofa. 'Did she let you see the portrait?'

'When I asked, she shrugged. She didn't seem to care. She didn't even ask me what I thought.'

'What did you think?' She held the pencil up; the lead was broken.

'It's good. She won't flatter me, but I don't think she would be wantonly vindictive.'

'Unlike you, you mean?' She hauled herself back up onto her feet.

'You seem to have a very low opinion of me, Dorothy.'

'I'm just uneasy. I don't think you have the least idea of what you're taking on with Stanley.'

'I'm just sitting for a portrait.'

She looked keenly at me: 'You'll be going back?'

'It takes more than an afternoon to paint a portrait, you know.'

She sniffed. What she wanted was for me to own up that I shouldn't have embarked upon it in the first place and in many ways I wished I hadn't. It had not turned out to be a comfortable experience for either me or Hilda.

'We'll be seeing your face on the walls at Tooth's then?'

'If I play my cards right it won't only be my face that ends up on the walls.' I took the pencil stub from her. 'I doubt there's much lead left in this. I'll treat you to a new one when I'm in the newsagent's tomorrow.'

She looked unimpressed. She wasn't going to be bought off by a pencil.

'We shall have to hope that Hilda hasn't rumbled you,' she called over her shoulder as she left the room. 'Or that she keeps the painting in the attic if she has.'

VIII

As Dorothy was quick to point out, when she saw it, it was not the sort of portrait you'd want hanging in your living-room. She told me I looked like a fly-blown, slightly goggle-eyed Madonna. Stanley thought it wonderful, of course.

His expectation that the portrait would cement the three of us, turned out to be naively optimistic. In the weeks that followed, Hilda spent less time in Cookham than she had before. My fear that she might turn up without warning and that I'd be lying naked on a mattress when she did, proved groundless. If decamping to her mother's was designed to demonstrate to Stanley that by making me his muse he'd crossed a line, the line remained crossed. Hilda, it appeared, was not in a forgiving mood and Stanley, starved of the unqualified affection he demanded, was becoming unpredictable in his behaviour. I sensed we were building up to something, but the *something* when it happened wasn't what I'd been expecting.

I'd warned Stanley not to call at Moor Thatch after dark, so when at ten o'clock one night there was a hammering on the front door, Dorothy and I ignored it. Both of us were in our dressing gowns. It was November and like animals we tended to get up when it got light and were in bed by nine o'clock most nights.

The hammering continued. It was Dorothy who finally went down the passage and unlocked the front door.

'Stanley. We were just about to go to bed.'

There's no one as adept as Dorothy at making someone feel unwelcome when she puts her mind to it. There was a pause whilst Stanley took stock.

'Well?' said Dorothy.

He shifted his weight to the other foot but stood his ground. 'The baby came today. I thought you'd like to know.'

I felt as if a door had swung back in my face and knocked me over. Hilda's absence meant her pregnancy had almost ceased to feature as an item for consideration in my dealings with her husband. I might fail to take account of Hilda but a baby was a different matter. Stanley would inevitably be drawn back into the family and away from me.

'That's wonderful news, Stanley,' Dorothy said finally. 'We're both so pleased for you. What is it?' He frowned. 'Boy or girl?'

'A girl. We've called her Unity.' He rubbed his eyes. 'That's Hilda's name for her.'

'And what's your name for her?' said Dorothy.

He scratched his neck under his collar. '*Unity*'s all right,' he said.

I wondered whether Hilda might be sending him a message with the name.

'So you'll be going up to London,' Dorothy said, closing the door marginally between them. 'Do give our congratulations to your wife.'

He blinked. 'I shan't be going yet. I'm halfway through a painting. Hilda's got her mother and the people from the Christian Science Movement popping round. They're in and out there all the time.'

I'd known by then, of course, that Stanley had his own ideas about the things that mattered, but his ruthlessness surprised me. Dorothy was grappling to come to terms with it as well.

'You surely want to see your daughter?' she said.

'Hilda says she's very ugly but don't babies all look ugly when they're born. She'll probably get better.'

'Don't you think you ought to be there?' Dorothy persisted. 'You're her father, after all. You can't act as if you have no responsibilities.'

He looked surprised, as if this was the way he'd always acted and he saw no cause to change now. 'Hilda knows I need to be in Cookham. And it's where Patricia is.' My breath caught in my throat.

'Patricia?' Dorothy stepped back. 'What has Patricia got to do with it?'

'Patricia is my muse.'

'And when did you decide that?' Dorothy said patiently, as if it was the first she'd heard of it.

'I knew when I first saw her that day in The Copper Kettle.'

Dorothy glanced sideways at me.

'Stanley, I was only filling in for Ida Buckpitt.' Whilst it was rewarding knowing that I hadn't been eclipsed, I wasn't looking forward to the grilling I would get from Dorothy once we'd got rid of Stanley. I gave him a hard stare. 'If you'd come the next day, you'd have missed me.'

'Don't you see, though, that's what makes it so miraculous,' insisted Stanley, who'd completely missed the point. 'You feel a bond with Cookham, just like I do.' He turned back to Dorothy. 'It's all right. Hilda understands.'

'It's not all right,' said Dorothy. 'It's not all right at all.'

He frowned. 'What's wrong with it?'

'You can't go taking what you want without regard to other people, Stanley. As I understood, you asked Patricia if she'd sit for you and she agreed. It was a situation that was meant to last a few weeks at the most. Now suddenly you're talking as if she's signed on for life. That's not the way it works.'

'I can't stop now. I need her for my painting.' His eyes passed from Dorothy to me and back again.

'She has her own life, Stanley. You have yours and it's with Hilda. Come to terms with it,' said Dorothy.

It wasn't the reception he'd anticipated and he wasn't sure how to react. 'We've talked about it,' he said. 'I've explained. Patricia doesn't need to change or give up anything. She only has to be herself.'

'Patricia's never been herself,' said Dorothy, dismissively. 'She wouldn't know where to begin.'

IX

'I think this farce has gone on long enough, don't you?'

The two of us were sitting at the table with the empty plates from dinner waiting to be taken out into the kitchen. Stanley had just left.

With Hilda's blessing, or at least with her collusion, he had put off going up to London till he'd finished working on his latest painting. Hilda planned to motor down to Cookham with the children to spend Christmas Day at Lindworth but on Christmas Eve he'd got a call to say her brother George, who had been ill for months, had died. She couldn't leave her mother and since there were no trains running, Stanley was stuck in the village.

We'd agreed we couldn't leave him on his own on Christmas Day, though Dorothy was adamant that having him to lunch did not imply a change of attitude on her part. On the few occasions when she had met

Hilda, Dorothy said she reminded her of a mule buckling underneath the load it was required to carry, but she still felt Stanley should be shouldering the burden with her, not imposing one on us.

That Christmas was our fourth in Cookham. Dorothy and I had never made a big thing out of Christmas, although since this was the last one of the decade it was likely to prove memorable for that. December had crept up on us without my noticing. I'd gone into the General Store one day and there were paper chains suspended from the ceiling and a bunch of holly with a bit of mistletoe taped to the light above the counter. Sergeant-Major Arkwright, teetering precariously on a ladder in the corner, held up one end of a paper streamer, gazing at the ceiling for a spot to pin it to.

The air outside was taut with winter. We had bought the house in spring and moved in whilst the weather was still clement. For the next six months it had been downhill all the way. The track that ran beside Moor Thatch was pock-marked with deep ruts and holes where icy pools collected overnight. There was a constant drip of water from the loose tile in the porch and when we did a wash, the house was swathed in laundry. If we hung the washing on the line outside, the sheets would be like cardboard in the morning. We had strung a make-shift washing-line across the kitchen by the range which meant we couldn't warm ourselves in front of it and had to keep the fire lit in the living-room. Moor Thatch was not a place where anyone would spend the winter if they had the choice.

We'd gone to church on Christmas morning. Although we thought Stanley would be there, at Dorothy's insistence we had not invited him to join us. In the church, there was a festive atmosphere. The aisles and choir stalls were hung with holly and christingles and the tableau of carved wooden figures representing the Nativity was laid out on a trestle table in the nave. As they came into church the Reverend Beeston handed every child an item from the tableau. One got 'Joseph' and another one the 'Star of Bethlehem' and so on, those who came last having to make do with miniature straw bales or shepherds' crooks. The idea was that, later in the service, Reverend Beeston would invite the children to come down the aisle with their bit of the tableau and re-build it.

Cookham, like most villages in England, had its 'dafties', as the local population called them. On the whole they blended in: the little ones accommodated them, the older ones tormented them. In this way they received the necessary preparation for the life they would be living after they had left school. They were happy to be part of what was happening even if they weren't sure what it was. They joined in, swaying, nodding to the music, their lips moving to the words that had already been and gone.

When it was time to put the figures back onto the table, one child who had spent the previous hour licking paint off her Wise Man, decided that she didn't want to give him up. A scuffle had ensued before the Reverend Beeston, looking like a man who'd signed a contract without looking at the small print, gave in, re-positioning the two remaining Wise Men to fill up the gap.

'I think there might have been a lesson there,' said Dorothy, as we emerged into the crisp light of a winter morning. 'Other than the one delivered from the pulpit, I mean. What a shame the pubs aren't open.'

There had been another snowfall in the night and as we walked across the moor, we saw a group of children climbing Cockmarsh Hill, dragging a sheet of corrugated metal for a sled. Their shrieks as they sped down the hill rose to a pitch when at the bottom the sledge hit the track and summersaulted over.

Back at Moor Thatch, Dorothy poured both of us a sherry whilst I brought in more logs for the fire and we sat down to wait for Stanley to arrive. An hour later, when I glanced out of the window, he was sitting on the stile. He'd stopped to watch the children sledging, clapping every time the sledge tipped over at the bottom and its occupant was pitched onto the verge, his high-pitched laughter mingling with theirs. He seemed to feel a bond with other people's children that was missing with his own.

He knocked on our door half an hour later. Stanley didn't drink but he had brought a bottle of *Glenfiddich*, which he gave to Dorothy.

We had another sherry before lunch and listened to the broadcast afterwards. The wireless is free-standing, housed in a wooden cabinet with a carved fretwork pattern over the loudspeaker. It stands like a sentry in a corner of the room and we sat in a semi-circle facing it as we might at a lecture. Stanley shuffled his chair forward, sitting with his hands clasped and a serious expression on his face.

I'd cooked a roast and following the custom in the North had served the Yorkshire pudding separately from the main meal. It was as I brought the joint to table afterwards that Stanley suddenly announced that vice had always had a hold on him. I looked at Dorothy to make it clear that I was no more party to whatever vice he was referring to than her.

'I worry that my vision will be snatched away from me,' he said. 'I need to channel my desires.'

'Good luck with that,' said Dorothy.

Oblivious to any hint of disapproval and assuming Dorothy was still an ally, Stanley ploughed on recklessly.

'I have these *memory-feelings*; things that happened to me when I was a boy. You know the sort of thing: you see a girl's legs and you suddenly feel differently about them from the way you felt before.'

'That's just called growing up.' I said.

'But I want all those feelings and sensations that I had then to be elevated into a new mystical experience.'

I passed a plate to Dorothy and offered Stanley his. He'd got that fixed expression on his face. 'I wish I could have been a mother,' he said. I replaced the serving spoon and put the lid back on the vegetables. 'I'd like to have been male and female at the same time, to know how it felt to be at the beginning of creation.'

'Oh for goodness' sake,' said Dorothy. She crumpled up her serviette. 'You don't think life is difficult enough already? Why make everything so complicated?'

'But it wouldn't be,' said Stanley, 'it would be much simpler if the two were fused. When I first married Hilda I was conscious of her *you-ness* and how much it differed from my *me-ness* but as time went on her *you-ness* and my *me-ness* fused into *you-me-ness*. It was wonderful. It was sublime, but Hilda felt that her identity was being swallowed up.'

'I see her point,' said Dorothy.

'But don't you see, that is the point. You can't be fused and separate at the same time.'

'If you can be male and female at the same time, why can't you be fused and separate?'

'But you can't be male and female, can you?' Stanley said dejectedly.

'I'll miss out on the pudding if you don't mind,' Dorothy said.

Stanley's plate was swimming with the gravy he'd poured on his meat and then left. There were peas and bits of Yorkshire pudding floating in it. When he talked, he would be crumbling bread or tapping out tunes with his fork or playing with the cruet so the area around his plate was like a battlefield.

'Well, that's a Christmas day I shan't forget,' said Dorothy when we'd got rid of him at last. We sat around the dining table, staring at the debris.

'We had to invite him, Dorothy.'

'Agreed. We had no choice. We do however have a choice about what happens now. The fact that Stanley has spent Christmas Day in Cookham without Hilda and the children, her continued absence from what's still the family home and your continued presence there, will soon get out. You can't afford a reputation as a marriage-wrecker, not in a village this size and not with a man like Stanley who thinks sex, whatever form it takes, is indistinguishable from religion. Either he's insane or he's extremely clever. Either way he's dangerous.'

I reached across her and began to put the plates into a pile. 'The one thing that he's not, is devious. You always know what's going on in Stanley's head.'

'I'd worry about what was going on in Stanley's head, if I were you.'

A blob of gravy fell onto the table cloth. I spooned it back onto the plate. 'Let's keep him on-side for a little longer. Things are moving, Dorothy. His membership of The Academy will give a huge boost to his reputation.'

'It's your reputation that concerns me. What if Hilda does come down to Cookham and she finds you in the studio with Stanley.'

'It's not likely we would coincide. I only go there twice a week. I'm sure she'd let him know that she was coming, anyway.'

'I think I would be more inclined to turn up unexpectedly. That, after all is how you find out what is going on.'

'There's nothing going on,' I said. She grunted. 'Come on, Dorothy, it's Christmas day. Let's not fall out. You must admit the jewellery he bought has come in useful. He'd have been worth knowing, just for that. It's meant that we can start the New Year with a clean slate.' I got up and went around the back of her. I looped my arms around her neck. 'Next year is going to be wonderful. I know it. I think we should open that last bottle of champagne we brought from Paris. Then I think we ought to go to bed. Why don't we take the bottle of champagne to bed with us?' I buried my face in her neck.

'You have the quaintest notions,' Dorothy said, drily.

X

As her birthday falls on the last day of December, Dorothy and I have tended to make more of New Year than we do of Christmas. Since we moved to Cookham it's become a ritual for us to spend her birthday at the cinema in Maidenhead.

I love those cinemas that look like Maharajah's palaces. There's one in Tooting that's a cross between a Gothic folly in the foyer and a Romanesque cathedral in the auditorium. Ours looks more like a power house from outside. You could walk past thinking that it was a factory, though it hardly matters once you're in there.

I like films that take me to another place, like *Sally in our Alley* whereas Dorothy prefers the sort that make you think. The feature this time was *The Broadway Melody*, the latest smash hit from America. It was the story of two girls in Vaudeville who want to make it big in Hollywood.

The cinema is always popular. It was a bitingly cold day and we had joined a queue so long we were afraid we might not get in. As we reached the doors, a rush of hot air hit us.

'Shall I buy the sweets before we go in?' I said, when we'd got our tickets.

'No, let's find our seats. I need to sit down and thaw out a bit.'

There was a *Pathé* newsreel on the screen which showed somebody jumping out of an American apartment block and then a short film featuring a potter living in St Ives. During the interval, the curtains came across the screen, the organ rose up from the pit and there was a recital, ending as it always did with *In a Persian Garden* .

When the usherette came down the aisle I put my hand up and she shone her torch on us. I'd made sure we were sitting in the middle of the row. If you sat at the end, the chances were you would be asked to purchase something from the tray and then to pass the money up and take the change and pass that back along the row so you could end up missing whole chunks of the film.

I snuggled up to Dorothy. The back two rows were full of courting couples but because she has strict views about the right way to behave in public, we confined ourselves to holding hands and eating sweets. I curled my thumb around her palm and ran it up and down her life-line. My skin might not be as sensitive as hers but by imagining what she was feeling I could feel it too and we had the advantage over couples in the back row that at least we saw the film as well.

It wasn't till the next day that we learnt that whilst we had been sitting in the cinema in Maidenhead, a picture house in Paisley had burnt down during a matinee performance. Upwards of a thousand children had been queuing at the cinema that day. Most of them would have got the penny for a ticket in the stalls by getting the deposit back on empty bottles. The film they were showing was *The Crowd*, a silent movie Dorothy and I had seen a fortnight earlier. It was preceded by a Western showing Tom Mix as a bareback-riding, lassoo-twirling cowboy.

Halfway through the second reel, a battery connecting with a metal cannister in the projection room short-circuited and toxic smoke began to billow down into the auditorium. A shout went up of 'Fire!' and there was a stampede towards the exits, children trampling over one another in their efforts to escape. That's when they found the doors were padlocked.

Rescuers were met by the appalling sight of children's bodies piled on top of one another, mislaid shoes, torn clothes and comics, upturned seats and pools of blood. There were reports of fathers breaking down doors, smashing their way through the stained-glass windows of the cinema and carrying their lifeless children out onto the pavements. They ranged from an eighteen-month old baby to a girl of thirteen.

The disaster would be news for weeks to come. The city was already famous for its woollen shawls with their distinctive 'tear-drop' pattern but as Dorothy knew from her own experience, the textile industry was fickle. Half the town was unemployed. The decade we were entering had not looked good for Paisley anyway. Now 1930 had brought tragedy on top of hardship.

A relief fund was set up and Dorothy insisted we contribute to it, although goodness knows we hadn't anything to spare. Still, it was something that a lot of people clearly felt they had to do since by the time it closed the fund had raised more than £5000.

In Cookham there were prayers in church for the bereaved, a box into which school children were asked to put a portion of their pocket money to buy toys for the survivors, and an outcry from the same school children when their parents tried to stop them going to the cinema on Saturdays incase it caught fire and the doors were padlocked. Fear that they might lose their children was soon superseded by the problem of four million children nationwide denied the one event that they looked forward to throughout the week.

Life gradually returned to normal and the cinemas filled up again. It wasn't possible to go on grieving in the abstract. Local gossip, in which I already had a walk-on part, was more immediate and there was not the same degree of reverence required.

XI

Although I wouldn't have admitted it to Dorothy I worried, too, that Hilda might turn up at Lindworth unexpectedly whilst I was modelling for Stanley. It would be a challenge to respond with dignity if I was naked and she had her hat and coat on. How the village would respond to Stanley's paintings of me in the nude, was also preying on my mind.

'I've got to live here, Stanley. I don't want to go into the General Store for quarter of a pound of lard and know that Sergeant-Major Arkwright's seeing me without my clothes on.'

I had called in at the store a few days earlier for some of his cured ham. His wife, who normally served front of shop, was in the Midlands visiting her sister. Having run the store for four years whilst her husband was on active service, Mrs Arkwright knew the business inside out, who could be given credit, how much and for how long, how much gossip she could pass on before nobody confided in her anymore, how far she was entitled to express an attitude towards the Government, the Royal Family or the problems she was having with the cash till they'd bought second-hand. So far she hadn't got the knack of it and was still adding up the purchases inside her head and using the machine as back-up. The majority of customers who shopped there thought it wouldn't take on, but her husband had insisted they must keep up with the times so she had left him on his own to get the hang of it.

Unlike his wife who was devoid of charm and had a face like putty framed by shoulder-length straight hair secured on either side by Kirby grips, ex-Sergeant-Major Arkwright had a reputation as a bit of a Lothario. He sidled up to favoured customers and put the purchases into their baskets, resting one hand casually on an elbow or the wicker handle. *Is there anything else I can get you?* he inquired, his lazy bloodhound eyes with their red-rimmed and sagging lower lids suggestively perusing the terrain in front of him. *A bit of bacon fat, perhaps?*

I wondered what it would be like to wake up next to such a man, especially on a Sunday when the choice was hearing about Hell at Morning Service or experiencing it first hand in the upstairs bedroom.

'I want him to share my joy,' insisted Stanley.

'Fine. But I don't want him sharing mine. Why can't you paint me dressed?' Apart from all the other inconveniences, Stanley's studio was not much warmer than the living-room at Moor Thatch. Stanley lit the stove each morning, adding more dust to the atmosphere.

Smoke belched into the room in small puffs and sparks shot onto the floor or onto books and sketches, sometimes even landing on the bed before they fizzled out.

'I often paint you dressed.'

'In black lace, with a ribbon in my hair and your head somehow always in the bottom right hand corner, looking up my fanny.'

'I adore your fanny.'

'Stanley you're a pervert. You're a puritan at heart and you have all these dirty thoughts. You want to reconcile them so you turn them into something mystical, but deep down they're still dirty thoughts.'

The latest painting featured me and several of our neighbours standing in the High Street with the local dustman, Archie Ferris, hoisted up onto my hip and Stanley and a girl who looked like Elsie offering up bits of rubbish from the dustbins.

Dorothy was scathing when I told her what the painting was about.

'You're saying Stanley's married you to Archie Ferris?'

'In the picture he's ascending up to Heaven. I'm just there to help him on his way.'

'Unfortunately, what the butcher and that bloodhound, Sergeant-Major Arkright will see when they look at it, is you and Archie Ferris having it away in Cookham High Street. What do you suppose they'll make of that?'

'Apparently the bits of rubbish - cabbage leaves, an old tin can, a teapot with a crack in it - have mystical significance.'

'For Stanley everything has mystical significance,' said Dorothy.

Like her, I'd have been happy not to see the painting on the walls of Tooth's but I had other reasons for not wanting to cut loose from Stanley, at least until Hilda had made her position clear.

A fortnight into January, she had still not put in an appearance. Stanley didn't seem to think her absence was significant. He had been up to London early in the year to see the family and reported back that Unity was now presentable and everyone was very happy with her. He was back within three days, however. Cookham was his work base and he didn't want to be away from it. He'd gone up twice more and come back the same day.

XII

When at last, one Thursday afternoon, the door did suddenly fly open, it was Elsie and not Hilda who burst in.

Since Dorothy and I arrived in Cookham at the end of 1927, I had probably encountered Elsie five or six times, mainly from a distance, once or twice when I was standing in the queue behind her in the village shop and that time on the High Street when we had our only proper conversation.

Since then I'd been running into her at every turn. She recognised me and was always friendly but she bustled past as if she had a huge amount to do and every second counted. I had wondered how she managed Stanley on his own. He didn't need a lot of looking after but she was the sort of girl who made work if she hadn't got enough to do.

The one place that was out of bounds to anyone who wasn't part of Stanley's inner circle was the studio, so when she burst in like that it came as a shock to both of us. I grabbed my wrap. She glanced at me and flung herself at Stanley. Tears were pouring down her face.

'Oh, Mr Spencer!' she cried. 'Something dreadful's happened.'

Stanley put his brushes down. We waited whilst she struggled to compose herself. Each time she tried to speak the words were swallowed up.

I reached out for my clothes as inconspicuously as I could, but then it struck me that she was less likely to have recognised me with my clothes off. I'd be just another one of Mr Spencer's ladies.

Stanley patted both his pockets for a handkerchief and held the paint rag out. She pressed it to her mouth and when she let it drop she had a green stripe on her top lip.

'I don't want to tell you,' she wailed. 'You'll be so upset.'

By now I'd started thinking either Hilda or one of the children had been struck down and if it was that bad, I would rather not be there to catch the fall-out. Surreptitiously I slid my arms into my shirt.

'It's Tiddles,' Elsie sobbed. 'He's....'

'Dead?' I offered. I was starting to feel cold and there were other things I could be doing.

Elsie looked at me aghast as if what had been just an awful possibility, had now become a fact in consequence of being said out loud. She turned to Stanley and he put his arms around her awkwardly. There was a reverence about the way he touched her that was different from the way he touched me. Stanley's fingers were like eyes; they saw things. They crept over me like slugs but when she was on the receiving end of them they never quite made contact. She was one of the most ordinary people I had ever met. I doubted she had ever had a thought that didn't start and end in Cookham and yet Stanley treated her like some sort of religious icon.

'Is it true?' he whispered.

Elsie gave vent to another burst of noisy grief. 'Yes, oh it's dreadful.'

'Tell me,' Stanley said. She bit her lip. 'What happened, Elsie?'

'Archie Ferris ran him over in the dustcart,' Elsie sobbed.

I rolled my eyes. The very dustman Stanley claimed to have transfigured in *The Lovers or the Dustman* had turned out to be his nemesis or rather Tiddles' nemesis. It would be devastating news for Dorothy. I'd never liked the cat and it detested me, but still I wouldn't have wished that on it.

I looked at Stanley. It was hard to know what he was thinking. Animals responded to him but he was oblivious to other creature's needs, which was why Tiddles came across to ours whenever he was hungry. Stanley patted Elsie's shoulder.

'Is the cat still there?' I interrupted.

'Archie's laid him by the verge,' said Elsie. 'We thought you would want to see him.' She saw Stanley's pained expression. 'I'll help bury him,' she murmured.

'You're a good girl, Elsie,' Stanley said.

'I'm really sorry, Mr Spencer.'

'I'll leave you two to get on with it, then,' I said. Stanley stood there dumbly. 'I'd be no use; I can't stand the sight of blood.' I patted down my hair and slipped past Elsie who'd left trails of snot on Stanley's shoulder and was patting at the white stains.

I had been about to ask her where the dustcart was so that I could go back to Moor Thatch by another route, but when I looked back at the door, I saw that they'd forgotten me already. Stanley's head was bent and Elsie's hand was resting on his shoulder. They looked like a pair of lovers bidding one another farewell in a painting by Augustus Egg.

I slipped out silently.

I wondered how to break the news to Dorothy. I found her kneeling on the grass verge, weeding the lawn of meadow grass and hen bit. Weeding was her favourite occupation, which said quite a lot about her. Nettles were piled up along the path.

I squatted down beside her. 'I'm so sorry, Dorothy. I've got some bad news. Something's happened.'

'I heard.' She shook loose earth off a clump of meadow grass and threw it on the pile.

'Christ, you can't blow a raspberry in this village without methane fallout.'

'I believe that's true.' She dug the trowel into the earth and got up off her knees. 'I happened to be in the garden when Miss Barrett came past on her way back from the library. She told me.'

Dorothy took off her gardening jacket and went down the path ahead of me. Her shoulders had a downward slope to them. She hung the jacket on the peg inside the door and sat down at the kitchen table. 'Be a love and put the kettle on.' She coughed into her handkerchief. When she was upset it brought on her asthma.

'Yes, of course.' I filled the kettle from the tap and put out cups. When I turned, she was sitting in her *Buddha* pose, so still you felt like checking for a pulse. I added one more scoop of tea leaves to the pot.

'I'm really sorry, Dorothy. I know how fond you were of Tiddles.'

'I just wish he'd had a more heroic end.'

I brought the pot to table and sat opposite her. 'Do you think cats care about that sort of thing?'

'I'm sure they don't.'

'Still, I know what you mean. I gather Archie Ferris was upset, too. He was in the van when Tiddles ran into the road.' I pushed the cup across to her. Her hand was shaking as she picked it up.

'Would you like me to put a spot of brandy in there, Dorothy?'

'Let's not go overboard.' She fumbled for the handkerchief and blew her nose. She hated me to see her cry, so I pretended that I hadn't noticed.

She sniffed. 'Who told Stanley?'

'Elsie. She was utterly distraught. He had to comfort her.'

'That cat was Shirin's.'

'Well, yes, but it's always lived in Cookham and for most of that time Shirin's been in London with her mother. Actually the cat spent more time at Moor Thatch than it did at Lindworth.'

'Given how fast bad news travels, I expect the mice will all be back here by tomorrow.'

'I'm not sure they ever went away. The cat was never much of a deterrent. It was too well fed.'

We sat there for a moment in companionable silence, Dorothy relieved that I had not tried to foist comfort onto her, me grateful that the cat's death had provided an excuse for us to come together.

Dorothy sat back: 'Do you think Stanley will need help to bury him?'

'I offered. Elsie said she'd pitch in. I think you and I would just be in the way. Of course if you would like to be there…'

Dorothy shrugged. 'I expect between the two of them they'll manage.' She peered down into her cup and swilled the dregs around in case there was a message in the tea leaves. 'Thank you, that was very welcome.'

'You're not going back into the garden?'

'I was halfway through the weeding. In an hour it'll be too dark to see.'

'Shall I come out and help?'

'No thank you. Murdering a few weeds is exactly what I need in terms of a distraction.'

Part Three
Treachery

I

Although we were not aware of it then, Tiddles' death marked the beginning of a change in Stanley's fortunes. I called in one morning with some parsley from the garden and he'd got *The Lovers or the Dustman* on the easel. He was making alterations to the face of Archie Ferris.

'He's not joyful any longer,' Stanley said, but what he meant was that *he* wasn't joyful any longer. 'I've been trying to do something with the mouth.'

'I think you ought to leave it as it is,' I said. He took no notice. There was something manic in the dustman's smile now. This was not my favourite painting and I had been hoping Stanley would consign it to the rack.

He went on dabbing at the surface, trying to reintroduce a semblance of the dustman's ecstasy into his placid, dough-like face. It was a losing battle. Stanley was incapable of distancing himself from his creations.

Elsie was the other one who found it hard to cope. She needed to be comforted in every shop she went into, which meant that shopping took whoever was behind her twice as long. If Stanley went into the Newsagent's to buy a paper, people treated him as if he'd lost a relative. This was a village where they didn't think twice about killing badgers, shooting foxes and as recently as 1650, drowning witches.

I knew Dorothy was pining but at least she did it privately. I wondered whether I should start to lure in neighbours' cats with food. It was when she was reading in the evenings that she'd feel the absence of that reassuring ball of fluff the most.

I left the parsley I'd brought Stanley on the bench. I wasn't due to sit for him that morning and the air of gloom inside the studio was getting to me. I glanced at a letter on the work bench which was splashed with tea stains. I was used to seeing scraps of paper scattered everywhere with bits of writing on them, but the writing usually was Stanley's. This one caught my eye because the envelope was headed 'Inland Revenue' in thick black lettering designed to be intimidating.

'What's this?'

Stanley glanced over his shoulder. 'It was in the post box last weekend. I don't know what they want. They keep on writing to me.'

Where the tea had soaked into the print, the words had faded off the page. I held it to the light. 'When you get letters from the Inland Revenue it's normally because they think you owe them something.' I looked down the page. It took a moment for the contents to sink in. 'Is this true, Stanley?'

'What?'

'It says here that according to their records they have never had a tax return from you.'

He went on tinkering with Archie's face.

'Is that right?'

He inclined his head. 'I can't remember.' He shrugged. 'I've been busy.'

'Don't you keep a record of your correspondence?'

'Hilda is the only one I write to.'

'But you must send letters out to other people. What about your dealers?'

He half turned. I waved the letter at him. 'Dudley Tooth, for instance.'

'Dudley writes me letters sometimes.'

'And presumably you write back? Don't you keep your business correspondence in a file?'

He gave me that besieged look. This was not a conversation that he wanted to be having.

'You know that if you earn money you're expected to pay tax on it? The Inland Revenue could fine you. People have been put in prison for not paying tax.'

'I haven't earned that much,' he said, defensively.

'They clearly think you have. You've bought a house, for god's sake. How did you afford that?'

'When I asked them at the bank, they said I had enough in there to cover it.'

'You didn't bother looking at your statements to see what was going in and out?' He stared back, blankly. Since a lot of what had gone out recently had made its way in my direction, I decided not to press the point too heavily. It might be best to focus on what had been coming in.

'What happens when you sell a picture? Take the one The Tate bought. You must have a vague idea of what they paid you for it?'

He frowned: 'You would have to ask John Rothenstein.'

'*I'd* have to ask him? It's not me the Inland Revenue is after, Stanley.'

He was starting to look anxious. 'What do you think I should do?'

'It says here that they've written to you three times. Have they?'

'Maybe. I don't always open letters when they're in brown envelopes. They don't seem very interesting.'

'I think you and Dorothy must have been hatched out of the same egg. You may not find letters like that interesting but they're clearly interested in you. They've given you a deadline of the thirteenth to get back to them. That's only two weeks off!'

'What happens if I don't? You really think I could be put in prison? What about my painting?'

'Frankly, this is one occasion when your painting doesn't count for much.'

'I've had this business of the cat to deal with,' he said. 'Couldn't I explain?' He raked the handles of his brushes through his hair.

I put the letter on the work bench. 'I'm afraid it doesn't work like that. Dead cats don't count as an excuse.' I nudged the letter over to him. 'What you need is an accountant.'

'Where would I find one of those?'

I paused just long enough for it to look as if I'd given it some thought. 'I handle Dorothy's accounts. She's hopeless at that sort of thing. I dare say I could have a look at yours.'

He spread his hands out: 'Would you? I just don't feel I can cope with all that at the moment.'

'I can't promise anything. We'd have to sit down and make out a list of everything you've earned and then make out a separate list of your expenses. You'll need to go back over your correspondence for the past five years for any references to pictures sold or money you've received.'

'I thought you just said you were doing all that for me.'

'I'm not psychic, Stanley. I don't know what's happening unless you tell me.'

'All right. But you'll sort it out?'

'I'll help you sort it out.' I picked the letter up and slipped it in my pocket. 'I'm not guaranteeing anything, just that I'll look at it.'

He pressed my fingers to his lips. I glanced over his shoulder at the painting on the easel. Archie looked less like a dustman and more like a medieval saint who'd just spent three days on the rack. 'You'd better put the tops back on your paints. You'll need to start now.'

'Can't I finish what I'm doing?'

'Stanley!'

'All right, yes.' He put his hands up.

'I'll call back this afternoon to see how far you've got with it.' I tucked the letter in my satchel. Stanley wandered over to the window. At the door I glanced back. He was gazing at the sky as if he thought God was about to leap out of the heavens at him.

'What are you staring at?'

'Imagine everything that's going on up there,' said Stanley, narrowing his eyes.

I closed the door behind me and then opened it again and slammed it hard.

II

'How does he seem?'

'A bit low. Elsie's planted Christmas roses on the grave.'

'No sign of Hilda, then?'

'Not yet, but at the moment he's got other things to think about. The Inland Revenue are after him.'

She blew her cheeks out. 'Once those weasels get a hold of you, they never let go.'

Although she professes to be left-wing, Dorothy's reluctant to accept that people who earn money should be taxed, especially if they're artists. Her suggestion is that since most of them earn so little, it would be a fairer system if the rich ones gave a portion of their income to the others and forgot about taxation altogether.

When I told her one day that I'd read the King was giving £50,000 away, however, she'd had trouble seeing the connection.

'For a start, the money isn't his; it's his allowance from the Civil List and he's not giving it to charity; he simply isn't claiming it.'

'Which means it could be given to the unemployed.'

'It could be.' Dorothy looked sceptical. 'It doesn't mean it will be.'

'Well I think it's very nice of him,' I'd said. 'It shows he cares.'

That really got to her: 'Let's not forget it was the King who advocated sending in the Army to resolve the

General Strike. He gets £9,000 a week. That's ninety years pay for a miner.'

You can't win an argument with Dorothy. She's never at a loss for a statistic.

I shook out my mackintosh and hung it on the peg. It had been raining for the past three days. The common was a swamp and in the scullery the water had been seeping underneath the door. Moor Thatch was at the bottom of a slight incline, a feature neither of us took into account when we were buying it.

'He asked me if I thought they might accept the death of Tiddles as a reason for him failing to fill in his tax returns.'

'Ah. Bless.'

I passed a cloth over the boots I'd taken off and lined them up inside the door. 'He wants me to help sort out his accounts.' I kept my eyes down. 'After all, it's what I'm good at. I've looked after yours for twenty years.' I felt her eyes on me.

'You don't think you ought to declare an interest if you're going to have access to his bank accounts.'

'He asked me, Dorothy. It wasn't my idea.'

'Can't an accountant get him off the hook?'

'That's what I'm offering to do. At least I'll try. It's in our interests as well as his.' I folded up the cloth and draped it on the wooden handle of the mangle.

'So you've swapped the role of muse for that of business manager.' She made a face but didn't comment. She had probably decided that as Stanley's business manager I was less likely to end up in bed with him.

'Needs must.' I wouldn't say I was a genius at mathematics but I liked to play with figures. It had been the idea rather than the love of art that drew me to the Slade. I recognised, too, that I was unlikely to find others like me in the business world. That notwithstanding, I preferred to spend the evening with a balance sheet in front of me than listening to a concert. Stanley thought that I was doing him a favour and that suited me just fine.

III

When I called in the next time, I was gratified to find him sitting at a small desk that had come out of the school-room at Fernlea and which we'd moved into the studio a couple of days earlier. He sat hunched on a stool infront of it, his knees bunched underneath his chin. There was a pile of papers on the desk and he was writing with a stubby pencil. I had caught him doodling once or twice and given him a rap across the knuckles. I'd slid seamlessly into the part of dominatrix which was not a role I often got to play with Dorothy.

My foray into Stanley's finances confirmed that on face value he was doing very well. He had an exhibition every year at Tooth's and now he was a member of The Royal Academy, whatever he exhibited would sell. He ought to have been able to support a family and live easily on what he earned. When I asked jokingly if he'd been stuffing pound notes in the mattress, he took time to think about it and then took an empty tin of *Twinings* off the shelf and handed me a wad of notes.

'I had forgotten those were there,' he said.

'But Stanley, there must be at least three hundred pounds here.'

'That's good, isn't it?'

'Have you got other places where you've hidden notes away?'

'I might have left some in that empty paint box over there.'

'Why?'

'If I keep it on me and I take my handkerchief out, money falls out with it.'

We ransacked the house and came up with another thirty pounds in notes and seven pounds in silver. I took Stanley's cheque book for safe-keeping, getting him to sign a handful of them first to cover any incidentals. It was when I sat down to go through the statements from the bank and saw the items on the debit list, however, that I realised where the bulk of Stanley's income for that year had gone.

It didn't make for comfortable reading. Stanley didn't spend much on himself and nor did Hilda. Elsie's weekly wage of 17s 6d was the only regular expenditure. The other items, which were mainly clothes and jewellery were what he'd bought for me. He never bothered looking at the price tag before buying something. If I liked it, he said that was all that mattered.

Hilda, if she ever got to see the list, would know at once who was responsible.

IV

It struck me that if Stanley's fortunes weren't, as I'd anticipated, on the way up but the way down, it would be as well to cash in on him now. I'd asked him several times if he'd put in a word in for us with the director at Lefevre's. They showed living artists and the gallery was well-placed in a part of London popular with the intelligentsia. It was the gallery he had suggested when I first brought up the subject, although it was clear that Stanley wasn't going to do anything to further my career or Dorothy's unless I piled the pressure on. He hadn't once asked how our work was going or if we had any exhibitions lined up. At least now that I was helping him with his accounts, I had a lever. I was doing him a favour, so why couldn't he do me one.

'You don't understand, Patricia.' He stopped writing and the pencil stub, robbed of its purpose, hovered in the air a moment and then started doodling in the margins like a lively dog let off the lead. 'That isn't how it's done. I can't approach MacNeill. You have to wait to be invited.'

I put one hand over his to rein the pencil in. 'Invite him to invite us, then.' I eased him round to face me. 'Dorothy and I can't go on living at Moor Thatch unless we find a gallery where we can sell our work and if we have to move, I couldn't go on sitting for you. Heaven knows where we'd end up. I'd have to get a job. We both would.'

'I'll ask Hilda if she'll reconsider letting you and Dorothy move into Lindworth.'

'That's no good. I told you Dorothy won't do it. She said she would rather walk to Rome in sackcloth on her knees. You've no idea how proud she is.'

'She doesn't mind me sucking up to the director at Lefévre's, though,' he said, resentfully.

'All you need do is tell MacNeill that you've discovered two new artists who you think he ought to look at.'

'You're my muse,' said Stanley. 'I don't want him looking at you.'

'It's not me he would be looking at, you muffin, it's my work. It's not as if you've bothered looking at it.

'Yes, all right, I'll do it,' he said. 'I'll ask him to look at what you've done.'

'I hope you'll put it to him more enthusiastically than that. You wouldn't sell a life raft to a drowning man with that pitch.'

'I don't know what you expect of me,' he whined. 'I worship you. I want to paint you. Isn't it enough?'

'For you maybe. You've got a gallery; you've got an income; you've got Hilda, you're a Royal Academician and you've got my services as an accountant. Sod you, Stanley, you've got everything.'

He looked hurt: 'Don't swear, please, Patricia. I don't like it. It's not ladylike.'

'Oh……bugger off.' I was halfway along the path when Stanley caught me up.

'Don't go. I'll tell MacNeill he has to take you on. I'll tell him you're my muse and that I have to have you for my work. He'll understand.'

I threw my arms up in despair: 'No, Stanley!'

'No?'

'Just ask him whether I can bring some work in. I can do the rest myself.'

V

A fortnight later, Stanley travelled up to London on the train with me. I had told Dorothy that I was going on my own and till the day of the appointment it looked as if this might be the case. When I suggested Stanley put in an appearance or at least help carry my portfolio onto the train, he hummed and ha-ed but finally gave in.

He spent the journey hunched up in his seat, his hands wedged underneath his arm-pits, staring out the window. The train rattled on through Slough, past those unending rows of terraced houses with their scruffy back yards and long gardens leading to the railway line. As it emerged into the countryside, we passed the new estates - prim little villas with neat gardens and names that suggested something grander - Meadow Rise, The Laurels or their owner's names entwined – Gladbert or Ethelroy, or some like 'Mon Repos' that hinted at a better class of resident. I fancied I saw reproductions of *The Laughing Cavalier* hung from the curtain rails on more than one wall as we sped past.

Dodo laughed when I'd suggested sending for the reproduction so that I could offer it to Mrs Arkwright in exchange for one week's groceries, although you had to pick your targets carefully with Dorothy. She'd seen what poverty was like whilst she was growing up in Lancashire. She took an interest in the housing schemes the government was putting forward, but she hated the pretensions of the lower middle class with aspirations to be better than their neighbours.

I no longer had the cigarette card with Fleur Laycock's number on it. I'd been on the point of ringing her once, after Dorothy and I had had a row, but when I searched the pockets of the jacket I'd been wearing at the Carline's soirée, it had disappeared. I told myself I wouldn't have rung anyway. It wasn't likely Fleur would still be camping out with Freddy in Park Lane.

At Paddington, we took a cab. It cruised down Green Park, slowing down outside The Ritz, where carriages were dropping off their fares, then turning onto King Street and St James' with its row of elegant Italianate facades. I felt intimidated suddenly. The cab drew up outside the gallery.

'I'll wait,' said Stanley.

'You're not coming in with me?'

'I'll keep the taxi. It'll save us having to flag down another one.'

'I could be in there for an hour.'

'I don't mind.' He gave a wan smile.

'Suit yourself.' I hauled out a portfolio and crossed the road.

I hoped the man behind the leather desk was the director and I wouldn't be obliged to waste my time with minions first. As I went through the glass door of the gallery with its expensive, polished floor, he glanced up. Seeing the portfolio, his face took on that guarded look I'd seen a hundred times before.

There was no question Dorothy had talent. If she had been born a man, she would have been a household name. Her paintings weren't incomprehensible, like Stanley's. They were still lifes, beautifully painted with an other-worldly quality that had a lot to do with how she mixed her colours. There were lots of pearly-greys and whites with hints of blue or orange. When you looked at them, you had a sense of time arrested. Her still lifes were so still that they made you want to hold your breath for fear of ruffling the creases in a table-cloth or breaking up the shadow underneath an egg. Her paintings reassured me that the chaos of the outside world was under Dorothy's control and so was I as long as I was under her protection.

As he reached into the drawer beside him for a magnifying glass, MacNeill sighed, as if he'd been pushed to breaking point by the demands on him. He stretched his hand to pull the sleeve up from his wrist and passed the magnifying glass painstakingly across the drawing. I was curious to wonder what he saw that he could not see with the naked eye and that would tell him whether this was or was not an artist.

He had black hair, slicked back and immaculately cut, but as he bent his head to peer more closely at a patch of colour I saw that the hair was thinning on the crown and that the roots bore just the faintest hint of grey. He picked another sketch out, then a water-colour. Once or twice he cleared his throat.

He glanced up, looking at me for the first time, and smiled briskly.

'These are good.' He rubbed his thumb and forefinger against each other, as if he'd decided that I owed him something and was docketing it up. 'I gather you were at the Slade?'

'That's right. I spent some time in Paris afterwards. I studied under André Lhôte.'

I wondered whether I should mention Dorothy. But to what end? He'd never get to meet her. She refused to take part in negotiations; all that side of it was left to me. If we'd been partners in a restaurant she would have been the chef and I'd have been the *maitre d'*. She'd rather spend an evening with her head down the latrine than have to talk about her work in front of other people.

When I met her at the Slade, I thought that painting was the thing we had in common. I imagined us companionably chatting about this and that as we daubed paint onto our canvasses. And then I realised that the one time we were not together was when Dorothy was painting. Then, she wouldn't talk to anybody. You could tell her that the world was coming to an end in fifteen minutes and she wouldn't even hear you. I don't think I've ever felt as lonely as I did then.

I'd assumed all artists were like that, but Stanley wasn't. Stanley needed to communicate. He had to have his audience on-side. I don't think Dorothy cared either way. But what I'd recognised over the past months was that she had more in common with him than she'd ever had with me.

MacNeill put down his magnifying glass. 'Do you know Roger Fry?'

'I haven't met him but of course I've heard of him.'

'I'll introduce you. I think Roger would be rather taken with these.'

When I finally emerged an hour later, Stanley was still sitting hunched up in the taxi, looking like a man who had been sleeping rough. I felt relieved that he had not come in with me. I'd half imagined that he would have gone by now.

'How did it go?' he said.

'Fine.' I leaned back into the padded seat.

'What happened?'

'The director thought the work was stunning. We'll be on the list for next year.'

'That's good,' he said. 'Did he mention me?'

I yawned. 'You know, I don't think your name cropped up once.'

VI

The news that her career might finally be up and running had elicited a grunt of recognition for my efforts out of Dorothy and a polite inquiry as to whether I thought it appropriate to step back now and leave the Spencers to repair their marriage. I still felt some reservations at the thought that once I'd handed back control of Stanley's finances there was a risk of Hilda finding out how much of their joint income had been spent on me. However, keeping Stanley at arm's length whilst not discouraging him altogether, had been time-consuming and exhausting. I was almost ready to let Hilda have her husband back. It came as something of a shock to find she wasn't as forgiving as I'd thought.

'A friend of Hilda's said she'd seen us coming out of that department store in Maidenhead,' said Stanley on the telephone.

'But that must have been months ago.' I pressed my mouth to the receiver and glanced up the stairs to make sure Dorothy was out of ear-shot. We'd arranged to have the phone installed in January. Dorothy and I traditionally saw the New Year in by giving one another something jointly that we couldn't have afforded individually. This year it was a telephone, though it was Stanley indirectly who had paid for it. There was a public phone box just outside the railway station but you often had to queue for it and anyone outside could overhear what you were saying.

'Hilda hadn't seen her for a long time. They were catching up.'

'But all that's history, Stanley. Surely Hilda isn't going to kick up a fuss about it now.'

'I think it was the high heels that she took exception to. I told her I got an erection when I saw you walking down the street in them.'

'For god's sake, Stanley. What did you say that for?'

'It was true. I wouldn't lie to Hilda.'

'But you surely don't have to tell Hilda everything!'

'I talk to her to get things straight inside my head.' His voice dropped. 'I need her to understand.'

'And did she?'

'No. She's left me.'

Something in his voice suggested that on this occasion Hilda hadn't simply got into the car and driven off.

Upstairs there's was a 'thunk' as something dropped onto the floor in Dodo's studio. I didn't think she'd heard the telephone ring, but I whispered into the receiver.

'Hilda's hardly been here for the past year, Stanley. You can still see her in London, I presume.'

'But Cookham's where my work is.'

'You had better ask her to come back then.'

'She won't.'

'You once told me Hilda would do anything you asked.'

He sniffed. 'We still love one another but it's difficult. She says that what she always valued was my purity. She thinks there are two Stanleys. There's the up-in-heaven Stanley, which she loves, then there's the day-to-day one which she sometimes finds it hard to understand.'

'She isn't asking you for a divorce or anything like that?'

There was a shocked pause. 'No.'

As far as Stanley was concerned, the idea was unthinkable. I felt exasperated. It was time that Stanley made his mind up which of us he wanted. I sank down onto the chair and rested my arm on the table. I decided to play devil's advocate to see if I could tease out the required response. 'It sounds as if it would simpler, Stanley, easier for both of you, if I stopped coming to the studio?'

'Of course not. No. You can't, Patricia! It would be unbearable!'

This was more like it. For an instant, I felt quite benign towards him.

I had wondered whether Hilda's ultimatum was a strategy on her part to reclaim him, but I'd realised during those long afternoons when she was painting me that Hilda, like her husband, was incapable of subterfuge. She'd left him, not because she couldn't bear to share him but because she wouldn't share him with a woman like me. If he had me, he could not have her.

But Stanley hadn't had me and therein the problem lay. Now that he couldn't find the refuge and forgiveness and of course the satisfaction that he craved in her arms, he would look to me for it. A peak inside the diary at that moment would have been revealing. Until recently he'd had two women at his beck and call. Now it seemed he had neither.

If I slept with Stanley, I risked losing Dorothy and if I didn't, I risked Stanley going elsewhere for the things he needed, taking with him things that I might need. With all the other problems he was having to contend with, he was growing desperate.

Since I gave up sitting for him so that I could concentrate on his accounts, the work he had been doing had become more flagrantly erotic. There was a direct connection, I'd decided, between Stanley's brain and what he had between his legs.

'Please promise me that you won't go, Patricia.'

'But you've always said that Hilda was your soul-mate. Are you telling me you don't mind that she's left you?'

'Yes, of course I mind.'

I wrapped my fingers round the flex: 'So what do you intend to do about it?'

'I need to make Hilda understand that both of you are necessary to my art. I can't let either of you go. It isn't fair of her to ask me to. She'll see that in the end.'

There was a pause. 'I wouldn't count on it,' I said.

VII

'It isn't my fault Hilda's left him, Dorothy. I would have been quite happy to step back once I had got this exhibition for us at Lefevre's, but it would mean leaving

Stanley on his own and he would never sort out this mess with the Inland Revenue without someone to help him.'

We were in the garden, folding sheets that had been drying on the washing line. You have to bring them in whilst they're still marginally damp so that the creases come out when you iron them, but not so wet that they've started to go mouldy when you finally get round to it. The garden wasn't big enough for us to pull the sheet out to its full length without one or other of us standing in the flower-beds. I gave my end a tug and Dorothy let go her corner.

'Can't you pass him on to an accountant?' she said, grappling for it.

'An accountant wouldn't solve his other problems.'

'Nor would you, I hope.'

We'd got the sheet four-square again and shook it out.

'It must be obvious that he isn't getting anything from anyone at present,' I said, thinking that I'd rather get this conversation over with whilst we were in the open. 'I think this stuff he's producing now - these phallic altar pieces and huge women crushing little men who go on looking up at them adoringly – it's part of his frustration.'

'I think we can safely say you're part of his frustration,' Dorothy responded, gruffly.

Each of us now had two corners of the sheet. We folded it along its length and walked the ends towards each other.

'Stanley is a masochist where women are concerned. It suits him to be treated badly. He's excited by it.'

I took both ends so that Dorothy had to bend down to take the folded edge. The gesture wasn't lost on her. She straightened. 'If you make it clear to Stanley that he has no future with you, he'll go back to Hilda. Men can't bear to be alone. What matters is that Stanley doesn't see you as a substitute for Hilda and that Cookham doesn't, either. We're not living in Montmartre now, Patricia.'

'More's the pity.'

'It was your idea to come here. There are other options.'

'Are there? I don't know of any.'

'The world doesn't just consist of Paris or the English counties.'

'No. They say that Africa is cheap, although when they found out about us we would probably be executed.'

'You could end up being crucified here too, if you're not careful. What you're doing isn't fair to Hilda and it isn't fair to Stanley.'

'He'll be all right. Hilda loves him.'

'You talk as if you know what that means.'

'I love you. I know what that means.'

Dorothy's lips twitched. Now that the sheet had been reduced in size, it could be folded into quarters ready to go on the pile of laundry in the scullery. I squinted at the sky. It looked like rain and there were still another two sheets waiting to be taken down and folded.

'Did you ever hear from Richard Carline after that night at the Palais?' Dorothy looked sideways at me:

'No.' I started to un-peg another sheet.

'You don't think he's said anything?'

'Why would he? He's the one who'd been behaving badly.'

'I'm not talking about his behaviour. I'm referring to what he might have deduced from yours.' I waited for the slight tug on the lead I knew was coming. 'As you found out that night, it takes more to reinvent yourself than fish-net stockings and a new frock.'

Dorothy took over from me, working her way down the line, un-picking pegs and throwing them into the basket whilst I draped the sheet across my arms. 'At least the only thing you sacrificed on that occasion was an evening and your pride. You won't get off so lightly when it comes to Stanley.'

'When I told him I was going to stop seeing him, he broke down. He won't hear of it.'

'Then you had better come clean and tell Stanley what you are.' She glanced over her shoulder at me. 'Unless you think Richard Carline has already done that.'

VIII

It was not long before word got around that Hilda had left Stanley. Ten days later I received a note from Jas Wood asking whether I'd be free to have tea with him in The Copper Kettle that weekend. He was already there when I arrived.

'Patricia.' He held out his hand. 'How nice to see you. I believe the last time was the picnic.'

'That's a while back.'

'Yes.'

I'd been surprised to get his call. I wondered for a moment whether he'd been sent by Hilda and if he'd been told about the incident with Richard. Women talked to one another. Men were more inclined to boast but Jas was older than the rest of that set and he didn't strike me as the sort who gossiped.

He pulled out a chair and we sat. I saw Ida watching from behind the counter. If I went in on my own, she let me serve myself, but he'd already ordered. She came over with a plate of pastries and a pot of tea.

'Perhaps you'd like a sandwich or a slice of quiche to start with?' Jas said.

'No, thanks. Just tea would have been enough.'

'You're looking thin. We need to build you up.' He smiled. His face was like a room that had been occupied by several people, all of whom had left a mark, but who'd stopped short of scrawling their graffiti on the walls or carving their names in the woodwork.

'I'll pour, shall I?' he said.

'Thank you.'

He filled both cups and then reached out for the sugar bowl. I gave a little smirk as he put four cubes in his cup.

He saw me looking at him. 'They say you can always tell a man who lives alone.'

I didn't know he lived alone. I noticed that there was a white smudge on his waistcoat where he'd tried to get a stain out and a button had been sewn on using yellow cotton whereas all the other buttons were sewn on with black thread.

I had wondered briefly whether he was queer. There were so many of them in the art world. But Jas had a charm that was peculiarly male. He liked the company of women and was interested in them but unlike most men his interest wasn't predatory. He put the spoon back in the saucer and leant forward.

'We don't want to interfere in Stanley's life,' he said, 'but we're a bit concerned; his friends, that is. We wondered what you had in mind for him.'

I coughed. The tea had gone the wrong way. 'Oh dear,' Jas said, handing me his serviette. 'I hope that isn't my fault.' He paused, waiting for the coughing to subside.

'I'm sorry.' I sat back.

'Oh, my dear, don't apologise.'

'I'm just surprised that you'd think I had anything in mind for Stanley. After all, he's married.'

The door opened and swung back again. The café was beginning to fill up. I realised we were sitting at the table Stanley and Hilda had chosen when they came into the café that day. Maybe, some time in the future there would be a plaque above it.

'Quite. There was a time when we thought he was never going to get round to marrying.' He laughed.

'It took six years for him to make his mind up, I believe.'

He nodded. 'Yes, that's Stanley. He needs to be absolutely sure when he commits himself to something that he can incorporate it in his vision. Stanley is a very special person. You and I, we're ordinary by comparison.' He held his hand up. 'I don't mean that we're less valuable as human beings. If I'd been allowed to choose I would have chosen to be how I am. You know, the sort who bumbles through life, hopefully not doing too much harm but not achieving that much either.'

'You're not doing justice to yourself.'

'I think I am. The thing is,' he sat back and looked up at the ceiling. 'The thing is, Patricia, that a man like Stanley isn't someone you can pick up and put down again. He's like a rare plant. You can't just tip water on him now and then and hope that he'll survive. To own a plant like Stanley carries a responsibility.'

'It's just as well that I don't own him, then.' I felt resentful. Stanley's friends accepted his peculiarities without complaint. They went on loving him in spite of them. Why could I never feel that I was loved in spite of mine?

A couple sat down at the table next to ours. A woman who occasionally helped out at the village stores had come in with her sister. It was soon apparent that they found our conversation more enthralling than their own. Their whispers were designed to leave the air waves open for whatever titbits came their way. The sight of me with yet another man who looked as if he could be someone else's was enough to send a frisson through the gossiping community.

Jas smiled. 'I merely wondered how you would respond if such a situation happened to arise.'

'Has somebody been talking?'

'There is rarely any need where Stanley is concerned.'

'All right. So what has he been saying?'

'Stanley is infatuated. He has not made any secret of the fact. Unfortunately.'

'But you just said he would not commit himself to anything unless he knew he could incorporate it in his vision.'

'He's convinced himself he can.' Jas spread his hands.

One of the women whispered something and the other one turned round as if to re-adjust the handbag looped over the chair-back and glanced surreptitiously my way.

'It didn't take him six years this time, then.' I tapped my fingers on the table-top. I'd varnished my nails that day with the new shade, *Regimental Red.* I didn't want the effort to be wasted. 'I want you to know, Jas, that this isn't something I've encouraged. I met Stanley here. He was with Hilda and the baby. All I did was serve them lunch.'

'Of course. I understand. It's not your fault, Patricia. Stanley saw something in you that he's persuaded himself he can't do without. I, we, just wanted to be reassured that you would treat him gently.'

Though he never raised his voice, I guessed it carried easily between the tables, several of which were now occupied. I wondered whether to suggest we leave, but walking down the High Street or across the common we were just as likely to be seen.

'Has Stanley done this sort of thing before?'

'No, actually. I know that Hilda's his Supreme Muse. No one can replace her. It's the first time he's been seriously distracted. Hilda's worried. She felt she had no choice but to make a stand.'

'There wasn't any need for her to be concerned.' Though saying no-one could take Hilda's place was tantamount to throwing down a glove.

'She isn't worried for herself. It's Stanley she's concerned for. Hilda loves him.' He shrugged, in a gesture that implied the whole thing was a mystery to him. But it wasn't. Jas knew what it was about. He'd been there.

'Did you know I'd once proposed to Hilda?' he said, and then seeing my surprise he gave a modest smile and cleared his throat. 'She turned me down, of course.'

I wiped the serviette across my mouth. It seemed that Hilda had been quite a go-er in her time. I wondered what the ladies on the table next to us would make of that.

'I ought to add it happened years ago, before she had been introduced to Stanley. I just mentioned it to emphasize that what exists between those two is very special. It's not something anyone would interfere with lightly.'

'I'm not interested in Stanley,' I said.

'Not at all?' he looked surprised.

'Why would you think I was?'

He took a muffin from the plate and broke it into pieces, nibbling at the crumbs. 'He's quite an interesting character, I would have thought.'

'You make it sound as if I ought to have been interested in him.'

'As a painter vis-à-vis another painter, you have quite a lot in common.'

I considered. Jas at least appreciated that I was a painter too and not, as Stanley seemed to think, there just to service his needs. 'Actually I'm not a fan of Stanley's work.'

He looked bemused: 'You're saying you don't like it?'

'No, I don't.'

'You don't think Stanley's vision is a bit like William Blake's?'

I was flattered that he thought me capable of making that sort of comparison but I knew better than to take him up on it. I took my bag onto my lap. 'Please tell your friends they don't have anything to fear from me.'

He looked pained. 'I've upset you. Please forgive me.'

'No, you haven't. But I'm not sure what this is about.'

He leant across the table, putting his hand over mine. The gesture didn't go unnoticed at the tables either side of us.

'I've made you feel uncomfortable. I'm sorry. What you've said will reassure those of us who are trying to look after Stanley. It's not always easy. In the wrong hands he could be destroyed.' He put his hand back in his lap. 'I'm glad we've had this conversation.'

As I watched him topping up my cup, I wished we *hadn't* had this conversation. In the future I suspected that it would come back to haunt me.

IX

Dorothy was sitting with her head bent in an attitude suggesting that she was asleep except for one ear cocked towards the conversation taking place. At one point she made an adjustment to her glasses. This was not in order to see better. Dorothy saw very well. She knew exactly what was going on. We all did. Even Stanley, jumping up and down and ranting in the middle of the room, knew in his heart that it was all a pantomime with lines that he'd rehearsed a dozen times over the past weeks.

'I thought Hilda was my soul-mate,' he raged. 'She's betrayed me.' He screwed up the envelope and tossed it in the air. 'She's written here that Unity is the result, not of a union with me but of a union with God!'

'I wouldn't have said Unity was all that saintly,' Dorothy said wearily.

'My marriage has turned into a primeval slime!' said Stanley, furiously.

When he had discovered that on this occasion Hilda wasn't going to immediately cave in to his wishes, Stanley had been first of all perplexed, then angry. This was not the Hilda who had always shown a willingness to see things from his point of view. He didn't understand, as I did, that it wasn't her who'd changed; it was the nature of the threat. She knew what Stanley was about.

She made allowances. But she was not prepared to make allowances for me.

A part of me felt vindicated. I preferred to be regarded as a danger rather than an inconvenience that Hilda felt obliged to work around. Our brief acquaintance, inconclusive as it had been, had apparently confirmed her reservations. Looking back, I was surprised she had allowed the situation to develop to the point it had. She may have thought that leaving Stanley on his own would do the trick, of course, that he would come to a decision by himself without the need for her to do so.

I wished that the circumstances hadn't been so ignominious. I had felt bad enough about those shopping trips to Maidenhead. The thought that someone might have seen me tottering up and down in front of Stanley in my undergarments and reported back to Hilda, was humiliating, but I still thought she would compromise if the alternative was losing Stanley altogether. It turned out that all of us had underestimated Stanley's stubborn faith in his divine right as an artist to do as he pleased, however. As time passed his attitude became increasingly implacable and judging by his own accounts of their exchanges, so did hers.

We soon discovered that we weren't the only ones he was reporting back to. It seemed everyone in Cookham knew that this time Hilda wasn't coming back. They looked at me and, not surprisingly, concluded that I was the reason why she'd left him. I was tarred, no matter what I did next. If I put a foot outside the door of Moor Thatch I risked being stoned.

Over the past weeks, Hilda had been sending Stanley letters from the elders in the Christian Science Movement, criticising his behaviour and suggesting ways in which he might improve. They'd told her she should give up having sexual relations with him altogether, which was possibly the thing he minded most. His rage was genuine but at the same time he seemed to be cherishing the insult to his pride as something precious. Hilda's unfair treatment of him had become a symbol of his lingering attachment to her.

Dorothy sighed. Like me, she was anxious that if Hilda wasn't catering for Stanley's needs, he was more likely to start looking seriously elsewhere.

'If you want to know what I think, Stanley,' she said, mildly, 'what you need is not a wife, but an obliging slave who'll let you do exactly as you want.'

Unfortunately, Stanley was impervious to irony. He made no secret of the fact that he thought life ought to consist of satisfying one's desires, although as he was quick to point out nobody was satisfying his at present.

'How is Hilda managing financially?' said Dorothy.

'I send her money when I can. I've told her that I can't afford to give her any more at present. Anyway, Patricia's got my cheque book.'

Dorothy looked sideways at me. She let out a sigh which Stanley misinterpreted as one of sympathy. He went to speak but Dorothy held up her hand. 'Enough.' She levered herself up onto her feet. As Stanley followed her into the hall, I heard her say 'You have to stop this, Stanley. You're a married man with children.'

'But it's Hilda who's refusing to come back to me.'

'The reason she's refusing to come back is that she thinks she has a rival in Patricia.'

'I've explained to Hilda that I need them both. Patricia's necessary for my painting.'

'No she isn't, Stanley. All your pictures are the same. The ones you did before Patricia came along aren't any different from the ones you're doing now.'

'But I had Hilda then and now I have Patricia.'

'You won't ever have Patricia, Stanley. Stop this nonsense. It will decimate you both.'

X

I knew she'd seen me. She was standing in the courtyard of the farm with Pyke, when I went passed. I started to cross over and I saw Pyke nod in my direction. She half turned and then looked quickly one way then the other, like a rabbit in the glare of headlights not sure which direction offered an escape.

'I'm glad I caught you,' I said, 'I was hoping for a word.'

I glanced at Pyke who put his fingers to his cap and turned to Elsie. 'I'll be getting on then,' he said. 'Give your mother my regards.'

She looked at him and then at me: 'I'm sorry, Miss Preece, I'm afraid I can't stop now.' There wasn't any of the warmth she'd shown the first time we spoke.

'Which way are you going? I'll walk with you.'

She took on the rabbit-look again, then recognised that it was immaterial which way she went, since that was the direction I'd be going in as well. She turned towards the common.

I'd assumed that Elsie would have been appraised by Hilda of the fact that she would not be coming back to Lindworth. This put Elsie in a difficult position. There was no doubt she was genuinely fond of Stanley and would hesitate to leave him in the lurch, but to continue working for a man who was to all intents and purposes now living in the house alone, would not be doing much for Elsie's reputation either.

Since the day she brought the news of Tiddles' death, she'd not set foot inside the studio. I knew which days she came to Lindworth and I'd made sure that they didn't coincide with mine, but still that one occasion would have been enough to tell her that the rumours circulating in the village weren't mere gossip. There was no point trying to dissimulate.

'I gather Mrs Spencer has decided to remain in London for the moment, Elsie.' She looked guarded. 'That must make things difficult for you.'

She hesitated, not sure possibly how much I knew already and not wanting to add fuel to the fire, but then deciding, given what she'd seen of me, that probably I knew as much as her. 'It does. I shall be giving in my notice at the end of this month.'

'You've told Mrs Spencer, have you?'

Elsie crossed her arms in front of her protectively. 'Not yet.'

I felt a rush of irritation. Surely Hilda could have seen this coming. She and Stanley carried on as if the outside world did not exist. If Hilda wasn't coming back to Lindworth, it put me in a more difficult position than the one that Elsie found herself in. I might still prefer the label 'scarlet woman' to its less desirable alternative but I did not want to lose Dorothy or be left to assume sole charge of Stanley.

'Might you be prepared to wait a little longer? You see I think Mrs Spencer may well change her mind and I know how much she relies on you. Well, so does Mr Spencer.'

Elsie gave a modest little shrug. At least I was acknowledging her contribution to the running of the Spencer household. She'd need more than that, however.

'That's all very well,' she said, 'but I've got Ken to think about. When Mr Spencer took me on, he said I would be working for the family. That was the arrangement.'

'Yes, of course. It's just that it would be an extra blow for Mr Spencer, losing you as well. He needs somebody to look after him.'

I smiled as if we were colluding but the look she gave me questioned why I wasn't looking after him myself since everyone in Cookham thought I was already catering for Stanley's baser needs.

'Of course, I'll serve my notice,' she said, 'And if Mrs Spencer does come back, well then I'll reconsider if I've not found something in the meantime.'

'That seems very reasonable,' I said and added. 'You're a good girl, Elsie.'

Her look clearly asked what right I had to make that sort of value judgement even when it happened to be in her favour. She was wondering exactly what my role was in the drama of the Spencer's marriage. So was I.

XI

The small scar over Dorothy's left eye where she had fallen on a gravel pathway as a child, ballooned to twice its size as she held up her spectacles to check for smudges.

I sank down onto my knees beside her, laying both hands on her knees and staring up into her face until her eyes met mine.

'Go on then,' she said.

Now that I had her full attention I wished I could get up. I felt at a disadvantage on my knees.

The day before, we had been looking through the paintings Dorothy was putting in the exhibition and deciding what to send off to the framer's. 'Bourlet' was the firm used both by Tooth's and by Lefevre's. I'd been shocked when I discovered what they charged. We wouldn't have to pay the bill for several months and if we put it through the gallery, they would deduct it from the profits and we wouldn't see the bill at all. But they would also charge us for their trouble and unless the exhibition did well, we could end up at a deficit.

I'd wondered if we could negotiate a price based on the quantity of paintings they were framing, but the bill would come direct to us then and they might want a deposit. I'd used up the blank cheques signed by Stanley when I took charge of his cheque book and I felt uneasy about asking him to sign another one.

'I know you'd rather I detached myself from Stanley altogether, Dorothy, but I think we should wait at least until the exhibition is behind us. I might need to ask him for a loan to tide us over.'

'Stanley won't have any money either if the Inland Revenue gets its way,' Dorothy said sceptically.

'He earns ten times as much as we do, or at least he does in theory. Why else would the tax authorities be interested in him? God knows what he's done with it.'

'He seemed at one point to be spending quite a lot of it on you. That necklace you brought back from Asprey's must have cost the best part of five hundred pounds.'

'It actually cost seven hundred and before you ask, I cashed it in six weeks ago and used the proceeds to pay off last month's arrears.'

'We'll have to hope he doesn't ask you for it back, then.'

I leant my head on her knee. 'I hate this scratching round for money, Dodo. I go into Arkrights and they look at me when I pick out a bunch of broccoli as if they're waiting to be asked for credit. For a bunch of broccoli!'

'That isn't why they look at you.'

'Why do they, then?'

'You've taken Stanley from them. He's a child of Cookham. He belongs here and you don't. Of course they'll take his side. The way you've been behaving recently, we'll soon have no choice but to leave here altogether.'

She turned down the corner of the page she had been reading. Several sentences were scored out. I'd been shocked when I first lived with Dorothy, to see the way she treated books, until I realised that it was the same way that she treated human beings. If she didn't like them she ignored them. They would be passed on to someone else without a mark on them. If on the other hand she felt they had something to offer her, she would reciprocate by treating them as an extension of herself. It was a sign of her regard for what she read that nobody who read it afterwards could possibly be unaware that Dorothy had been there first.

'That wouldn't be so dreadful would it? There are other options, as you pointed out. We could go back to France if we had money.'

'We could go back anyway if money is the only thing that's stopping you. It's cheap enough to live there.'

'Cheap is what I've had enough of.'

She looked keenly at me: 'Yes, that's what I thought.'

Although it had been my suggestion to come back to England, at the time I sensed that Dorothy was of the same mind. In the end, there was too much of everything in Paris. Things had reached a crisis when, after a raucous evening at *Le Monocle,* I woke up in the night, my body clammy and my forehead burning. Dodo always left a mug of water by the bed on her side. I'd reached over for it. She stirred.

'What's the matter, sweetheart?'

'I don't know. I feel odd.'

She turned over, pressing one hand to my forehead. It was wet. She got up on her elbow. 'When did this start? You were all right earlier.'

The room we rented in *rue Lamarck* had no windows, just a skylight, which meant it was never fully dark or light there. We existed in a twilight world. I could see Dodo's outline in the dusk. I sank onto the pillow.

She got out of bed and I could hear her fumbling with the matches as she tried to get the stove to light. I fell asleep and when I woke up she was holding out a beaker of warm milk. I turned my head away. 'I want to sleep.'

'You've been asleep for hours. Come along now. Take a sip of this. You need to keep your strength up.'

For the next ten days I slept and dreamed and ranted as the fever worked its way out of my system. Every time I woke up, Dorothy was there with mugs of milk or beef tea, urging me to take a sip to please her.

'How long was I ill for?' I asked afterwards.

'Three weeks.'

Although we didn't talk about it then, what preyed on my mind was that Dorothy would have been physically unable to survive the sort of illness she had nursed me through. With her weak lungs she was susceptible not just to the appalling winters in the capital but to infections and diseases common amongst those who lived as we did.

Gretha Mathurin had died that winter of an overdose. It wasn't known if it was accidental or intended or indeed exactly what she'd taken. At *Le Monocle* as long as you had money, you were spoilt for choice.

Our paths had crossed occasionally. The queer community in Paris was close-knit and flourishing, at least according to the people in it, but it wasn't large. The turn-over was brisk so if you hadn't seen somebody for a month or two you could assume that they had either left the capital or left the world.

The smile that Gretha Mathurin reserved for Dorothy whenever we ran into her, told me that she was waiting for the call and ready to respond to it, but also that it hadn't come yet. I was never quite sure whether Dorothy was loyal to me out of principle, because she didn't have the energy or appetite to be unfaithful, or because she loved me, but I felt that it was something I could count on.

We were at a party in the 16th at the flat of Romaine Brooks when we first heard the news. A porter had discovered Gretha when a friend arrived and was unable to get into her apartment. She'd been dead for three days. I glanced round at Dorothy but her face wasn't giving anything away. I asked her if she'd like to talk about it and she said no. Neither of us had referred to it since then.

We had seen Gretha's parents at the funeral. Her mother clung onto her father's arm, a screwed-up handkerchief in one hand which she dabbed continually on her nose. She didn't raise her eyes once and he kept his own eyes straight ahead. They didn't look like the descendants of a Saint and they were clearly ill at ease amongst their daughter's friends.

On her last journey Gretha was accompanied by those she had been closest to in life: a line of women, some of them in men's clothes although they did not exhibit any of their usual flamboyance and the women they were with hung onto them like drowning sailors clinging to a raft. I wondered which of them had given her the cocktail of amphetamines that killed her.

Ordinary Parisians came out to watch the coffin pass and some jeered when they realised that not all the men were men. At one point, as the cortège turned into a narrow street, somebody threw a soft tomato and it splattered on the black suit of a mourner.

In the cemetery it started raining so hard that in minutes water had begun to fill the grave. A number of the mourners surreptitiously began to drift away until there were no more than half-a-dozen standing at the graveside as the clogged earth spattered down onto the coffin. All in all, it was a dismal afternoon.

Once the idea of going back to England had been mooted, it was self-perpetuating. Quietly, we began to close down all the avenues we'd been so anxious to explore when we arrived. We still accepted invitations, but less often. I did not enrol at André Lhôte's Academy the next term, although Dorothy continued studying with Colarossi.

When we started to discuss where we might move to, it was I who had suggested Cookham. To return to London, having left our friends behind there five years earlier, would carry the inevitable whiff of failure with it. I was anxious to avoid the feeling that we had returned to England with our tails between our legs.

I knew that Dorothy was not concerned to live in London. As she said, it was like Paris but without the compensations. I remembered Cookham as a place where I'd been reasonably happy but where nobody would recognise me; near enough to London that we didn't feel cut off but far enough away from the temptations of the city.

I was not prepared for the small-minded bigotry of England's country villages. We'd barely been back six months before we were bickering. I strafed at the restrictions whereas Dorothy believed that it was what went on inside your head that mattered. You could compromise outside as long as you kept faith with what you were. She saw no point in causing ructions. Where we differed was that she was not ashamed of what she was. If she'd been outed she would not have cared much, whereas I would have been mortified. She knew this and occasionally she taunted me. It was a game we played where I pretended that I wanted to declare myself in order to be reassured that Dorothy would not allow me to. We batted threats across the net to keep ourselves in shape. But every now and then the argument grew bitter. Recently that had been happening more and more.

I rested one hand on her knee to give myself some leverage and started hauling myself up onto my feet. 'At least in Paris we could be ourselves!' I threw out, irritably.' It was a complaint I often voiced and usually, knowing it would escalate into a row, she let it pass. Not this time.

She took my hand firmly from her knee and let it go. I sank back on my heels. I had no choice now but to hear her out. She closed the book she had been reading, placing her hand on it palm down, like somebody on the witness stand.

'You can be yourself here as long as you're prepared to take the consequences.'

'You're the one who's been insisting that we shouldn't draw attention to ourselves.'

'Not in the way that you've been doing. If that's an example of you being what you are, God help us.'

'What's happening now is Hilda's fault as much as anybody else's, you know.'

'How so?'

'She encouraged Stanley to think he could have as many women as he wanted…as he needed.'

'I imagine she thought she was giving him creative freedom.'

'More fool her.'

'You think she should have been less generous?'

'I don't know. I don't care.'

'You don't think that, as a beneficiary, you ought to care?'

'The person who stands to gain most from our association with him, Dorothy, is you.'

I once picked up a bucketful of water I'd left underneath the sink when it was leaking and unthinkingly upended it into the sink again. There is a second when you think it might be possible to turn back time, to put the water back into the bucket. Then you feel it sloshing round your ankles.

'Me?'

'Your work would sink without trace if it wasn't for my efforts to promote it.'

'But I like to think I would continue doing it, whereas you'd be completely at a loss. What would you have to recommend you, after all? You're thirty-seven and the only jobs you have at present are that of a part-time waitress in The Copper Kettle and an unpaid model for a grubby little man whose idea of a good time is to have you tottering up and down in front of him in high heels and to paint you copulating with the local dustman.' Both of us were treading water now.

'You told me you thought Stanley was a genius.'

'What I object to is the smell of garbage that you have on you when you come back here after seeing him.' She stuck her chin out.

I was kneeling in the middle of the floor as if I needed her permission to get up. I thought how bland our rows had been before they found a focal point in Stanley. She got up. I didn't want her leaving me there on the carpet like a penitent.

'He's not important, Dorothy,' I shouted after her. 'He doesn't matter.'

At the door she hesitated for a second before coming back. She leaned across me to pick up her book. As she went out, she called over her shoulder. 'I'm afraid old girl, he does.'

XII

Just how much Stanley mattered, to himself at any rate, would soon become clear. Although they no longer spoke to one another, he and Hilda still wrote letters to each other every day. In one, she wrote that she'd consulted God about their future and was waiting for an answer.

Stanley argued that since God agreed with everything he'd done, he didn't see why Hilda needed to consult Him first. Until now, she had gone along with this so her unreasonable attitude of late had been another subject of complaint. We looked on as he inched his way relentlessly towards the edge of the abyss.

To crown his troubles, he'd received an answer from the Inland Revenue. He brought the envelope to me unopened. Inside was a tax demand for payment going back five years. The fine for not submitting his returns was seven hundred pounds.

He looked at me aghast: 'I thought you'd written to them.'

'I did write to them. I put your case as clearly as I could but frankly Stanley there was not much I could offer them by way of an excuse except that it had slipped your mind. We can appeal. That way you'll get a few months' grace but in the end you'll have to pay up.'

'I'm already struggling to find Hilda's maintenance. I send her money and she gives it to the Christian Scientists! She tells me it's important to keep in with them because they have a direct link to God. I've told her there's no need – I have a direct link to God.'

'I don't know which of you is barmier. What's Hilda living on, then?'

'That's the trouble. She says she can't keep herself and both the girls on what I'm giving her.'

'I'm not surprised if half of it is going to the Christian Scientists.' I tap my fingers on the envelope. 'Your assets at the moment, Stanley, leaving out the paintings, would appear to be the house, the car and the piano. Could you manage to get by without the car and the piano?'

'I could do without the car.'

'Where is it, incidentally?'

'In Hampstead. Hilda's got it.'

'Are you sure she hasn't made a present of it to the Christian Science Movement?'

He looked bilious. I held out the letter. 'Does she know about this?' Since the two of them were writing to each other twice a day, you'd think he might have mentioned it but it seemed their discussions focused more on what was happening above than what went on below. 'You need to tell her. It's important she stops giving things away.'

'I'll tell her.'

'When you next write, say you need to sell the car. If it's been standing outside all this time, the battery has probably gone flat in any case.'

He looked bemused. I doubted that he'd ever looked under the bonnet of a car.

'Where did the Bechstein come from?'

'I can't sell that,' he said, panicking.

'Why not?'

'When I'm not sleeping, I play Bach. It keeps me company.' He frowned. 'Is there no other way?'

'The fewer assets you have, Stanley, the less they can take away from you. The more you have, the more you stand to lose and by off-loading items like the car you can release a bit of cash. You're obviously capable of earning money. You just need to go on doing it. You told me once that you could paint a landscape in a fortnight and they always sold. Why don't you do some more of those?'

'They're not my real work.'

'They might have to be until you've paid off what you owe.' I didn't add what I was thinking, that if landscapes offered Stanley a distraction from the kind of pictures he'd been painting recently, the current crisis might turn out to be a blessing in disguise.

He sighed. 'It's all so difficult.' He sat with his hands pressed against his temples.

'You'll feel better once you've knuckled down to sorting out the mess.'

'I know. It's just....' He shook his head. Decisive action wasn't Stanley's strong point. Reckless, maybe, but decisive, no. I, on the other hand, was on a roll.

'Another thing you might consider doing is transferring some of your more valuable possessions into someone else's name so that you won't be liable for tax on them. At present everything's in your name which means you're responsible.'

I looked round for a scrap of paper and dug out a pencil from the bottom of my bag. 'Why don't we write down what you've got and mark the items that you could and couldn't do without and then decide what should be done with them.' I patted the low chair in front of Stanley's desk and he came meekly over and sat down.

XIII

'You're telling me that Stanley has signed Lindworth over to you!' Dodo wasn't often at a loss for words. 'How did you manage that?' she said at last.

'It was the only answer. By off-loading Lindworth he'll have fewer liabilities for tax and there'll be less for him to pay in maintenance for Hilda if she doesn't come back. An accountant would have said the same.'

She stared at me incredulously. 'Dare one ask what you gave Stanley in return?'

'The benefit of my advice.'

In truth, I'd been as shocked as she was by this unexpected change of fortune. From a part share in a leaky cottage on the edge of Cookham, I was now the owner of a house on three floors with a tennis court. And I'd not even had to fight for it.

I wondered how soon Hilda would discover what had happened. Should I write and tell her I had simply wanted to keep Lindworth from the Inland Revenue? Or would her answer be that she would have preferred the Inland Revenue to have it. I was quite surprised she hadn't made it over to the Christian Scientists but then of course as long as it remained in Stanley's name, she couldn't.

He had signed the documents without a murmur. It was then I realised that his work was all he cared about. He would fight tooth and nail for that. If signing over Lindworth meant that he no longer had to think about the Inland Revenue, then it was worth the sacrifice in his terms.

Certainly the work he had been doing recently would not have got him out of trouble on its own. I had been leafing through his sketchbook one day and discovered drawings of half-naked women, several of them recognisable as me, embracing telegraph poles sticking up between their legs.

I tore a couple of the pages out when Stanley wasn't looking. Although there was a waste-paper basket in the studio, the floor was where most of the rubbish ended up and from there much of it eventually made its way back to the workbench, so I slipped the sketches in my satchel to dispose of later.

When I called the next time, I found Stanley thumbing through the sketchbook.

'There are pages missing,' he said.

Given what a mess the studio was in, I hadn't thought he'd notice. He shook out the pages. Bits of debris – bus tickets, receipts from Arkwright's store and scraps of paper on which Stanley's thoughts had been recorded for posterity - cascaded down onto the floorboards. So far, buying him a diary so that it was all in one place didn't seem to have had much effect.

He looked up. 'Someone's torn the page out. Who would do that?'

'If what's missing is that obscene drawing of a woman in a feather boa with her legs wrapped round a telegraph pole, it was me who took it.'

'Why?' He looked perplexed.

'Because if anybody saw it, Stanley, you would be arrested.'

He put one hand palm down where the missing page had been: 'Where has it gone?'

I hesitated. 'I believe I threw it in the bin.'

He stared at me: 'You threw my work away?'

'Believe me, I was doing you a favour. You've already fallen foul of the authorities over your tax affairs. You don't want to fall foul of them over your morals. Do you have to drag sex into everything?'

'It's there in all we do,' insisted Stanley.

'It's not there in everything I do. It isn't normal to be so obsessed.' When I arrived I had intended sitting down with Stanley to work out a draft of his appeal but this exchange had thrown me out of kilter.

'How would you know?' Stanley said. He ran a finger down the torn edge where the sketch had been ripped out.

'You're not suggesting I'm the one that's odd!'

He turned on me: 'You won't make love with me and nor will Hilda. What am I supposed to do? I'm going mad! The drawings are the only way I can express myself.'

'Does Hilda think we've had sex? Is it something you've discussed?'

'I said you wouldn't. She said it was probably because of Dorothy.'

'She said that! How dare you discuss me with your wife like that.'

'You talk to Dorothy about me.'

'No, I don't and if I hear you've talked to her about us, Stanley, that's it. It'll be all over.'

'How can it be over?' he said, harshly. 'Nothing's happened.'

I felt suddenly as if I had been arbitrarily dismissed from a position I thought was a sinecure. I wondered whether he regretted having signed over his house to me so easily and whether he was thinking he should have been offered something in return. If I'd shown gratitude it would imply that he was doing me a favour rather than me doing him one. Stanley was naïve on many levels but he wasn't stupid. It was not the loss of Lindworth but the desecration of his sketchbook that had brought the other issues to the surface.

When I'm challenged, I become aggressive. As a ploy it hardly ever worked with Dorothy and I did not think it would work here, but I needed time to think and hitting back at Stanley was the only way I could defend myself.

'You're telling me that all the times I've sat for you, the endless boring afternoons you've spent at Moor Thatch, taking up our time, complaining to us about Hilda, all the effort I've been putting in to put you on the right side of the Inland Revenue, all that time you were simply angling for a fuck?'

'It wasn't like that,' he said, shocked.

'That's what it sounds like.'

'You're my muse. I want us to be up-in-heaven. Can't you understand?'

I looked at him. Perhaps things weren't as bad as I had feared. I was still Stanley's muse. It was important not to spoil what had already been accomplished. I put down my bag. 'What do you want to do about it, then?'

'You know what I want, but you say it's not what you want. You don't even like my work.' He kicked out at the table leg.

I ought to have anticipated this. I once poured coffee accidentally over a drawing Dorothy was showing me. If there had been a weapon handy, I might not have lived to tell the tale.

'Of course I like your work. And so does Dorothy. We think you're very talented.' I bit my tongue. 'And both of us are very fond of you.'

He stood there with his shoulders hunched. I patted him. 'You're feeling low. It's not surprising, losing Tiddles, all this trouble with the Inland Revenue and Hilda being difficult. I just don't think this is the moment for us to become emotionally involved.'

He looked at me. His eyes were like a dog's that went on trusting in its owner, even knowing that it was about to be abandoned. Stanley hadn't been emotionally *un*-involved since he was born. I might have got away with it on this occasion but I knew that I was running out of time.

XIV

As I'd anticipated, it was not long before Hilda got wind of the fact that if she did return to Lindworth, she would be returning to a house that, legally, was not hers any longer.

Normally I'd turn up at the studio and let myself in but the next time I arrived at Lindworth I found Stanley's car parked in the drive. The muffled sound of voices drifted from the studio. I was about to creep away again when I heard my name mentioned. It was hard to make out what was being said but then the voices rose and I heard Hilda say:

'How could you, Stanley? You signed our house, *our house*, over to that woman?'

Stanley's silhouette appeared against the window as he backed away. 'Patricia said it would be better if I didn't have too many assets to declare now that the Inland Revenue is on my back.'

'You didn't think to speak to me or a solicitor?'

'Solicitors cost money, Hilda.'

'From what I've heard, so does she. I know about those trips you made to Asprey's. Whilst I'm struggling to find money for our daughter to have music lessons, you've been frittering away your fortune on that woman.'

'She's a friend.'

'She's nothing of the sort. Your *friend* has robbed our family of its inheritance. We loved you, Stanley, and now you've betrayed us.'

'Don't say that; it's horrible. I feel the world's attacking me from all sides.'

'Why do you think that is! When you told me that you had to have her for your painting, I accepted that. I didn't think she would be taking over every aspect of our lives. It's weeks since Unity and Shirin saw you. Unity's not certain any longer who her father is.'

'You left me, Hilda. It was your decision. You could spend more time in Cookham.'

'In a house that's not mine anymore? No thank you, Stanley. What would be the point of coming back in any case whilst you're besotted with Patricia.'

'I want both of you,' said Stanley. 'My lust's all churned up inside me. I can't concentrate on anything. I can't work; I feel impotent.'

'She's stopping you from working. Don't you think that's odd if she's your muse?'

'It's complicated, Hilda.'

'You don't love her, Stanley. You're infatuated with her. Jas says...'

'Jas! I thought he was my friend!'

'He is your friend. He's our friend. He wants us to stay together.'

'I want that, too.'

'But you've said you want Patricia as your mistress, as your muse. And now, as if that wasn't bad enough, she owns our house. How do you think that makes me feel?'

'Oh Hilda, don't you understand?'

'No, Stanley. I'm afraid I don't.'

I crept away. I didn't need to hear more and I was afraid that if she suddenly walked out on Stanley, Hilda would discover me outside the window, lurking, and I would feel even more humiliated.

I went for a walk on Odney Common to give her a chance to get away. From one side I could hear the shouts of children swimming in the river; from the other, the low cheers of the spectators at a cricket match. It was so long since I'd indulged in any past-time simply for the pleasure of it, that I felt quite tearful.

I walked down towards the river, following the shouts and laughter. By the bridge at Cookham Lock a family was picnicking. Three boys in shorts and striped vests took turns to skim pebbles in the water. A black Labrador rushed in to fetch them, barking joyfully and sending white spume up into the air as pebbles landed next to it and disappeared.

A woman in a broad-brimmed hat sat with a baby underneath a parasol a short way off. In half an hour when the sun began to go down, she would pack the baby and the rug into the stroller, call the boys and make her way back to their modest house in Cookham Dean to wait for the arrival of her husband on the train from Maidenhead or Reading. She would talk about her day and he would tell her about his. Perhaps they'd listen to a concert on the radio before they went to bed. This was the way that normal people lived. Though Stanley and his wife had never lived a normal life in the accepted sense, without me they would still have something that approximated to it.

The Saloon had gone when I returned. I had expected to find Stanley devastated after Hilda's visit but I found him sitting quietly by the window, staring out over the garden.

'Hilda's leaving me for good,' he said. 'She's going to divorce me.'

'I'm sure Hilda wouldn't go to those lengths,' I said, shakily. 'She wants to frighten you, that's all.'

Although it wasn't unexpected or unreasonable in the circumstances, I could not see Hilda leaving Stanley permanently. She might want to punish him but if she left him altogether it was she who would be suffering as much as him. And who else would take Stanley on? I hoped she didn't think it would be me or, worse, that he did.

I had boxed myself into a corner. I could hardly walk away now that he had signed Lindworth over to me, not without his friends assuming that my motives had been mercenary all along.

I had felt flushed with victory in the wake of that achievement. We'd gained so much more from Stanley than I had originally hoped for. Dorothy's career would get the boost it needed from the exhibition at Lefevre's; thanks to Stanley's presents of expensive jewellery, we'd paid off the arrears on Moor Thatch and although I hadn't got as far as thinking what I'd do with it, our assets now effectively included a three-storey house. All this with Stanley still in thrall to me.

And yet I had the feeling Dorothy was disappointed. Why should she be grateful for my having given her what she had never asked for in the first place: that would be her argument. Once she began to reap the benefits, however, she would soon come round. From worrying that we were on a plateau none of us was going to escape from, now I worried that a sudden movement on the part of one or other of the players could begin an avalanche that would sweep everybody off the mountain.

'Better that you don't say anything to Hilda at the moment, Stanley. You don't want her doing something you might both regret.'

'I won't have her dictating who I love.'

'She is your wife.'

He looked at me as if he couldn't see what relevance that had. 'I feel I'm married to all women I experience a *oneness* with.'

'But that's not quite the same as being married to them, is it?'

'No, it isn't,' he said, meaningfully.

I felt it was safer not to go too far along this path. I didn't like the look in Stanley's eye.

'If Hilda's going to divorce me, there's no reason why we shouldn't be emotionally involved,' said Stanley.

I would have to be more careful what I said to him.

'There are a lot of reasons, Stanley. For a start she's only *said* she's going to divorce you. Hilda could have changed her mind before she reached the front gate. Getting a divorce involves a huge upheaval and expense. Once she's consulted a solicitor she'll soon discover that.'

'But spiritually we've already parted.'

'*Spiritually* doesn't cut the mustard either, I'm afraid.'

'You're saying that you still won't sleep with me?' He looked affronted. 'I signed my house over to you, thinking we would live in it together. That's the reason Hilda is divorcing me.'

'The point of putting Lindworth into someone else's name was so the Inland Revenue could not include it in your assets. Dorothy and I already have a house. We don't need yours.'

'You're saying you would rather I had given it to someone else?'

'Of course not. I'm your business manager. I'm handling your affairs. But it will look odd if the minute you sign Lindworth over to me, we start acting like a couple.'

Stanley shook his head. 'I thought we were a couple. Hilda thinks that we're a couple. Whether she divorces me or not, she isn't going to come back now. If you still won't sleep with me I shan't have anyone.'

This was the situation I had dreaded finding myself in, whereby I couldn't think of any reason not to go to bed with Stanley other than a natural repugnance. I did not want his friends thinking I had engineered the break-up of his marriage, then refused to sleep with him because my inclinations lay elsewhere. I wasn't likely to be credited with finer motives even if I'd had them.

I breathed in and in that instant wondered what would happen if I didn't bother breathing out again, so by the time I did, my head and body seemed to have detached themselves from one another.

'If it's that important to you, Stanley, I might be prepared to give ground.'

Stanley tipped his head to one side, like a sparrow that had seen a worm move in the corner of its eye. 'How?'

'I might go to bed with you, just once to tide you over.' Had I just said what I thought I'd said? The strange thing was that once I'd said it and the thing was out there in the open, it seemed less outrageous.

Stanley went to speak and stopped. There was a long pause. 'Are you saying that we can be joyful after all?'

I hesitated. Was it too soon to start having second thoughts? A part of me was thinking that what didn't work with Richard Carline wasn't likely to work here with somebody whose main attraction was that he could offer me and Dorothy a ticket out of poverty. But I'd invested so much time in him already and endured so much that I could not bear to relinquish what ground I'd already gained.

'There'd be no question of me staying overnight, I want to make that clear. And don't think I intend to make a habit of it.'

His eyes searched my face. 'Now?' His hands wandered to the buttons of his shirt.

'No. Maybe Thursday afternoon.' That was the day when Dorothy returned her library books and took another set out. She'd be there until the library closed at five. At least it put a time limit on my experiments with Stanley.

'Couldn't we lie down for quarter of an hour now?'

'No, Stanley. I shall need time to prepare myself.'

'But we can be together?' he said, his hands clawing at the air. 'That's wonderful.'

I wished he wouldn't grin at me like that. 'We can use any time left over afterwards to write your letter to the Inland Revenue.' I slid the bag over my arm. I couldn't concentrate on letters to the Inland Revenue after the conversation we'd just had.

He followed me out of the shed. 'You will come, won't you? Thursday afternoon?'

'I've said I'll be here and I will. Stop pressuring me.'

He fell back but I could hear him panting slightly. At the gate I turned around. 'And maybe you could change the sheets before I come.'

He frowned: 'I'm not sure where to find the clean ones.'

'In a drawer maybe. The airing cupboard?'

'I'll ask Hilda.'

'Oh for God's sake, Stanley. Are you mad?'

'I'll look for them. I promise. Only tell me you won't change your mind.'

'Just get the sheets changed, Stanley.'

He curled both hands round the gate and swung it back towards him. 'I'm so happy,' he said. 'I can't wait. It's going to be bliss.'

Part Four
Paradiso

I

I'd spent the next week wondering how to get out of the situation I had put myself in. I could picture Stanley in the studio, naively trying to create the sort of ambience that was conducive to an afternoon of passion. I imagined lying on that horrible brass bed whilst Stanley fumbled his way through the preliminaries. I did not think he would prove to be an expert lover, even if he did spend most of his time thinking about sex.

On Thursday morning I told Dorothy I would be going into Maidenhead that afternoon. I'd kept back half-a-dozen items from my last excursion, mindful that I'd need to bring back evidence of purchases if I was using shopping outings as a reason for my absence. This time I took less care over my appearance.

I heard Stanley humming as I turned into the drive at Lindworth. He'd arranged a bunch of poppies in a jam-jar on the window-sill.

'You came.' His face broke out into a smile.

'I said I would.'

He nodded: 'Shall I make some tea?'

'No thank you.'

I saw Stanley's fingers stray towards the work bench and withdraw again. He wiped them on his trousers. 'Would you like to sit down?'

He was acting as if this was my first visit to the studio, as if I'd never taken off my clothes infront of him, as if he'd never made that gross remark that he would like to crawl across me like an ant. He knew the landscape of my body better than I did myself, yet he was acting as if we had never met before.

I threw my handbag on the bed and kicked my shoes off. Plonking myself on the mattress, I sat with my arms pressed to my sides.

There was a pause and Stanley came and sat beside me. He put one arm round my shoulders and leaned over, giving me a chaste peck on the cheek. We sat like that a moment, neither of us certain where to go from there.

'I changed the sheets,' said Stanley.

'So I see.'

'Why don't you get in?'

Recognising that I'd have to make a move at some point, I stood up, unfastening the belt that held my skirt. It fell down in a heap around my ankles. I took off my stockings and undid the buttons on my blouse.

The look on Stanley's face was one of dreamy expectation, quite unlike the piercing gaze he wore when he was painting me. He had made no attempt to take off any of his own clothes. As the final item dropped onto the mat, he put a hand up to adjust his spectacles. He stood up, drawing back the covers, smoothing out the bottom sheet.

I slid into the gap. I'd hoped that Stanley wouldn't start by taking off his trousers. There's a protocol about these things which he was clearly unaware of. He not only took his trousers off first, but he left his vest and socks on. Having changed the sheets, I'd hoped it might occur to him to change his vest and socks too, but the vest was grey and I had long suspected that he only had one pair of socks.

I shunted sideways to make room for him and he got in beside me. We sat stiffly like two teenagers, each waiting for the other one to make a move. The longer we sat there in silence, the more difficult it was to break it. Stanley finally leaned over, pressing me against the pillows, and began to lever himself onto me. The sudden flurry of activity was so abrupt, it took a moment for me to appreciate that we had started.

Stanley's wet lips nibbled at my shoulder and moved down onto my breast. The slug-trail his lips left behind brought bile into my throat.

He glanced up. He still had his glasses on. The eyes behind them were unfocused. 'This is wonderful.' he said. 'You don't know what it means to me.'

I felt his hand against my stomach. Things were escalating out of my control. There was a moment when I thought we might get through it. I looked round the room. I needed something else to focus my attention on. The poppies on the window-sill were swaying in the draft. As if on cue, the petals started dropping off them, spiralling towards the floor. I saw an ear-wig running up the table-leg. Once it had reached the top, it made a bee-line for the loaf of bread and disappeared inside it, burrowing its way into the dough, its back legs thrusting at the air. The floor was strewn with screwed up bits of paper. There was nothing in the room that offered any respite. I felt Stanley nibbling at my thigh, just as the ear-wig poked its head out of the loaf.

'It's no good, Stanley. Please stop. I can't bear it!'

II

I am trying not to break into a run as I turn out onto the main road. People in the street glance curiously at me. I must look as if I've just been roughed up in an alleyway. My hair is wild and I am holding up my skirt with one hand, having lost the belt under the bed and been in too much of a rush to search for it.

I turn onto the path across the moor. I'm desperate to get back to Moor Thatch before Dorothy comes home. I need to have a bath and scrub myself from head to foot. I couldn't bear the thought of sitting opposite her over tea with Stanley's finger-prints all over me.

The house is empty. I fill up the bath and empty half a jar of bath salts into it. And then I sink down with my head under the water and remain there till I have no choice but to come up again.

Although he hadn't tried to stop me leaving, the exchange we'd had whilst I was pulling on my clothes had finally brought home to me how utterly impossible the whole thing was. The afternoon had mercilessly pointed up our incompatibility as lovers. No one, even Stanley with his boundless optimism with regard to sex, could want to go through that again. The mere thought was enough to send me sliding back under the water.

Dorothy was right. The time had come to put an end to this charade. The next time I saw Stanley, I'd explain that it had been nice knowing him but that his future lay with Hilda. I'd put Lindworth back in his name. Dorothy and I would go back to the life we had before. We'd struggle to make ends meet and lose patience with each other when we couldn't buy the things that made life bearable. I would smoke forty cigarettes a week instead of twenty-five a day and Dorothy would have to water down her whisky.

We still had the exhibition to look forward to, of course, though without Stanley's contacts it might be our only chance to break into the art world. I knew how to put myself about, but telling people I was Stanley's friend had given me a context, one I'd have to do without in future.

I turn on the hot tap and there is another burst of heat around my ankles. Little rivulets of water lap against my thighs. My heart-beat's slowing down. I'm starting to feel calmer. Maybe after all it would be sensible to wait. Each time I reach the point of thinking there is nothing to be gained by our continuing association with him, something else pops up into my head, like that three-page spread in *The Times* last week on underrated British artists. It suggested Stanley's work was undergoing a resurgence and so were the prices it was fetching. One of Stanley's *Views of Cookham* had sold recently for just over £200. It seemed his friends were right about him. Stanley was an artist who was going places.

It would be a shame to cut loose just as things were starting to improve.

An hour later when the front door slams and I hear Dorothy call 'Coo-ee' from the passage, I am sitting at the kitchen table with a glass of whisky and a cigarette, attempting to appear relaxed. She dumps the pile of books she's carrying onto the table next to me and pecks me on the cheek.

'How was it at the library?'

'Miss Barrett tried to throw out poor old Walter Orbell, who was laid off from the timber merchant's last month. He fell fast asleep over the Situations Vacant column. She's determined not to let them turn the library into a doss-house but where else are they supposed to go?' She takes another three books from her bucket bag and lays them on the pile. She always brings back eight, the maximum that she's allowed. When I said inadvisedly one day that no one could read eight books in a week, she clearly felt obliged to prove me wrong. Because I only read one book a fortnight, she insists I'm not a reader.

'I thought you believed in quality, not quantity,' I'd said.

'I do,' said Dorothy. She'd whipped my magazine away from me. '*The Shadow*'. She held it away from her as if she was afraid it might have germs. The Shadow's a detective who can read minds, hypnotize his enemies and make himself invisible. At least there is a story to it. I had once made the mistake of saying there was not much plot in *Mrs Dalloway*.

'I don't think I can dignify that with an answer,' Dorothy had said.

When I found out she'd been subscribing to a left-wing book club which charged members 2s 6d a month to take a book out, I was furious, however.

'You can take out books for nothing from the Lending Library, Dorothy!'

'They don't have any of the radical new publications. When I ordered Orwell's latest book, I had to wait ten weeks for it.'

'But 2s 6d a month!'

'Foyle's has set up a *Right Book Club* in opposition. This is war, Patricia.'

I pull out a volume from the stack she's plonked down next to me and turn it over to see what they say about the author. I wish they had photos on the back. It's how I'd choose which ones to read. As Dorothy was quick to point out, it's as well the literary world does not depend on me to pick the big names, though from what I've heard most of the people who it does depend on would employ the same criteria.

I'm humming, something I do automatically when I feel agitated. I sound like the cat when he was angling to get Dorothy to take him on her lap. I stop and jiggle one foot up and down across my knee instead.

She hovers for a moment and then crosses over to the sink and pours herself a glass of water. As I'm leafing through the pages of her book, I realise she is watching me. There's something not right in the way I am behaving. I can feel it, too.

'I gather Hilda's been down?' she says casually. 'I heard Miss Barrett say she'd seen the car parked in the drive at Lindworth. Did you know about it?'

'Stanley said she'd called in. Tuesday I believe it was. Apparently she didn't stay long.'

'Long enough to tell him she was going to divorce him.'

I keep my eyes on the book. 'You obviously know more than I do.'

'Stanley went into the village shop on Saturday and bared his soul to Mrs Arkwright. He might just as well have broadcast the news on the radio. He didn't say what prompted her decision, fortunately.'

'Do we know what prompted it?'

'Discovering her rival had the deeds to her house might have had some bearing on the matter.' Dorothy leans over, takes the book out of my hands and puts it back onto the pile.

'You know why I took over Lindworth Dorothy.'

'Tell that to Hilda.'

'Stanley said he'd square it with her. Either she misunderstood or he did.'

'You had better go and see her. Put her straight, then. If she sues him for divorce it will be us who end up dealing with the consequences.'

'Go and see her!' The idea of facing Hilda now that I'm to all intents and purposes her husband's mistress, brings the sweat out on my upper lip. I am more prone to sudden flushes when I've had a bath; the pores stay open. 'I would rather not get too embroiled.' I smooth my dress down.

Dorothy lets out a bark. She gathers up the pile of books and tucks them underneath her arm.

'Where are you going?'

'I was thinking I might have a bath.' She lumbers over to the door.

I stare at her: 'You never have a bath at this time.'

'Well today I feel like one. I'm sticky. It's the weather. Neither one thing nor the other.'

'I'm afraid there's no hot water in the tank.'

She stops. 'The boiler's been on all day, hasn't it?'

I wonder whether I should lie and tell her I forgot to turn it on this morning, but she only has to go into the bathroom, check the towels and see the condensation on the mirror.

'I felt sticky, too. You're right, the weather's odd. The water won't take long to heat up. Leave it until after supper.'

She stands for a moment with the books stacked up against her chest, her head on one side, contemplating. Then she glances at me, gives a short nod, turns and leaves the room.

III

It turns out even bad sex, even sex that's so bad it gives sex a bad name, is still worthy of inclusion on the list of Stanley's *up-in-heaven* moments. Not just worth recording either, but repeating. Listening to him, I'm not sure we're even talking of the same event. That *incident* (I can't persuade myself to give it any other title) signified for Stanley my promotion to the status of

Supreme Muse. My surrender, which I'd hoped would stabilise a situation that was threatening to get out of hand, has had the opposite effect.

Now I've succeeded to the throne in Stanley's terms, the idea of divorce which would have been unthinkable three months ago is an eventuality he positively welcomes. I have given him an anchor when I should have left him drifting in the open sea.

He stands there in the middle of the parlour, holding out a letter. My heart sinks. I hope, whatever it contains, that my threats will suffice to stop him saying anything infront of Dorothy about *that* afternoon. He puts the letter on the table.

'Hilda's written to me,' he says. 'She's seen a solicitor. She's going to proceed with the divorce.'

We stand there looking at him. Neither of us goes to pick the letter up.

'Well, Stanley,' Dorothy says finally. 'You've got yourself into a right old pickle, haven't you?'

He looks from Dorothy to me. There's a *what now* expression on his face. I feel I'm on a tightrope over an abyss with a sheer drop not just beneath me but at either end.

'What does she ask for in return?' I say, assuming that it must be something quite substantial.

'Nothing. She says here that she just wants me to be happy.'

Dorothy sits tapping with her fingers on the table. 'What a beacon of self-sacrifice,' she murmurs. Whilst she might have sympathy for Hilda, she's annoyed that Hilda has effectively passed Stanley onto us. She looks at him: 'So what are your plans now?'

He frowns. His eyes dart back and forth as if they're not sure where to settle. Finally, they light on me. 'We shall get married,' he says.

For the first time in a long time, Dorothy is speechless. Then I see her hackles rising. 'I don't like to say this, Stanley, but you really are a very silly little man. If this divorce is something that you've engineered assuming that Patricia will conveniently move into the gap, you're very much mistaken.'

Now it's Stanley who is speechless. 'She said she would only marry me if I got a divorce from Hilda,' he protests.

It's me who's lost for words now. I ought to have taken minutes of our conversations. I go back over the last months in my mind. 'No, Stanley,' I say with as much conviction as I'm capable of, 'what I said was that I wasn't going to play second fiddle to your wife. I never said that I would marry you.'

'But I thought….'

'You don't think, though. That's the trouble.'

He stands with his arms hung limply at his sides. I have to get him out of here. I take his arm to lead him out into the hall but he seems rooted to the spot. I give his arm a little tug. 'You have to go home, Stanley. Dorothy and I have things to talk about.'

He pulls his arm back. 'I have things to talk about.'

'We can discuss those things tomorrow.' I edge him in the direction of the hall. If I can get him to the front door, there's a chance that I can put him on the other side of it. 'I'm sorry there's been a misunderstanding.'

'No there hasn't,' he says, stubbornly.

'Yes, Stanley, I'm afraid there has. I never said at any point that I would marry you.' I look back to make sure that Dorothy is out of earshot.

'I thought we were going to make love again. You said we could be joyful.'

'Oh for God's sake, Stanley. Couldn't you at least speak proper English?'

'Why, what's wrong with joyful?'

'It's so…. medieval.'

'There's no point in me divorcing Hilda so that I can marry you if you won't marry me.'

'You should have asked me first. You should have told me that's why you were doing it. You can't spring something like this on me, Stanley. It's not fair. I'd no idea that's what you had in mind.'

'You're saying no?' His face looks like a bomb-site when the last remaining building is about to crumble.

Am I? Well, of course I am. The thought that I could marry Stanley is ridiculous, especially now when anyone with half an eye can see the differences between us are irreconcilable. The fact that Stanley doesn't think so, merely shows how out of step he is with ordinary life.

I wonder, fleetingly, if he has told his friends of his intentions. Richard Carline will have tried to talk him out of it, but that could be interpreted as pique on his part. Putting up with Stanley is one way of getting back at Richard. On the other hand, I wonder what Jas thinks about it. Will he have decided marriage was what I was angling for from the beginning? Maybe when I saw him he already knew what Stanley had in mind and that's why he was so concerned. If he had said so then, I could have reassured him.

But there's something undeniably rewarding in receiving a proposal. Dorothy can't claim that Stanley simply wants to get me into bed with him or even that he simply wants me as his muse. He's asking me to marry him. I can't help wanting to hang onto that a little longer.

'I'll come to the studio tomorrow. We can talk about it then.' I nudge him down the path and blow a kiss in his direction. When I hear the front gate squeak, I close the door and take a deep breath before going back into the living-room.

'I'm sorry about that.' I rummage in the left drawer of the dresser for a cigarette. This time I need one and that's all there is to it. I hope that Dorothy's not watching as I light it. My hand's trembling so much that it takes three goes to get it lit.

'Did you encourage him to think you'd marry him?'

'Of course not. It's another of his fantasies. Now all his friends will think I'm out to milk him of his money and destroy his marriage.'

'I was rather under that impression too.'

'Don't worry, I'll go round and sort it out tomorrow.'

She looks stonily ahead of her. I sit down on the arm of her chair, facing her, and smooth the collar of her shirt. 'Please don't be angry, Dorothy. I hate it when you're cross with me.'

'Well I'm afraid you'll just have to get used to it.'

'You know what Stanley's like. When he decides he wants something, it's tantamount to thinking that he's got it.'

'You should never have agreed to sit for him. You must have known he'd take it as a sign that you and he meant something to each other.'

'He's had lots of sitters. He's not tried to marry any of the others.'

'He was not in a position to, while Hilda was his wife. The fact that she's been driven to a point where she is willing to divorce him is entirely your fault. Give her back her house. Perhaps she'll reconsider.'

'What if she doesn't?' I pretend to be preoccupied with a loose thread I've discovered in the neck-line of her shirt. 'You know, as crazy as it sounds, there might be some advantages in being married to him.' She turns her head round to face me but I keep my eyes down, winding the thread around my finger. 'For a start, I'd be entitled to a half share of his income. Once his tax affairs are sorted out he'll be a wealthy man.'

'Have you completely lost your mind?'

I give the thread a little tug and raise my eyes to meet her gaze. 'Why don't you think about it for a moment, Dorothy, instead of sounding off at me the minute I suggest something.'

'I don't think you've been listening to a thing I've said.'

'I have. I have been listening. He's the one who is insisting we get married. I just wondered if it would be worth considering as a solution.'

Dorothy's top lip curls: 'A solution?' Sometimes, rather than respond to something I've said, Dorothy will let the word hang in the air till gravity takes over and it spirals like a dead leaf to the floor. 'Apart from the small matter of betraying every principle that I thought our relationship was based on, you'd be marrying him for his money and his contacts. That's not only cynical; you would be taking an enormous risk.'

'You know I'd never risk destroying our relationship.'

'You have already,' Dorothy says bluntly. 'You can't carve a path through other peoples' lives and think there'll be no consequences. It's a dangerous game you're playing. You don't seem to understand how dangerous it is.'

'It's not a game. I know that, Dorothy.' I let my thumb creep back under the neck-line of her shirt, but she shrugs off my hand impatiently.

'You might not think much of his work, but other people do. Whatever defects Stanley may have as a human being don't have any bearing on his talents as an artist and you'd do well to remember that. He could be one of England's greatest painters.'

'All the better surely...'

Her hand curls around my wrist. 'Do you want to be cited as the woman who seduced him, wrecked his marriage, married him for what she could get out of it and then abandoned him? Or have I under-estimated you? Would marriage signal the beginning of a life of cosy domesticity, perhaps?'

'I'd never live with Stanley.'

'Right. So what would he be getting out of it? You seem to think he's stupid. What that does is cast doubt on your own intelligence.'

'I sometimes think you like him more than you like me.'

'Oh, now who's being childish.'

'I wish I had never met him, if you must know.'

'So do I.'

'But do you wish that *you* had never met him?'

There's a long pause. 'No,' she says. 'I couldn't say that.'

We lapse into silence.

'Well,' says Dorothy eventually. 'You've got six months to think about it.'

'I don't need to think about it.'

'Yes, you do.' She hauls herself up.

'Dorothy....'

She bats my hand away. 'I don't want to discuss it any more. I shall forget we've had this conversation, but I hope that you won't. There's a good deal hanging on it.'

She picks up her cardigan. The sleeve has somehow found its way into the ash-tray. As she turns away she throws the cardigan across her shoulders and a line of grey dust dribbles down her back.

IV

When I arrive outside the studio the next day, Stanley's waiting by the door. I take it as a sign of his obsession that he hasn't even started painting. His eyes follow me imploringly as I take off my coat and drape it on a chair back.

'Well?'

'Well what?'

He's trailing after me around the room. 'Have you decided if you'll marry me?'

I stand next to the window with my back to him and run my finger absently across the grimy pane. 'We've got six months to mull it over, Stanley. It'll take that long for the divorce to go through.'

'But I need to know. I can't bear this uncertainty.'

'Well I'm afraid you'll have to.' If I've learnt one thing from my exchange with Dorothy last night it's that I'd better keep my mouth shut if I want to keep my options open.

'Anything could happen in the next six months,' I say. 'You might decide you're not in love with me.'

'I won't.'

'I might decide I'm not in love with you.'

'That would be terrible,' he whispers.

'Hilda might decide to come back. One of us might die. Let's face it, Stanley, anything could happen.'

'But suppose it doesn't.'

'Well then, I suppose in six month's time we'll have to come to a decision. In the meantime you can get on with your painting. Write your thoughts down in the diary. You could give this place a spring clean. Heaven knows it needs one.'

Through the window I see Elsie scurrying across the lawn. I wonder if she knows it's now official: Hilda isn't coming back. But knowing Hilda she might well come back. How would I feel then?

This year won't just be remembered as the year that Stanley made me a proposal; it's the year that I turn forty. I know that unless I marry Stanley, it's unlikely I shall marry anybody else. Although I don't attach much weight to it, I'd like to know if being married made a difference. Would I feel that I belonged to Stanley in a way that I did not belong to Dorothy, for instance. She thinks marriage is a form of slavery, but having been around so long it must have something going for it.

I turn back into the room. He's standing there dejectedly.

'Cheer up. Six months may seem a long time but believe me it will soon pass.'

He smiles hopefully: 'And then you'll marry me?'

'Who knows?' I pat him on the cheek and wipe my hand across the shoulder of the brown suit.

'It's our destiny to be together,' he insists.

'Then we shall be together,' I say, thinking that if that's the case we can blame destiny, whatever happens.

V

In the village, nobody is speaking to us. They might not have put much store by Hilda but she is the injured party. They see Stanley as an innocent who has been led astray. The next time I pass Elsie in the street, I say hello and she just nods.

There's been no further reference to him in the conversations I have had with Dorothy. She's said her piece and now she's leaving me to mull it over. Dorothy is very good at saying nothing and implying everything. The very fact that marriage has been mentioned without either of us ending up in hospital, however, might suggest that Dorothy is not quite as inflexible as I'd expected.

I know that in order to keep her on-side, I need to look as if I am at least attempting to bring Stanley and his wife together. Lindworth was a crucial factor in the break-up and returning it is probably the only thing that might lure Hilda back. I write to her and say I'm sorry she and Stanley haven't managed to resolve their differences and that I hope I'm not the cause of them.

I manage to imply that putting Lindworth in my name was Stanley's idea and I had agreed with it to help him out. I had assumed that he'd consulted her about it. I stop short of offering to hand the house back. There is no reply.

Dorothy and I settle back into a routine not unlike the one we knew before the Spencers came into our lives. The paintings we've selected for the exhibition at Lefevre's have come back from the framer's and we spend our evenings choosing titles, making lists and writing labels. I occasionally think about what I might do when the divorce comes through. In spite of what I said to Stanley, six months seems a long way off, however, and the year is shaping up to be a busy one.

Since George V came to the throne a quarter of a century ago, the public hasn't seen much of him, so his Silver Jubilee in May attracts a good deal of attention. Photographs show huge crowds cheering the procession down the Mall. The King looks hesitant, as if he isn't certain the applause is meant for him.

'He's waiting for an anarchist to lob a bomb into his carriage,' Dorothy remarks.

'They wouldn't, Dorothy. The people love him.'

Although she's pretending to be bored by all the hoo-ha, Dodo likes the idea of the Monarchy, just as she warms to the idea of God. It's only that she doesn't necessarily believe in either.

Every village has its own events to mark the Jubilee. The celebrations go on for a week. In Cookham there's a grand finale on the last day which includes a tug o' war, sack races and a Father's Pram Race on the village green, a brass band, boats festooned with bunting advertising pleasure trips and free teas for the village children laid on by the Women's Institute.

It's as we're walking back to Moor Thatch down the High Street afterwards that I see Stanley propped against the railings outside Ovey's Farm. He's making drawings of the village children sitting at the trestle tables in their paper hats with streamers round their necks and torn flags littering the ground beside them. No one's taking any notice of him. We pause. Dorothy has seen him too.

When I last spoke to Stanley, I suggested we should not be seen together whilst he waits for his divorce to come through. If it looked as if we were consorting and the rumours got to Hilda and her lawyer, it might influence the settlement. It wasn't welcome news for Stanley but so far he's stayed away.

The tables are awash with the remains of jelly, fish paste sandwiches, spilt lemonade and shredded serviettes. Bees, woken by the warmth of early spring, buzz lazily amongst the carnage. There's a dead fly floating in a jelly. Typical of Stanley not to get here till it's over. He should have been there at the beginning when it was all set out nicely.

There are two boys pitching cake crumbs rolled up into pellets back and forth across one of the tables. Miss O'Hearn, the primary school teacher trying to keep order, hits one of the boys across the shoulder with a rolled-up copy of the afternoon's events and when that doesn't work, gives him a clip across the ears. George Hatch, the farmer who donated half a pig to the occasion, stands and watches. One of the two boys is his. His wife, in a hat with artificial daisies round the brim, makes shoo-ing noises at them. A small girl screws up her face and lifts her hem up as a puddle forms around her feet. She gazes at it helplessly, her fists bunched up against her frock. The day, like many that start joyfully and full of expectation, is about to end in tears.

I wait for Stanley to replace his pencil in the pocket of the brown suit and move on but he remains there, hunched over his drawing, his lips pursed, a look of furious concentration on his face, and suddenly I'm looking at the scene through his eyes as he dredges it out of the ether for posterity.

The little girl who's wet her knickers will still be there in a hundred years' time, staring at the puddle forming in the dust, whilst yards away the two boys, their grey pullovers now streaked with dribbling lines of jelly and ice-cream continue to pitch pellets at each other for eternity. I'm living through a moment that's been crystallised in time.

I lift my face up to the sun. A wave of happiness sweeps over me. It's quarter past four on the afternoon of May 13th, 1935 and unbeknown to Stanley, we've just shared an up-in-heaven moment.

VI

'Shall I wear the red shirt or the green one?' I stand back a few feet from the glass and smooth my skirt down.

'How about the red,' says Dodo, giving me a glance that's so peremptory she might as well not bother.

'It's just that my shoes look better with the green.'

'Why don't you wear the green, then?'

'But the red is more dynamic, don't you think?'

'The red is very nice, dear. So's the green.' She's halfway to the door.

'Where are you going?'

'Upstairs.'

'Dorothy, I'm trying to decide how best to represent you at your exhibition. You could take a bit more interest!'

'You look splendid, darling. I'm sure everybody there will be delighted with you.'

'It's not me I'm selling, it's your work.'

'In that case, wouldn't it be less distracting if you stayed at home. They'd have a chance to see what's on the walls.'

'You clearly don't appreciate how these things work. Why don't you come along for once?'

'As what, your minder? You could wear the red shirt and I'll trail behind you with the green one draped across my arm in case you change your mind.'

I toss my head back petulantly: 'I don't think I'll bother going.'

Dorothy sighs and then comes around the back of me. She cups my shoulders in her hands. She looks at my reflection in the mirror and our eyes meet. 'You look lovely.' she says, brushing my neck with her lips. She picks my coat up from the arm of the settee and holds it out.

The cab turns into Sussex Place and toots the horn as it goes past The Alexandria. It's raining and the pavements look like hammered silver.

At the gallery, I pause outside to look at my reflection in the window. Dorothy was right. I look sophisticated, even glamorous. There are a dozen people inside, chattering to one another. As I enter they all turn around to see who has arrived, except for one man looking at a painting on the far wall of the gallery who keeps his back to me.

'Patricia!' The director comes across. 'You're looking wonderful, my dear.' Since taking me onto his books, MacNeill's become much friendlier.

I offer him my cheek. He looks around the gallery. 'There are so many people here who want to meet you, it's a challenge to know where to start.'

He introduces me to Duncan Grant who's vague and charming and insists I meet Vanessa Bell who introduces me to someone else. The talk is all about the Prince of Wales' current floozy. I'm asked my opinion. I don't care that she's American or that she's married, but I don't see why he couldn't have picked someone English to have an affair with. After all, the country isn't short of women.

'You're the artist, I believe?' This is the man who had his back to me when I came in and was the only person so engrossed in looking at the paintings that he didn't turn around. He's in a suit and wears a monocle; he's clearly not an artist turning up to private views to take advantage of the wine on offer.

'I congratulate you; it's a splendid show.' He smiles, urbanely. 'Let me introduce myself. I'm Eddie Marsh.' He takes my hand and lifts it lightly to his lips. 'I'm very taken with your still lifes.'

'Thank you. I've been complimented on my greys… not something many women would take as a compliment.'

'Nobody's ever complimented me on mine. I wish they would. But certainly they're nowhere near as good as yours.'

'Are you a diplomat?'

He laughs: 'I try to be.'

He must be well into his sixties but he has that well-preserved look that the upper classes can afford to cultivate. He twinkles at me with those grey eyes and I think how different Stanley is from men like this. The last time I saw Stanley at a private view of someone else's work, he pigeon-holed one of the guests and treated him to a description of the *Church of Me* he plans to build in Cookham as a hymn of celebration to the women in his life. It went on for three-quarters of an hour. No-one invites Stanley to their exhibitions anymore.

He takes a silver case cigarette case from his pocket. 'Do you smoke?'

I take one, gratefully. Because he doesn't smoke, MacNeill neglects to put out ash-trays at his private views, but a retainer rushes forward with one when he sees us lighting up. We both pause to enjoy the brief rush of adrenalin you get when you've been longing for a cigarette and finally you have one.

'I see you're a dedicated smoker.' He laughs.

I feel thoroughly at home with Eddie Marsh. I'd heard he was in love with Rupert Brooke and paid for his work to be published privately after he died. He's clearly had an interesting career but there has never been a whiff of gossip, which suggests he's either very good at managing his life or that his friends are very loyal.

'Have you met Roger Fry?'

'Not yet.'

'Those still lifes are exactly Roger's thing. They're what he'd call *significant*.' He taps his nose to indicate that we are sharing a joke at Roger Fry's expense. He's always writing articles about how form must be significant. Nobody seems to know exactly what it means. When I asked Dorothy, she said it was a feeling you got when the objects in a picture were arranged in such a way that nothing could be changed.

'What sort of feeling?' I asked and she pondered for a moment.

'Bliss,' she said. I told her she'd been spending too much time with Stanley and she laughed. Those were the early days of our association with him.

The glass door swings open and it's as if an enormous draught has blown into the room. All heads turn. Eddie Marsh looks past me.

'It's Augustus,' he says.

I have not yet met Augustus John, although like Dorothy and me he was a student at the Slade. He has a presence, there's no doubt about it. As with Stanley you feel that his energy is sexual and anything he does is an expression of that energy.

He takes a turn around the room whilst everyone waits breathlessly and then he takes up a position in the centre:

'I declare Miss Preece to be one of the six great female modern painters,' he announces. There's a stiff pause followed by polite applause from Eddie Marsh which is then taken up by other people in the room. Now they are diving for their cheque-books, anxious not to miss out on the chance to buy something.

Although he has a personality fuelled by testosterone, Augustus has a reputation for appreciating women painters. He believes his sister Gwen to be the better artist of the two of them but she's like Dorothy, she won't appear in public if she can avoid it so it's hard for anybody to promote her.

'Thank you, that was very kind of you,' I say, when we eventually come face to face.

'No need to thank me; it's God's truth,' he says and then leans forwards: 'But don't let the *Bloomsberries* get a hold of you. They'll suck the marrow from your bones.'

'I thought you liked them.'

He lets out a guffaw: 'I adore them. What's that got to do with it?'

'It was amazing, Dodo. We sold eighteen paintings! The director's offered us a second exhibition.'

'Well done, darling.' Dorothy is in her dressing gown. It's after midnight. Usually she's in bed by ten. 'I don't suppose you got a cheque?'

'I asked if I could have £10 as an advance. We can at least afford to eat now for a bit.'

'And drink.'

'And smoke.' We giggle. I sink down into the arm-chair. 'God, my feet ache.'

Dorothy draws up a footstool. She bends down to lift my foot into her lap and eases off my shoe.

I flex my toes. 'Vanessa Bell was so impressed with that small drawing you did, which I said was a self-portrait, that she's asking me to do one of a friend of hers, Dame Ethel Smythe.'

'Grief, is she still alive?'

'Apparently.'

'She must be in her nineties.' Dorothy rests one hand on my ankle and then with the other starts to knead the toes. She curls her fingers round the foot to give her hand some purchase and her thumb moves down between each toe in turn.

I watch her fingers with their square nails digging down into the flesh and teasing out the tension and I think of Stanley's fingers curling around Hilda's breast. She gives each toe a little tug until the bones crack.

'Better?

'Lovely,' I say wiggling my toes.

She puts the foot down and picks up the other one. 'She's got an interesting face.'

'That's not the point though is it?'

Dorothy grunts. 'Do you want to have a go at painting her?'

'Do you?'

'I'm not the one Vanessa Bell is asking.'

'Yes, you are.'

'Dear heart, if Ethel Smythe comes here, she may be doddery and half blind but I think she'll notice it's not you behind the easel.'

'Shall I turn it down, then?'

'Seems you'll have to.'

'What excuse shall I give?

'Say you're inundated by commissions.'

'Very funny.'

'What would you suggest?'

There is an edge to both our voices now. The tensions of the past months have been simmering beneath the surface. There are lots of things we argue over, but it isn't usual for us to argue over this. I don't feel guilty in the least if I'm rewarded for a job I haven't done, but every now and then if Dorothy gets the idea I'm taking her for granted she'll get crabby, I'll bite back and then it turns into a dog-fight.

She plonks my foot on the floor and sits back. 'Personally, I think you should accept.' She gives an irritating little smirk. The hours of sitting here alone have clearly got to her. 'Let's face it, this is your one chance to be creative.'

Here we go again. I could sell my work if I wanted to; I got into the Slade. The fact that I left with a Pass and she left with a First Class Honours, set the scene from then on. When we moved to Paris, it was Dorothy whose work was taken seriously; I was the flighty one.

I am about to answer back but Dorothy's decided that on this occasion it's not worth an argument. I have brought back a cheque for £10 after all.

'I wondered whether we should put the cheque towards a few days in Dieppe,' I say. It was a favourite stomping ground of ours when we were desperate to get out of Paris and it has fond memories for both of us. As far as Dorothy's concerned we would be going there to celebrate my birthday and her show, but it would also be an opportunity for us to shore up our relationship before it has to face another battering from Stanley. Soon, he will be free to marry me. I need to get away. I'm even wondering if Dieppe is far enough.

'You think £10 will cover it?'

'No, but there'll be more coming from Lefevre's later.'

'How much later? That's the thing.'

'We'd only be there three or four days and it will be cheaper out of season.'

Dorothy is wavering. 'I dare say I could cash in that antique ring Mummy left me.'

'Not the sapphire in the silver setting?'

'I don't wear it. It's been sitting in a drawer for fifteen years.'

'But it has sentimental value, Dorothy. I've always liked that ring. I hate the idea of you getting rid of it. Don't. I'll sell off the last of Stanley's jewellery.'

'I thought you had.'

'I kept back one brooch.'

'Stanley will be paying for our trip, in other words.'

'He won't know that he is and I would rather that your mother didn't have to pay for it.' I run my finger down her cheek. 'I'll take the cheque into the bank in Maidenhead tomorrow and call at the travel agent's whilst I'm there.'

VII

I've always relished being in a foreign place with Dorothy. Because she gives so little of herself to other people, she is not fragmented in the way that I am when she is transplanted onto unfamiliar terrain. When we first met I used to look at her and wonder what I saw in her. She's not conventionally attractive, other than her eyes; she makes it obvious from the clothes she wears that she's not interested in fashion. She has never bothered going to a hairdresser and she has never in her life worn make-up.

There's a photograph of her – one of the few she's kept - that shows her at the age of twelve or thirteen in a less than flattering school uniform: the blazer's too big and the skirt's too small. Her head is lowered and she's scowling at the camera. She's determined nobody will find her pretty and she makes it clear that if they did she would despise them for it. Everything about her radiates rejection.

Maybe that's what drew me in, the fact that she made no attempt to court me. I decided on a whim that I would make her fall in love with me and I suppose I did, but in the process it was me who fell for her.

Over the past two decades, I've occasionally looked to other people for the things I couldn't get from Dorothy. You could say Stanley was a case in point. But in the end I didn't want those things from anybody else; I wanted them from her. Once I'd accepted that I couldn't have them, I became demanding, childish and unreasonable and Dorothy would no doubt tell you I've been that way ever since.

The fact is that I can't imagine life without her. She would struggle to get by without me, too, of course. I'm her protection from the outside world. All Dorothy's required to do, is paint. And love me.

Our trip starts off well. At a bookstall in the Gare du Nord, I come across a first edition of *Enduring Passion*. Marie Stopes is not someone I'd go out of my way to read; she's notable for saying 'homosexual vice' - her term for same-sex love - is not included in the passion she refers to. Since the book's been banned in the UK, however, it's a *must-have*. When we lived in Paris, I went to enormous lengths to get hold of a copy of *The Well of Loneliness* which turned out to be dreariness incarnate, even though it was specifically about the vice that Marie Stopes abjures. Since that had been banned too, however, the mere fact of having it was something of a coup.

If I tell Dorothy, she'll want to get her hands on it at once, but I can't help myself. I rush back to the train with a baguette and Marie Stopes tucked underneath my arm.

'What would you rather have: *Enduring Passion* or a ham and cheese baguette?'

'I'll have the ham and cheese baguette, please. But I wouldn't mind a look at this, too. Clever girl.' She turns it over.

'We shall have to hope it's got a bit more going for it than *The Well of Loneliness.*'

I'd heard that even though they gave it their support, the *Bloomsberries* didn't think much of the book, so this is one of those occasions when I don't see why I should pretend. As for *Enduring Passion*, I remembered someone telling me that Marie Stopes was not a gynaecologist at all. Her speciality was fossil plants. When I told Dorothy, she roared with laugher.

On the voyage out, I'd decided to present myself, as far as possible, the way I had when we first met: flirtatious but not inappropriately so, solicitous but not ingratiating, smart but not obsessed with how I looked. I'd dyed my hair, though I was careful to select a shade close to the one I have already.

If she noticed, would she laud the fact that I had tried to make myself attractive for her or would she disdain my efforts? She once said she liked the fact that I was pretty but it wasn't on her list of necessary attributes. I asked her what was on the list and she refused to tell me. She said if she did, I'd either try to manufacture virtues that I didn't have or lose the ones I did have by exaggerating them.

'So should I simply be myself?' I asked.

'I wouldn't go as far as that,' she said, with the result that I have never been sure whether I'm enough for Dorothy because I'm not sure what she wants. I wonder if this insecurity exists in all relationships.

I once accused her of deliberately trying to destroy my confidence. 'I haven't said a thing,' she said. 'But that's exactly what I mean,' I said, at which point she gave me a detailed list of all those areas where I fell short, thereby reducing me to tears and her to a renewal of her vow of silence.

When we finally arrive that evening at the *pension,* we find we're booked into a room with twin-beds. I wait for her to suggest we push the two together but she tells me I can take the one next to the window.

It would have been easy to ask why we shouldn't put the beds together but instead I go into a sulk until she asks me what the matter is. She knows exactly what the matter is, so I snap back at her and we end up by sitting through our evening meal in silence.

When the waiter puts our plates infront of us, I see him glance towards my left hand and I'm grateful for the ring that's on it. After I'd insisted that she shouldn't sell her mother's ring, Dodo had asked me if I'd like to have it as a present. There was no suggestion that she was intending to go down on one knee, but I took the offer as a sign that she was not still angry with me. I had seen her glance up as I slipped the ring onto the wedding finger of my left hand. I held up the hand so she could see it.

She smiled back but didn't comment.

She has brought her art things with her and she spends the morning of the first day sitting in the window, making sketches of the port. There was a painting she did in Dieppe one summer ten or fifteen years ago which showed the two of us in deckchairs gazing out to sea. The beach appeared to be deserted but for us. However, looking closer you could see another figure on the shoreline. It consisted of a single upright stroke of lemon yellow and was, like the figures in the deckchairs, virtually invisible. All that defined us was the faint suggestion of a purple band around a yellow hat, a smudge of orange to suggest a blouse, a patch of lilac underneath a deckchair. As was usually the case with Dorothy, what had been left unsaid had most significance.

It was my favourite painting. I was devastated when she told me she had sold it to the *patron* of the *pension* where we were staying.

I am tempted to suggest to Dorothy that we go back to find out whether it is still there, but the port is crowded with small lodging houses and I'm not sure which of them was ours.

The next day is my birthday. It was not one I'd been looking forward to, although I hadn't said as much to Dorothy. For her it's just another anniversary, important only in as much as it could be the last one I spend as a single woman, which as far as Dorothy's concerned, means it'll be the last one that I spend with her. These thoughts are never far from either of our minds.

We have lunch in a little restaurant along the quay, where we drink rather more than usual, take a siesta in the afternoon and wander through the old town in the evening. That night we make love, but there is still an underlying tension in the air. I'd hoped that coming to Dieppe would be an opportunity to get away from Stanley but he's there in everything that we don't talk about.

VIII

The day of our return, the weather breaks. It's blustery and as the ferry leaves the harbour at Dieppe, waves pound against the bulwark. Passengers are warned not to go out on deck and Dorothy and I decide to spend the crossing in the restaurant. Two women on the table next to ours are in the middle of a conversation.

'Let him please himself, I say,' says one of them. 'Whose business is it who he goes about with?'

'She's not worthy of him,' says the other one. 'She isn't even pretty.'

'Still, she's got style,' says the first one grudgingly, then feels obliged to qualify it. 'It's the accent I can't stand.'

Her companion looks around, gives me a hard stare and then whispers to her neighbour. 'I heard that she'd spent time in a brothel in Shanghai.'

'Well, you'd pick up a few hints in a place like that, I dare say.' There is muffled laughter.

I look wearily at Dorothy, who gives a slight nod. We rise wordlessly and leave the restaurant.

We've barely had time to unpack when news breaks that the King is dead. There is a momentary paralysis whilst everyone absorbs the shock before the Nation is plunged into mourning. George V's death overshadows that of Rudyard Kipling hours earlier, which Dorothy seems more upset by.

I had cut out pictures from the Jubilee of King George waving to the crowds and pasted them into a scrapbook. Now I cut out pictures of his coffin on its journey to Westminster Hall, draped with the royal standard and the crown on top of it, the King's sons following behind. I can't help thinking they're a sorry-looking lot, apart from Edward who I'd always rather fancied. When the Maltese Cross falls off the crown and is picked up out of the gutter by a Guardsman, you can feel a ripple going through the crowd. They're frightened it's an omen.

IX

I take out the suet from the meat safe and secure the wire mesh window that is meant to keep out insects. Nothing keeps out ants, however. As I take the wrapping off the fat, three scurry out and drop onto the floor. I tread on them. I draw the line at anything that eats food I have earmarked for myself.

'You've had six months to think about it. What have you decided?'

Dorothy is sitting at the kitchen table. It's my turn to cook, although since Dorothy is better at it she will often sit there offering advice until I ask her if she'd like to do the meal herself. Sometimes she says yes but this evening supper is the last thing on our minds. Today we heard that the divorce had come through. Stanley is a free man.

'What I want has never been in question.' I select a couple of potatoes and tip the tomatoes and a pepper out onto the work-top. After six months I ought to be primed for this discussion but I feel rushed. It's as if no time at all has passed since we last talked about it. 'I would never think of leaving you for Stanley.'

'You've told him you're not prepared to marry him?'

I rub my thumb across the pepper and the bloom comes off on it.

'Patricia?'

'Not yet.'

She tilts back her head. 'You're thinking that you might *give it a shot* perhaps, in spite of everything you've said?' She says it lightly but she's fixing me.

I take a taper from the box under the sink. I feel I'm standing on a fault-line that has just begun to open up.

'If I did marry Stanley, it would be a tactical manoeuvre, nothing more.' There is a pause whilst both of us take stock of what I've just said. *And in any case I wouldn't*, is what I'd meant to imply. It's what I should have said. The phrase was meant to be conditional but that's not how it sounds. My first thought when I heard the words was that somebody else had said them.

I put down the pepper and then pick it up again. I need a solid object in my hands but this one with its thick stalk and louche curves is not the vegetable of choice. The silence carries on for so long that I'm wondering if Dorothy is waiting for me to say something else. I need to qualify what I've already said but I'm afraid whatever I say next will just compound it. I glance sideways. Dorothy's expression is unfathomable.

'If you married Stanley, it would be a marriage, not a *tactical manoeuvre,*' she says, her voice thick with condescension. She goes over to the pantry, fetching down the whisky bottle. 'Don't think you can circumvent the laws of our society to suit yourself. You would be bound to him. You would be living in his house and sharing his bed. He would own you in effect.'

I run the pepper underneath the tap and start to quarter it. At least she's willing to discuss it then.

'I'd never live with Stanley and I'd never share his bed. Call it a marriage if you like; it would still be a marriage of convenience.' Now that the word's been introduced into the conversation without bringing down the ceiling, I am wondering how we managed to negotiate those other conversations without ever saying it out loud.

'It sounds extremely inconvenient if you'll forgive me saying so,' says Dorothy. She takes a tumbler from the drainer and leans past me at the sink to pour a splash of water into it. 'You realise if you marry Stanley, we can't possibly remain together. There would be no question of us even being friends.'

I light the gas and it explodes under the pan. 'Why not?' I hold the taper till the flame goes out. 'I've told you. I would never let him have me.'

Dorothy puts down the tumbler and leans back against the draining-board. She folds an arm across her chest and leans the elbow of the other arm on it in order to support her chin. She looks up at the ceiling for a moment. 'So how do you see yourself negotiating your way round a marriage?' she says, sweetly. 'You don't mind me asking? You see I think you might not have thought this through.'

'I have an idea.' I feel like a schoolgirl trying to explain away some misdemeanour.

'Good,' says Dorothy. 'That's a relief.'

'If Stanley married me, we could ask Hilda to come back. She'd be his wife again in all but name.' When Dorothy is quiet it's usually because she's giving me a chance to damn myself, thus saving her the trouble. We've not talked about this once in six months but I'm suddenly aware that all that time it's been fermenting in my head. I may not want to marry Stanley but the idea stubbornly persists that my best interests might be served by doing so. 'He's tied to Hilda and she's still devoted to him. I'm sure when she threatened him with a divorce she never thought he would agree to it. What Stanley really wants is to have both of us. He's said so.'

'What he wants, is not the issue. What do you want?' She tops up her glass but doesn't offer me one.

'I was not prepared to under-study Hilda, but I could accept her as his mistress. That way everybody would get what they wanted: Hilda would have Stanley back, I would have access to his fortune, we would have an income and I could go back to smoking twenty cigarettes a day.'

'There had to be a down-side.' She is giving me that look of hers. 'You've clearly got it all worked out.' She holds the tumbler to the light. 'He knows you would be entering the marriage as a business partner rather than a wife?'

'If Hilda were to come back, Stanley wouldn't need a wife.'

'But why would Hilda come back now? She's spent the last six months divorcing him.'

'They write to one another twice a day. I don't think those two can survive without each other. They're like us.'

'You think so. In what way?' She bends to pick up a potato peeling from the floor and lays it on the work-top. Why can't she just put it straight into the bin?

'We couldn't live without each other.'

'Really?'

'You know that we couldn't, Dorothy.'

'How would we know until we tried?'

Is it a provocation or a threat? Unlike me, Dorothy does not speak without thinking first. She chooses her words carefully. I sense that whilst I put off planning my next move she has been giving quite a lot of thought to hers.

Still, she seems less unyielding than she was six months ago. The idea, previously inconceivable, that I might marry Stanley, has become acceptable by virtue of its having been around a long time. Whilst it wouldn't be the outcome that she'd hoped for, I see Dorothy harrumphing like a walrus on a mud flat before giving in to gravity and letting the in-coming tide wash over her.

I dry my hands. I tend to get aggressive when I drink but whisky has the opposite effect on Dorothy. I'm glad now that I didn't have one. 'It seemed like an option worth considering, that's all. I'd never have suggested it if I thought it would drive a wedge between us.'

She is close enough that we are almost touching. I can smell the *Lifebuoy* soap she scrubs her hands with when she comes out of the studio. I found a bar of it in

Stanley's kitchen once and took it. I did not want him and Dorothy to share the same scent.

She is looking sideways at me. I stand staring down into the sink and we remain like that for several seconds, like cows in a field when they stand motionless under a tree to shelter from the glare of sunlight.

She puts out her hand. My sleeves are rolled up and she runs a finger up and down my arm. When Stanley touches me I feel as if a worm is crawling up my arm; with Dorothy it's like a feather being brushed against my skin; my stomach starts to flicker.

'Swear to me that you won't sleep with him.'

'Of course I wouldn't. Never.'

'Even if you married him? No matter how much pressure you were under?'

'Nothing would induce me to get into bed with that man. Trust me, Dorothy, you don't have anything to fear on that score.'

I loop one arm round her waist and tuck my face into her neck. I feel her ear against my mouth. The saucepan's boiling over. I can hear it spitting as the water sizzles on the stove.

'It's not myself I'm frightened for, Patricia. It's you.'

X

'You will!' He throws back his head and roars. 'Hurrah!'

'Hush, Stanley. Everyone in Cookham will be rushing over here to find out what's the matter.'

Stanley throws his arms around me and because I'm not expecting it, he manages to plant a wet kiss on my lips. He swings me round. We knock into the work-bench and a jar of brushes topples off onto the floor and smashes. Stanley goes on whirling, crunching glass into the floor-boards.

Finally he steps back, gazes at me for a moment and then links his finger-tips in prayer-mode and drops down onto his knees. His lips move silently. Eventually he whispers 'Amen'.

'Did you feel you ought to bring God up to date with what's been going on?' I say.

'I wanted to say thank you to him. I knew that he wouldn't let me down.'

I doubt that Hilda will be seeing it like that, but it seems that for once she is the last thing on his mind.

'It's wonderful,' he whispers. 'I'm so happy. We'll get married straightaway.'

'You've only just got a divorce. You don't think we should wait a bit?'

'Why wait? We could be married next weekend. You could be *Mrs Spencer.* Just think!'

I stare at the glass shards scattered on the floor between us and I see the genie that was previously in the jam jar, tip-toeing across the boards and slipping out the door to freedom.

XI

Although I've told Dorothy that marriage won't affect our lives, I feel I ought to make a token gesture to acknowledge that I'm getting married for the first and last time in my life.

I buy a new dress for the ceremony and decide to have a clear-out of the wardrobe. There are clothes in there that go back to our time in Paris. I decide to jettison all those that fasten using hooks and eyes. Three cheers for the invention of the zip. That man deserves to feature on the New Year's Honours List if anybody does.

I pile the clothes up in the middle of the bedroom. Those that still have wear in them can go into the local jumble sale. My clothes outnumber Dorothy's by ten to one. We share a wardrobe but I occupy three quarters of it. When the wardrobe door is open, it lets out a heady scent of lavender and moth-balls. My frocks, although there are never more than three at any one time, simper next to Dorothy's tweed jacket and thick, pleated skirt. She stores her brogues in there, too, and it's quite unnerving to throw back the door and be confronted by a headless Dorothy. I turned the shoes around but the effect was even more disturbing.

At the far end of the wardrobe is the satin dress and short-sleeved jacket that I'd worn the evening of the Carline's soirée. As I shake the jacket, something falls out. It's a cigarette card. Scrawled across the front is *Mayfair 167*. It must have been wedged into the lining.

I kneel on the carpet for a moment, looking at the loopy writing, wondering how long ago that number ceased to be the current one. Fleur will have half-a-dozen follow-up addresses tucked under her belt by now.

I drape the jacket on my knees and stroke it with the palm of one hand. It's like skin. I run my finger-tip over the buttons and depress the collar lightly with my nail. It leaves a ridge that disappears after a second. When I bunch the jacket up against my mouth, there is the faintest residue of cigarette smoke lingering in the fabric, mingled with the perfume Fleur was wearing that night at the Carline's party. It's the only bit of her that's left.

I stuff the heap of clothes into the bag. When there is nothing left to throw away except the jacket, I unfold it and return it to the wardrobe.

XII

'Mr Spencer says you've given in your notice, Elsie.' We've run into one another outside Arkwright's and though neither of us welcomes the encounter, courtesy demands that we acknowledge one another. 'That's a pity. I don't know how he'll get by without you after all this time.'

'He'll manage, I expect.' She sticks her chin out. In the past months, Elsie's face has hardened, unless it's a look she's putting on for me.

The Lovers and the Dustman

'Let's hope so. You know Mr Spencer and his wife are now divorced.'

'I had heard.'

'He's asked me to marry him. Perhaps you'd heard that, too.'

She doesn't answer. I lay one hand on her arm. 'I'm only saying that to reassure you that the situation wouldn't be that different from the way it was before. You won't be working for a single man. There will still be a *Mrs Spencer*; only not the current one.'

She looks at my hand as if it's a pigeon dropping that's just landed on her sleeve. I had assumed that Elsie would defer to me – somebody older, more sophisticated, better educated, dare I say it better looking - but the look she's giving me is almost pitying.

'I couldn't work for you,' she says.

'Why not?' I say, then wish I hadn't. 'I would probably not spend a lot of time in Lindworth anyway. My friend Miss Hepworth will continue living at Moor Thatch….' I tail off.

'I'd be leaving soon in any case,' says Elsie. 'Me and Ken are going to get married.'

'But I thought you had to save up first.'

'Ken says we'll manage.'

'Well, that's good.' I give a weak smile. 'But that won't be happening quite yet, will it?'

'I've told Mr Spencer I'll help in whatever way I can. I don't mind staying till the wedding, but I won't stay on beyond that.'

'When you say *the wedding,* Elsie, is that yours or mine?'

'Yours,' she says bluntly. 'Now, if you'll forgive me.' This time she seems not to be in doubt about which way she's going. She turns on her heels and strides off in the opposite direction.

XIII

'Why don't we ask Hilda if she'd like to join us on the honeymoon?'

There is a hoot from Dorothy. She knows I'm panicking. I'm sitting in the middle of the living room with piles of sketch books, paints, an easel and assorted boxes full of charcoal, crayons and brushes on the mat in front of me. I'm ticking off the items we'll be taking with us to St Ives. 'We've said we're going on a painting holiday. Why shouldn't she come?'

Dorothy looks up and glances briefly at the pile.

'What do you think?'

'You wouldn't want to know.'

'Well frankly if you're coming I don't see why Hilda shouldn't,' I say, sulkily. I'm feeling agitated and not just about the wedding.

I wait as she turns the page. 'What makes you think I would be coming?'

'Because if you don't, I shan't go either.' Most of what is laid out on the floor infront of us is hers in any case. What does she mean, she *isn't coming*.

She adjusts her glasses. 'You'd send Stanley off on honeymoon alone? It will be interesting to see what Cookham makes of that.'

'I doubt that things could be much worse as far as Cookham is concerned.'

She lets the book she's reading sink onto her lap. 'Me coming on the honeymoon was never part of the agreement.'

'You enjoyed our four days in Dieppe. Imagine spending six weeks in St Ives.'

'You think I would enjoy accompanying you on your honeymoon? Come off it, Pet. Why are you so reluctant to be on your own with Stanley anyway?'

This kind of banter would have been beyond the pale a year ago. It's as if Dorothy suspected all along that this was how things would pan out. Now it's a *fait accompli*, she's behaving almost as if it was her idea. And why would she object? She's benefited just as much as I have from our friendship with the Spencers. She might not enjoy attention but she likes her work to be appreciated. And then there's the whisky. The occasional egg cupful has become a nightly ritual and now she has it in a beaker. And she has the added bonus that she hasn't had to lift a finger to acquire it. She'll still say *I told you so* if it goes wrong, of course, but at the moment I'm just grateful that she's put the gloves aside.

'There is a sense in which you're always on your own with Stanley,' I say. 'He's on stage, you're in the audience.'

'But as his wife you have a duty to provide an audience if that's what he requires.' She sounds smug.

'What about the other services he might expect me to provide?' I've touched a nerve there. Dorothy adjusts her glasses. Since I promised her I wouldn't sleep with Stanley we've not talked about it, but the idea that she'd let me go off on my honeymoon and not say anything is ludicrous.

'You told me you could handle that.' She looks at me over her glasses.

'I can.' I put down the list. 'It doesn't mean I wouldn't like a bit of help. It isn't easy for me either, Dorothy. At least you're not obliged to cosy up to Stanley.'

'Nor are you.'

'I'm his fiancé.'

'So?'

'I feel obliged to give him something,' I say, carelessly, as if the *something* is so insignificant it's not worth mentioning.

She goes on looking at me, but her eyes have that alert intensity that cats have when they have seen something moving in the undergrowth.

I feel the colour rising in my cheeks. 'Why are you staring at me like that?'

She looks down the page to find her place. 'I'm not.'

'What are you reading?

'*Saint Augustine's Letters*. Stanley leant it to me months ago. It's time I gave it back.'

'He's probably forgotten all about it. It sounds very boring.'

'Yes, to you it would be.'

'Are you disappointed?'

'In the book? No, Saint Augustine got it right, I think.'

'I meant us.'

'Ah well,' she grunts. 'As to that…' She gives the pile of art materials another glance. 'Are you expecting to get all that on the train?'

'We'll have to be especially charming to the guard.'

'I think that's your role,' Dorothy says, tersely.

'You can be nice when you want to.'

'So can you, dear.' She sniffs. 'If I were to come, I'd need the folder with the cold-pressed cotton watercolour paper and some drawing ink, *Sennelier* by preference. And the Faber sketch pad.'

'Is that all?' I sit back on my heels.

'A drawing board and palette, maybe? And I'll need the monk strap shoes I wear for standing at the easel.'

She takes off her spectacles and gives a little yawn.

'You're finding this quite entertaining, aren't you?'

'The idea that you would take your current lover and your husband's ex-wife on your honeymoon does have a certain jolly eccentricity about it. What will Hilda think to that, I wonder.' She gets up and smoothes her shirt down, tucking *Saint Augustine's Letters* underneath her arm. 'How many bedrooms are there in the cottage?'

'Two.'

She makes a little twirling gesture with her index finger in the air and gazes at the ceiling as if she is doing calculations in her head. She nods and gives her head a brief shake as she leaves the room.

I hear her mutter 'Lunacy' as she goes up the stairs.

XIV

'You'd need to stay behind a few days anyway, to finish off those landscapes. Dudley's only given you a loan. He's going to want something in return for that cheque.'

I'd expected Stanley to put up a fight when I suggested he remain in Cookham following the wedding, but he seems confused about which hoops to jump through and which ones to stall in front of.

'Can't you wait and we'll go down together?' he says. 'It's our honeymoon, Patricia.'

'We'll be in St Ives for six weeks, Stanley. I'd have thought a week was neither here nor there. We'll get the place aired and the beds made up.'

'I thought it would be just the two of us,' he says resentfully.

'You're not suggesting Dorothy should stay behind? We're going on a painting expedition. Dorothy's a painter, too. So's Hilda, if it comes to that. Why don't you ask her if she'd like to come?'

'You want me to ask Hilda on our honeymoon?'

'I wish you wouldn't keep referring to it like that.'

'Why? It's what it is. When Dudley gave me that cheque, he said it was an advance to see me through the honeymoon.'

'You make it sound as if we'll spend the whole time staring into one another's eyes.'

'I did that on my honeymoon with Hilda. It was…'

'Don't! Don't tell me it was joyful, Stanley, or I'll scream.'

'What's wrong with joyful?'

'For a start it's very time-consuming. You owe Dudley £86. Hilda's last two cheques were sent by him as well. You'll need to concentrate on painting landscapes whilst we're in St Ives. At least we know that you can sell those.'

'But they're not my real work. Dudley knows that.'

'He still needs to make a living from your painting, Stanley. So do we. This is a working holiday we're going on. Ask Hilda if she wants to come. She'll need to clear the rest of her things out of Lindworth anyway. I'd rather that she did it when I wasn't there.'

'There's not much, other than the letters.'

'She'll need several boxes and a cart to transport those. Why not invite her to call by and pick them up and whilst she's there you can suggest she comes down to St Ives. She would be company for Dorothy.'

'I don't think she and Dorothy have much in common.'

'Well, she can be company for you, then.'

XV

'What time is it?'

'Thirty seconds later than the last time you asked.'

I reach for her hand. 'It will be all right, won't it?'

Dorothy lets out a sigh that sounds like air escaping from a tyre. 'We shall have to hope so.'

'I'll be fine as soon we get on the train. Six weeks in Cornwall. What bliss!'

'Mmm.' She pats her handbag. 'What could possibly go wrong?'

As the taxi rounds the corner we see Jas and Stanley waiting on the pavement.

'Oh God, look at him. He surely didn't have to wear that old felt hat to marry me in. He looks like a toadstool.'

'At least Jas is reasonably turned out.'

'I don't think that much of his hat either.'

'Men don't care about these things as much as women. Let's get out here.' Dorothy leans forward, rapping her fingers on the glass screen, and the driver pulls into the kerb outside the Town Hall. It's one of those harsh, new, geometric buildings that are everywhere in Maidenhead.

Jas comes towards us holding out his hand to help me down onto the pavement. Stanley just stands with his arms hung at his sides and grins. I glance at Jas to try and work out what he's thinking. I would rather he was not best man but he is Stanley's closest friend and it's quite possible that no one else was keen to step into the role.

We haven't spoken since our meeting in The Copper Kettle that day, when he warned me to tread carefully where Stanley was concerned. I'm looking at him now for signs of disapproval but his face is empty.

'Hello, Jas, how are you?'

'Nervous.' He smiles. 'It's the first time I've been asked to serve in this capacity.'

'You weren't at Stanley's wedding when he married Hilda?'

'I was there, but not as best man.' He guides me across the pavement. When he lets go of my arm, I wish he hadn't. I need somebody to talk me through this. Stanley hasn't got a clue. He stands there beaming.

'Can we go inside,' I say. 'I feel a bit exposed out here.'

Jas holds his hand out. We're directed to the first floor. There's a vase of wilting flowers on the landing. It feels cold out of the sun and all I'm wearing is a summer dress. The clerk gives us the briefest glance and nods towards the waiting area.

There is a copy of the previous day's *Times* left on the chair. Three days ago, the Duke of Windsor, as he now is, joined his mistress in the South of France. His face stares up at me, one eyebrow slightly raised as if he's asked a question he's still waiting for an answer to. He gave up everything for love. I wonder what that's like. I go to pick the paper up but Stanley sits on it. A moment later, we're called.

Given that he's been through all this once before, you'd think that Stanley was the novice, stumbling over his responses, having to repeat himself and generally acting as if he has no idea what getting married is about. Jas is the soul of patience.

When the registrar asks whether we would like a photograph, I say no.

Stanley's face falls. 'Don't you want a record of our marriage?'

'The certificate will do.'

'Oh come on,' Dorothy says, irritably. 'You must have a photograph. Let's get it over with.'

We leave the building through the back door and line up against the wall. We're standing outside the solicitors. When I look down I realise that we're straddling a grille. This isn't how I'd want to be remembered. Jas and I look reasonably presentable, except for his flat cap, but Dorothy's still wearing that old cardigan that came out of her father's knitwear factory – you can take family loyalty too far – and Stanley would look more at home amongst the seven dwarves.

The camera-man looks through the lens and then looks up at us as if he can't believe what he's just seen in there. He gives a coy laugh.

'Right then,' he says. 'Smile.'

There is a click and it's all over.

We go to a restaurant for cocktails. It's a rite of passage. Stanley doesn't drink and Dorothy prefers beer. I'll drink anything that's alcoholic but I know if I have more than one I shall be tipsy. Dorothy and Stanley have their heads together.

'You've decided to spend six weeks down in Cornwall for your honeymoon, I gather,' Jas says, conversationally. 'Do you know that part of England?'

'No, I've never been.'

'If you're a landscape artist, it's a dream, but I thought still life was your metier.'

'It is, but after all we are on our honeymoon. We won't be painting all the time.'

'Quite.' He gives an embarrassed little laugh. I'm almost drunk enough, but not quite, to tell Jas that Hilda's going to be joining us, but I think that might be a bridge too far for Jas and I'd want him to think that it was Stanley's idea, not mine, so instead I nibble on a cheese straw. 'Stanley's promised Dudley to do half a dozen landscapes whilst we're there. He's financing the trip.'

'Yes, I heard. Good old Dudley,' Jas says, mildly.

'And it won't do Stanley any harm to paint the landscape whilst he's there. You've just said it's a dream.'

'Yes,' Jas says, genially. 'Cornwall's very pleasant. But it isn't Cookham.'

'Well, of course it isn't,' I say, more impatiently than I'd intended. 'But don't you think it's about time Stanley broadened his horizons?'

'I expect he will eventually. He can't stop painting. Stanley will do what's required. But don't ask too much of him.'

'It's not me that's asking, Jas. It's Dudley.'

He smiles: 'Dudley's not a fool. Give Stanley space, Patricia. Let him have his head. It's always dangerous to come between an artist and his vision.'

He picks up his glass and clicks the rim against mine. 'I hope that you'll both be very happy.'

XVI

I love trains; that sense of going somewhere; being whisked away in comfort to a place you've never been before. At Maidenhead a young man dressed in overalls with a bandanna round his neck had got onto the train. We'd watched him saying goodbye on the platform to his mother.

'Don't go, Harry,' she wailed, hanging onto him.

The guard paused with his flag half-raised to wave the train off.

'It's all right, Mum.' The boy tore himself away and climbed into the nearest carriage, which unfortunately happened to be ours. His mother tottered down the platform, keeping one hand on the carriage door until the train lurched forward and she had to let go.

'You take care now, Harry,' she called, her voice hanging on the air a moment before being sucked into the roaring vortex.

He leant out the window, waving back until she was a dark smudge in the distance and then sank down in his seat.

'My mum.' He gave a shy laugh which became a rictus.

Dorothy put down her book. 'It sounds as if she'll miss you.'

'Yes.' He wiped his hand across his nose. I glanced at Dorothy over my magazine. She crooked an eyebrow. He sat back and shoved his hands into his pockets, humming. Dorothy picked up her book again.

'Do you know where I'd go to get the train to Portsmouth?' His fists jiggled nervously inside his pockets.

'Change at Reading. You might have to take the footbridge, but it will be clearly signed.'

'Right. Thanks.' He took a cigarette pack from his haversack and offered one to Dorothy.

'No thank you.'

When he offered me one, I saw that he only had three left. I shook my head.

He lit the cigarette and took a long draw, tapping it repeatedly so that the ash cascaded to the floor. He cleared his throat.

'I'm going out to Spain.'

He took a crumpled slip of paper from the pocket of his overalls and smoothed it out. '*The International Brigade*, that's where I'm going. Barcelona.'

'Good for you,' said Dorothy. She put the book aside again.

'I was meant to be going with a mate, but he dropped out.' He blew a stream of smoke towards the window.

'I'm sure they'll be glad to have you. Spain's not getting much help from the British Government.'

He leaned across the gap and put his elbows on his knees. The hair fell in a wave across his forehead and he swept it back. I wondered if he'd thought to pack a comb. The haversack he carried wouldn't have accommodated much more than his packed lunch.

He took several quick puffs at the cigarette which was about to burn his fingers. They were stained with nicotine. 'The war's between the Fascists and the Communists, like here. I told my Mum, we can't win this war if we don't win that one.'

'You may well be right,' said Dorothy.

'You think it's good, then, what I'm doing?'

Dorothy smiled: 'Absolutely.'

'Do you think you ought to have encouraged him like that?' I say when we've arrived at Reading and he's gone to look for his connection.

'At his age you don't need much encouragement to fight for futile causes,' she says.

We climb up the iron stairs to the bridge and down the other side. The sky is leaden but the sun shines briefly from behind a cloud before it disappears again.

'What did he mean, we can't win this war if we don't win that one? I thought Hitler was the problem.'

Dorothy puts down her bags and looks up at the noticeboard. A crowd has gathered on the platform which suggests our train is due. Across the line I get a glimpse of Harry, holding out his little slip of paper to a woman standing next to him. She pats his arm. There is a rattle as the slates change on the notice-board.

'That's why the government's not in a rush to help the Spanish. Baldwin says the English hate the Fascists but they hate the Bolsheviks as much so why not let them kill each other off.' She squints up at the board. 'Poor Harry may be in for quite a hard slog.'

There's a whistle in the distance and a puff of smoke on the horizon. 'I think that's our train,' she says.

XVII

We have the carriage to ourselves till we reach Taunton. Dorothy and I sit opposite each other. Both of us doze intermittently. I'd rather she was sitting next to me, but then another family gets in. I smile at her. She tries to keep a straight face. She knows what I'm thinking.

At St Erth, we change trains for the Cornish Riviera Express. Posters in the carriage offer us a glimpse of the delights the South West has to offer: rugged fishermen in roll-neck sweaters heaving lobster pots onto a slipway, sandy beaches populated with contented, laughing children bending over rock pools with their fishing nets or making castles in the sand.

Whilst we were waiting at St Erth, I'd bought the new *Shell Guide to Cornwall* for the giddy sum of 2s 6d. After all, this is my honeymoon. The booklet's edited by Betjeman and it includes a recipe for *Cornish pasty* as distinct from the *Stargazy Pie* made only in St Ives. He makes St Ives sound like another country altogether.

The wheels grind and lock and there's a shrill shriek of the whistle as we cross the bridge over the churning waters of the Tamar. After Truro, woods give way to gorseland, heather-covered hills and low stone walls. I stare out of the window. Dorothy, who spent her childhood holidays in Torquay and has seen it all before, continues reading.

'What are those mounds and depressions in the earth? The landscape's peppered with them.'

Dorothy squints up over her glasses. 'They're called burrows. They're abandoned mineshafts. Cornwall was awash with natural resources till they closed the copper mines in 1870 and then ten years ago, they closed the tin mines. Unemployment here is worse than Wales.'

It's typical of Dorothy to have that sort of information at her finger-tips. A homeless man persuaded her to buy a copy of *The Sunday Worker* on the Strand once and she brought it home with her. She said she'd read it on the train and she agreed with every word. And she says I'm naïve. I thought she'd be delighted when the Labour Party got in but they're still not radical enough for Dorothy. Still, I am not about to start an argument on politics. The countryside is beautiful and for the next six weeks we have the freedom to enjoy it. What more could you ask?

'Vanessa Bell said Cornwall was the in-place for the arty crowd,' I say, though it's the last thing Dorothy would be concerned about. 'That fisherman-turned-painter everyone's so keen on. Doesn't he live in St Ives?'

'Do you mean Alfred Wallis?'

'That's the one. They had a picture of him in *The Daily Herald*. He's quite old. He said he'd started painting when his wife died, for the company. He paints on cardboard. Well, apparently he paints on anything he can lay hands on.'

'How quaint,' Dorothy says.

'Maybe we could call on him?'

'I'm sure he'd hate that.'

'Don't you think he might be flattered if we asked to look at what he'd done.'

'You've got one artist sucking up to you, Patricia. Why can't you be satisfied with that?'

There is a woman with a small boy sitting at the far end of the carriage. She looks nervously across at us.

'I only want to see the man's work, Dorothy. I'm interested in his art.'

'You're not. You want to gawp at him, like everybody else. The arty set is only interested him as a novelty. They'll rob him of his innocence and then when they get bored they'll simply throw him overboard.'

'All right. We won't go. Who cares anyway?'

'But that's the whole point. No one does, not really. From the sound of it, he's just like Stanley, someone who has no idea where their creative power comes from, only that it's there and they have no choice but to follow it. They're ciphers through which something else is working.'

'You don't seriously believe that clap-trap do you?'

'Yes, I do.'

'As far as Stanley is concerned, I'd hoped we might forget about him for a few days?'

'That's an odd thing to say about your husband of...,' she glances at her watch and does a calculation, 'thirty-seven hours and eleven minutes.'

'We left him behind so that he'd have a chance to talk to Hilda.'

'What if Hilda doesn't want him anymore?'

'A woman in her forties with two children isn't likely to be inundated with proposals, even from the Christian Science Movement. Hilda's made her point. Why would she want to go on punishing them both?'

I lean across to Dorothy and take her hand. The woman at the far end of the carriage holds my eye a moment and then turns back to the boy and takes a pack of sandwiches out of the linen bag beside her. She spreads out a handkerchief across her knees and he brings his knees forward to create a table. As she takes the grease-proof paper off the sandwiches the scent of fish-paste fills the air inside the carriage.

'Come on, Dorothy,' I whisper. 'Let's not spoil the first day of our holiday by fretting over Stanley. This may be the only time we have.'

She gives a slight nod. As the train begins its slow descent towards St Ives, the lights inside the carriage flicker.

There's a grey, low-hanging cloud over the estuary but as the train goes through a cutting and comes out the other side, so does the sun. A second later we are treated to our first glimpse of the sea. The scent of fish-paste in the carriage mingles with the salty air outside. We take our cases from the rack and shunt them out into the corridor. The train grinds slowly to a halt. I pull the window down and lean out.

Dusk has fallen by the time the horse and cart we've hired has brought us to our destination on the far side of St Ives. The village is a warren of dark, crooked alley ways and narrow cobbled streets.

Our cottage is the first of six stone dwellings built around a central courtyard, accessed by a passageway between two houses. There's a large drain in the middle of the yard and fishing nets draped over the facades. The smell of fish is everywhere.

The cottage offers us a view across Porthmeor Beach and the Godrevy Lighthouse and behind the town there is a narrow footpath up a hill topped by a medieval chapel dedicated to the patron saint of Mariners.

We stand together at the window till the light fades altogether and the intermittent strafing of the water from the searchlight on the promontory is the only interruption to the darkness.

For the next three days we sleep late. Dorothy spends every morning painting. In the afternoon, we go for long walks on the beach or bicycle to Carbis Bay. I've been collecting shells to make frames for my mirrors. One day when I'm on the beach alone, I catch a glimpse of someone standing underneath the cliff and gazing out to sea. He has one of those raddled, oak-brown faces testifying to a lifetime at the mercy of the elements and a moustache that curls down scruffily on both sides of his face. He wears an old blue pullover with threadbare elbows and a roll neck and I wonder whether this is Alfred Wallis. He ignores me and I can sense even from a distance that he wouldn't welcome an approach so I walk on.

Each morning when the fishermen bring in their catch and load the lobster pots and wicker baskets onto carts, we're waiting on the slipway with the other women to select a crab or lobster fresh out of the water. In the evening we sit in the window watching as the sun goes down over the harbour. Stanley's presence hovers like a sword of Damocles above our heads but we've avoided any mention of him.

'Isn't this idyllic?' I say.

'Certainly it has a lot to recommend it.'

'And we're renting this place for two bob a week. We could afford to live here.'

'You might not find it as pleasant in December'

'Cookham's not that pleasant in December.'

'True.'

'At least admit you're glad that I persuaded you to come.'

'I'm glad to be here. I'm not sure you ought to have persuaded me.'

'We can't keep feeling guilty, Dorothy. It's not as if I pressured Stanley into marrying me; he insisted it was what he wanted.'

There is no reply from Dorothy.

XVIII

When we receive the telegram that tells us Stanley's on his way, I can't believe it's been a whole week since we got here. I tell Dorothy he'll have to find his own way to the house but she insists I go to meet him at the station.

I see him a good ten seconds before he sees me. He's on his own so I know straightaway that something's wrong. He hesitates a moment when he catches sight of me, then lifts his hand. I don't wave back. We haven't even spoken yet and I'm already feeling angry.

'What ho!' he says nervously. I nod. He goes to kiss me and I turn my head. The kiss lands on my ear.

'How was the journey?'

'Bit of a wait at Maidenhead, but all right otherwise.'

'You haven't brought much with you.'

'I thought you'd brought everything.'

'We had to hire a cart to get us from the station.'

'That's all right. I'll settle up.'

'The woman who is renting us the cottage came round yesterday. I said you'd call.'

'Right.'

'So where's Hilda?'

'Hilda couldn't come. She didn't want to.'

'Why not? When we last spoke you said you were sure you could persuade her.'

'I did try.' He shrugs as if the whole thing is a mystery to him. 'Hilda wasn't having it. She said that having been a wife, she wasn't playing second fiddle to another one.'

My first response is *Good for you*. She's only said what I said, after all. But then I realise where this leaves us. I imagine Stanley pointing out that this is what God wants and Hilda, having been primed by her Christian Science friends, interpreting his teaching in a rather different way.

He doesn't seem put out by her refusal. He'll just have another go at her at some point. He's convinced he'll get her to see things his way eventually. He doesn't understand how hugely inconvenient this is for me and Dorothy.

'We both agreed that Hilda would be joining us and now you say she isn't.'

Stanley shifts from one foot to the other. 'Hilda thought it wasn't right for her to be there on our honeymoon. I told her it was your idea and she said that was even odder.'

'How am I supposed to manage Dorothy? She'll feel left out.'

'So what?' Those girlish lips of Stanley's settle in a pout that makes him look about sixteen again. 'I don't know what she's doing here in any case. You'd think she might have made herself scarce on our honeymoon.'

'I don't think you appreciate how hard it's been for Dorothy. It was her parents' money from the knitwear factory that provided the deposit for Moor Thatch. When the firm went bust it killed her father. Dorothy was suicidal.'

'All right, but she isn't suicidal now. Can't she go back to Cookham?'

'Isn't that just like you, Stanley? Not a thought for anybody else.'

He puts his hands out. 'Darling.'

'Don't. I'm not your darling.'

'I just want you. You're so beautiful. I ache for you. I'll go down on my knees for you.' He parts the two flaps of his mackintosh as a preliminary to going down onto his knees, a gesture that reminds me of a flasher getting ready to expose himself.

'Oh stop it,' I say, and I turn my back on him. 'I bet that's what you said to Hilda.'

Dorothy is working in the little patch of garden at the front when we get back. She glances up, sees Stanley's on his own and looks at me. I shake my head. She digs the trowel into the earth and gets up off her knees. I go ahead of Stanley. Dorothy smiles graciously at him as I squeeze past her.

'Stanley. Did you get your landscapes finished?'

'One of them. Tooth sent a car for it this morning.'

'They can't wait to get you on their walls.'

'The landscapes always sell well but I don't like doing them. They're not my real work.'

I don't want to listen to a litany of his complaints when I've got several of my own I'd like to voice. 'Still, now you've got two families to support you could be doing quite a few of them,' I say.

'You're painting, Stanley. That's the main thing,' Dorothy says. I won't hesitate to kick a man when he is down but Dorothy will wait at least until he's halfway up.

I leave them on the path. I need to speak to Dorothy to tell her that I'm putting Stanley in the spare room. I don't want her offering to move out of ours. But for the moment Stanley's clinging to her like a limpet.

Over tea, he tells us what's been happening at Lindworth. Hilda turned up as expected after we had gone, to pick up those possessions of hers still remaining in the house. He'd left the letters they had written to each other since their courtship, separated into *his* and *her* piles and arranged chronologically. He had decided not to be there when she came, but had returned to find her sitting in an armchair reading through the letters. Hilda told him that she didn't have the heart to take them. They had spent the rest of that day reading them aloud to one another.

Now that he's divorced it's probably inevitable that he's reinstated Hilda back amongst the angels. It's the price we'll have to pay for having her on board. But I am not prepared for what comes next. They'd gone on talking till the light failed and then Stanley had suggested she might stay the night since they were getting on so well and Hilda hated driving in the dark.

He takes a mouthful of the tea and puts his cup back in the saucer. There is silence round the table.

'You asked Hilda if she'd stay the night?' He nods. 'And did she?'

He smiles. 'Yes, she did.'

I glance at Dorothy who's fingering her napkin.

There's a pause whilst I absorb what Stanley has just told us and decide what I can do with it. 'You're saying Hilda slept in your bed…our bed?'

'She said it was wonderful to find me just the same, to find that we still loved each other in the same way; that we could still talk to one another. It was a reaffirmation.'

'So you slept together,' I snap. 'And what happened in the morning?'

'I thought after what had happened, Hilda would be keen to come down to St Ives with me.' He rubs his eyes. No wonder he's tired. 'I said we'd all be together. It was what I'd dreamed of, having both of you. That's when she said that having been a wife, she couldn't be a mistress. I tried to persuade her but she wasn't having it.' He picks a crumb up absently and puts it in his mouth.

'You realise, Stanley, that what you've owned up to is adultery?'

There is a sound from Dorothy, a cross between a whimper and a groan. She's following the thread. It's clear, though, Stanley isn't.

'I thought that was what you wanted, for me to persuade her to come down here.'

'We get married and no sooner have I left the house than you move your divorced wife back in, spend the night in our bed and then join me on our honeymoon assuming everything will be all right?'

'You've still got Dorothy.'

My eyes shift sideways. I am never certain how much Stanley has deduced about the nature of my ties with Dorothy. She has her eyes fixed on the table-cloth. 'That's different. I'm her agent. I'm responsible for handling her affairs. It makes sense that we go on living under one roof.'

'You're not just her agent,' he insists, aware now that the ground he's standing on is not secure.

'This isn't about Dorothy. We're talking about you and Hilda.'

'Well, why shouldn't I make love to Hilda if I want to? As an artist I must be completely free. I owe it to my painting.'

'Well you and your painting will have to make alternative arrangements. Don't expect to sleep with me now. I could have this marriage declared null and void.'

'Patricia!'

'Don't *Patricia* me'. You're like a spoilt child. You don't only want a slice of cake, you want the whole lot. You can move your stuff into the spare room. In the morning you can go out painting. It's time you got down to reimbursing Dudley for that cheque.'

XIX

'Well, dear, you managed that superbly. I was tempted to break out into applause at one point.' We watch Stanley struggling across the yard, his easel strapped onto his back, a carrier bag full of paints in one hand and a fold-up chair tucked underneath his arm.

'It's damage limitation, Dorothy.'

'You didn't have to send him out into the rain this morning. Don't you think that was a bit harsh?'

Dorothy has colonised the landing as her studio and started on a still life. I would rather that she didn't work in spaces where she can be overlooked, though Stanley is so self-obsessed I doubt he notices what's going on around him.'

'Better that he's out than getting underneath our feet.'

'He'll catch his death of cold. I heard him sneezing last night.'

'He's been writing letters on that roll of wall-paper we found under the stairs. He's telling Hilda he's not sure that Cornwall is the place for him. He'd rather be in Cookham and of course he'd rather be with Hilda.'

'You read Stanley's letters?'

'I'm the only one who will. He won't be able to get that into an envelope.' I laugh. 'It's just as well. He'd be arrested for indecency if they saw what he wrote about his *father* thing and what he wanted to imagine Hilda doing to herself. When I called up the stairs to ask him if he'd like a cup of tea, he said that he was coming! Then I heard him say *I wish*.'

It goes on raining for the next ten days. The water's running in the gutters. When it rains in Cornwall, there's no doubt about it.

'Can't I miss a day,' says Stanley, desperately. 'It's pouring.'

'Wear your hat.'

'The canvas will get wet.'

'We lugged those canvasses along so you could paint on them. According to the forecast, Thursday will be dry.'

'But that's four days away. You're not insisting Dorothy goes out.'

'She's not a landscape painter.'

'Nor am I,' says Stanley, wretchedly.

Part Five
Purgatorio

I

We're back in Cookham six weeks later. Stanley has four landscapes ready to deliver which will cover the advance from Dudley Tooth, although I don't know what will happen after that. I'll need to intercept whatever mail the postman brings to Lindworth incase there are cheques inside.

Of course there is a letter from the Inland Revenue. They've turned down his appeal but they're prepared to spread out the repayments over two years. It's not quite enough to justify the opening of a bottle of champagne but it means that when money does come in it won't all go on paying off the debts.

We find that Hilda has been in and spring-cleaned. She has tidied Stanley's clothes away. He leaves a trail of them behind him everywhere he goes inside the house – shoes, socks, vests - Stanley's wardrobe is the floor and any other surface he can find. Until now I've refused to pick them up on principle but I feel momentarily ashamed that Hilda will have thought I wasn't looking after him. The feeling only lasts a second till I realise how ridiculous it is. I've never felt the slightest inclination to take care of anyone. I much prefer to be the one who's taken care of.

'Look,' says Stanley. 'Hilda's even washed the curtains.'

'Lovely.'

'And she's cleaned the windows.' He goes over to the window and stares out over the garden. It's waist high with grass and a profusion of wild flowers. It looks more attractive than it has for ages. But inside the house there is a feeling of decay, as if nobody's lived there for some time and even when they did they didn't love the place.

'I won't be staying here, you know.'

'Why not?'

'We're formally estranged. I couldn't possibly live here with you. I'm going back to Moor Thatch.'

'Please don't.'

'Sorry Stanley.'

'You're my wife but you won't sleep with me.'

'Please don't let's go through that again. I wouldn't sleep with you on principle now, but in any case it didn't work. You know that.'

He goes over to the kitchen table and picks up a knife to gouge the whorls out in the wood. Whatever's going on in Stanley's head immediately finds an outlet through his fingers. 'Hilda thinks you ought to see a gynaecologist,' he says.

'What! You told Hilda what had happened when we tried to make love?'

'I tell Hilda everything. Why wouldn't I?'

'Because there are some things between a man and his wife that you don't share, Stanley.'

He adjusts his glasses. 'Hilda was my wife for twelve years. You've not been my wife at all.'

'How dare you say that!'

'I thought when I married you that we'd be in a state of bliss,' says Stanley, bitterly. 'We would be making love on Cookham Common. I would be reclaiming all those places I loved as a boy. My painting would be reinvigorated.'

In the end the idea that he wasn't being well-served by his marriage was bound to occur to Stanley. I've been put on the defensive. 'There are people in this village, Stanley, who think you should be locked up.'

'Love can't be bad, Patricia.'

'Yes, it can, when it's miss-placed.'

'How can you say it's miss-placed when I gave up Hilda for you?'

'But you didn't, did you, Stanley. In the circumstances I suggest you go to Hampstead and persuade your wife to come back.'

'Hilda's not my wife.'

'She's more your wife than I am and she wants to be with you, whereas quite frankly I don't.'

There's a painting on the easel which shows me in high heels and a bolero – a bit of fluff that doesn't even hide my breasts - parading up and down before a looking-glass. The wall-paper has hearts on it. I'm heavily made up and smoking from a fashionably long holder.

This is not the sort of thing I'd do infront of Stanley. He hates women smoking and he doesn't like to see them made-up. It confuses him. He's sitting naked on the floor behind me, the droop of his penis mimicking my drooping cigarette. The floor is tipped up and it looks as if he's sliding down a slope. He's tiny. It's not flattering to either of us. Thank God Elsie's not here.

'I thought the idea was that you'd stay behind to finish off the landscapes you were doing.'

'I had no choice but to come home once it got dark. I was on my own. The painting kept me company. It's us.'

'Yes, I can see that. So will everybody else. Is nothing intimate enough for you to feel it might be inappropriate to offer it up for the world to gawp at?' I snap. 'What did Hilda say about it?'

'I told Hilda that I hadn't found a way yet to incorporate you in my Cookham image. You know how it works for me. Somewhere along the way it turns into a vision. Hilda said she couldn't see that happening here. There wasn't any love in it.'

There is a bowl of dead pinks on the table and he starts to pull the petals off and make a pattern of them. 'Hilda thinks...'

'Stop, Stanley.' I can feel a migraine coming on. 'I haven't time to listen to you, and in any case I've heard it all before.'

He's looking at the letter in my hand: 'Is that from...?'

'Yes.' I take the letter from the envelope and lay it on the table. The light draft sends half a dozen petals skittering onto the floorboards. 'They'll spread out the payments, but there's no chance of you being let off. I did warn you.'

'Why is everybody hounding me like this?' he moans.

'They aren't. Nobody else is hounding you.'

'But what am I to do! I'm struggling to pay maintenance for Hilda as it is.'

'You'll have to sell the Bechstein. You can hardly claim it as essential.'

'It's essential when I can't sleep.'

'What do you suggest then?'

'I don't know.' He looks round as if searching for a hole to disappear into.

'There is one way of bringing money in. This house is far too big for one. You hardly use it anyway. Why don't you move out and we'll rent it. '

Stanley's mouth falls open. 'You're suggesting I move out of Lindworth. I can't do that. It's my home. It's our home.'

'It's not my home and we can't afford to run it, Stanley.' I go over to the wall and put my finger on a bloom of mould that's virtually the only decoration this room has to offer. 'We would need to put in electricity, of course. Nobody these days lives in houses lit by gas with kitchen ranges that you have to light each morning.'

'We did.'

'Yes, well you and Hilda aren't exactly typical. And you had Elsie.'

'It was me who lit the fire each morning.'

'But you won't be there to light the fire.' His face falls. 'Well what else is there? You can't run three homes. At the moment you can't even run one.'

'I could move into Moor Thatch with you.'

Blood rushes to my head. 'I don't think that would work.'

'So where am I supposed to go?'

'You only use the shed in any case. Why don't you stay there?'

'Thank you very much.'

'Don't think I'm happy with the situation, Stanley. You've let everybody down.'

He turns on me and for the first time there's real anger in his face. 'I gave up everything for you, you harpy.'

Part of me is thinking that I get along with Stanley better when he isn't trying to accommodate me. There are times when I wish I could give myself a good slap and not have to wait for someone else to do it. I can't risk him taking his complaints outside, however.

'That's what you'll be telling everyone in Cookham, I suppose. You really think the village wants to hear what's going on between the three of us? Well yes, they do. They're all agog. But don't you think it would have been more sensible to leave them out of it?'

'I can't hide what I am.'

'No, more's the pity.'

'Hilda understood that.'

'Oh, we've got to that stage, have we? My new wife can't understand me like the old one did. Stop being so pathetic, Stanley. You can hardly pass yourself off as the injured party, even if you think that's what you are.'

II

I had left Dorothy at Moor Thatch with a cup of coffee to plough through the huge back-log of mail and newspapers we hadn't cancelled. I don't see the point of news when it's no longer new but Dorothy says it's more interesting when it's history and you have a perspective on it.

She'd pre-empted me when I came in by showing me a headline in *The Daily Herald*. '*The first British casualty....*' it read.

'Felicia Browne. Remember her? She was a student at the Slade.'

The photograph is faded. 'Wasn't she that rather unattractive girl who cropped her hair? She wore an Army greatcoat, even in the summer.' I peer at the photograph. 'I'm sure that's her.'

'It was her.' Dorothy says, riffling through the papers to see whether any of the others have reported it. 'She's dead.'

'Oh gosh. Poor thing. I take it back; she wasn't unattractive.'

'I doubt that on this occasion your opinion would have mattered much.'

'How did she die?'

'Shot.'

'Shot!'

'In Spain. It says here she was killed whilst taking first aid to an injured fighter. They retrieved her sketchbook but they had to leave her body. She'll be famous now. There's nothing like a tragedy to bolster one's career.'

'Do we know whose side was she on?'

'She was a paid-up member of the Communists so we can probably assume that she was on the side of the Republicans.'

'I wonder what became of that boy we met on the train to Reading?'

Dorothy sighs. 'It's not going well out there, especially now that Hitler's put his oar in.'

'Someone told me that Vanessa's son had joined up as a medic.'

'All that means is that unlike the other volunteers he won't have anything to fight with. There's no safe place in a war.' She checks another paper for the date and puts it back. 'The trouble with not keeping up with what's been going on, is that when you eventually get round to it, it overwhelms you.'

Dorothy will not, as I do, simply turn her back on news that bothers her. When I suggested we stop ordering a daily paper since it always put her in a bad mood, Dorothy put in an order for an extra one to be delivered every day. She said the only way to deal with bad news was to have a balanced view of it.

It angered her that Britain hadn't gone to Spain's defence, but when reports of Stalin's purges leaked into the British press, it seemed that Baldwin might have had a point – there didn't seem to be a lot to choose between the Fascists and the Bolsheviks.

'It's surely easier to let them fight it out between themselves in that case?'

'What that means is that whoever wins, we'll have to fight them,' she says.

Does she mean there'll be a war? And if there is, what will that mean for us? Will we remain in Cookham? Will we have a choice? The last war was exciting. I was in my twenties. I had a fiancé. There were endless dances. And when it was over, there was Dorothy. But would it be like that the next time?

'If you think that, shouldn't we be making preparations?' I say.

'Sandbags underneath the windows, you mean? Stocking up with tins of corned beef? At least we're too old to be conscripted. We can sit the war out in the comfort of our living-room.'

I snort: 'The comfort of our living-room!'

I watch her as she folds the paper round the image of Felicia and tears the photograph out. 'You'll be glad you're not in London when the bombs start dropping.' She looks at the photograph a moment and then slides it inbetween the pages of her book. 'Or Paris, if it comes to that.'

'Why do you want to keep that photograph?' I say.

'You cut out pictures from the papers for your scrapbook.'

'Yes, but you don't.'

'I thought I might write a letter to her mother. I believe Fe was her only child.' She glances at me. 'You've off-loaded Stanley at the family home, I take it. Or will he be joining us for tea?'

'I hope not. He and I have been discussing what to do with Lindworth. Since at present it's his only asset...'

'Don't you mean your only asset,' Dorothy says, drily.

I ignore her. 'I've decided we shall rent it out.'

Her mouth drops. 'Rent it out?'

'He needs the money, Dorothy. He's struggling to pay maintenance, his dealer's having to advance him money against paintings that he hasn't done yet. Elsie's gone and he's been racketing around in that house on his own for months.'

'It seems he's not the catch you thought he was,' says Dorothy. 'Are you intending to rent out the house with Stanley in it?'

'Hardly. I've told Stanley he will have to move out.'

She grunts. 'Please don't tell me he'll be moving in with us.'

'Of course he won't. As long as he's in Cookham Stanley's not that bothered where he lives. He's got the studio.'

'You mean the garden shed.'

'He often sleeps there. He pees in the flower beds. It's not as if he uses the facilities.'

'You don't think anyone who rents it might be put off by the sight of Stanley peeing in the flower beds?'

'I'll have a word with him. To rent the place out makes sense, Dorothy.'

'But still, evicting him from his own home….' She looks up over her glasses.

'It's not his home, is it? Not now.'

'History might not see it quite the way that you do, Sweetie. What do you suppose his friends will think when they discover that he's living in the shed and we're still living as a couple in Moor Thatch?'

'All right, so what would your advice be?' It's unhelpful, when I know the ground I'm on is shaky, to have Dorothy confirm the fact.

'It's obvious you were wrong in thinking Hilda would come back.' She puts the paper on the pile. 'She looks on the Almighty as a second husband and he's more reliable than Stanley.'

'She could still take some responsibility for him.'

'Why should she?'

'If it weren't for me, her maintenance would probably have dried up altogether.'

'If it weren't for you, she wouldn't be in need of maintenance. You sold this marriage to me on the grounds that everyone would benefit. As far as I can see, not only has it benefited no one but the very people you professed to want to help are worse off than they were before. I don't want to seem critical but frankly, Pet, you've got a lot to answer for.'

III

'Did you know Hilda would be coming?'

Stanley makes one of those hopeless gestures that suggests the world's too much for him to cope with and he's on the point of throwing in the towel. 'I thought you wanted me to get her down here. I invited her to lunch.'

Although I've never lived at Lindworth I've been spending time there, getting the house ready to let and occasionally, if it's more convenient, it's where we have lunch.

There had been a spate of warm days and the long French windows facing on the garden at the back were open. As I came around the side wall, I'd heard what I thought at first was Stanley talking to himself. The gramophone was playing somewhere in the house, a record by Cole Porter that I liked but which was not a favourite of his. I wondered if he'd put it on for me, and it was then that I heard Hilda's voice. It felt surreally as if I had slipped back in time to that day when I'd stood outside the studio and listened to her telling Stanley she was leaving him, except that Hilda was now standing in a place I'd come to think of as my own.

I said a curt hello to her and nodded Stanley out into the passage.

'All right, you invited her to lunch. But what's she doing in our kitchen?'

'She asked whether she could help peel the potatoes.'

'Christ Almighty!' I hiss. 'Why is everything you do so…. inappropriate!'

'I thought you two should have an opportunity to get together. It was you who wanted her to come to Cornwall with us.'

'On a painting holiday. It's not the same as finding her with her hands sunk up to the elbows at the kitchen sink. You've heard about the territorial imperative?'

'It was her kitchen first,' says Stanley, reasonably.

'But that's precisely why it's inappropriate for her to be there. Get her to come through into the parlour.' My exasperation is compounded by the fact that I know my objections are unreasonable. It's not as if I'm jealous, although listening to that record playing, for a moment what I envied was that easy domesticity that came so naturally to them and which was alien to me.

I wait whilst Stanley goes into the kitchen. There's a whispered conversation and then Hilda comes into the parlour rolling down her sleeves.

'Come in and sit down, Hilda,' I say, making it clear which of us is hosting this event. 'Perhaps you'd like a drink.'

'No thank you,' she says. 'Stanley made a cup of tea when I arrived.'

I pour myself a gin and tonic. 'Well at least sit down. You're not obliged to earn your lunch by peeling the potatoes.'

'I don't mind.'

It's obvious that she hasn't bothered dressing up for the occasion. That old dress she's wearing is the one she had on in The Copper Kettle that day and my eyes drift automatically towards her right breast. I reach for the tonic bottle. I can hear it fizzing as I take the top off.

'How are Unity and Shirin?' I say, thinking that we'd better get the courtesies out of the way.

She gives a little shrug. 'They miss their father.'

I wait, thinking that she's offering a way into the conversation, but she goes on. 'Richard spends as much time as he can with them. He likes to draw the children.'

I remember seeing Richard's painting of five members of the family and their friends all standing in a group at Downshire Hill to have their portraits painted. Though I'd rather not give Richard Carline praise for anything, I must admit it was a cracking picture. I find it more difficult than Dorothy, to separate the artist from the work. Not liking one, means that I automatically have difficulty with the other. Dorothy's not like this, which is why she still persists in thinking Stanley is a genius.

The tonic's warm. In this heat it would have been more refreshing to drink water from the tap. I add more gin to bulk it out, then wish I hadn't. I'm already feeling woozy and now that I've got a taste for it I'll want another one as soon as this one's finished.

Hilda's sitting, her hands folded in her lap, her head bent, as if she's in church. This is the woman Stanley claims he spent a decade up-in-heaven with. She must have something going for her.

'Did you ever go out dancing when you were a young girl, Hilda?' I say on an impulse.

'Dancing?'

'You know,' I gyrate my hips and flap my hands.

'I know what dancing is,' she says.

'Well, did you?'

'Yes, when we were at the Slade. My brothers liked to dance.'

I think of Richard on the dance floor at the Palais, shimmying with me in unison. My mouth feels dry.

'And what about you? You were eighteen, Hilda. Did you have fun? Did you ever get drunk? Did you ever wake up in the morning wondering what you'd done the night before?' I knock the gin back. It tastes horrible. I might as well be drinking bleach. I had a headache when I woke up and I know that by the time today is over, I shall have a worse one.

Hilda's looking at me: 'No,' she says. 'I never did that.'

I throw up my arms, triumphantly: 'I rest my case.'

She tilts her head. 'What case is that?'

'I find it hard to work you out, that's all.' Is it too soon to get myself another drink? 'I'm wondering what excites you. What things make you want to laugh and throw your arms about. What gives you joy?'

She's looking at me steadily. Not for the first time I suspect I've underestimated Hilda.

'You took everything that gave me joy,' she says.

'If you mean Stanley…'

'You've got all you wanted,' she says, fixing me. 'Why aren't you happy?'

Stanley's banging pots around inside the kitchen. *I* would have been listening at the door, but Stanley thinks he's doing us a favour by allowing us to beard each other in his den.

'I am.'

'You don't appear to be.'

'Well, after all, what's happiness? Can anybody say they're happy? What about you?'

'No,' she says. 'No, I'm not happy.'

Her tone doesn't seem to be implying blame but I feel guilty anyway. She's had that careworn look about her ever since we first met but she wears it like a suit of armour now. It's her defence against the world.

I sit down next to her: 'I have a proposition for you, Hilda. I accept that you and Stanley had a very deep relationship. He talks about you all the time. He'll never feel the same way about me, I know that.'

'Love is something that you have to earn.'

'In my experience love happens when you're least expecting it,' I say. 'You don't have time to earn it and it doesn't have a lot to do with worth.'

She gazes at me. 'Who do you love?' she says.

'Well of course I'm fond of Stanley. I would never willingly do anything to hurt him.'

'So why have you?'

'Hilda, he came after me.'

'You could have told him that you didn't want him.'

'But that isn't how it was. I'm simply saying that I didn't set the pace. You know what Stanley's like. He talked himself into believing I was crucial to his work. That's all it was.'

'His work is everything.'

'Well, obviously his work's important, which is why I gave in. But beyond that…' Is she going to sit there and wait for me to spell it out, 'We're really not all that compatible.' I pour myself another gin and hold the bottle up. She shakes her head.

'Have you tried sleeping with him?' From her voice, she could be asking me if I had brushed my teeth that morning.

'Yes, of course. I mean, how would I know unless I had?'

'Perhaps you ought to see someone.'

'You think a Christian Scientist might do the trick?' I say, impatiently.

A beam of light with what looks like a million dust motes dancing in it, slants across the rug between us.

'They've helped me,' says Hilda.

'I was under the impression you and Stanley didn't need help. You were up-in-heaven from the start.'

'We all need help.'

I'm wondering, if I call for Stanley, whether that will make this situation easier or harder. I lean forward, as if what I am about to say is confidential. 'Hilda, let's not argue. We are on the same side after all.'

She jerks her head back: 'How can we be on the same side?'

'In the sense that we both want the best for Stanley. You believe in him. You share his vision. So do I. Why don't we work together? That way we can manage him.'

She looks at me. 'I don't need help to manage Stanley.'

'Yes, you do,' I say, my patience finally unravelling. 'Because in spite of all the difficulties, which believe me I'm not minimising, he still thinks I'm necessary to his vision and since we're now married he has to run everything he does past me.'

I wish I hadn't said that. Up till then, I think I almost had her on side. 'I'm inviting you to come back, Hilda.'

'What as?' She looks baldly at me.

'As....well, I don't know, his lover, his companion, his...' I shrug my shoulders.

'I was Stanley's wife,' says Hilda.

'But you're not his wife now!'

'I am more his wife than you are.' She gets up. 'I'm more his wife than you will ever be.'

As if he has just got his curtain call, the pandemonium inside the kitchen ceases. Stanley puts his head around the door: 'Is everything all right?'

IV

'You won't believe what Stanley's done!'

I thrust the paper at her. Since our lunch with Hilda, Stanley had kept to himself at Lindworth, finally accepting possibly that there was no chance of a reconciliation between me and Hilda. It seemed that the honeymoon had been a watershed in other ways, too. He no longer saw me as a confidante. I was more likely to discover what was happening from the gossip in the General Stores or, as on this occasion, from the *Letters* column in *The Times*.

'Why don't you tell me,' Dorothy says, calmly.

'Stanley has withdrawn the pictures he put into The Academy because they've turned down two of them and now he's threatening to resign. It's sheer pique,' I say, furiously.

There's a spitting as the contents of a saucepan on the hob begin to bubble over. Dorothy re-lights the gas-jet which has gone out. She's been making jam. The kitchen is awash with orange peel and pulp, three saucepans simmering with more fruit in them, paper sacks of sugar, muslin bags, a chopping board with shredded orange peel to go into the next preserving pan and half a dozen kilner jars lined up along the work-top.

'Have they said why they rejected them?' She goes on chopping up the mandarins. A steamy vapour rises from the saucepans, adding to the heavy, perfume-laden atmosphere. The kitchen's like a Turkish Bath.

'According to *The Times* the members felt that showing them would adversely affect their reputation in the art world. We all know what that means. His *St Francis and the Birds* shows Old Pa Spencer in his dressing gown and slippers. He's been painted over what was previously Hilda in a haystack, which is why he's such an odd shape.'

'What's the other one?'

'*The Lovers or the Dustman.*'

'Well we should be grateful that one's not on show.' She tests the jam for sweetness, skimming off a teaspoonful of liquid from the scummy surface. She holds out the spoon for me to taste. 'More sugar?'

'Just a touch.' Each of the saucepans on the stove is boiling at a different rate so that the contents don't set simultaneously. I don't know how she can concentrate on everything that's going on and still give half her mind to me.

'He could have shown the other four,' I say. 'He would have sold those easily. Why does it have to be a case of all or nothing?'

'He has principles.'

'He can't afford them.'

'Dudley is still championing him, isn't he?' She starts to spoon the jam into the kilner jars, allowing time for it to settle after every spoonful.

'He sends Stanley money every month.' I peer over her shoulder. 'Can I have the saucepan when you've finished?'

She hands me the spoon. 'It's hot. Be careful.'

I don't bother with the spoon. I scoop the jam out from the bottom of the saucepan with my finger and then lick my tongue around the rim. My lips are burning. I can see a blister forming on my finger but the taste gives me a blast of happiness.

'Bliss. It's like being wrapped up in a blanket with my favourite teddy and a bag of sweets.'

'You'll make yourself sick if you carry on like that,' says Dodo. 'Be a good girl, put the saucepan in the sink. You've had enough.'

I have a last scrape round the pan and hand it over. 'Without Dudley, Stanley would be stumped.' I run my fingers underneath the tap. 'Small wonder that he's getting twitchy when the only paintings Stanley's interested in doing are unsaleable.'

'Not all of them, presumably.'

'I managed to persuade him to cut off the more offensive sections of two paintings he was putting in his next show.'

Dorothy frowns. 'You should not have done that. You may not agree with it, but you don't have the right to interfere with his creative process.'

'Dorothy, the paintings were obscene.' I shake the water off my hands.

'Then they would probably have been rejected, but at least they wouldn't be emasculated.'

'I don't think you realise how bad things are.'

'That's why it's important not to make them worse.' She edges me aside. The cosy moment we have just enjoyed is over.

I pick up the paper and leaf through the pages, sulkily.

She looks over her shoulder. 'If you've finished with *The Times*, perhaps you'd leave it out for me.'

'I thought you'd read it.'

'I glanced at *The Herald* earlier.'

I smooth the pages so the paper doesn't have that limp look. 'I don't know how you can bear to read the same thing half-a-dozen times,'

'It compensates for you not bothering to read it once.'

'I always read one paper.'

'Really? What's today's news?'

I glance at the front page. 'Hitler's marched into the Rhineland.'

'Quite. I think that might rate equal in importance to your husband's resignation from The Royal Academy, don't you? '

It's when she's really cross that Dorothy refers to Stanley as my 'husband'. She's upset because she has been forced to side with him on principle and she blames me.

'I don't know what the fuss is all about. All Hitler's done is take back what was his already.'

Dorothy lets out a 'tch' of disbelief.

'Well, hasn't he? Correct me if I'm wrong.'

She bangs the saucepan on the draining board.

'You're wrong,' she says.

V

'You know that I'm already giving Stanley £7 a week so that he can continue paying Hilda her allowance?'

I'd decided against telling Dudley Tooth that I was coming in to see him. I know from the gossip that's leaked back that he holds me responsible for Stanley's current situation. To say anything in Stanley's absence could be seen as disloyal and men tend to stick together, even when it's not to their advantage.

'I know. Stanley says you've been extremely generous.'

'What I'm giving him is an advance. As long as Stanley can produce the work at some point, that's fine. I don't want to pressure him.' He taps a finger to his lips. He has a slightly puffy face with very soft skin that has clearly benefited from persistent moisturising. When he smiles, there is a glow to it which is a bit like candle wax when it begins to melt.

'I think you need to pressure him a bit. The trouble is, he'd rather not be painting landscapes but they sell well and his visionary work is so bizarre that nobody will buy it.'

'But the visionary work is what he'll be remembered for. That's where his brilliance lies. It's vital that he doesn't stop work on those pictures altogether. Stanley's not a hack. I wouldn't want to turn him into one.'

'I wouldn't want to either, but he has to find a way to make ends meet.'

Although he's only in his thirties, Dudley has a reputation in the art world for exhibiting live painters as opposed to dead ones. It's a risky business and he wouldn't do it if he wasn't certain he could get back his original investment. He thinks Stanley is a genius and who am I to disagree? That's not the point though.

'Have you seen what Stanley's painting now? The Royal Academy has turned down two of his most recent pictures. Stanley's threatening to withdraw the other four in protest.'

Dudley runs his finger underneath the cuff of his immaculate white shirt and gives his chest a reassuring little pat. He isn't someone who gives way to indiscretion as a rule but this is an exception: 'Munnings is a fool,' he says. 'They'll rue the day they made him President.'

When I took issue with him, Stanley said he'd read an article suggesting that of twelve contemporary painters asked if they would put work into The Academy, ten had suggested that they wouldn't: the Academy was out of touch and closed to innovation. What concerned me was the fact that Stanley wasn't even asked for his opinion. He seems to have slipped between two stools, he hasn't anything to offer the Surrealists but his work is too weird for the dinosaurs in the Academy.

'I wondered if you'd seen the paintings. One of them, *Saint Francis*, shows the saint as a decrepit old man in a dressing gown and carpet slippers feeding chickens in a farmyard.'

'His work isn't always easy to appreciate; I grant you that.'

'The other picture shows a dustman being hoisted up to heaven by a woman who could pass for me or Hilda or the two of us together, whilst a group of village yokels offer him up bits of rubbish from the dustbins.'

Dudley clears his throat and nods.

'There is some money coming in, of course, apart from what you're giving him. But he's not very good at organising his affairs so he's asked me to do it for him. I'm already acting as a business partner to another artist and I handle all my own accounts.'

'He's having to support two families; that's the biggest problem. Not to mention two homes, three if you count Lindworth.' He looks meaningfully at me.

I smile. Dudley's walked right into it. 'I wondered whether we could rent out Lindworth as an extra source of income.'

'Moor Thatch would become your married home, you mean?'

My face remains blank. It's as well he can't see what's behind it.

'That seems sensible,' says Dudley, misinterpreting my silence. 'Although I believe you have a sitting tenant at Moor Thatch?'

I wonder just who he's been talking to. 'For Stanley what's important is the studio at Lindworth, but it's separate from the house. The problem is that there's no electricity in Lindworth at the moment.'

'Good God, how did he and Hilda see their way around?'

'There are a lot of burnt-out wicks about the place. It's a substantial house; it just needs work. I doubt if anyone would want to live there at the moment. We were wondering if you would be prepared to front the cost of putting in electrics and recouping it in rent.'

Too late, he sees he's walked into the trap. He taps his fingers on the desk. He's wearing an exquisite onyx signet ring.

'Excuse me for a moment.' He goes over to the shelves behind his desk and takes a file down. He leafs through it, stopping at one point and going down a list of numbers with a pencil. If these figures are a record of the loans he's given Stanley in the past year, Stanley's more indebted to him than I thought.

He turns the page and glances up at me. He's not sure whether I'm a lighthouse guiding him to safety or a siren luring him onto the rocks.

'As things stand at the moment, leaving out the incidentals, Stanley owes me £86 for the trip to Cornwall, £15 for Hilda's maintenance and £8 which I leant him for his framing costs. I've so far had four paintings back from him.'

'Quite. I saw renting Lindworth as a way of utilising Stanley's assets to repay a bit of what he owes'.

'What would it cost to put in electricity at Lindworth?'

'I would have to make inquiries. Shall I do that and get back to you?'

He hesitates. 'I'd need to know what was implied. I'm not a charity.' He goes to close the file. Then, as an afterthought, he scribbles something on the page. 'I take it Stanley knows you've come to see me.'

'I thought it was best to wait until we'd spoken. Obviously I'll tell him when I get back.'

'But he knows about your plans for Lindworth?'

'Stanley is my husband. I would hardly rent the house out without saying anything. We came up with the plan together.'

Dudley looks abashed. 'Forgive me, Mrs Spencer, I ought to have offered my congratulations on your marriage. I hope you and Stanley will be very happy.'

'Thank you.'

'You're both painters. You have that in common. Although so was Stanley's first wife,' he says, thoughtfully.

'We were all students at the Slade….tarred by the same brush,' I say, lightly.

'I believe you had an exhibition at Lefevre's some time back.'

'Yes, it sold well. I'd hoped to have another solo exhibition this year. Any money coming in from my work goes into the joint pot, naturally, and it leaves Stanley free to concentrate on what he calls his *visionary* paintings.'

An extremely well-dressed couple have just come into the gallery and started looking round. The work on show is by a painter championed by Roger Fry. You can't get anywhere unless you have the blessing of the *Bloomsberries* these days.

Dudley is distracted. He will leave the couple to make up their own minds but he'll stay on the alert so that he recognises when they have.

'Perhaps you'd care to see the work I did in Cornwall,' I say, casually.

He glances at me: 'Sorry?'

'I was wondering if you'd care to see some of the work I did in Cornwall.'

'Your work?'

'My work,' I say, patiently. 'I think I have enough there to put on a show.'

He's going back over the conversation, wondering how we managed to get on to this. There is a moment when I think I'd have been wiser not to push my luck. But then he gives a brisk smile. 'Bring a couple in with you next time you call. I'll have a look. We're booked up till the autumn, but there might be something in October or November.'

'Thank you. Duncan Grant's agreed to write the introduction.'

'Duncan?' Dudley gives a wheezing laugh. 'I didn't realise he could write. He once told me he'd had no education whatsoever.'

I smile. 'He was probably exaggerating.'

'Yes, I dare say. Well, if that's all.' He holds out his hand. He's anxious to get rid of me before I think of something else to ask for and the couple in the gallery appear to have decided what they want to buy.

As I shake hands with Dudley, I can feel the imprint of the onyx ring against my palm. He may not like me, I can cope with that, but he respects me. He's aware that he has been manipulated but he's too well-bred to show resentment. I can deal with Dudley.

'I'll get back to you about the estimate.'

He purses his lips. 'Estimate?'

'For Lindworth.'

'Ah, yes. Pass on my regards to Stanley.'

'Certainly. It's been a pleasure.'

As I make my way down Piccadilly, people stand aside for me. The men look back over their shoulders. I walk as if I am going somewhere. I know just how Hitler felt as his troops marched into the Rhineland.

On my way back to the station, I stop off and buy a packet of my favourite Turkish cigarettes. I'll have to smoke them out of sight of Dorothy, but I don't mind that. I like doing things in secret.

I get back expecting to find Dorothy behind the closed door of her studio. Instead, I find she's commandeered the kitchen for the second time that week. Like Stanley, Dorothy is only really interested in painting. If it's going well, she's utterly absorbed and if it's not she's looking for a razor blade to cut her wrists with. Or, and for some reason I resent this most, she'll suddenly acquire an interest in domestic duties. Naturally she's choosy about what she does. It's most unlikely that you'll find her chipping seven years of grease stains from the inside of the cooker. She's not interested in doing what needs to be done; the exercise is to distract her from the void she's in.

In consequence, she'll sometimes get bored halfway through or have an idea for a painting or a sudden yen to have a brush in one hand but without the bother of a dustpan in the other. She'll abandon everything and disappear into her own room, problem solved. When she felt she had made enough jam, she left two tureens still bubbling on the stove and several pounds of fruit already chopped and curling at the edges. I turned off the gas but left the tureens there as a reminder, the scum on the surface looking less inviting as the days passed and the dust took over.

This time when I get back she is sitting at the kitchen table with a tin of brasso and a chammy leather, polishing the cutlery. She's humming. It's the humming that annoys me most, suggesting as it does that she has found the satisfaction she was seeking doing the one job I like to do myself.

She glances up: 'Successful trip? Have you come back with shares in Dudley's gallery?'

'Not quite but we might get an exhibition out of him and I've persuaded him to pay for electricity to be installed at Lindworth.' I sit down and move the tray of cutlery aside.

'Well done you.' She holds up a spoon and looks at her reflection. Cleaning silver is rewarding in as much as you get an immediate result. What thirty seconds earlier was dull and tarnished, suddenly reveals itself as sparkling, bright and full of optimism. Whereas neither Dorothy nor I have looked behind the Aga since we moved in, the brass knocker on the door of Moor Thatch has been polished to the thinness of an egg-shell. One day someone, and let's face it Stanley's the most likely candidate, will grasp it like he did with Hilda's right breast and it will disintegrate.

'I told him Duncan Grant would write an introduction for the catalogue.'

'I didn't realise he could write.' She takes a fork and slides the duster in between the prongs.

'No, nor did Dudley. It was when we had that exhibition at Lefevre's that he offered. He was drunk, of course.'

'You said Jas Wood once told you it had taken him six months to write a letter.' She holds up the fork and twists it in the air to catch the light.

'It's probably enough that Dudley *thinks* he'll write the introduction.' My hand creeps towards the pile of cutlery. I look to see if there's another duster on the table.

'Shouldn't you have talked to Stanley before seeing Dudley?'

'Absolutely not. He might have wanted to come with me and that would have ruined everything. You can't negotiate with someone if it looks as if you're begging.'

'Even if you are.' She puts the fork down.

'Dudley wouldn't be supporting Stanley if it wasn't in his interests.'

'You persuaded Dudley Tooth that it was in his interests to go on giving Stanley money?' She looks sideways at me. 'Honestly, Patricia, you're the end.'

'He's giving Stanley money anyway. At least now there's a plan.'

'And what is that, pray?'

'Stanley needs to be persuaded to leave Lindworth altogether. Even if the house is viable, you're right, no one will want to rent it once they find a tramp is living in a shed in their back garden.'

There's a pause. The fork stays upright in her hand. She's holding it the way a child does when they've never used a knife and fork before. The sight is oddly touching.

'But you promised Stanley he could stay there. It's his studio.'

'He'll have to find another one. As long as there's a wall to pin his canvas to and light to see by, Stanley will be fine. He's blind to his environment.'

She's looking at the fork as if she can't remember what it's doing there. 'I wish I shared your optimism.' She picks up the duster, but the task seems to have lost its purpose. 'It just seems that Stanley's bearing an unfair proportion of the blame for his financial situation.'

'That's because he is to blame for his financial situation.' I lean over and pick up the fork she's just put down. I hold my hand out and she passes me the duster. 'It's not just the cost of the divorce, although that's bad enough. If he'd persuaded Hilda to come back to him, at least he wouldn't have to pay her maintenance.'

'He'd still have to support her and the children.'

'But he wouldn't have to do it from a distance and there wouldn't have been any need to bring in a solicitor.'

I tip a little of the cleaning fluid out onto a corner of the duster. Dorothy looks on distractedly.

'The name of his solicitor is *Evill*, incidentally.' I laugh. 'He could end up in one of Stanley's paintings with a name like that.'

'I don't like the idea of Stanley having to give up the studio.' She spreads her fingers out. They're at a loss now she's relinquished both the duster and the fork. 'I know how much it means to have a space you can rely on.'

'Maybe you would care to have him share your studio.'

'No thank you.'

I get up and hand her back the duster. 'Well then.'

VI

'It's impossible. I can't! I'm halfway through the series. How can I move all these paintings? And I haven't anywhere to move them to.'

'It won't be happening straight away. The first job is to get the electricians in.'

'I can't believe you're doing this.' He picks a paint rag up distractedly and tries to clean his glasses.

In the studio it's hot and airless, even with the window open. There's been no rain for a month; it's been more like mid-summer than the tail-end of September. In the shed heat tends to incubate under the corrugated iron roof.

'There's no need to panic, Stanley. I just thought it best to keep you up to date with what was happening.'

I take in the pictures stacked against the walls. Although I haven't wanted to complain too much to Dorothy, who'll tell me I'm to blame, I'm horrified by almost everything that Stanley's painted since we came back from St Ives. If it was left to me, I'd put the whole lot on the fire.

The paintings are six deep in places. I pull one or two out from the back. One canvas shows a couple licking one another's tongues, there are huge women dwarfing tiny men, a little man on all fours who is clearly Stanley in a collar, being dragged along the pavement by a woman who bears an uncomfortable resemblance to me.

Stanley trails round after me. 'What do you think of them? They're my *Beatitudes.*'

I clear a pile of newspapers and sketches off the only chair and sit down. 'I hope you're not thinking of exhibiting them.'

'They're for Church House. They'll be going in the transepts.'

So far Stanley's *Church of Me* has been a figment of imagination, even if the paintings Stanley wants to put in it are real. When he showed one of them to Eddie Marsh and asked him what he thought, for once he didn't get a diplomatic answer. 'Terrible', was the response.

There is another painting leaning up against the wall with a gross overweight man carrying a long stick with a small man holding onto it.

'They're about different kinds of love,' says Stanley. 'That man's Kench, the Sergeant-Major in my unit in Salonika.'

'And that's you hanging on his stick, presumably. Do you think Dudley would continue to support you if he saw these?'

'Dudley's said I have to keep up with the visionary paintings.'

'These aren't visionary. If there is a message here, it's that the painter's sexually frustrated and a masochist to boot.'

'Whose fault is that? I've got two wives and neither of them wants to sleep with me. I have to masturbate or I'd go crazy. Now you say I've got to move out of the studio.' He's blustering. 'Perhaps you'd like me to set up my easel on the common!'

'Please don't. If the village got a whiff of what you're doing now, we'd be a laughing stock. You might as well be smearing excrement across the walls.'

'How dare you criticise my work!'

I'm frightened suddenly. He's never looked at me like this before.

'You haven't got the first idea of what it means to be an artist,' he shouts.

I can see the whites around his eyes. The red veins in his cheeks are bulging. It's so rare for Stanley to get angry that I put my hands up to defend myself. As I discovered when I tore the drawing from his sketchbook that day, Stanley drew the line at criticism of his work.

He makes a gesture as if swatting flies away. 'What makes you think you have the right to talk to me this way. What have you painted that's so wonderful?'

'I've got an exhibition planned for later this year,' I say, put on the defensive by his outburst. 'Dudley's looking at the work I did in Cornwall.'

Stanley blinks. 'What work? The whole time we were there, I never saw you with a paintbrush in your hand.'

'Why would you? You were outside doing landscapes every day.'

'You know when somebody's been painting. You can smell it on them.'

'You resent the fact that Dudley might be interested in what I'm doing? He'll have more luck selling my work than he will with your *Beatitudes*.' I bite my tongue. I still don't like the look in Stanley's eyes.

'I don't know how I'm managing to paint at all with everything that's going on around me.' He kicks at the pile of paint rags on the floor. They flutter and subside.

He bunches up his hands again. 'I think God must have sent you to torment me, like he sent the devil to Saint Anthony.' He beats his fists against his forehead. He is in a worse state than I thought.

'Stop shouting and calm down.' The shed is set back from the road but there is just a hedge between us and the main road and there's always someone in the courtyard of The Railway Arms. 'No one's tormenting you. We want to help you. If you think about it, renting Lindworth is the only sensible solution. Dudley thinks so, too. The house will be worth much more after it's been renovated. Later on, we might consider selling it.'

'But you said I could keep the studio. This is my home!'

'We'll find you somewhere else. Be sensible now. Come and have a cuddle.'

He scowls and starts picking out the paint from underneath his nails. His anger has gone limp on him. He stands there like a lost soul in the middle of the room, surrounded by these awful paintings. For an instant I feel almost sorry for him.

'Come along.' I pat my knees.

He hesitates and then comes over and kneels down beside me. I attempt to brush the hair back from his eyes but that ridiculously puerile hair cut means it just falls back again. He peers at me short-sightedly with those soft spaniel eyes of his. I run my fingers through his fringe, then rub my hand across my sleeve to show him that the cuddle's over.

'There, that's better, isn't it?'

'Why don't we take our clothes off and lie down.' He starts to paw my lap.

'Not now. I'm busy, Stanley. There's a lot to organise.'

'Why don't you come back later?'

'Maybe. Why don't you go out and get some fresh air? Take a canvas and your paints.'

His face falls: 'You want me to paint another landscape?'

Anything to stop him working on his current pictures, I think. 'Well, it's not a bad idea. It's better to be occupied. I'll bet you haven't put your nose outside all day.' I get up briskly. 'I'll find out how soon the electricians can begin work. Then at least we'll have a time-scale.'

VII

I leave Stanley on his knees. That afternoon I take the bus to Maidenhead. I need to get away from Cookham for an hour or two. My brain is scrambling in the heat.

At Moor Thatch we've been leaving all the doors and windows open, channelling what little breeze there is, but it's as if the oxygen is being sucked out of the air. Although the sun is setting earlier each day it leaves a heaviness behind it and the nights are almost as oppressive as the days.

The heat seems to insinuate itself into the thatch and linger, adding to the next day's quota. At night Dorothy and I lie naked on the mattress with a sheet that ends up in the middle of the bed because we've both discarded it. Out in the garden, bees buzz dozily amongst the wilting shrubs. We're like those countries that await the monsoon with a mixture of relief and terror, knowing that the more extreme the heat has been the more extreme the weather will be afterwards.

At least whilst I am sitting on the bus there is a cool breeze coming from the window vent. I spend an hour window shopping and then treat myself to a vanilla ice-cream in a café on the High Street.

I get back to find the pram with Stanley's paints and easel in it parked outside the door of Moor Thatch and hear his voice coming from the parlour.

'Can't you talk to her?' he says.

I fancy Dorothy has heard the front door click, whereas when Stanley's talking he's oblivious to everything.

'I'm sorry, Stanley, I'm afraid I can't. She wouldn't listen to me, anyway.'

I creep along the hall.

'I thought that you two....'

'What?'

'That you were close. She wants me to move out of Lindworth altogether. I'll be homeless.'

His voice sinks into a whine. I realise leaving Stanley on his own this afternoon was a mistake. He's spent the last four hours festering and now he's looking for a sympathetic ear. A part of him still thinks of Dodo as an ally. I suspect a part of her does, too.

She starts off neutrally: 'You know enough rich people, Stanley. Can't you talk to Dudley or John Rothenstein?'

'It isn't just this business of the house. She acts as if it's me she's trying to get rid of.' His voice breaks. 'I thought she wanted me; that's why she was insisting I leave Hilda. I've made everybody miserable and now that I've signed over all my assets to Patricia, she won't let me near her.'

He tails off. There is a pause in which I sense that Dorothy is struggling to provide an adequate response.

'I don't think she expected you to foist yourself upon her quite so forcefully,' she says at last.

'She hasn't given me a chance to foist myself on her,' he says, resentfully. 'It's never been what you'd call joyful, not the way it was with Hilda, although even Hilda…' he stops, as if suddenly aware of who he's talking to.

'You mean it didn't work with Hilda either?' There's a hint of curiosity in Dodo's voice.

'Oh goodness, yes. With Hilda I was up-in-heaven all the time. But this group she belongs to - Christian

Scientists - they don't believe in birth control so it was always somehow incomplete, if you know what I mean. Well no, I don't suppose you do.'

'You seem to have been either rather reckless or exceedingly unlucky in your choice of women, Stanley,' Dorothy says, gently.

'You don't choose the women who inspire you, Dorothy. God sends them to you.'

'You think God's responsible for sending you Patricia? Isn't it more likely, Stanley, that Patricia crossed your path at just the moment when you were beginning to find fault with Hilda?'

Stanley looks as if the idea that he might find fault with Hilda is ridiculous. He seems to have forgotten that a year ago he kept us up till midnight ranting about her iniquities.

'You said your marriage had turned into a primeval slime.'

His voice is lathered with resentment. 'That's just what my marriage to Patricia seems to have turned into. When we did make love, she put her head under a pillow.

It was as if she was renting bits of herself out but at a price she knew would be beyond my means.'

There is another pause 'I thought you said you hadn't made love to Patricia.'

'We tried, but she wasn't keen.'

'I see,' says Dorothy with that edge in her voice that I have come to dread. 'But you went through the motions? Did you think that after you were married, you'd get better at it?'

'It's not something you should need to practise. Dogs don't.'

I should interrupt them now, before this gets worse. As I'm moving down the passage, I hear Dorothy say, sweetly. 'For you to have ended up in a primeval slime on both occasions, Stanley, might suggest it's where you feel at home.'

'At least with Hilda it's not where I started off. Her trouble was that she could never let herself go. That's what I thought was so wonderful about Patricia. It seems I was wrong about her.'

'It seems both of us were wrong about Patricia,' Dorothy says. Stanley grunts. 'You haven't only come to ask me if I'll intercede for you so that you can stay on at Lindworth, have you?'

'No', says Stanley, taking courage from the way the conversation's going. 'I've decided that I've had enough of this. Patricia is my wife. It's time that she behaved like one.'

I've reached the door into the living-room. Just as I push it open, I hear Dorothy say:

'You know what, on this occasion, Stanley, I agree with you.'

VIII

'Please, Dorothy. At least say we can talk about it.'

'What is there to talk about? Accept that you're a married woman. You owe Stanley that much.'

'You expect me to move out of here and in with him?' I follow her upstairs. She clumps along the passage to the bedroom, picking up a stool and standing on it to take down a suitcase from the wardrobe. They've been up there since we came to Moor Thatch. As she lifts hers down, there is a draft of hot air and dust billows up towards the ceiling.

'It's considered normal for a wife to occupy the same house as her husband.'

'Stanley's not a normal husband.'

'And you're not behaving like a normal wife.' She takes the suitcase over to the bed and starts to take her clothes out of the chest of drawers.

'You're not suggesting I should sleep with him?' That's usually enough to focus her attention.

'It would seem you have already. Since the line's been crossed, you might as well make someone happy.' She holds up a faded blue shirt and then puts it back into the drawer.

'And what will you do?' I feel breathless.

'I shan't be here anyway. I'm leaving.'

Does she mean it? Panic sweeps up from my stomach. 'Just like that? You'd take his word against mine?'

'Yes, of course I would. I realised long ago that you were someone who would rather lie than tell the truth.'

'I've never lied to you about important things.'

'Quite.' She gives me a long look. 'I've known for some time, Patricia, that fidelity is not important to you.'

'That's not what I meant. If Stanley mattered to me, I'd have left you long ago and gone to live with him.'

'Well now you can. What's stopping you?'

'You are. I love you and I don't love Stanley.' I start taking things out of the case and scrunching them up in my hands. She grabs them and there is a tug-of-war before I let go.

'But you let him trifle with you, nonetheless,' she says.

'It never came to anything. I found it utterly revolting if you want to know.'

'I don't.' She waves me to the side and takes a jacket from the hook behind the door. Because she has so few possessions she could actually walk out of here with everything she owns, except the paintings. She would need a lorry to transport those. I feel shivery, despite the heat. We've had these rows before, but it's the first time that it's got to this point. I put one hand on her arm. She shakes it off.

'I've called a cab to take me into Maidenhead. That way the whole of Cookham won't be privileged to see me go. It might be less humiliating for us both.'

'You can't leave, Dorothy. You know you can't.'

'I can.' She shuts the case and loops the fasteners, tucking in the ends.

'What will you do in Maidenhead?' My voice is shrill.

'I'll catch a train to London. I can stay with friends until I find digs.'

'What friends?'

'If I told you, you might turn up at the door and to be honest, I would rather not see you again.' She lifts the case onto the floor and drags it back along the passage and downstairs.

'You're angry. You don't mean that.'

'I am angry. I've just wasted twenty years of my life on a woman who has no integrity. I'm incandescent if you must know.'

I feel tight inside. 'How can you say your life's been wasted? That's like saying you wish we had never met.'

She looks up at the ceiling with her lips pursed and then nods. 'That is what it amounts to, I suppose.'

I'm stunned. She's never been this cruel before. She picks her keys up from the table in the hall and throws them down again. 'I shan't need those.'

'Why don't you take them just in case you change your mind?'

'I shan't.' The taxi hoots outside. 'Goodbye, Patricia. I hope you and Stanley will be very happy, though if you behave with him the way that you've behaved with me, I have my doubts.'

She hoiks the suitcase over to the door.

'If you go, Dorothy, I'll kill myself.'

She turns to face me, wearily: 'Of course you won't.'

I reach out for the paper knife that's lying on the table. 'I will, Dorothy, I'll cut my wrists infront of you.'

Outside the taxi hoots again. She looks at me. 'You'd have to hack away for half an hour to get through the skin with that knife. It won't even open envelopes efficiently.'

She's right. The knife is made of ivory and has a rounded blade. I didn't want to cry, but suddenly I know I'm going to. The tears are running down my face.

'For heaven's sake, girl, pull yourself together,' she says. 'Do you want the whole of Cookham seeing you in this state?'

'I don't care. What does it matter if you're not here? What does any of it matter?'

She goes to the door and signals to the taxi-driver that she knows he's there and that she's coming. She puts down her case. 'How could you let him near you? Just explain it to me.'

'He kept going on about us being up-in-heaven; sex was vital to the process. He said that he couldn't paint without it. I'm a vehicle for his beastly fantasies. He doesn't even bother trying to excuse them. The *Beatitudes* are just filth. They're not even dressed up to be art.'

'Did you allow him to make love to you, Patricia, yes or no?'

'No! I agreed to go along with it to prove to him that it was no good. In the end, he saw that. Stanley's cross because at present he's not getting anything from either me or Hilda.'

'Have you any idea of the damage you've done?'

'It's not all my fault, you know.'

'Forgive me, but it is. If you had not encouraged him at the beginning, it would not have happened.'

'You liked Stanley at the start, too.'

'There's a difference between liking someone and encouraging them to become infatuated. What's so dreadful about you, Patricia, is that you have the ability to teeter on the edge of an abyss for so long that when you begin to slide you're not aware of it. You go on thinking you're on solid ground, but once you start to sink, you can't stop. There is no halfway. You go immediately to the bottom. Down you go, still waving, still convinced it isn't you that's tilting but the world. Can't you at least take some responsibility for what you do?'

'Yes, all right, I admit I've been a naughty girl. I'm sorry. But I don't deserve this. You don't have to leave me. Can't you punish me some other way?'

'Off-hand, I can't think of a punishment that fits the crime.'

'I'll go across to Lindworth and tell Stanley that it's over. You and I can go away somewhere. There'll only be the two of us.'

'You can't make Stanley disappear now, just because it suits you. You've caused untold misery to everyone involved. When he went up to London, Stanley told me he'd found Hilda living on her own with Unity. She's given Shirin to a relative in Epsom to look after. She sits in a corner all day staring into space whilst Unity plays with her dolls. She thinks she's dying. The poor woman has been driven crazy. You say her solicitors are threatening action. Stanley could end up in prison, then he wouldn't have the chance to paint at all.'

'At least he'd have a roof over his head.'

'Excuse me.' Dorothy picks up her case again.

'I'm sorry, Dorothy, I didn't mean that. I know some of it is my fault, but I couldn't live with Stanley, I just couldn't. There must be some other way. Why don't we have another go at getting Hilda back?'

'I think it's rather late for that.'

'Well let's at least discuss it. Send the cab away. I can't think with the engine running like that. Let me go and settle up with him. Why don't you pour us both a whisky? Dorothy?'

She lifts her sleeve to see her watch. 'I've missed the train. I'll take the cab as far as Maidenhead and book into *The Swan*. I'll be there till tomorrow afternoon. If by then you have made the situation clear to Stanley and by that I mean you've put him straight about the nature of your ties with me, we might discuss it further. Otherwise I shall be on the 4 o'clock train into London.'

IX

'How could you tell Dorothy we'd been to bed together, Stanley!'

He screws up his eyes. 'I thought we had.'

'I don't mean simply getting into bed. I mean...the other things.'

'The other things were what I said I wasn't getting.'

'But you made it clear you'd had a go...that you'd had several goes in fact. Now Dorothy's insisting that I either leave you or she'll leave me.' My voice breaks. 'She has left me in fact. She went last night. She took a taxi into Maidenhead after you'd gone.'

I sound hysterical. My eyes are red and puffy. I've been up all night. Outside, rain's hammering against the corrugated iron roof of the shed. As I ran from the house this morning, right on cue the weather broke. There was the faintest rumble in the distance, as a warning of what was to come. If Tiddles was still here, he'd have been searching for a cupboard or an open drawer to dive into and vomit up the latest meal, a process that might be repeated four or five times as he scoured the house for safety. Once, after a storm, I'd found a pile of dried sick at the bottom of my sock drawer three days later.

The first rain-drop plopped onto my head as I ran down the path. I looked at it and for a moment I thought that was it. There was a lull and then another drop. Then suddenly the heavens opened. All I had on was the flimsy dress I'd worn the day before. In seconds I was drenched; the path had turned into a stream. Had Dorothy been there, we would have rushed out of the cottage and stood in the deluge with our arms outstretched, our faces lifted up towards the heavens as the rain poured over us and seeped into the parched earth.

As it is, I might as well be naked. I look as if I've been wrapped in gauze. I'll have to borrow Stanley's jacket or an old coat Hilda's left behind, before I leave. His eyes pass up and down my body but he doesn't comment.

'You can't stay in Cookham, Stanley. You'd be leaving Lindworth soon in any case, so why not just go somewhere else now?'

'Where else?'

'Oh for goodness' sake,' I press my fists against my forehead. 'Does it matter? Anywhere.' I'm conscious of the steady drip of water from the gutter as the downpour starts to ease.

'If Dorothy's not there, why can't I live with you at Moor Thatch?'

'Are you mad! You think I'd live with you now, after all you've done.'

'What have I done?'

'It's your fault Dorothy's gone, Stanley. If you hadn't kicked up such a stink over the sex thing, we could have resolved this amicably.'

'She thought you should start behaving like a proper wife,' says Stanley, bullishly. The previous day's conversation is beginning to come back to him.

'How can I be a wife to you when I'm already married, or as good as?'

'You've already got a husband?' Stanley frowns.

'Oh Stanley, work it out. I've lived with Dorothy for nigh on twenty years. What Hilda is to you, she is to me.'

'But she's a woman.'

'Christ!' I throw my arms up in the air. 'I give up.'

'So it's true what Hilda's brother told me?' His eyes harden.

'You're not telling me you wouldn't have suspected, even without Richard bloody Carline putting in his oar.'

'I thought you'd married me because you loved me.' He puts down his brushes and then picks them up again as if he needs them for protection. He stares glumly at the floor. He hasn't got the energy to go on arguing and nor have I. In terms of our shared misery we probably have more in common at this moment than we've ever had before.

'I'm sorry if you're disappointed, Stanley. I was fond of you. It's just that Dorothy....'

'I thought if we were both prepared to go on trying, it would be all right.'

'It's not a case of how much practise you put in. You're either that way or you're not.'

'Why did you marry me, in that case?'

'You insisted.'

Stanley waves the brushes at me in a final gesture of defiance. 'I put up with your shenanigans with Dorothy because you told me I could still have Hilda.'

'You *can* still have Hilda.'

'Hilda doesn't want me.'

'Maybe if she knows you're homeless, she'll take pity on you.'

'I don't want her taking pity on me,' he says, heatedly.

'All right, I'll tell you what I'll do. I'll go to Hampstead. 'I'll tell Hilda that I'm stepping down, that she can have you to herself. She'll be your wife in all but name. How's that?'

He shrugs. 'She says she won't come back whilst you're there.'

'But that's what I'm saying, Stanley. I won't be there. I'll tell Hilda that I'm going. In return, can I tell Dorothy that you've gone, too; that you're agreeing to a separation.'

'You mean not be married anymore?'

'Of course we'll still be married.'

'What's the point of being married if we're separated?'

'Marriage isn't just about what happens in the bedroom, Stanley. I shall still be handling the accounts.'

'Who cares about those?' he says, sullenly.

'Somebody has to. I don't think you realise what a hole you're in.'

'If you're my wife, you should be in it with me.'

'Listen to me, Stanley. Try to understand. I couldn't function without Dorothy. I'd be no good to you.'

He backs away. 'You've been no good to me in any case,' he says. 'I might as well have been cast out into the wilderness.'

'Don't play the prima donna. All I'm asking you to do is make yourself scarce until I've persuaded Dorothy to come back.'

'And what then?'

'I don't know. It depends on Dorothy.'

'It looks like everything depends on Dorothy.' He's swinging his arms, peevishly.

'Please, Stanley, say you will. You don't know what it means to me.' He hunches up his shoulders. I reach out and kiss him on the cheek. It's grey and stubbly. There's no doubt that Stanley needs a woman to look after him, but it was never going to be me. 'I won't forget this, Stanley.'

'Nor shall I,' he says.

I leave the studio to find that summer has turned into autumn in the space of half an hour. It's stopped raining but the cyclone whipped up by the storm has stripped the trees of leaves. They're heaped in drifts against the hedges; children on their way to school are tossing sodden armfuls in the air. A wintry sunshine shimmers on the cobwebs clinging to the branches of the trees. I feel as if I've slipped into a time warp. There's a moment when I wonder not just whether Dorothy has gone, but whether she was ever here.

X

'I'm going up to London in the morning, Dorothy.' I had to hear her voice, although the tone of it does nothing to reduce the distance separating us. I draw breath. 'Why not spend an extra night in Maidenhead and I'll call at the hotel on my way back?'

'I've already booked myself onto the afternoon train.'

'Can't you change the ticket? I'm not sure I can see Hilda and get back in time.'

'You'll miss me then.'

I try to keep the edge out of my voice. 'Our future is at stake here, Dorothy.'

'It's good that you're aware of that.'

There is a pause. 'I can't believe you're doing this,' I whisper.

'What was that, Pet?'

'I said that I can't believe you're doing this.'

The aim in offering to see Hilda was to forestall Dorothy's attempts to leave. Once she's in London, I know it will be more difficult to get her back. I know, too, that there's no point in me promising to do something until I've done it. I might manage to dissimulate where

Stanley is concerned and I might even manage it with Hilda. But not Dorothy.

'I told you my intentions when I left,' says Dorothy. 'By all means visit Hilda. I'm sure she'll appreciate it. So will Unity, I dare say. Life can't be that good for her at present. Take your time. It's no good rushing it. When you know categorically what's happening; when it's happened, rather, you can let me know.'

'So you're determined that you won't come back tonight, whatever answer Hilda gives me?'

'Having failed to get the answer you want out of Hilda so far, I would be surprised if she caved in now.'

'Stanley has agreed that, even if she doesn't, he'll leave Cookham.'

'Well, you have been busy.'

'So if you could see your way to cutting me a bit of slack....'

'Of course, I've just said take your time.'

'But I want us to be together. Couldn't you....'

She sighs. 'You haven't understood, Patricia. I am not averse to compromise. I recognise that all relationships depend on it. But if the compromise is all on one side, the relationship is undermined and in the end it breaks down. That's what's happened here. You've grudgingly admitted that the thing you promised me would never happen, happened.'

'No.'

'Please hear me out. If you had owned up straightaway, perhaps I'd have forgiven you, although I can't be certain of it. But your grief was not in consequence of your betrayal, it was a result of being found out. There is something skewed in your morality, Patricia, and unless you can accept that, there is no way forward.'

'I admit it. I was wrong.'

'You were, but not for the reasons you think. You've insisted that you don't love Stanley, which makes your behaviour the more reprehensible. You toyed with his affections and you toyed with mine. You can't rely on Hilda to make good and certainly it isn't something that can be accomplished in an afternoon.'

'How will I know where I can get in touch with you?'

'I'll let you have a poste-restante address in London once I'm settled.'

'You don't trust me to know where you're living?'

'No, dear.'

'But what if…' a noise comes out of the receiver. Something's happened on the line. I listen to the dialling tone. She's gone.

XI

'Who is it, Unity?' The voice is papery and thin. Along the hall, the passage opens up into a living-room and through the door I see part of an armchair with a stockinged leg stretched out across the gap. There is a pile of newspapers beside it on the mat.

After my call to Dorothy I'd spent the morning at the kitchen window staring out over the garden, watching as the sun crept round, illuminating the hydrangeas and the roses Dorothy had staked the week before to stop them falling over and which now lay in a tangled heap. It felt as if the storm that signalled her departure had already drawn a line under our life there.

Midday came and went. The afternoon unravelled silently. At 4 o'clock the light began to fade. I pictured Dorothy boarding the train at Maidenhead, the statutory newspaper under her arm, seeking out a carriage where she could be on her own and coming into Paddington an hour later, summoning a porter, getting in a cab to go... where?

She was right in thinking that the chances of persuading Hilda to go back to Stanley now were negligible. And in any case, as Dorothy had pointed out, the issue wasn't Stanley; it was me.

I went back over our last conversation: Even if my mission was a lost cause, at least it would show that I was trying to atone, whilst if I went on sitting there, it would be me who was the lost cause. I thought I might also draw some consolation from an hour in the presence of a woman whose position was, if anything, less enviable than my own.

The house where Hilda is now living, is a stone's throw from the Carline's house. It's on a similar wide, leafy road, but like most of the Spencer homes it has a run-down and neglected air. The feeling I get as I enter isn't so much of a life in progress as one that's already run its course.

The child who's standing in the door is very pale with two enormous eyes that seem to take up half her face. The last time I saw Unity she was a bump in Hilda's stomach. It comes home to me how long this saga has been going on.

'My name's Patricia.' I smile briskly. 'Has your mother mentioned me?'

'You're Daddy's floozy.' she says without any trace of irony. When she grows up, she'll have the sort of face that you could strike a match on.

'Actually, I'm Mrs Spencer, although you can go on calling me Patricia.' She looks blankly at me. 'Maybe you could tell your mother that I'm here.'

There is a murmured conversation and then Unity comes back. 'She's in the parlour.'

'Thank you, dear.' I make my way along the passage. Hilda glances at me with her hall-mark lack of curiosity but there's a wariness about her that suggests my visit isn't unexpected.

'Don't get up,' I say, unnecessarily. I fetch a chair and shuffle the legs through the pile of papers till it's facing her. Scrunched up around the chair leg is a picture of the Duke of Windsor shaking hands with Hitler. I can picture Dorothy's response to that. She thought he was a toe-rag even when he was the King.

I glance at Unity and then at Hilda. 'I was wondering if you'd heard from Stanley recently?'

'He writes to Mummy every day,' says Unity. She has gone back to playing with her doll but she is clearly capable of multi-tasking.

'That's good.' I lean forward to reduce the distance between me and Hilda. 'Stanley's missed out on a couple of your payments recently, I gather. He's been finding it struggle. I just wanted you to know I've taken over his accounts, so if you could be patient …'

'Mummy says we can't afford the music lessons Mrs Harter's giving Shirin.' Unity is combing out the tangles in her doll's hair.

It seems there is no chance of a private conversation between me and Hilda. Looking at her, I suspect it might be better if I simply talked to Unity directly. She seems more clued up as to what's going on.

'That seems a pity. Shirin is a talented musician, I believe.' I keep my eyes on Hilda in the hope that she might take some interest in the conversation.

'Mummy's sending me to stay with Mrs Harter, too.'

I don't know what to say. I had assumed that sending Shirin out to Epsom was a temporary measure not the first stage of a general evacuation.

'We'll be going on the bus.'

'Gosh, how exciting. I love travelling on the bus. I always take the front seat at the top.'

I'd heard that it's what children do, but Unity is looking at me as if I'm the reason why she's never found the top seat free. I can remember Stanley telling us that Hilda thought she was the product of a union between herself and God and looking at her now, it doesn't seem so far-fetched.

'What would you want, if you had the choice?'

'I want my Daddy back,' she says. More fool me, then, for asking.

I turn slightly in the chair so that I'm sitting with my back towards her. 'Hilda, as I said before, I bear you no ill will. I realise you and Stanley need to be there for the children and that you're important for his work. He's always said so. Why don't you invite him up to London? Or come down to Cookham for the day to talk things over.'

Unity perks up, but Hilda goes on staring at me, listlessly. It seems a day-return to Cookham isn't much of an inducement. 'Or the three of you can stay at Lindworth, temporarily,' I say, reluctantly.

'And where would you be?'

'I can stay at Moor Thatch where I lived before our marriage.'

'What of Stanley?'

'He would be with you…wherever you are.'

She regards me, beadily: 'Why aren't you living with him?'

'I am, on and off. It's just….' This is ridiculous. I feel as if I'm having to apologise to Hilda for not sleeping with her former husband. 'We don't have the same kind of relationship that you and Stanley had. It's not…' I glance at Unity and catch her eye. She's sensed a frisson in the air and is now paying close attention. 'Let's just say it's different.'

'He says you won't sleep with him,' says Hilda, bluntly.

'He's exaggerating. Look, I really think this conversation ought to be between the two of us, don't you?' I tilt my head at Unity.

'Why did you take him from me if you didn't want him?' Hilda's staring at me as if it's a question that's perplexing her.

'I thought I'd just explained that, Hilda. I've come here to offer you an olive branch. Since we each occupy a different role in Stanley's life, there isn't any reason why we shouldn't divvy the responsibilities. My dealings with him won't encroach on yours and frankly I'd be happy for him to take what he needs from you.' I hesitate. 'We'll separate entirely. He'll be yours.'

'No,' Hilda says.

'You'd rather live like this in poverty and on your own, except for Unity, when I've said I'd be happy to accommodate you - on your terms - as part of the arrangement.'

'Part of the arrangement?' Hilda looks at me, contemptuously. 'I'm not part of an arrangement.'

'Hilda….'

'I was Stanley's wife. I told you the last time you asked me, I would never come back as his mistress.' She has hardly moved her body but the anger's radiating out of her.

'I thought if Stanley and I separated, if I wasn't there at all, then once you'd had a chance to think about it, you might change your mind. Let's face it, Hilda, how you're living at the moment isn't doing anybody any good. If you go on like this you won't have just lost Stanley, you'll risk losing both the girls as well.'

'We were all right before you came along.'

'You can't blame me for your financial difficulties, Hilda.'

'Yes, I can,' she says. 'I've seen those things he bought you – bits of frippery.'

'Believe me, those weren't bought at my behest.' I feel embarrassed. Hilda knows what Stanley's like; she must do after all this time. But she blames me for catering to that side of his nature. I sit back.

'I'm sorry, Hilda. I'd hoped that we might work something out between us. I can see how terribly unsatisfactory this has been for you.'

'Unsatisfactory. Yes.' Her mouth twists in a grim smile. 'I think you had better go.' She nods at Unity who scrambles to her feet.

I get up, shuffling back the chair. The Duke of Windsor's looking crumpled and there is a skid mark from his hair-line to his chin. I glance at Hilda. Do we shake hands or am I expected to bend down and kiss her on the cheek? In the event, I don't do either. Neither seems appropriate. I loop my bag over my arm. 'I'll try and make sure that you get your payments, Hilda.'

'You'll be paying me?' she says, ironically. 'It'll be your name on the cheques, then? I suppose you'll make them out to *Mrs Spencer* and then sign them *Mrs Spencer.*'

'Unless you would rather leave it up to Stanley. You might find me more reliable.'

'Yes,' she says, almost to herself. 'I dare say.'

XII

As when I allowed myself to be persuaded into bed with Stanley, I'm aware that all this latest face-to-face with Hilda has done is to emphasize the gulf between us. We could never have been friends. It isn't only Stanley who's the sticking point. Without him, I'd have been the sort of person Hilda tolerated; not someone she loved, or even liked.

There's no point in me trying to be good, I have decided. All it is does is emphasize my failings. Goodness isn't inextricably a part of me, the way it is with Hilda. It's a piece of clothing I invest in when my wardrobe needs a boost and it is rarely made to measure. Like shoes, if they're glamorous they tend to pinch and if they're comfortable they're dowdy. And however much I'm complimented on the change they make to my appearance, when I take them off what's underneath is still the same.

I glance into the window of the house next door as I am leaving. There's a single oil lamp on the table and the room is bathed in soft light. I pause by the railings and step back. A maid is clearing dishes from the table, stacking them into a pile to carry out.

A man in tweeds with a clipped, military moustache stands with one foot against the fender. A log rolls out of the fire onto the hearth and he bends down and kicks it back before the sparks fly out and singe the carpet. Firelight shimmers on the paintings hanging from the curtain rail and flickers over the expensive raised flock wall-paper.

Why do those lives we glimpse as we are on our way to somewhere else seem so much more inviting than our own?

The man takes out his pocket watch and flips the lid back. He gives it a little shake and holds it to his ear, then tucks it back into his waistcoat pocket. The maid balances the dishes and removes the top one from the pile. I watch the man step out into the room and slip his arms around her waist. She gives a little squeal. He laughs. She tosses back her head and goes out, looping her foot around the door to close it after her. The man takes a cigar out of its box and lights it with a taper from the fire.

I've time to spare before the train leaves Paddington so I decide to walk through Belsize Park. The trees are now black skeletons, etched eerily against the dusk. Vague shapes are huddled by the railings and a young man with a dog, a scruffy terrier with scabby fur whose eyes are gummed up, asks if I can spare some change. There is a tin beside him with a few coins in the bottom. Anything will do, he says, a few pence so that he can buy his dog some food.

Once you catch someone's eye, you're lost. I rummage in my handbag. There's a shilling in the lining. True I didn't know I had it, but a shilling is a lot.

He is probably no more than twenty-one. His shirt is open and there is a scarf tied loosely round his neck. The jacket he is wearing has no buttons and there are stains down the front of it. It's obvious this has been his day and nightwear for some time. There is a rank smell coming from him.

He delves in the waistcoat pocket and takes out a woodbine. I'm still rummaging inside my bag. I've surely got a few coins somewhere. The idea that I could walk three miles to save the fare and then hand over three times what it would have cost to this man, is absurd.

'I'm sorry,' I say. 'This is all I have. I need it for a taxi at the other end.'

'A taxi?' he says with a slow smile. He has crooked teeth and when he speaks he draws the *a* out like elastic.

If I don't go now, I'll miss the train. 'All right,' I hold the shilling out, expecting him to offer me his palm so that we don't touch. But he takes it with his thumb and forefinger and squints at it as if he thinks it might be counterfeit. He smiles again. There is a hint of pity in the smile. The dog appears to know that a transaction's taken place. It lifts its leg and piddles on the pavement.

A thin stream of urine snakes across the paving-stones in my direction.

XIII

When I get back to the cottage, it's in darkness. Well, of course it is; what else did I expect, but still a bit of me was hoping that as I went past the War Memorial and caught my first glimpse of the house I'd see a light on in the porch. The weather has been cold and drizzly since the storm and it smells damp and uninviting as I hang my coat up in the scullery. This is the first time since we moved to Cookham that I've come home without knowing Dorothy would be there.

I turn all the lights on, fill the kettle and take what remains of the stale loaf out of the bin. I'll make myself a proper sandwich and a cup of cocoa, I decide, which is what I'd have done if Dorothy was here. And then I'll listen to the wireless whilst I'm eating it.

But as I'm lathering the bread with dripping, I decide I won't have cocoa after all, I'll have the sandwich with a whisky from the bottle Dorothy has left behind and maybe smoke a cigarette.

The night she left, I got through twenty cigarettes. The next day, I went down to Arkwright's and bought all the cigarettes they had in stock. I can't afford to go on living on my own; at this rate, I'll be destitute. I wish I hadn't handed over my last shilling to the young man in the park. He'll only do what I'd have done and use it to buy cigarettes or alcohol.

I wake up in the morning and the whisky bottle's empty. There are half-a-dozen cigarette stubs in the ash tray and another which has fallen off onto the table leaving a long trail of ash and a brown burn mark underneath it. I don't know what's woken me. There is a pounding in my head like a persistent drum-beat. I'm about to let my forehead sink onto the table when I realise that the pounding isn't only in my head. There's someone furiously rapping on the window. Stanley's face is pressed against the glass.

'I couldn't make you hear me. I've been outside knocking on the door for quarter of an hour.' He looks at the whisky bottle and the ash tray. 'Did you speak to Hilda?'

Normally I would have given Stanley short shrift, but we have to have this conversation some time. I go through into the kitchen. Stanley follows me. I fill the kettle, wincing at the noise the water's making as it gushes from the tap.

As Stanley's mackintosh thaws out, a faint mist starts to rise from it. I wonder whether to suggest he takes it off, but I would rather that he didn't make himself at home here.

'Yes. She wasn't having it. I'm sorry, Stanley.' I wave him towards a chair and put out cups.

'How is she?' he says.

'Not good. Maybe you can talk some sense into her. I had the impression she spends all day staring into space.' Since I was doing this myself less than a week ago, I have some sympathy for Hilda. Staring into space is not the answer, although getting drunk and leaving cigarettes to burn out in the ash tray isn't a solution either.

'I've been writing to her every day,' says Stanley, as if opening his letters constitutes a worthwhile occupation. 'Hilda doesn't always write back, but it's not because she doesn't love me.'

'Surely you can see you need to get her out of that house, Stanley.'

He stares at the patch of floor between his knees. 'I wondered whether I should take her down to Wangford,' he says. 'Wangford's where we spent our honeymoon. I've got the address of the boarding house we stayed in. Mrs Lambert – that's the woman who was running it - is still there.'

I nod. 'Worth a try.' At least it gets him out of Cookham, which fulfils the first of Dorothy's demands. 'A second honeymoon sounds just the thing'.

He's drawing with his index finger on the knot of wood next to his cup. 'There was a maize field near the boarding house,' he says. 'We walked through it, the morning after we arrived, and I remember thinking that it was a symbol of our married life together reaching out ahead of us. I longed to wander through it, scattering my *me-things* in amongst the maize.'

'Who knows, perhaps they're still there,' I say, stifling a yawn.

'Time seemed to slow down to the pace that we were walking. I felt joy between myself and everything around me. Hilda said she felt like that, too. I completed her and she completed me.'

He rambles on, his hands together and his fingers touching in an arc. I look at him. My headache's pounding in the background.

'I wrote to her that night. Twenty pages.'

'On your wedding night?'

'I wanted her to know what that day had been like for me.'

I get up. The last thing I need this morning is a blow-by-blow account of Stanley's honeymoon. 'How long would you be taking her to Wangford for?'

He shrugs. 'Two weeks?'

'Why don't you make it three?' I push the chair into the table. 'Hilda needs to get away from London. You can paint the landscape whilst you're there?' I usher him towards the door. As soon as I've got rid of him, I go in search of aspirin.

XIV

'How have you been, Dorothy?'

'Fine, thank you.' We are sitting at a table on the 1st floor of Lyons Corner House on Coventry Street, a meeting place that Dorothy has chosen. It's the first time since she left that we've met face to face. She's thinner and she has that grey look everyone who lives in London seems to have. Her cough is worse. The smog's been terrible. Apparently the warm air suddenly colliding with the cold air is what causes it. But it's the sulphur from the coal they burn that's poisoning the air. I tied a handkerchief over my mouth when I got off the train and half an hour later when I took it off you couldn't see the pattern on it for the grit. Imagine all that in your lungs.

When I ask Dorothy what she's been doing, she says she went to the rally for the latest hunger march in Hyde Park at the weekend.

'That sounds fun,' I say. No wonder she looks peaky.

'You would not believe what those men went through,' she says.

'Don't you want to take your coat off?'

She unbuttons it and slides her arms out of the sleeves. So far, a nod when she arrived is all I've had by way of an acknowledgement. 'They'd walked from Scotland, some of them, and when they got to Hyde Park they were met by mounted police with batons. They were having to tear up the railings to defend themselves.'

'Did they get what they wanted?'

'No, of course they didn't, but they do have some important people on their side.' She reaches for the tea-pot. 'H.G.Wells and E.M.Forster were amongst the speakers.'

'Wasn't Wells the one who thought it might be a solution to the unemployment problem if the South Wales miners used their slopes for growing vines?'

'The very fact that people like him came, will make a difference,' she says, pouring out a cup. 'The Labour Party wouldn't give the Union support before, because they thought it was a front for Communists.' She hooks the strainer over my cup. 'Now that Atlee and Nye Bevan have agreed they have a case, it represents a huge step forward.'

'Good.' I listen with a vague smile as she tells me police brutality is being monitored by Civil Liberties. She hasn't talked this much in ages. I wait for the talk to get around to us.

A Nippy in the regulation black dress with pearl buttons down the front and starched white pinafore, brings a selection from the pastry trolley. There's a quartet of musicians playing in the background. If she'd chosen Blackpool seafront for a meeting Dorothy could not have picked a venue less conducive to a private conversation.

A man with a loud tie on the table next to us is nervously demolishing a rock bun, crumbling it between his fingers and then licking them to garner up the crumbs. A young man in a shabby suit comes in and sits down opposite him. They exchange a few words and the boy gets up and moves on to another table.

'You know what they call this place?' I say. *'The Lily Pond'*.

She takes a sip of tea and puts the cup back in the saucer. 'Do they? Why?' She dabs the serviette against her mouth.

'It's where the *Dilly* boys come for a pick-up on a Sunday afternoon. They buy a cup of tea and then hop from one table to the next.'

'Good heavens,' she says lightly. 'And in one of Joe Lyon's restaurants. Whatever next?'

I realise she knew very well what it was known as. That was why she chose it. The boy sits down opposite a man who looks like an insurance salesman. He leans forward and says something and a moment later they get up and leave.

'It looks as if the frog has found his prince,' says Dorothy.

'The frog becomes a prince if you remember.'

'Well as long as it ends happily,' says Dorothy. 'That's all that matters, isn't it? She's toying with an almond slice. 'How's Stanley?' She rakes through the crumbs and tries the fork out on the pastry.

'He's in London. He was hoping he and Hilda could rekindle their love by returning to the village where they'd had their honeymoon, but she refused to go.'

'So Stanley is still on his own?'

'They both are. Stanley said he couldn't bear to stay with her if they were not *together*. Hilda has sent Unity to join her sister. Epsom's fast developing into a dumping-ground for Stanley's cast-off children.'

'That's not fair, Patricia. Stanley loves the girls. And so does Hilda, come to that. Why is she sending Unity away?'

'She can't cope, I suppose. Mind you, I wouldn't want to spend unlimited amounts of time with Unity.

She has a look that could freeze lava coming out of a volcano.'

Dorothy puts down the fork. She sees me glancing at the remnants of her almond slice and nods. I reach across and scoop it onto my plate. 'Thanks.'

'You're welcome,' she says, putting her plate to one side. 'What's Stanley doing now, then?'

'In the end, he asked the Rothensteins for help. He turned up on their doorstep looking like a down and out. He had used one of Shirin's nappy pins to hold the two flaps of his mackintosh together.'

She looks shocked. 'Are things that bad?'

'Of course they're not. He did spend three years in the Army; he knows how to sew a button on. The maid told him to go away or she would call the police, but Mrs Rothenstein took pity on him. I imagine she regrets it now. He's living in their spare room.'

'When you say he's living there....?'

'He's turned the room into a studio. He's working on a series of *Christ in the Wilderness*. No prizes for deducing what that's all about.'

'You're still in touch, then?'

'I can't stop him writing to me.' I drain my cup. Dorothy has finished hers. 'More tea?' I tilt the pot towards her.

'Just a splash.'

I serve her and then serve myself. I glance across the table and our eyes meet. 'What's important, surely, is that Stanley's not in Cookham anymore.'

'Important?' Dorothy picks up her serviette. 'To whom?'

'To us. Those were your terms, if you remember.'

'I said you would need to separate before I would consider coming back.'

'All right, we have.'

'Not quite. You said he writes to you.'

'That's hardly my fault.'

'No dear, as you've said on numerous occasions, none of it is your fault.'

'What I meant, is that I'm not encouraging him.'

'You could send his letters back unopened.'

'Oh come off it, Dorothy. If I did that, he'd turn up on the doorstep wanting to know why I was avoiding him.'

'But that's just it. He ought to know why you're avoiding him. You're either separated or you're not.'

'We're separated in as much as we are not cohabiting.'

'But then you never were. That might be part of what is meant by *separation*, but it's not the whole of it.' She signals to the waitress.

'Won't you come back, Dorothy?'

She reaches for her jacket. 'No dear, I don't think so.'

'What's the point of Stanley living in the Rothenstein's spare room if I'm still on my own in Cookham?' I lean forward. 'Dorothy, I'm begging you.'

A couple at a nearby table glance at us and whisper to each other.

'You had better keep your voice down if you don't want to attract attention,' Dorothy says.

'I had something else to tell you,' I blurt out. She hesitates.

'Well?'

'You remember when I had that interview with Dudley, he agreed to look at what we'd brought back from St Ives. I had a postcard from him last week. He's prepared to let us have an exhibition next year. Isn't that good news?'

She lowers herself back into her chair. 'How did he get to see the work?'

'I took some paintings from your studio. I didn't think you'd want me to pass up an opportunity like that. He's moved another artist out in order to accommodate you. That's how much he liked the pictures.'

'We could hardly have an exhibition in the gallery where Stanley shows?'

'I don't see why we shouldn't. If it does well, everyone will benefit.'

'But that's just it. We shall be more embroiled than ever. Anyway, I haven't got enough work.'

'You've got nearly eight months to prepare for it.'

She clears her throat and suddenly I know what this is all about. 'You don't have anywhere to paint. Is that it?'

'This is London, darling. People don't have studios. They live in boxes.'

'Oh for Christ's sake, Dorothy. This is ridiculous. I'm living by myself in Moor Thatch where there is a dedicated studio, now empty, and you're living in a shoe-box. If you're really so averse to living with me, let's swap. I'll live in the shoe-box.'

'Thank you but that won't be necessary.'

'Are you seriously telling me you would turn down the opportunity to show your work at Tooth's in order to uphold a principle?'

'I happen to believe it's an important principle.'

'All right, but is it really more important than your work. You must be going crazy without anywhere to paint. At present, you're worse off than Stanley. Maybe I should introduce you to the Rothensteins.'

'I think the Rothensteins have suffered enough.'

'Where are you living, out of interest?'

'I would rather not say.'

'Could it be with Dora Gibbons?'

Dora was a friend of Dorothy's when they were at the Slade. I don't know why I didn't think of it before. She is the only person Dorothy has corresponded with, outside the family. Her cheeks have turned pink so I know I'm right. I've never visited her house in Watford but since Dora lives there with her aged father, an unmarried brother and two lurchers, I imagine it would have its drawbacks for a person who liked privacy.

'I can't believe you'd say no to the offer of an exhibition that could turn our fortunes round. It's not just me you would be punishing; it's all of us. Tooth's gone out of his way to make room in the schedule because he likes the work so much. The *Bloomsberries* will be there in force and they determine everything that's happening in the art world. I reminded Duncan that he said he'd write an introduction to the catalogue. You can't back out now.'

When it's not myself I'm rooting for, I can be quite persuasive. Dorothy is wavering. She might be willing to let me go to the wall; she's willing to go there herself if needs be. But she is an artist – she won't sacrifice her work.

There is a pause. 'I'll think about it,' she says.

When she calls the next day she tells me she's thought about it and decided she's not ready to come back. The argument is heated and I end up shouting into the receiver, although Dorothy remains calm, as if she's the grown-up and it's me who's making the unreasonable demands.

'You may not feel you owe me anything,' I yell at her, 'but if you upset Dudley he could end up ditching Stanley, too!'

That brought her up short. Dorothy's relationship with Stanley is a complicated one. She feels he's been unfairly treated and now that she's made so much of sticking by her principles, she doesn't want to look as if she's sacrificing them for her career, though judging by the look of her she could be sacrificing more than that if she remains in Watford.

The next time we speak I'm careful not to lose my temper or burst into tears. I tell her Dudley is assuming that the show is on and if it's not, I'll leave it up to her to let him know.

'But he thinks it's your exhibition,' she says.

'You need paintings to put on an exhibition, Dorothy. I've done my bit in finding you a venue. I'm not having any more to do with Dudley than is strictly necessary.'

There is silence at the other end. I take a deep breath. I'm assuming that she will be paying Dora something in the way of rent, so she'll be strapped for cash. 'There's something else you ought to know. The next instalment of the mortgage on Moor Thatch is due in ten day's time. I can't afford to pay it on my own. If you're not coming back, I'll have to move out.'

There's a long pause. 'I'll put something in the post to you before the end of this week.'

'Why not bring it with you?'

'You know why. It would be wrong to make decisions based on economic reasons.'

Would it? Most of the decisions I've made in my life have been for economic reasons. Only not the one I made to live with Dorothy.

'You told me you were renting Lindworth,' she says. 'That must bring in something.'

'No one's there at present. If you don't come back I dare say I could live in it myself but then I wouldn't have an income, nor would Stanley, other than his painting and he can't support a family of two children and three adults on the strength of work he hasn't done yet.'

She sighs.

'Don't you miss Moor Thatch,' I say.

'Of course I do.'

'You haven't seen the garden recently. The hyacinths are doing wonderfully.' There's no reply. I wonder whether the receiver's swinging on its flex and Dorothy's already halfway down the road. I know that she's been ringing from a call-box. The last time she called I heard her feeding coins into the slot.

'We'll live like sisters, Dorothy. I promise not to make demands.'

If she says nothing or if she says 'No' now, I don't know what I can say to bring her back. I'll just have to accept it's over. There's a silence which seems to go on forever. I stand with my knuckles pressed against my mouth.

'If I moved back to Cookham, I'd be living in the studio,' she says. 'I want to make that clear.'

I punch the air. My mouth is gaping silently. Has Dorothy just said she's willing to come back? There is a pause. I realise she is waiting for an answer.

'Is that clear, Patricia?'

'Absolutely,' I say. I need to get off the phone so I can shriek. I feel ridiculously happy, suddenly. 'Whatever you want, Dorothy.'

Part Six
Limbo

I

A fortnight later Dorothy is back in Moor Thatch. When the cab draws up outside I don't give in to the temptation to fling open the front door and rush to meet her. I wait till she's paid the driver and the cab has driven off.

She hauls her suitcase up the path. We meet halfway and hug each other awkwardly.

'Good journey?'

'No heat in the carriages but otherwise all right.'

I try to take her suitcase but she waves me off.

There isn't a spare room at Moor Thatch; Dorothy is still insisting she'll sleep on the sofa in her studio.

'You realise you'll be breathing paint fumes in all night as well as all day.'

'I'll sleep with the window open.'

'If you do, you'll catch pneumonia.'

Because it waited so long before making an appearance, winter's come as something of a shock. The air is taut and sullen. Even in the house it's cold enough to see your own breath hanging in the air. There is a layer of thin ice on the water trough and when I look out of the kitchen window in the morning, frost is sparkling on the fields. But there is still sun, even if there isn't any warmth in it.

I let her take her own case upstairs. She stands in the doorway of the studio and casts her eye around it. Whilst she's been away I've tried to make the house attractive, running up new curtains for the downstairs windows from material I picked up at a jumble sale and washing down the walls. But this room is the way she left it. Sometimes, when the loneliness became unbearable, I slept in here myself, deliberately breathing in the paint fumes that I'm wanting to protect her from, or taking out her paintings from the rack and spreading them around the walls. But otherwise it has remained untouched, down to the brushes left to stay moist in a jar of turpentine that has long-since evaporated.

She looks round and her eyes settle on the pile of paint rags by the door.

'I've missed this room,' she says.

She's up at dawn the next day, sifting through the objects in the pantry for the items she needs for a still life. She picks out two pewter dishes and a jug.

'I've just made coffee. Will you have some?'

'Pour me out a beaker and I'll take it up with me.' She balances the pewter dishes so that she has one hand free.

'I'll bring you up a sandwich later.'

Once she's in the studio, she'll often be there all day. When she does emerge, she hasn't got the energy to have a conversation. Unlike Stanley, she has no desire to talk about her work. If I'm asked questions by potential buyers, I have to make up the answers. I know more or less where Dorothy is coming from and, having studied art myself, I speak the language. In the past I've felt neglected when she's working but now I'm just glad she's up there.

'If you leave it on the landing, I'll be out at some point,' she says. 'Have a good day.' She scoots up the stairs and clomps along the corridor. There is a pause and then the studio door slams behind her. I'm alone.

II

We carry on like this into the spring. At my insistence, Stanley's been addressing all his letters to the studio at Lindworth. There's a couple living in the house now, but they have no interest - other than a passing curiosity - about the studio. The postman puts the letters through the door and when I'm passing I call and collect them.

Stanley's had an offer from a gallery in Covent Garden that pays cash up-front for pictures and he says he's coming down to Cookham to pick up some work. Although she doesn't often go into the village, Dorothy will sometimes take a walk across the common when she's finished working and is certain to run into someone who will tell her Stanley's here. It's better if it comes from me.

At six o'clock, the studio door opens and she comes downstairs. I pour her out a whisky. 'I saw Mrs Arkwright when I went into the shop this afternoon,' I say. 'She tells me Stanley's coming down to Cookham to collect some pictures.'

I'm not sure if Dorothy's embargo on my seeing Stanley runs to an embargo on him being here at all. She is still sleeping in the room she paints in, although we've made love on three occasions, twice in what is now my bed, once in the studio.

Each time, I thought it was a breakthrough, but the next night she was back there on her own. There has been no discussion and the way she's looking at me now, as if she's never heard of Stanley, I am wondering if she's forgotten why we separated in the first place. I am on the point of saying 'You remember Stanley? He's the reason why you left me,' but it's always risky making jokes of these things.

'Has he got an exhibition coming up?' she says at last.

'Not that I know of. I believe there's a new gallery in Covent Garden: Zwemmer's. I remember Stanley mentioned them when I last saw him. They're prepared to buy work outright and pay cash for it.'

She pours an inch of water in the whisky. 'Isn't Stanley under contract to give all his work to Tooth?'

'I can't see Dudley kicking up a fuss. He'll be relieved that Stanley's made some money. It'll take the pressure off him.'

She holds up the glass to check the level. 'Don't you think his attitude might be that, after keeping Stanley's head above the water all this time, he ought at least to be consulted?'

'It would be the first break Stanley's had for months.'

She adds another splash of water to the beaker. 'I don't think you should encourage him to break his contract.'

'Me? I shan't encourage anything. I doubt we'll even meet.'

'I don't see how you can avoid it if he's here.'

'You wouldn't mind… if we ran into one another, that is?'

Dorothy tilts back her head and takes a slow gulp of the whisky. 'Since as far as I'm aware you're still his wife, you ought at least to pass the time of day.'

I'm stunned. It's typical of Dorothy to suddenly decide that what was a condition of our getting back together has become irrelevant, but without bothering to tell me, leaving me to catch up as and when I can.

'Right.' For the past months I've been pussy-footing round a topic which it would appear is not of interest to her any longer. Dorothy's so single-minded when she's working, nothing else exists. It's possible not only that she has forgotten why she left me, but that she's forgotten that she did.

'It wasn't Stanley I was taking issue with, Patricia,' she says, as if she has read my mind. 'It's your behaviour, not his, that's the problem.'

I nod. I'm not in the mood to have an argument. 'How is the painting going?'

She smiles: 'Rather well.' It's rare for Dorothy to own up that her work is going well, which must mean that it's going very well indeed. Those months of enforced idleness in Watford must have been a blessing in disguise as far as she's concerned.

'That's good.'

She lumbers over to the window and stands staring out onto the garden. There's a full moon with clouds scudding over it. The outlines of the trees are etched against the sky. An owl hoots and a second or two later there's an answering 'twit twoo' from Quarry Woods.

She turns and holds her glass out. 'Put another splash in there, dear, would you?'

III

When I next see Stanley he looks chastened. Dudley, on discovering that he'd been selling work behind his back to Zwemmer, wrote a letter threatening to withdraw the weekly cheques he has been sending. Stanley's having to go back to Dudley on his knees and promise that in future all his work will go through him.

'Apparently, when Dudley asked to buy back two of Stanley's pictures, Zwemmer charged him three times what he'd paid for them.'

'Ouch,' Dorothy says. 'Still, you can't blame Zwemmer. Stanley had no right to take his work there in the first place.' She's on Tooth's side, since he's now her dealer, too.

A month before her exhibition she has eighteen paintings ready. She leaves me to sign them. As things stand, we can't afford to frame more than a dozen and that will depend on Dudley selling Stanley's latest painting. It's as well that Stanley doesn't know we need his landscapes to fund Dorothy's still lifes.

She props a painting up against the wall and stands back so that she can see it properly. 'I'm not sure whether to put that one in or not.'

I glance at it. 'Yes, put it in.'

'That will be nineteen. Didn't you say twelve?'

'We'll get an estimate from Bourlet. Maybe they would be prepared to offer us a discount if we put in more.'

'Right then,' says Dorothy. She's taking it for granted which of us will be negotiating for the discount.

I come back from an excursion to the post office to find out what it will cost to crate up and deliver fifteen paintings and discover Dorothy hunched over at the kitchen table with the newspaper spread out in front of her. She growls.

'What is it?' I'd stopped bothering to keep abreast of world events since learning that Felicia had died. I felt I had enough to cope with on the home front.

'Hitler's made another land-grab.'

'What's he taken this time?'

'Part of Austria.'

Oh well, I think, At least it isn't Dorset or the Cornish Riviera.

'Why would that affect us?' I pick up the paper. 'Look, it says here the *Sudetenland* is mainly German.'

'Liverpool is mainly Irish. It's still part of England.' She gets up and reaches for the biscuit tin. I watch her prize the lid off. Sometimes if the news is bad, we'll see off a whole packet of digestives. 'Hitler says he's reuniting Germans with their homeland.' She holds out the tin. I take one. 'What about the Austrians who'd rather not be *reunited*? What if Ireland did take over Liverpool so that the Irish felt at home? What would that mean for Liverpudlians?'

Now that she's finished working for her exhibition, Dorothy is at a loose end. She can now give over all her time to worrying about the international situation. I slip off my coat. I couldn't find it in my heart to care that much if Ireland did decide to annex Liverpool.

'I still don't see why everybody's making such a fuss. Can't we leave them to sort it out?'

'That seems to be the attitude of our Prime Minister.'

'With whom you naturally do not agree.' I take the tin and tip the biscuits out onto a plate. When Dorothy bit into it, the biscuit crumbled down her cardigan. I've swept the kitchen once today.

'It won't stop there. Before you know it everyone will be embroiled. The Czechs have an alliance with the French. If Germany attacks France we'll have no choice but to pitch in.'

'Why would Germany attack France, knowing that?'

'Because their leader is a nasty little bully boy who's punching way above his weight and he won't stop till someone blacks his eye. Unfortunately, it'll take a man with more clout than the haberdashery assistant to do that.'

The 'haberdashery assistant' was how Dorothy referred to Neville Chamberlain. Compared with heavyweights like Hitler, Franco, Mussolini and the man they called the 'Russian Bear', the little man with the umbrella and the bowler hat looked like an understudy for a Chaplin film.

The latest one we'd seen was *Modern Times*. It was another one of Chaplin's silent movies. On the whole, I found the 'Talkies' disappointing. Actors you had fancied for their looks invariably turned out to have voices that were too high, too posh, too rough or just not what you'd expected.

I loved all the Chaplin films and this one had looked promising. The opening showed a flock of sheep dissolving into crowds of workers hurrying through factory gates. When we saw Charlie Chaplin stretched out on a giant cog wheel in the factory, I thought it was meant to be a joke but no one laughed.

'What did you think of it?' said Dorothy when we came out.

'It's not as funny as his other films,' I said.

She sighed: 'Sometimes, Patricia, I despair of you.'

IV

When Chamberlain leaves on another diplomatic mission to try and negotiate a settlement with Hitler, he's boo-ed at the airport, though in Germany they wave the British flag and yell 'Heil Chamberlain'.

'He's certainly gone down well with the Germans,' Dorothy says.

'Why are they so keen on him?'

'Because each time he pays a visit to the Führer he gives up another piece of land that isn't his.'

'The Duke of Windsor has been boasting that he's stopped the British acting against Germany.'

'The little worm,' says Dorothy. 'They should have locked him in the Tower when they had the chance.'

This time, however, the proposals Germany puts forward are rejected. *Sergeant-Major* Arkwright, now a paid-up member of the ARP, is given the green light to make the necessary preparations in case there's a war. What seemed too far away to matter suddenly feels very close indeed.

Within a fortnight, Cookham is transformed with trenches, sandbags outside public buildings, and the trunks of trees along the roads out of the village white-washed in anticipation of the black-out.

'Sergeant-Major Arkwright seems to think we're on a par with Chelsea when it comes to risk of aerial bombardment,' Dorothy says, acidly.

'We're not that far from London, Dorothy.'

Although we haven't talked about it, I am wondering whether Dodo's exhibition will take place at all now. Most of London's Art is going in the opposite direction.

'The Tate Gallery's selected fifty-five of its most treasured paintings to remove to safety,' I say, leafing through *The Times*.

'Is Stanley's *Resurrection* one of them?'

'It doesn't say.' I wonder if they'll show the same concern over the artist as they're showing for his work.

In *Picture Post* there is a photograph of elephants from London Zoo linked trunk to tail as they set out to walk the thirty miles to Whipsnade. People gather at the roadside cheering.

Dorothy leans over. 'Does it say what's happening to the other creatures in the Zoo?'

'They're boiling the Black Widows and Tarantulas and cutting off the heads of all the snakes except the giant python. If its cage is wrecked, they say the cold will make it sleepy.'

'That's all right, then,' Dorothy says, shuddering theatrically. 'I dare say if you're being bombed, a poisonous snake or two is neither here nor there.'

She seems much calmer now that things are moving, whereas I'm still reeling from the shock of having to accept that if there is a war, it might affect me, too.

When gas masks are distributed, we queue alongside everybody else to learn how they are fitted and discover they are all the same size. What is worse, however, is that there are none for children under four. This leads to tearful and occasionally hysterical exchanges as young mothers are advised to wrap their babies in a blanket and make for the nearest gas-proof shelter if there is a raid.

The leaflets that begin arriving through the door contain advice on how to build an air raid shelter in the garden. One of the mechanics at the garage in the High Street spends an afternoon erecting it. It looks like a truncated poly-tunnel, dark and poky with a corrugated iron roof and a concrete floor. It's dug into the ground so that you step down into it, but even in the middle there's no room to stand up.

'You would think they might have put a window in it,' I say.

'What do you suppose would happen to the window if a bomb dropped?'

'Can't we move it farther down the garden?'

'Next to where the compost is at present?' Dorothy says mildly. 'Won't you find it rather smelly?'

'We're not likely to be gardening if we're in the shelter.'

'True. It takes a stretch of the imagination to assume we'll be alive at all.'

'Oh don't be such a party-pooper, Dorothy.' It frightened me when she was in this mood and she'd been in it now for weeks.

'A party-pooper?' Dorothy's tongue moves around the inside of her mouth as if it's looking for a light switch in the dark. 'Is there a party going on? You should have said.'

Another leaflet offers 'Opportunities for Women' if they volunteer for service. I was rather taken with the uniform, but Dorothy insisted that she wasn't taking orders from the likes of Sergeant-Major Arkwright. 'And I'm not about to join a knitting circle, thank you very much,' she says. So that's that.

But one leaflet which arrives is not so easy to dismiss. It's asking how many evacuees we would be able to take in. There's talk of bringing Jewish children out of Germany and if war comes they will evacuate the youngest children from the East End.

If we took in refugees, the only room that we could put them in was Dodo's studio. The idea that she would give up her private space to strangers was unthinkable, but the idea that we could carry on as normal in the face of all that horror, was unthinkable as well.

'Perhaps we could adapt another room,' I say.

'Do you mean turn the scullery into a bedroom; make a bed up in the sink, perhaps? Why not? The draining board could double as a bedside table.'

'I'm just trying to find a solution.'

She nods grudgingly. We both know it's the studio or nothing.

'I heard Ovey's Farm was offering to take three children from the East End.'

'So did I. George Hatch is specifying that they must be male and older than thirteen. Why's that, I wonder.'

'You think George is looking for cheap labour on the farm?' It wasn't only Dorothy who questioned George's motives. What concerned me was that if we took in children, they might question ours.

'There's always Lindworth,' Dorothy said. 'You could fit in several families there.'

'We've only just found somebody to take it over, Dorothy, and at the moment they're our only source of income. Anyway, I can't see Hilda wanting to remain in London with the children, if the situation worsens. We might have to turn the tenants out of Lindworth, so that they can have it.'

'It's ironic, isn't it, that after all the effort you went to in order to acquire that house, you might have no choice but to give it back.'

'The point is, Dorothy, that I do have the choice. If Hilda and the children want to move back into Lindworth, they will have to ask me.'

Dorothy gives me one of her long looks. She shakes out the paper she is reading. And that's when she sees it.

'Oh, dear God.'

'What is it?'

'Barcelona's fallen.' She lifts up the paper so it's level with her eyes. She can't believe what's printed there.

'The Government's decided to acknowledge Franco.' Dorothy sits back. 'That means the end of Spain, then. Poor Felicia. It seems she died for nothing.' She takes off her glasses, rubbing at the crease between her eyebrows with her middle finger. If I didn't know her better, I could almost think it wasn't Spain that she was mourning for but its first casualty. 'At least, before, her mother could take comfort from her daughter having made a contribution to the cause of freedom.' Dorothy picks up the paper, loops the glasses on her nose again and then as if she can't bear to read any more she tosses it aside.

I turn the newspaper towards me. 'Did you stay in contact with Felicia after we left the Slade?'

'I got a letter every now and then.'

Which meant Felicia would have received a letter every now and then from Dorothy. 'You never said.'

'The letters were political, not personal. I didn't think you would be interested.' She waves a hand towards the newspaper. 'There'll be a bloodbath. The two sides will massacre each other.'

'Hasn't Franco won the war in any case if Barcelona's fallen?' I say.

'It's the fact of us legitimising it that's shameful,' Dorothy says. 'It's a diplomatic coup for Mosley's *biff-boys*. He's already saying Britons won't die to support a Jewish quarrel.'

'Is the war in Spain a Jewish quarrel?'

'No, the war in Germany is shaping up to be one, though.'

'We're not at war with Germany.'

'We will be now,' says Dorothy.

V

The possibility of war is uppermost in everybody's mind, but at least at the moment people are still going out. The exhibition at his gallery will go ahead as planned, says Dudley.

I'd designed a business card after the exhibition at Lefevre's, which I gave to anyone who might be useful to us. Dudley naturally has his own list, so between us we've got most of London's glitterati at the private view of Dodo's show.

The Rothensteins ignore me. Rumour has it they hold me responsible for foisting Stanley onto them. His visit lasted four months. He would probably still be there if Jas hadn't found a bed-sit for him in Swiss Cottage and contributed towards the rent. The Rothensteins leant him some furniture and other friends chipped in. He's always managed to pull in the punters when he puts his mind to it.

I realised from the way heads turned towards me as I came into the gallery, that everybody knew I was the woman Stanley Spencer had divorced his wife for. Naturally, the *Bloomsberries* are delighted by the scandal. They don't care what anybody does as long as no one has a hissy-fit about it. They might not care much for Stanley – Duncan Grant confided that they found him rather 'quaint' - but they adore the notion of us all existing in a great big stew.

I catch a brief glimpse of Vanessa Bell and am about to go across to her when it occurs to me that she's not looking at me; she is glassy-eyed. Then I remember hearing that her son had been another casualty in Spain.

I ought to go across and speak to her, but I can't face it. I see Eddie Marsh who has just finished talking to a couple keen to canvas his opinion on one of the smaller paintings. As he turns away, I catch his eye. He gives a little wave and I make my way over to him. I know that, whatever he thinks privately, he'll feel obliged to be polite to me. Somebody told me he was Winston

Churchill's private secretary, so he'd meant it when he said he was a diplomat.

'Patricia.' He gives me a kiss on both cheeks. 'Are you here alone?' I nod. 'How's Stanley? I heard there had been a fall-out between him and Dudley.' Eddie looks at me, inquisitively.

'It was a misunderstanding. Stanley heard that Zwemmer's was prepared to pay its artists cash advances. Stanley took some pictures in and Zwemmer bought them. Dudley took exception. It's a pity Stanley didn't ask me first; I'd have advised him not to do it.'

'Aren't you acting as his business manager?' He gives me an oblique look. Am I acting as his wife is what he really wants to know.

'I handle the accounts. Whatever anybody thinks of Stanley's work, he's not a genius with money, I'm afraid. He's also fallen out with The Academy again. The President has threatened to have Stanley prosecuted for some drawings he thinks are obscene. It looks as if he might have to resign again.'

'I must admit I thought that *The Beatitudes* were dreadful and I told him so. I've never liked art that was purely self-expression. They were not up to his usual standard. He'd have recognised that later. He was suffering at the time and painting was the only way he could find out of it. He tried to justify them but you can't talk your way into art. It doesn't work like that.'

He must have seen the couple licking one another's tongues in *The Beatitudes*. Another drawing featured women bound and carried on men's shoulders with their heads behind so that the men would not be forced to listen to their protests. I'm embarrassed even thinking of the drawings when I'm standing next to this urbane, sophisticated man. I hope he hasn't recognised me as the model for them.

'Did you tell him not to show them?'

Eddie takes his cigarette out of the holder. 'I persuaded him to put them on one side and come back to them later when he wasn't so emotionally attached to them. If he had seen those, Munnings would have had a field day. Fortunately at the moment he's preoccupied with Eric Gill's supposedly disreputable sculptures for the BBC's new building. You'll have heard about that rumpus, I expect?'

'I think the whole of London has.'

'I used to walk through Portland Place whilst Gill was working on the scaffolding. He'd always worn a smock and sandals in his studio and didn't see why he should change the habit of a life-time just because he happened to be working fifteen foot above a London street. A member of the public, passing underneath, observed that he did not seem to be wearing underpants. That would have been enough for Munnings, but when Gill unveiled the figure he'd been carving, there was outrage at the generous amount of stone he'd given over to the genitals. There's a campaign afoot to have them filed down.' His eyes twinkle with amusement.

I imagine Dorothy at Moor Thatch with a cup of cocoa, listening to the wireless, wondering how it's going here. Not for the first time I think my role is the more attractive one.

Of course, the conversation's principally about the offer Hitler's just made, to attend an international conference. Is it a climb-down or a ploy to gain time? I'm surprised that almost everybody seems to think a settlement is possible and that the worst thing that could happen is for us to go to war. When I ask Eddie Marsh he says it's true that our defences would be smashed and that diplomacy could buy us time, though Churchill isn't of the same opinion and of course the Czechs feel let down. 'I believe there are three horses in the race', he tells me: 'peace with honour, peace without it, or a bloody war. The first is not an option any longer and the other two are neck and neck.'

I am about to ask him what a war would mean for people like us, but then Dudley interrupts us. They've begun to clear away the glasses. A quick tally of the red dots on the pictures and the look on Dudley's face suggest the exhibition has gone well.

'We've practically sold out,' he says. 'Two pictures are reserved and the Pryce-Carpenters are coming back tomorrow for another look. I'd better book you for the next show before other galleries get wind of you.'

There's half a bottle of wine on the table in between us and I'm wondering whether I'm allowed to help myself. As I'm deliberating, Dudley puts a cork in it. He's generous on many levels but not when he's dishing out the wine. Since I paid for the whisky I'd be interested to know where that's gone.

He takes down the ledger from the shelf behind him. It's the same one he consulted when I came to ask him whether he would front the bill for renovating Lindworth. He leafs through it, pausing to write something, and then taps the pen nib on the page. 'Forgive me asking, but are you and Stanley still together?'

'We collaborate. I'm still in charge of the financial side.'

'So any money goes into a joint account?'

Too late, I catch his drift. I suddenly see everything that Dorothy and I have made tonight evaporating into the elusive bubble that is Stanley's debt. This is the downside of exhibiting in Dudley's gallery. He holds the purse-strings and from what I know of him, he isn't going to let go of them. I have a joint account with Dorothy, but as he thinks that she's my 'sitting-tenant', Dudley's hardly likely to agree to paying into that.

I think how much I'd like to set light to the wick that I imagine running through the centre of that smug face, watching as the smooth flesh start to melt and sag.

'It would be nice to think not all the profits from this evening would be swallowed up,' I say.

'Still, getting Stanley back on track financially has got to be our first priority,' says Dudley, as if it's for Stanley's benefit and not his own. 'You realise that the contract stipulates that any work you do goes through me. Stanley seemed to be a bit confused on that score.'

'You mean his approach to Zwemmer's. I think Stanley saw it simply as a way of making money.'

'But in fact it turned out to be rather costly.' Dudley says it lightly, but I can detect an underlying petulance. 'I don't expect to have to buy work back from other galleries.'

'Quite.'

He smiles: 'I just thought I'd better point that out.'

VI

This time I wasn't able to elicit an advance from Dudley and I end up walking back towards the underground instead of waiting for a cab. I'd been invited to join Eddie Marsh for dinner at his club but, by the time I got away from Dudley, he'd made his apologies and left.

The streets are quiet and there's a tension in the air as if the city's bracing itself for the onslaught. As I walk down Piccadilly, I see sand-bags piled up in the courtyard of The Royal Academy and homeless people curled up in the trenches in Green Park.

There is a humming in the distance and a shadow looms out of the darkness. It turns out to be a crocodile of women and small children coming down the street towards me, spilling out across the road. The children carry small attaché cases made of cardboard and have labels tied around their wrists. They trudge behind each other in a line, the women chattering to one another in a foreign tongue, the children silent, clutching one another's hands. And then I see that they're accompanied by priests and I remember reading that four thousand refugees from Spain had come into Southampton from Bilbao on a boat called *the Habana*, lying head to tail along the bulkheads like sardines. They're obviously exhausted but the women have gay, coloured handkerchiefs around their necks and they are carrying bright blue enamel kettles filled presumably with gifts from charity. They take no notice of me and walk on obliviously, as if tramping through the streets of London is an everyday event for them.

I wait until they've passed. There's a young woman with a baby bringing up the rear and on an impulse I run back and grasp her arm. She turns on me with that defiant look the persecuted have when it's their only weapon and puts up her hand to ward me off. I press a pound note into it. She looks alarmed.

My eyes slide sideways to the baby and she pulls the shawl over its head. Does she imagine that I'm offering to buy the baby? She turns, sees she's being left behind and runs to catch up with the others, glancing back over her shoulder once she's safely reunited with them. They walk on.

The thought of being homeless, terrifies me. I attribute it to being constantly uprooted as a child. My father's Army postings meant I saw more of the world than other children my age, but I was too young to turn this into an advantage. All it meant for me was having constantly to reinvent myself. When I see other homeless people, I feel tearful and I overcompensate, like Freddy Ashworth, with misguided acts of generosity.

It's after ten o'clock when I get back to Moor Thatch. I am wondering how to break the news to Dorothy that although her show has exceeded everybody's expectations, we are likely to be just as hard up as we were before. From what I know of Dorothy, she'll be more philosophical than I am at this moment. She won't fret. She gets her satisfaction from the work she does whereas mine comes from the rewards, rewards that having dangled tantalisingly within reach have been snatched away again.

She's spread out on the sofa. I could hear her hacking as I came across the common. This place is so damp that sometimes you could wring the curtains out. It's worse when she's been working for an exhibition. Once she stops, she is completely drained.

I drop onto my knees beside her. 'Darling are you all right.'

She nods. There's a handkerchief pressed up against her mouth. She screws it up inside her fist. I'm terrified that one day when she takes the handkerchief away, I shall see blood on it.

'What can I get you? Water?'

She nods. I fill up a beaker from the sink. She takes a few sips.

'See what happens when you try to do without me? You spend two nights in that horrible hotel in

Maidenhead and three months camping out with Dora Gibbons and you come back with your health in tatters.'

She puts down the beaker but her hand's not steady and I catch it just in time. She grunts. 'Well fielded.' She lies back and folds her hands across her stomach. 'Was it fun this evening? Tell me all about it.'

'We did well. Twelve pictures sold. Another two have a reserve on them.'

I wonder whether to tell Dorothy about the refugees I saw and then decide to leave that for another day. We are meant to be celebrating, after all.

I put the beaker down: 'The Rothensteins are still recovering from Stanley's visit. Rothenstein told someone Stanley had a tendency to set his easel up in any room he found himself in and Elizabeth, his wife, was getting rather twitchy. His reluctance to take baths was something else she took exception to. As someone pointed out, there aren't too many baptisms in Stanley's pictures. At least now they know how difficult it is to live with him.'

'The Rothensteins don't have an obligation to him, though, whereas you do.'

I get up. When I've been out and left Dorothy alone, we often find ourselves at odds with one another when I come back.

'Dorothy, you were the one insisting that I leave him.'

'I was simply pointing out that you would have to choose between us.'

'All right. I chose you. There's no need to keep on going on about it.'

'And that you were not just free to choose, but free to take the consequences.'

'Sometimes, Dorothy, you sound like a headmistress.'

'Do I, dear? I think I'd probably have made a good one, though I wouldn't have wanted too many pupils like you.'

'I expect you would have found out how to keep us all in order.'

'I'm not even sure I've managed to keep you in order.'

I spread out my hands and step back: 'Look at me, I'm all compliance.'

'Mmm. I wonder why that makes me feel uneasy.' She hoists herself up onto her feet. 'I think I'll go to bed, dear, now you're back.'

'You know you didn't have to wait up.'

'I know, but I didn't want you coming back here after such a glittering occasion and discovering the house in darkness and no one to welcome you.'

'It wasn't all that glittering. One private view is very like another.'

'Is it? My experience is limited, thank goodness.'

'You know if your work takes off, the truth is certain to come out eventually.'

She shrugs. 'I don't see why it should.'

'You must want recognition.'

'If the work is well received, that's all I need.'

I take a deep breath. 'That's as well because it looks as if the lion's share of the profits from tonight will go to paying off the loans that Dudley's given Stanley. I did try to argue for the two things to be separate, but he wasn't passing up the opportunity to get some of it back.'

'So now we're all supporting Stanley. Ah well, I hope he appreciates the sacrifice.'

She is about to close the door behind her. 'Dorothy?' She turns. 'You know tomorrow is our anniversary.'

'You don't say? Anniversary of what?'

'That evening after we had graduated from the Slade, when we decided we would spend our lives together.'

She makes a pretence of thinking. 'Mmm. I do remember vaguely.'

'It was twenty years ago.'

'Good heavens, how time flies.'

'You don't regret it, do you?'

'Not a bit. Although the last five years have had their ups and downs.' She throws her cardigan across her shoulders.

'Dorothy.'

'Yes?'

'Won't you come and sleep in my room?'

'I'm afraid my cough would be a nuisance. I've not slept well recently.'

'The fumes those paints give off are poisoning your lungs.'

'You're worrying unnecessarily.'

'I'm not.'

'That's why you don't want me to go on sleeping in the studio…you think my health will suffer?'

'If you don't come back, *my* health will suffer.'

'How's that?'

'I can't live like this. I thought when you returned to Moor Thatch, we would be a couple like we were before.'

'You can't go back, Pet. We can never be the way we were before. Officially you would be guilty of adultery if you and I slept in the same bed.'

'We slept in the same bed on the honeymoon. And afterwards.'

'But then I didn't realise you and Stanley were an item.'

'We have never been an item.'

Dorothy picks up her cardigan and drapes it carefully across her arm: 'In that case, you're married in name only.'

'But that's what I've always said.'

'And it would be a simple matter, therefore, to divorce him.'

I'm not sure if it's a statement or a question. It's said in her usual quiet, dead-pan voice, but she is looking at me keenly and I realise that the silence is acquiring a significance.

I'm hoping my voice won't betray me. It's as if she's chosen to attack me from a different angle without giving me an opportunity to regroup my defences. I need time to think.

'Divorcing Stanley would be tantamount to owning up that we should never have been married in the first place,' I say.

'With respect, I think we've all arrived at that conclusion.'

'It's not something Stanley would agree to. He would fight it and the last thing we need is the hassle of a drawn-out legal wrangle. Lawyers are expensive.'

She nods. 'I expect you're right.' She pats my arm. 'Goodnight dear.' She yawns. 'Sleep well.'

She picks up her book and turns away. I hear her climb the wooden stairs up to the landing and a moment later her door clicks shut after her.

Although it's not the first time Dorothy has brought the word 'divorce' into the conversation, it's the first time she's appeared to be suggesting it as a condition of our getting back together. Just as Hilda won't go back to Stanley whilst he's married to another woman, Dorothy is now implying that she won't come back to me whilst I am married to him.

The idea of cutting loose from Stanley altogether, ought to come as a relief and at this stage might come as a relief to him too, though he's not suggested it. His fear is that if Hilda still refuses to accept him, he'll have lost us both. My fear is similar in that I question whether Dorothy is ever really going to come back and if she doesn't and I've sacrificed the only chip I have to bargain with, I shall be powerless and on my own.

Whilst I'm still married to him, Stanley is a weapon in my arsenal. Notwithstanding the frustrations, I have access to so many things I wouldn't otherwise have had, the opportunity to pass for normal being one of them.

If I were honest, I might have confessed to Dodo that I liked the idea of belonging to another human being, even somebody like Stanley. Being married made me feel safe for the first time in my life. He worships me and no one's ever worshipped me before. Occasionally men said they did, but you knew even as they said it that it wasn't true. In conflict with the urge to give up everything and throw my lot in with the only person I have ever really loved, some instinct urges me to *Hold on. Why should it be either/or? Why opt for less if you can have more?*

Although she would struggle to survive without her whisky, Dorothy would get by in a monastery as long as she was given paints and told that she could decorate the walls. In that sense, she's like Stanley so I don't know why she's so antagonistic to the idea of me staying married to him.

VII

I decide to wait for the result of Chamberlain's attempts to find a settlement before continuing to try and find one on my own behalf. If there's a war, we shall have other things to think about. As terrifying as the prospect is, it would force Dorothy to call a truce. You can't conduct a war on two fronts, not unless you're Hitler.

This time, when he lands at Munich there is no reception to mark Chamberlain's arrival. No one seems to be expecting anything to come out of the mission so when he returns twelve hours later with his piece of paper, he is greeted as a hero. Somebody suggests that his umbrella ought to be dismantled and the fragments sold as relics. Forty thousand letters, most of them congratulatory, flood into Downing Street.

The ARP is put on hold and when I call in at the village stores, I find the Sergeant-Major trying to chip black paint off his windows with a chisel. Every time the shop door opens, flakes are swept up in the draft and settle on the sleeves of customers so that when they emerge they look as if they've just walked through the back door of a crematorium. He's not a happy man. The truth is, Sergeant-Major Arkwright couldn't wait to go to war again.

When I get back to Moor Thatch, Dorothy is taking cuttings from the blue Kingfisher daisies in the garden. Is it a coincidence, I wonder, that the latter also happen to go by the name *Felicia*? She's planting them in flower-pots lined up along the trestle table in the yard. At least this indicates that she is planning to be here next year.

The sandbags are still piled against the back wall of the cottage. 'Couldn't we get rid of these now that the war's off?' I say.

'I would leave the sandbags where they are, if I were you,' says Dorothy. She lifts the tiny green leaves of the cutting whilst she presses the earth gently in around it.

'But they look so awful and we're always tripping over them.'

'I'm sure they'll come in useful.'

'What about the Anderson?'

'We'll keep that, too.'

'You're worse than Sergeant-Major Arkwright. He still thinks there'll be a war before the year's out.'

'Much as it grieves me to admit it, Sergeant-Major Arkwright's probably correct,' says Dorothy. She shakes the loose earth from her hands and tilts her head towards the door. 'A letter's come for you.'

I follow her into the scullery. The letter's lying on the draining board. It's been addressed to 'Mrs Spencer' which is one of Stanley's eccentricities. He introduces me as *Mrs Spencer* to his friends and colleagues as if I'm the wife of someone else. What is he doing, writing to me here?

I scan the contents. 'Stanley says that Dudley's furious because I put in an expenses claim for framing costs after the exhibition.'

'You sent him the bill from Bourlet's?'

'How else were we going to break even?'

'£125! God above, Patricia. I'm surprised the poor man didn't have a heart-attack.'

'All right, perhaps I should have asked him just to take the framing costs into account, instead of sending him the bill.'

'That would have been more diplomatic.' Dorothy kicks off her Wellingtons.

'I also charged him for the whisky I bought for the exhibition.'

Dorothy lets out a guffaw.

'It was worth a try. He's so mean, he was putting corks back in half empty bottles at the private view.'

'He's lucky he's not bankrupt after all these months of bailing Stanley out.'

'He's angling to take charge of the accounts. I'd like to see him make a better job of it.'

'You said yourself it felt odd writing cheques to Hilda. Wouldn't it be a relief to let it go?'

'If Dudley does assume responsibility for Stanley's finances, it means that he'll have access to the bank accounts. He wouldn't have to go back far to see what Stanley spent on jewellery and lingerie when we were courting, nor how many cheques he's made out to me since.'

She looks at me askance.

'How do you think I paid the coal man when he came last week? I also settled the account we'd run up at the butchers. Whilst I'm married, I can do that legally.'

She runs her hands under the tap and dries them on the towel. I turn away, assuming that the conversation's at an end, and go through to the living-room.

'It's not much of a reason to stay married,' she calls after me. 'I think I might prefer to be divorced, wear Long Johns and a vest and give up eating meat.'

VIII

'What is it, Stanley?'

It's the first time in weeks that I've seen Stanley. Yesterday I got a telephone call from him asking whether we could meet. I'm wondering what he's got to say that's so important he can't say it on the phone. The way he's ambling up and down outside the station, kicking up the gravel with his shoe, it's obvious he has something on his mind.

'We haven't seen you down here for some time,' I say.

'No, I've been living in a bed-sit Jas found for me in Swiss Cottage.'

I wait for him to continue but he stands there easing the mud off one shoe with the other. 'So what are you doing here?' I prompt.

'I had a talk with Dudley last week. He's asked whether you could see your way to cutting your allowance from three pounds to two.'

So that's what it's about. The bastard. 'Sorry, Stanley, I'm afraid not. I appreciate that money's tight, but Dorothy and I have got to live.'

His mouth sets in a sulky line. I've no doubt it was Dudley who suggested Stanley ought to tell me face to face what they'd cooked up. 'I don't mind paying you and Hilda an allowance, but I don't see why I should support her,' he says.

'As things stand, you're not supporting anyone. A rabbit couldn't live on what you're giving me.'

'You've got rent coming in from Lindworth. That's what Dudley says.'

'Well what about you. Your last exhibition did well.'

Stanley rubs his eyes. 'It did but it was like the last one; by the time I'd paid off Dudley, I got less than half of it. And now the tax authorities are onto me again.'

I stare. 'What is it this time?'

'I forgot to send a cheque last month.'

I roll my eyes. 'I warned you they'd be on your back if you defaulted on the payments.'

'I can't pay them what I haven't got. The bills are coming in from everywhere.'

'At least you're selling what you paint now.'

Stanley folds his arms across his chest. 'I've painted Cookham upside down and inside out, Patricia.'

'You've no other option if you want to clear your debts. If Dudley wants to argue over my allowance, he will have to get in touch with me himself. I don't think you appreciate the work involved in renting out a property. It's me who has to do the laundry and make sure repairs are carried out and that the tenants are behaving themselves. It's not easy, Stanley.'

He is chewing at the inside of his cheek. 'I think he's notified the bank already,' he says.

'You mean he's not even had the courtesy to tell me in advance! I'm meant to be in charge of your accounts!"

'He's been quite busy. He's persuaded my solicitor to take a painting rather than put in a bill. That helped. Since almost all my income comes through Dudley and since you and I are living separately, he's suggested he takes over.'

I draw breath. I feel as if the rug has suddenly been whipped away from underneath me. 'It would have been nice to have been notified of these negotiations, Stanley.'

'I'm just telling you what Dudley said. He's been in touch with Hilda and arranged for her to put her work into a couple of mixed exhibitions to bulk out her income.'

'Maybe he can find a way for me to bulk out mine.'

'I'll ask him, shall I?'

'No, don't bother. You can tell him that since we're officially still married and officially I'm still your business manager, whatever he's not paying you directly will still go through me. Don't look at me like that. We can't both be in charge of your accounts and I'm the one who's been negotiating for you with the tax authorities.'

He knocks the knuckles of his right hand on his forehead. 'I can't think with all this pressure on me.'

I bunch my fist over his and lower it, allowing it to rest inside my hand. I must be careful here. I don't want Stanley thinking Dudley is the port and I'm the storm.

'You're lucky to have someone like me acting for you, Stanley. Don't you think it's better that we keep it in the family? Bringing Dudley in is just confusing things.' I press his hand against his side. 'Leave it to me. All you need do is paint.'

'There's no point if I can't choose what to paint.'

'There's every point. You can go back to painting what you want when this is over.'

'I'll be dead by then,' says Stanley, bitterly.

'Of course you won't,' I say, more gently. 'This is just a blip. In five years, you'll be able to put all of it behind you.'

'Dudley thinks I ought to write my own biography. He thinks it would be good to get it off my chest and it would help to publicise my work.'

My blood runs cold. It's bad enough that Stanley's friends know what's been going on, without the whole world knowing. 'I'd be careful what you say about us, Stanley.'

He frowns. 'I shall only tell the truth.'

'I would think twice before you do that, too.'

'I thought you wanted me to make some money.'

'Stanley, I would only need to walk down Regent Street in my suspenders and a see-through blouse to make some money. There are limits to how far one is prepared to go.'

'But I like writing. I'd enjoy it.' He looks innocently at me.

I am wondering what he's written in the diary I so recklessly suggested he use as a vehicle for his frustrations. Stanley is the sort of person who should be discouraged from expressing himself other than on canvas, although even there some form of censorship ought to apply.

'You haven't started it yet?'

'I've put down some thoughts. I'm only on page sixty so far. It'll run to several thousand pages when I've finished.'

'Several thousand pages?' Like the *Church of Me*, I realise suddenly that this will almost certainly turn out to be another of those projects, lovingly conceived and nourished in the hot-house atmosphere of Stanley's mind, which is unlikely to survive outside the womb of his imagination.

'Well, good luck with that.' I turn to walk away. It's started raining and just now there are more pressing matters on my mind.

First Dorothy starts nudging me towards divorce, now Dudley puts his oar in. Stanley's not alone in feeling that the world's against him. The idea that I might lose control of his affairs entirely is disturbing and not only for the obvious reasons. Stanley is my husband. I feel I have rights of ownership where he's concerned. This is the kind of attitude that Dorothy despises so it takes a lot for me to own up that although ten minutes in his company can leave me gibbering, as things stand I need Stanley more than he needs me.

I'm wondering what he'll say about me in his memoirs. I'll have to persuade him that I'm more than just his business manager: I am his friend. We are still married after all.

I know what Dudley's game is. He sees himself as a patron nurturing a wayward genius and he thinks that's how Stanley will present him in his book. He won't. The only person who'll come out of Stanley's memoirs with a halo will be Stanley. Well, and Elsie, possibly. She has been sanctified already. He thinks if he tells the truth, he can't be criticised. He doesn't realise that the truth depends on who is looking at it.

As I cross the road to Arkwright's stores, I realise I am muttering to myself. I can't remember what it is that I've come in for. Fortunately there's a queue so I have time to think. A little clutch of women wearing headscarves and thick woollen coats are huddling just inside the door. They turn and nod. I noticed several of the conversations stopped as I came in but now at least the villagers have something else to talk about. The shop, which at the moment doubles as a 'Ministry of Information', issues daily bulletins through Sergeant-Major Arkwright and the latest bulletins have not been reassuring. No one wants to think that in a few weeks we could be at war.

Ahead of us an argument breaks out between Miss Barrett the librarian and old Tom Parry who has wandered over to collect his paper and who she claims was behind her in the queue. It isn't just me; everyone's on edge.

'I'm in a hurry,' says Miss Barrett, in a voice meant to remind us that she was the only person in her family to get the School Certificate. She's managed to intimidate Tom Parry, but Miss Barrett is in limbo like the rest of us. The truth is we are rushing around in circles waiting to discover which direction we should run in.

IX

Only days after the Munich summit, Hitler makes a speech in Nuremburg dismissing Chamberlain as 'an umbrella-wielding bourgeois' and suggesting that the German people will secure their rights by any means. The Peace Agreement starts to look as flimsy as the paper it is written on.

'If this is Hitler's peace,' says Dorothy, 'God help us when he's not in a conciliatory mood.'

'I've heard you calling Chamberlain a bourgeois,' I say.

'It's like Jewish jokes. Jews are the only ones who have a right to tell them.'

I think what she's saying is that this is no joke.

'Does it mean war's coming after all, then?' I say.

'Just be glad we kept the sandbags and the Anderson's still out the back,' says Dorothy.

Kristallnacht, Germany's retaliation for the shooting of a German embassy official by a Polish Jew, is front page news in all the papers. Photographs show Jewish-owned stores, homes and synagogues reduced to rubble by the Nazis. There is no official protest from the British Government, however, although Chamberlain is heard to say that he does not approve of Hitler's persecution of the Jews.

'You wonder why he bothers opening his mouth at all,' says Dorothy. It isn't until Baldwin launches his appeal to *Get them out before it's too late* that a rescue effort to bring Jewish children out of territories taken over by the Nazis finally gets under way and the first *Kindertransports* start arriving.

Dorothy retreats into herself. It's the uncertainty that's getting everybody down, the waiting to see how far Hitler is prepared to go.

In England, 1938 is shaping up to be the coldest winter ever. There is heavy snow at Christmas. Icicles a foot long dangle from the gutters. International tensions have done nothing to alleviate the problems on the home front. Unemployed men lie down in the road amongst the Christmas shoppers in the West End, chanting 'Work or Bread' and carry coffins through the streets with the 'remains' of those not eligible for relief. A Fascist rally noisily demands why there should be relief for Czechs, Basques, Austrians and Jews whilst Englishmen are starving.

For the first year since we came to Cookham, Dorothy says she would rather not go to the cinema in Maidenhead to celebrate her birthday. There does not seem to be much to celebrate. We spend the evening playing cards and listening to the wireless.

As the Church clock begins striking midnight I unlatch the window and lean out. The air is so crisp you could cut it with a knife. It catches in my throat.

'Here'. Dorothy holds out a whisky. I turn back into the room and shut the window. We clink glasses and I kiss her.

'So what should we drink to?' I say.

Dodo sighs. 'Let's drink to next year's New Year's Eve and hope we're here to see it.'

X

By the end of January over half the Jewish population has fled Nazi Germany. In Nuremburg and other cities, the drab day to day lives of the German people are transformed by massive torchlit rallies staged like operas and accompanied by military marches.

Listening to them on the radio, I feel that stirring in the loins that comes when you are moved in spite of knowing that what's moving you is pandering to instincts you'd do well to keep in check. I have the feeling, when I glance across at her, that Dorothy's not unaffected by it either.

Hitler is now turning his attention to the port of Danzig, currently a free state under the protection of the League of Nations. He is pressuring the Poles to hand it back to Nazi Germany. I'm wondering if Dorset's that safe, after all.

'Nowhere is safe,' says Dorothy.

I get a note from Dudley Tooth the next day which suggests she's right. According to an inventory that Stanley has provided, he says I appear to have four works of his in my possession. We have three of Stanley's paintings hanging on the walls and although it is true that none of them are paid for, one – a painting of Moor Thatch - was given to us, one which Dorothy expressed an admiration for is 'on loan' and the other I removed from Lindworth for safekeeping after it was rented.

I hope Dudley doesn't think I have designs on Stanley' work. I did sell off one of his landscapes without telling him, which is the Number 4 that Dudley mentions, so I'm hoping he won't follow that one up. In future, he says, any work of Stanley's is to go to him directly.

It's clear we have nothing more to gain from Dudley. He's decided he can't represent us both and, like me though in different ways, he has invested so much money, time and energy in Stanley that he is determined to see some reward for it. I write him a conciliatory note, not mentioning the paintings we already have, but recognising that as Stanley's dealer he should have first sight of anything he does. The last thing I need is a full-blown row with Dudley whilst I'm fighting to keep Dorothy and Stanley on-side.

It seems Hitler's reasoning is somewhat similar. In August, news comes through that he has signed a non-aggression pact with Stalin.

'Sergeant-Major Arkwright chipped the black paint off his windows too soon,' Dorothy remarks. 'Now Germany can wage war on whatever front it likes; the Soviets won't interfere.'

'I thought they were our allies.'

'So did everybody else in Britain,' Dorothy says, bitterly.

Days later, Hitler's tanks roll into Poland and a few days after that we're sitting down to listen to the PM's broadcast to the Nation. It's a lovely, balmy day, the kind you cling to when you don't know what the future might bring.

'Well,' says Dorothy, when we've switched off the wireless. 'At least war will solve the unemployment problem.'

XI

The arrival of the first evacuees in Cookham – seven children, all boys from the East End – generates the kind of curiosity that must have greeted the first sighting of an elephant in Europe. People crowd the railway station for a glimpse of them.

The boys are staying with a couple called the Sedgwicks. Mr Sedgwick is a labourer and they already have three children of their own. The new arrivals come with labels tied to them like bits of luggage and their gas masks slung over their shoulders.

Within days they're rampaging through Cookham like a raiding party. Sergeant-Major Arkwright won't let more than one of them inside the shop. He says one boy will set out to distract him whilst the others pilfer sweets.

They squat down playing 'Pitch and Toss' with marbles in the gravel by the War Memorial and swing on ropes looped over branches or the iron bars projecting from the lamp posts in the High Street. Their 'whoops' ricochet across the common. We've said we'll take two girls at a pinch but Mrs Arkwright reckons that the girls are just as bad.

When I hear Stanley's back in Cookham for the day, I gear myself up for the probability that he'll want Hilda and the children to move back to Lindworth whilst the war is on. I don't see how I can refuse, but I'm not letting go of Lindworth unconditionally. Dudley might have taken back control of Stanley's earnings from his paintings, but I'm still in charge on the domestic front.

Now that he doesn't have a house here, we are forced to meet outside. We're sitting on the bench next to the War Memorial which two of the evacuees seem to have taken over as a den. They've climbed over the railings, trampling through the marigolds, and sit bunched up together on the stone step underneath the plaque examining the scabs on one another's knees.

At least here in the open, we will not be overheard, a fact I'm grateful for when he tells me the object of his visit.

'You want a divorce!' I gape. I'm at a loss for words. I wonder for an instant whether this is something he's cooked up with Dorothy. 'I thought you were desperate for us to remain together!'

'But we aren't together, are we?' he says.

'We're still married. That was what you wanted.'

He is picking at a loose thread in his trousers. He would not look out of place between the two boys squatting opposite us.

'It was what I thought I wanted, but I've changed my mind.' His lips purse stubbornly. 'I can't put up with all this interruption to my train of thought. I want a bit of peace, Patricia.'

'You think getting a divorce will bring you peace?'

'Well why are you so keen for us to go on being married? You won't let me touch you. You say you're my business manager, but since we married I've been poorer than ever.'

'That's not my fault, Stanley,' I say, shakily. 'You won't listen to advice. You go your own way and then when it all goes wrong you blame me.'

'When? When have I gone my own way?'

A young couple saunter past and glance towards the bench. The man's in khaki. He'll be one of those who's been called up. They look as if they're going to sit down, but then the woman sees that we are in the middle of *a conversation* and tugs lightly at the man's sleeve.

'When you put those drawings in the Venice Biennale last year and the organisers called the police, for instance. One of the drawings was of me. You had no right to put it in the exhibition. How do you think I felt, having all those people gawping at me? As for the

Beatitudes, it didn't take a genius to see they'd get you into trouble.'

He sits forward with his hands locked round his knees. 'I needed to express the way I felt. I was in agony in Cornwall during that fiasco of a honeymoon.'

'If you had kept to your side of the bargain and brought Hilda down with you, we might have all enjoyed it more.' Because this wasn't what I'd been expecting, I don't know how to respond.

'You only wanted Hilda there so you could carry on with Dorothy.'

I'm really struggling now. 'Weren't you the one who said that every sort of love was blessed in the sight of God?'

'I wasn't getting any love at all!' says Stanley, wretchedly. 'I had to lie there in the spare room listening to you whispering and fondling one another. I knew what was going on. You think I don't have grounds for a divorce?'

I'm thinking *Thank God Dorothy's not witnessing this*, whilst another part of me is wondering how I'll get around it when she finds out she and Stanley are now on the same side.

'Think about it, Stanley. You've already been through one divorce. God might have overlooked the first one as an innocent mistake, but you can hardly claim that this time. When you married me you made a sacred promise.'

'So did you.' he says.

'All right. I'm willing to bear some responsibility for what's gone wrong. But cutting loose is not the answer, Stanley. You need my support. And God's.'

He's wavering. 'God understands.'

'Let's hope so. But I wouldn't try His patience any more, if I were you.'

I'm shaking as I make my way across the common. When I come within sight of Moor Thatch, I turn back. I need time to clear my head. The conversation I've just had with Stanley has put paid to any notion that I can manipulate events to suit myself. If Dorothy discovers that the only obstacle to a divorce is me, not Stanley, it will scupper any hope of reconciliation.

I could just give in. Say yes. Go home to Dorothy and celebrate. She'd have no reason not to take me back then. Why not?

Well, for one thing, I would feel humiliated. I imagine Richard Carline and his cronies jubilantly toasting my departure and pretending they knew all along that this would be the outcome. Who leaves who, if you're a woman, is the crucial factor in a separation.

When she finds out later that I've been to a solicitor and had my married name put on the deeds to Lindworth, Dorothy's response is typical.

'You don't think that's a trifle calculating?'

I avoid her eye. 'I thought it would be tidier and anyone examining the documents won't have to look for a connection. It means Stanley won't be able to move back to Lindworth and claim legal trespass.'

'Stanley's not that devious,' says Dorothy. Compared with me, is what she means.

XII

As soon as Stanley's back in London, I expect him to begin bombarding me with letters. If, once he has thought about it and is back under the influence of other people, he decides he still wants a divorce, he'll chip away until I give in just as he did in the days when he was desperate to marry me. I make sure I'm the first up next day, listening for the postman.

But a week goes by without word. When I phone his digs, I'm told that he's in Oxford. Finally, I call Jas Wood. If anybody knows what's going on, it will be him. He's cagey.

'I believe he's gone on holiday. Yes, I seem to remember that was what he said when I last saw him.'

'Stanley never goes on holiday and he would never go alone. He wouldn't trust himself to get off at the right stop.'

'It's a painting holiday. I'm sure he will be bringing back some landscapes.'

'Jas, I couldn't give a damn about the landscapes.'

'Really?'

'Something's cropped up and I need to get in touch. Where is he?'

'Let me see. He was a bit vague. Oxford, I believe. A place called Leonard Stanley.'

'Why would he take off to Leonard Stanley when the only place he's ever shown an interest in is Cookham.'

'He did say he'd rather not be back in Cookham at the moment.'

'Why?'

'I gather you and he met up there recently.'

'You've seen him in the last ten days then?'

I can hear Jas breathing. 'We spoke on the telephone.'

'Did Stanley tell you what we'd talked about?'

Jas hesitates. 'He said he'd asked for a divorce.'

Damn. If he's letting it be known that a divorce is what he wants, it's certain to get back to Dorothy before long.

'Jas, the last thing Stanley needs is a divorce. He isn't capable of living on his own.'

'He has been living on his own for some time,' Jas reminds me.

'I meant without anybody looking out for him. He'd be incapable of managing his own affairs.'

'He does have Dudley.'

'Dudley's only interested in himself. He wants to get his hands on Stanley's paintings.'

'Well, he is his dealer.'

'Stanley needs a woman, Jas.'

There is a long pause. I hear Jas take out a cigarette and light it.

'Who's he gone to Oxford with?'

He takes a long draw on the cigarette and clears his throat.

'Come on, Jas,' I persist. 'You might as well come clean and tell me.' A bizarre idea comes suddenly into my head. 'Is Stanley having an affair?'

I feel him squirming in the silence. 'Honestly, Patricia, I would rather not say.'

'You just have. Who is she?' He groans audibly. 'Who is it, Jas? You know I'll find out in the end.'

I brace myself. He sighs. 'It's really not my place to say, Patricia'. He hangs up.

XIII

'Is something on your mind, Pet?'

Dorothy is kneeling on the path next to the pocket handkerchief of land that she insists on calling the 'allotment'. This bit of the garden by the back fence is where we traditionally try and grow the vegetables we can't afford to buy from Arkwright's. Last year it produced three lettuces, thirteen potatoes and a pound of green beans. Dorothy says this is not the point and, all right, I accept that. Our back garden is where she confronts her demons.

Whilst I'm nervously anticipating Stanley's next move, she's been waiting for a letter from the Ministry informing us that we'll be taking in one of the next batch of evacuees. In her place I'd be sitting with a glass of whisky and the bottle within easy reach, but Dorothy's not like that. Nor can she take refuge in the studio, although we both know that she might not have it for much longer. Twenty minutes after Mr Chamberlain's announcement that we were at war, she was out in the garden pulling up the weeds.

I squat down next to her. Although I haven't had time to absorb the implications of what Jas has let slip, I need somebody to talk to and there isn't anyone apart from Dorothy.

'I have the feeling Stanley's up to something.'

'In what way?'

'He's told Jas Wood he doesn't want to be in Cookham. It's unknown for Stanley not to want to be in Cookham. It's like someone saying they don't want to enter Paradise because they've found a viable alternative.'

'Is it because you think he's found a viable alternative to Cookham that you're worried, or because you think he may have found a viable alternative to you?'

Trust Dorothy to get straight to the point. She can be irritatingly perceptive. I'm still trying to work through my feelings on discovering I had a rival. At the soirée in *rue Jacob* when I realised Gretha Mathurin had set her sights on Dorothy, I had felt blindly, madly jealous. The idea that I'd feel like that over Stanley was ridiculous. I'd never grudged him Hilda, after all, except on principle. Maybe that was because I was in the ascendant at the time, whereas now... I was angry that he had misled me, telling me he wanted a divorce so he could get on with his work. Why not just tell me he was having an affair? And what did he imagine God would say to that?

'If Stanley found another woman, that would be a good thing, wouldn't it?' said Dorothy.

It wasn't easy, trying to talk through the problem without letting on to Dorothy exactly what the problem was.

'Well, that depends. You know how vulnerable he is.' I'm thinking that the best way forward might be to imply that my concern is to protect my husband rather than to block his path to happiness.

'You're worried someone else might take advantage of him?' Dorothy says, her voice thick with irony. 'The way things are, it's hard to see what they would have to gain.'

'But that's just it, why would they bother?'

'Just because you're not attracted to him, doesn't necessarily mean no one else would be. He has a number of endearing qualities. I can imagine he would bring out the maternal instinct in a lot of women.'

'If you say so.'

'You're not jealous, surely?'

Damn her. 'No, of course I'm not. I'm just surprised. I can appreciate that Stanley might not care about upsetting me but I'm surprised he'd risk upsetting Hilda.'

'Still, it wouldn't be the first occasion,' Dorothy reminds me. 'I believe you were the other woman when it happened last time.'

She tips up the tray and empties the remaining crumbs of soil onto the earth, then places one hand on my arm to lever herself up. Because her mind is currently preoccupied with things she feels are more important,

Dorothy is less inclined to waste time looking at a situation from my point of view, although I'm not sure what my point of view is anymore.

She folds the mat she has been kneeling on and pats my shoulder. 'Stanley's never been much good at keeping secrets.' She stamps on the path to knock off any particles of earth still clinging to her shoes. 'I don't imagine you'll have long to wait before he tells you.'

Dorothy is right, of course. We get a letter from him three days later.

'He's in Oxford staying with the Jesuit Fathers.'

'That sounds lots of fun,' says Dorothy.

'They've brought him in to paint their chapel, but they are insisting that he does it their way. Father D'Arcy's given him a book about the Virgin Mary. Stanley says it's utterly depressing. He's been staying in a Temperance Hotel which he describes as like a glass of beer left on a window ledge for weeks in sunlight.'

'He's not happy then?'

'Yes, he's delirious,' I say, resentfully. 'He tells me on page 2 that he's in love.'

'So we were right. How touching.' Dorothy is trimming water-colours ready to slide in under the mount once they've been signed. After a week of grubbing in the compost and with no word from the Ministry regarding the arrival of the next batch of evacuees, she's finally gone back into the studio. She might not be much easier to live with when she's working but her moods are more predictable. 'Let's face it, love is Stanley's whole existence. It's what every brush-stroke is about.'

'This isn't universal love we're talking about, Dorothy. It has a name. She's Daphne Charlton.'

'Not George Charlton's wife?'

'Yes, do you know her?'

'I know him. He lectures at the Slade. She was a student of his years ago.'

'He says that George has given him his cast-offs,' I say, dully. 'That's his suits, apparently, not Daphne. They're too big for him, but Stanley doesn't care. He's up-in-heaven. *Holy* is how he's describing Daphne.'

Now that my determination to discover what was happening has been satisfied, I wish that Stanley didn't feel obliged to offer every scarifying detail. 'He says the collision of her shape with his shape has brought meaning to their lives. He hands bits of himself to her and she hands bits of herself back.'

Dorothy considers and then makes a face. 'The picture that it conjures in one's head is not that pleasant. Still,' she shrugs.

'She's clearly got him on a string,' I throw out, spitefully.

'You've had him on a string for years. I think it would be nice for Stanley to have somebody to care for him.'

'He says she cuts his fingernails.'

'Well there you are,' says Dorothy.

'I can appreciate that this has its amusing side for you.'

"Perhaps he'll want to marry her,' says Dorothy. She holds the trimmed sheet up against the frame.

My stomach takes a jolt. 'He can't if she's already married. Just as well. They'll soon get tired of one another.'

'Stanley's not as shallow as you think.' She tilts the lamp so that the light is concentrated on the drawing. We've wrapped thick brown paper around all the lights but Sergeant-Major Arkwright has had several run-ins with us for not being strict enough about the blackout.

'I don't think he's shallow. That's why I'm surprised he's doing this. He must have finally accepted Hilda's gone for good.' I turn the letter over. 'They've gone on a painting holiday to Gloucestershire – a place called Leonard Stanley.' It inevitably brings back memories of the 'painting holiday' we went on to St Ives.

'I spent a week in Leonard Stanley just after the war. It would have been, let's see now, 1921. Lucinda Barclay, that girl we knew at the Slade – she lived there.'

'They've got lodgings at The White Hart and the manager's let Stanley turn his room into a studio. Tooth sends him £1.15s every Saturday for board. I can't imagine what he's living on. Apparently they go for long walks in the countryside and lie in hammocks eating Cox's orange pippins.'

'It sounds like a very healthy diet. Stanley needed somebody to sort him out. Why not be pleased for him. You've spent the last year trying to persuade him to agree to a divorce. He's much more likely to agree if he's got someone else to go to.'

'But you know what Stanley's like. He went ahead with the divorce from Hilda without even checking that I was available. Suppose he does that this time?'

'You can hardly write to Daphne and ask whether she has honourable intentions. You want a divorce and now it would appear that he does.' She inclines her head in one direction and her mouth goes in the other. 'So for once the future seems to be plain sailing, well as far as that goes.'

I pretend to go on reading. 'He says he and Daphne were discovered sketching near an aircraft factory last weekend and taken in for questioning. The vicar had to come and vouch for them. One wonders what else they were doing. If that's an example of her looking after him, it hardly bodes well.'

XIV

Whereas Stanley would be more than capable of going through a war without acknowledging that anything unusual was happening, I would have expected his friends to alert him to the need to make contingency arrangements. It's soon clear, however, that the only thing on Stanley's mind is Daphne.

'You told me you wanted a divorce because you needed to be on your own,' I say. 'You couldn't work with everybody crowding in on you.'

'That was the reason.'

We are walking back across the common. Stanley's sauntering. He turns his face up to the sun. There is a dreamy look on it. He's more relaxed than he's been in a long time.

'I suppose the fact that you had started an affair just slipped your mind.'

He stops and looks at me, offended. 'At the time, I hadn't started it.'

'But you must have been working up to it. These things don't happen overnight.'

'You said you wouldn't grant me a divorce in any case. What does it matter why I wanted it?'

'So what do you suppose God – I presume you're still in touch with Him – makes of your latest infidelity?'

'It isn't infidelity if no one else is sleeping with me,' he says, stubbornly.

I have the feeling God is not the only one who Stanley has discussed this with. I had begun by asking him about the paintings he was doing for the Jesuit Chapel. He said Daphne thought what Father D'Arcy wanted him to do would be degrading to his talents.

As he starts explaining why, it's not his voice but Daphne's that I fancy I hear running like a leitmotiv through every sentence.

He picks up a pebble, skimming it along the path. He's warming to his theme. I put a hand out to restrain him.

'It's all very well for Daphne to decide that it's degrading to your talents, but she isn't paying you and Father D'Arcy is. This could turn out to be your last commission. It's all right for Daphne; after all, she's got a husband to fall back on.' If I keep on mentioning the husband, I am hoping to bring home to Stanley that, however all-absorbing this relationship might be, it hasn't got a future. 'Incidentally, where is her husband?'

'He's been helping to evacuate the Slade to Oxford,' Stanley says, so he's at least aware that preparations are in hand for war.

'Has he said what he thinks about all this?'

'George? He's a very understanding chap.'

'He must be.' We shall have to hope he doesn't prove too understanding, I think.

'Daphne's been a revelation to me.' Stanley's face lights up. 'I feel joy when I'm with her. Daphne's helped me to recover my lost self.'

'She's putting ideas in your head,' I mutter, crabbily, remembering that he had once said something similar about me.

Stanley looks insulted: 'I have plenty of my own ideas inside my head.'

'I don't mean those ideas. I mean ideas about the sort of work you should be doing. Not just landscapes, but the kind of pictures people understand.'

'You want me to be useful. Daphne's made me realise that my uselessness is where my purpose lies.'

The more I hear of Daphne, the less optimistic I become that the relationship will be of benefit to either of them. Clearly she has no idea how Stanley should be handled. Not that I've been having much success in that direction recently. I'm starting to appreciate how difficult it must have been for Hilda, having to contend with someone else encroaching on her territory.

'I told her I was like a broken pot that's been discarded and picked up by someone else who thinks it might be useful. They in turn discard it when they see it's broken. Daphne's helped me understand that it's my brokenness that gives my art its purpose.'

'Daphne wants you to be broken?'

'Daphne sees me as a vessel.'

'But a vessel's not much use to anybody if it leaks.'

'She says the good I have to give is through my brokennness. That is the path my soul treads.' He is gazing past me as if he's expecting Daphne to come wafting down the road towards us.

'Have you painted her?'

'Of course, I paint her all the time.'

'You've not suggested to the Jesuit fathers that you put a painting of her as the Virgin Mary in their chapel?'

If it hadn't yet occurred to him, it has now. His eyes swivel round to meet mine.

'That was not meant seriously, Stanley. Any thought of Daphne as the Virgin Mary would be sacrilegious.'

He grunts. We walk on until we reach the stile. He offers me his hand to cross it. This is where the paths diverge.

'Does Hilda know about this new relationship of yours?' I say as we're about to part.

'Of course. She's pleased for me. They're similar in some ways, her and Daphne. You must meet her. Dudley's putting on an exhibition next month. Come along.'

XV

The taxi, fitted with blue sidelights, crawls in darkness through the streets. Apart from the occasional pedestrian, the city seems deserted. It's like driving through a dream. The leaflets pinned to walls and lampposts offer details about air raid warnings and what signals to expect in the event of gas attacks, but they're already fraying at the edges. Sticky tape obscures the windows of big buildings and there are armed military police at railway stations. Everything's in place, but we're still waiting for the war to start.

The air raid sirens went off half an hour after the Prime Minister informed us that we were at war. We spent an hour in the Anderson but nothing happened. It's been like that ever since. A number of evacuees, including two of the boys boarding with the Sedgwicks, have gone back home to the East End and no new ones have arrived. In Piccadilly, shops and restaurants are open and behind the blackout in Tooth's gallery the latest Stanley Spencer exhibition is in full swing.

Dudley is polite, but frosty. Neither of us wants a row in public, so I occupy myself with looking at the paintings. One of the exhibits is *The Wool Shop*. It shows Stanley helping Daphne to match wool to make a cardigan. A tiny Stanley is enveloped in huge coils of wool. The difference in their sizes isn't that great in reality but there is something about Daphne that most men, unless they're masochists like Stanley, would find daunting. She has long blond hair and crimson lipstick and she's wearing an enormous hat which adds at least three inches to her height. A fox-fur stole is twined around her neck. If she were to pause long enough on a street corner, she could be mistaken for a lady of the night, albeit a high-class one. Any similarity with Hilda must lie well beneath the surface.

Stanley's clearly in over his head and loving every minute of it. There's a life-size painting called *The Tiger Rug* which shows him and a half-naked Daphne lying on a tiger rug and staring raptly at each other. I hear Stanley joyfully explaining to a couple of potential buyers that the rug which he and Daphne are wrapped up in is a chrysalis.

'What is it that you're turning into?' says the woman. Her expression of polite inquiry falters when he tells her the rug symbolises his return to potency. 'I'm being resurrected,' he says blithely.

Here we go again. George Charlton's distanced himself wisely on the outside of the circle. Daphne shadows Stanley as he moves around the room, not obviously stalking him but keeping him within sight. Once, I see her speak to him and then glance over at me. Stanley makes a move towards me but she draws him back to her. I had decided not to introduce myself in any case and she is clearly of the same mind.

I wait till she's moved away and Stanley's finished talking to another couple, before going over to him. His eyes flicker round the room till they alight on Daphne and he gives a little wave.

'Have you seen Hilda recently?' I say, reminding him he has an ex-wife and a current one towards whom he still owes some obligation. 'Has she joined the girls in Epsom?'

'No, she doesn't want to. She prefers to stay in London, but the house has been well barricaded.'

'Has the War Artists Committee found you anything?' His dealings with the Jesuit fathers ended with both sides withdrawing to their separate corners and remaining there. When he approached the War Artists Committee he discovered that he wasn't on the list of artists they were thinking of commissioning. He had gone back to Dudley who agreed to put a word in for him.

'Yes,' he says. 'I'm going to Port Glasgow to record life in the shipyard.'

My first thought is that I can't see Daphne in Port Glasgow, so perhaps the situation isn't quite as critical as I'd imagined.

XVI

The War Artist's Committee has commissioned Stanley to produce eleven paintings of the shipyard, rather fewer than the sixty-four he'd planned although they have agreed that they can be up to six metres long.

He's found digs with a couple on the outskirts of the city. The facilities are basic and the meals are frugal, but he's never lived extravagantly and his landlady is motherly, which Stanley likes.

He's just completed *Burners*, his first painting of the shipyard when the Blitz starts. Dorothy and I are in the garden at Moor Thatch. It's one of those late summer/early autumn days of clear skies and abundant sunshine. We're about to go indoors for tea when there's a sound like swarms of bees approaching. I glance up and see what looks to be a huge bird coming over the horizon. As it passes, we see it's a V-shaped squadron of about two dozen bombers with up to a hundred midge-like fighters in the air above them, the late afternoon sun glinting on their metal casings.

I assume the planes are ours, but then I realise they're not going in the right direction. As they plough their way relentlessly across the skies, birds scatter. There is no sound other than the deafening roar of engines overhead and the earth shuddering beneath. We stand there staring with a fascinated horror at the sky.

The planes are heading for the East End. There's a droning, heavy feeling in the air. The siren goes off and the anti-aircraft guns let loose. They manage to hit one of them and there's a screaming *zoom* as it begins its slow descent towards the earth. We hear a bang and then the sky's ablaze.

'Dear God,' says Dorothy. 'It's started.' There is an explosion and the sky lights up again. 'They're aiming for the docks.'

Dusk has already fallen. In a quarter of an hour it will be completely dark. But over London it's as if a light has been switched on; the city is illuminated. The incendiaries the planes drop so that they can see their targets, are no longer necessary.

I can feel the earth shake underneath my feet. I think about the families in their tenements, alert to what is happening, trying to find shelter and discovering there is none, that the bombs are falling all around. The noise is shattering from here. What must it be like to be underneath it, knowing there is no escape.

'Oh, Dorothy.' I reach behind me blindly and she takes my hand. The sky is streaked with red now like a sunset. 'Those poor people.'

The explosions carry on throughout the night as fires spread from one warehouse to the next. It looks like a spectacular display of fireworks. When the wind blows our way, there's a smell which has so many different things mixed up in it, it's hard to separate them: burning oil and rubber, dried fruit, rum and sugar as it turns to caramel.

We wait inside the Anderson until the sky begins to lighten overhead and then creep back into the house. It's cold. I kneel down in the hearth to light the fire and as I put a match to it and watch the spills catch, I think of the homes that have gone up in flames, the families that have nothing any longer, even in some cases one another.

I imagine Hilda on her own in Hampstead, staring from an upstairs window over London as it burns, her children out of reach and Stanley miles away in Glasgow.

I begin to shiver. There is something stuck inside my throat, a solid lump, irregular in shape like a home-grown potato, its skin grey and scored by bumps and craters with the earth still clinging to it. As I go to pile twigs on the fire, I feel it forcing its way to the surface, searching for a way out. My mouth opens. There's a pause and then a rush of air, then nothing.

Dorothy bends down and scoops my shoulders in her hands. I lean back on my heels and rest my head against her. We stay like that, staring at the fire until the flames begin to take.

She pats my arm. 'I'll go and fill the kettle.'

Part Seven
Inferno

I

The fire goes on raging for a week. The gas works and the Woolwich Arsenal have also suffered hits. The Germans dropped a thousand bombs that night, some strapped to oil drums which exploded. For the next ten days, the skies are blood red over London. There are over sixteen hundred casualties.

Eye-witnesses describe exploding barrels on Rum Quay creating blazing rivers and a heady, thick miasma. Roads out of the docks are covered in squashed currants and burnt fruit and for weeks afterwards the air is rank with it. In Poplar where a bomb dropped on a warehouse storing fifty tons of powdered milk, the area is bathed in white. Rats poured out of the burning buildings and where scorching sugar was turned into toffee by the firemen's hoses, labourers have started chipping wedges of it off the road to take home. One man talks of watching flames run up the ropes that tethered barges to the pier and seeing them float out to sea like Viking funerals.

Perhaps the most distressing story of them all is the report of bombed-out families taken to a school in Canning Town till buses could be sent to take them somewhere safe. Before the buses could arrive the *Luftwaffe* went back and bombed the school. Four hundred of them died.

The day after the first raid, when I can't get hold of Hilda, I phone Stanley at the port in Glasgow. He has heard about the raid, of course and he is desperate to get Hilda out of London but she won't go. Is she being reckless or heroic? Or does Hilda simply not care any longer what becomes of her?

When Churchill visits the East End with General Ismay, dockers line the pier: 'It's all right, Winnie, we can take it,' they shout.

'How can they be so brave, Dorothy?'

'When you have nothing left to lose, it's easier, I dare say.'

'What will we do if they come here?'

'The Germans?' she says. 'Seems they have.'

'Aren't you afraid?'

'It's all right,' she says, calmly. 'I've made certain we have what we need.'

'What we need to survive, you mean?' I thought she meant she had been stock-piling provisions.

'No, dear, that's not what I meant.'

I stare at her. Sometimes I think I don't know Dorothy at all and then I realise that I do and that's what I'm afraid of.

'That's all right, then,' I say, weakly. 'Thank you, Dorothy.'

'You're welcome,' she says.

'Those boys from the East End who were staying with the Sedgwicks...?'

She sighs. 'They went back. They didn't want to sit around and wait for it to start.'

She spreads her hand out on the table and then turns it palm up. I lean over and put my hand over it. We go on sitting like that till the light fades.

II

Now that it's begun, the Blitz continues battering the East End for another fifty-seven days. The next wave of evacuees is very different from the first. They disembark in silence from the train, some of the younger children clinging to their older siblings, snivelling into their sleeves. A quarter of the population leaves the capital over the next few weeks.

In Glasgow, faced with the Great Western Railway's understandable reluctance to assume responsibility for the safe carriage of his painting, Stanley brings it down to London on the train himself, ignoring Daphne's protestations that her vulnerable little artist will be risking death by going to the capital. The War Artists Committee won't hand over money till they've got the goods and Stanley's broke as usual.

'You got to the gallery in one piece, then?' I say next time we meet. I'm wondering whether to suggest he uses part of what they're paying him to buy a new shirt and a set of underwear. But I decide that Daphne might as well assume responsibility for such things, too.

'Have you seen Hilda?'

'Yes, of course. I went there after I'd seen Dudley.'

'And? How is she?'

He is silent for a moment. 'I'm not sure. She seemed a bit down.'

I lean forward. 'Stanley, Hilda's been *a bit down* all the time I've known her. But I think what's happening now is different.'

'Different in what way?'

'She sounds depressed.'

We're sitting in the back room of the bakery where you can take the buns you've bought and order tea. I watch as Stanley steadily demolishes his bun whilst he considers what I'm saying. 'It's the war,' he says. 'It's getting everybody down.'

'I think it's more than that. The way she's been behaving recently is not exactly rational.'

'She's had a lot to put up with,' he says, innocently.

I'd suggest that the arrival on the scene of Daphne won't have helped to lighten Hilda's mood, but Stanley has that vague expression on his face that tells me he's no longer listening. I change tack.

'Are you still writing your biography?'

'When I have time. The publishers are still insisting on it being edited. They want to cut bits out.'

'That's what an editor is for. You can't expect to be allowed to say exactly what you like.'

'I'd rather that they didn't publish it at all, then.'

Since I would prefer that, too, I don't take issue with him. Stanley's so adept at scuppering his own boat, there is rarely any need to send in a torpedo.

'And what's happening at the gallery?'

It's Stanley's turn to look depressed. 'It's empty. Dudley says there's been no trade for months. The war's scared everybody off. The gallery might have to close. He's waiting to be called up.'

'Does that mean he won't be acting for you any longer?'

'That's the way it looks,' says Stanley, bleakly. He picks up a fork and tests the prongs against his palm.

I take a cigarette out. 'Have you nothing coming in at present other than the money from the War Artist's Committee?'

'They've not paid me yet. John Rothenstein has bought a painting I did earlier this year of Daphne in a hat. He's given me a hundred pounds for it.'

'Can't Daphne throw something into the pot?'

He puts his tea spoon in his mouth. 'I don't like asking her?'

'You've never minded asking me.'

'It's different. You're my wife,' says Stanley. 'Wives are meant to be supportive.'

'You said Daphne had been looking after you. If your description's anything to go by, she's a candidate for sainthood.'

He looks glumly at the table-cloth. The waitress brings the bill. I wait for him to pick it up. He's looking at it as if he suspects that when he opens it he'll find a writ inside.

'My treat,' I say. I reach into my purse.

'Thanks.'

'How's it working out with Daphne?' I ask, casually.

'It's all right.' Stanley watches me sift through the change.

I take a pound note from my purse. 'You don't seem quite as joyful as you did the last time we met up.' He sniffs. 'Well?'

'Daphne wanted to look after me. I thought I needed looking after. Now I'm not so sure.' He hunches up his shoulders and I get a brief glimpse of the grey vest underneath his shirt. 'She overwhelms me.'

'I thought being overwhelmed was what you wanted.'

'Not like that.'

I'm not sure that I want to hear how Daphne overwhelms him, but *The Wool Shop*, with its tiny figure wrapped in coils of wool and pressed against a vast expanse of female flesh, comes back to mind. I know from bitter personal experience, that painting is the way that Stanley comes to terms with issues in his life.

'I feel more comfortable with women when they don't give in to me. I need to fantasize about them. When they're there, it just gets complicated.'

I reach for my gloves. 'You won't be seeing quite so much of her in future then?'

'The landlady is putting in a bill for broken crockery,' he says, as if that is sufficient explanation and perhaps it is.

III

Now that he isn't spending all his waking hours up-in-heaven, we begin receiving regular reports from Stanley. It seems Glasgow's also coming in for its fair share of bombing.

Since the war began in earnest, Germany's been making up for lost time. Every night, the skies are lit up over London. We are close enough to Windsor that a raid would certainly affect us, although there's a rumour Hitler's told the bombers to avoid the castle as he wants to live there when the war is over.

'How nice,' Dorothy remarks. 'He'll be a neighbour.'

'Do you think we'll still be living here, if he's in Windsor Castle.'

'No, dear.' She sighs. 'I imagine we'll have moved on.'

Silly me, for asking.

Whether by design or accident, one bomb falls right next to the barracks and another one lands next to Savile Gardens, leaving a 100' crater. Maidenhead becomes an Air Transport Auxiliary, transporting planes to factories and the front-line, so that has become a target, too. The bombs are dropped in sticks of eight and we get used to counting the explosions when we're in the Anderson. I've brought a rug to lay over the concrete floor and there's a blanket we can huddle under but it's cold and cramped and neither of us sleeps. Before we go to bed each night,

I heat the water to make tea and put some in the flask so that if there's a raid we have something to drink that's hopefully still warm. So far, thank goodness, no evacuees have been assigned to us.

Of course the shipyard at Port Glasgow is a target for the Germans. It's located on a long thin wedge of land and there are anti-aircraft batteries on both sides of the river. Since planes have to fly across the Clyde from side to side to get at it, they struggle to release their bombs in time and often hit the other bank instead, so up till now the damage has been minimal. The ARP build decoy fires on nearby hillsides to confuse the target.

Stanley writes about a street he regularly walked down from his lodgings which was totally demolished in a raid except for two red sandstone houses that remained untouched, as if the blast had passed round to the back of them, destroying those on either side. The houses have acquired a mystical significance, he says, and he's seen people chiselling at the brick-work for a souvenir or good luck token.

So far he has done over a hundred drawings of the shipyard and its workers using toilet rolls, which are more portable than sketch-pads. At the gatherings he's invited to, he's taken to unrolling them across the floor to entertain the guests.

The workers in the shipyard take an interest in his progress, crowding round him as he's working, arguing with one another about which of them is true to life and who has been 'transfigured'. He seems thoroughly at home.

His main complaint is that the Ministry of Information isn't paying him enough to buy boots or a set of waterproofs. He's having to walk three miles in the rain each day from where he's lodging to the shipyard and, since he needs to draw some views from the shore, he's treading water when the tide comes in. His landlord has been trying to find bits of leather to patch up his shoes.

When he comes home on leave it's obvious that although he now has money coming in, he's still not spending any of it on himself. He'd told us in a letter that he'd once been caught out in an air raid and the blast had lifted him six feet into the air. When he came down he must have looked a little as he does now.

'Well,' I venture, brightly. 'What does the Committee think about the work you're doing on the shipyard?'

He sighs: 'They bought *Burners* for £300 but they've turned down the next one.'

My heart sinks. 'I thought they had commissioned you to do eleven.' He shrugs. 'Have they said what's wrong with them?'

'The man who runs the shipyard thinks my workers are too homely.'

'Homely?'

'They want men of steel who'll terrify the enemy, not craftsmen wearing *Fair Isle* sweaters.'

'Can't you make your figures more heroic?'

He thinks for a moment and then shakes his head. 'No, I don't think I can. They're not withdrawing the commission,' he adds, quickly, before I can chip in with objections, 'but they've brought in somebody called Rushbury. I suppose they're hoping he'll come up with something more robust.'

'I see. How soon will you be going back?'

'Tomorrow.'

'But you said they've given you a month's leave. Given all that's happening in Glasgow, I'd have thought you'd want to spend a bit more time here or with Hilda.'

'I'm not going back directly to my digs,' says Stanley. 'I'll be spending four days with the Murrays.'

'Who are the Murrays?'

'Graham is a teacher at the Art School. Charlotte studied under Jung.'

'Is this you having treatment?'

'Not exactly, but we talk a lot. She's interested in religions. We've got lots of things in common. She was born in Germany and came to England as a refugee,' he adds, as if it's something else they have in common.

I sit back. 'You're not about to have another of your up-in-heaven moments, are you, Stanley?'

'Well, what if I am?' he says, defensively.

I can't believe this. Having waited whilst the 'Daphne' episode peaked and came down the other side, I had been looking forward to a restoration of the status-quo. I fold my arms.

'This is the second married woman that you've dallied with.'

'She isn't all that married.'

'What does that mean?'

'Graham, that's her husband, doesn't mind. We're soul-mates, me and Charlotte.'

'You've been soul-mates with every woman you've ever known, Stanley.'

'No, I haven't. There are lots of women that I wasn't up-in-heaven with.'

'But you'll admit you've not exactly been discriminating.'

'Why don't you divorce me, then?' he snaps, as a reminder that he hasn't given up on the idea.

'I'm simply pointing out that I'd have ample grounds for doing so if I decided that was what I wanted. If you're finding it a stretch to pay for Hilda, think what it would be like paying maintenance for two ex-wives and having to support a third one. At the rate you're going through them, you would probably be on to Woman Number 4 or 5 by that time.'

'If you hadn't come along, I'd still be on Wife No 1,' he throws out.

I feel winded by the unexpected parry, although it confirms what I still wanted to believe, that I had been the only woman he would ever have left Hilda for.

'Well I did come along and you did marry me. I'm sorry Stanley but I'm not divorcing you. It suits me for the moment to be Mrs Spencer.'

'You're not Mrs Spencer,' he says vehemently. This is not the man I'm used to bullying into submission. Daphne's influence or maybe now it's Charlotte's, must be more far-reaching than I'd thought or maybe it's a build-up of resentment over years of having his desires frustrated.

I give vent to my exasperation and then wish I hadn't. 'Sorry, ducky, I'm afraid I am. When you said Dudley wanted to take over running your affairs, it was the last straw. I saw a solicitor after that meeting and I've put the deeds for Lindworth in my married name.'

The look he gives me reassures me that he's no idea what that implies.

'It means we're bound together, Stanley, whether you like it or not.'

IV

'I gather she's a psycho-analyst.'

'That could be useful,' Dorothy says. 'More than Daphne and her knitting, anyway.'

'They have long conversations about Eastern mysticism.'

Dorothy sighs: 'Other people lead such interesting lives.' She turns back to her book.

I put the shirt I'm mending in the sewing-box. 'The next time he comes down, I'll mention the divorce.'

She doesn't look up from the page she's reading. 'As you wish, dear.'

'It's her husband, Graham, who could be the sticking point. He'd rather sit out the affair than lose her altogether. At least that was the impression I got.'

'And you think you owe it to her husband not to make her lover readily available.'

'I'm only thinking Stanley might decide that there's no point in him divorcing me if Charlotte's husband won't divorce her.'

'You could always take the reins and sue him for adultery.'

I realise I've been pulling the loose threads of raffia out of the sewing-box whilst we've been talking. 'Still, it would be better if we could resolve it amicably, don't you think?'

'In my experience, divorce is hardly ever amicable and particularly when the marriage hasn't been that friendly.' Dorothy shoots me the sort of glance that tells me she has got a whiff of bull-shit and if I persist on this tack I could end up face down in a cow-pat.

'Anyway, I'll have a go at him next time we meet.' I drop the threads of raffia in the waste-paper basket. Now the sewing-box won't fasten properly. I go to fold the shirt I've finished darning and discover when I prick my finger on it that the needle is still pinned onto the sleeve.

'Blast!' I suck on the finger. 'That hurts.'

'Oh dear, more bloodshed,' Dorothy says, languidly.

V

Towards the end of 1944, the Germans launch their last offensive. Now, the planes they send to bomb the capital aren't manned with pilots who might also die or hopefully might die instead of us; they are the bombs. Their engines sound like motor mowers in the sky, too insignificant to take account of till we see the damage they inflict. We soon learn that it's not the planes approaching that we have to fear, it is the silence when the engine stops.

They are replaced in turn by flying bombs a few months later. You hear two bangs: first the *phut* of the exhaust as it cuts out, then the explosion. Just as we thought we'd defeated them, the Germans launch a thousand V2 rockets from The Hague and kill nine thousand people who thought they'd survived the war.

Although the fighting is continuing in Asia, it's when Dorothy and I hear Paris has been liberated and see footage of the march along the Champs Elysées, that we feel the war is truly coming to an end. We dance around the kitchen. She's rejoicing because Paris was the city she felt most at home in. I'm rejoicing because I no longer have to worry that she'll kill me, thinking that she's doing me a favour. We've come through it and we're both alive.

So, too, of course, is Stanley. The last we heard, he'd completed his commission for the War Artists Committee. Thinking he'll be coming back to Cookham, I write telling him he can rent Lindworth if he cares to. It takes Stanley three weeks to reply. He says he can't afford the rent for Lindworth and is staying up in Glasgow to complete a painting of the *Resurrection* set in the Port Glasgow cemetery. He's looking for a canvas fifty feet across.

When finally he does return, we hear he's living in a small house near the station on the outskirts of the village. Cliveden View was built by his grandfather and is owned by his brother Percy. Percy's offered him the purchase of the house and Dudley has arranged a mortgage.

Shortly afterwards, I hear there's been a rumpus outside Arkwright's store. 'Two women fighting over one man. They went at it tooth and claw, apparently.' I hoist the bag of shopping up onto the work-top.

'How undignified,' says Dorothy. She disapproves of women who behave like men. 'And who's the prize bull? Do we know?'

'It's Stanley.' I reach underneath the work-top for the wire baskets where we keep the vegetables. I'm all for village gossip when I'm not the target of it.

She puts down her mug of coffee. 'Do you mean our Stanley?'

'Is there any other?'

'There are women fighting over Stanley Spencer?'

'Lots of women think that he's a genius.'

'I think that Stanley is a genius. It doesn't mean I'd sacrifice the laws of civilised society in his defence. This country's just been through a war. These women should be setting an example. Do they have names?'

'One of them is Daphne Charlton, George's wife.'

'I know who Daphne Charlton is. You said he'd finished with her.'

'Not as far as she's concerned, apparently. She'd come to Cookham hoping for a reconciliation, but she chose an awkward moment. Charlotte Murray had arrived on Friday. Daphne saw her coming out of Cliveden View and followed her into the shop.'

'I'm not sure Cookham can survive this level of excitement.' Dorothy turns on the tap and rinses out her mug. She's waiting for me to fill in the details. I wait for her curiosity to get the better of her. 'Who won?'

'Rumour has it Charlotte got a black eye. Daphne was a stretcher case.'

She peers at me. 'You're joking.'

'Yes. I gather there were several scratches but they'll both live.'

'What did Stanley do?' She's rooting through the shopping bag to see if I've brought some of Arkwright's broken biscuits back with me.

'He barricaded himself in the house. He's still there. If you're looking for the broken biscuits by the way, I couldn't get any.' She pouts. 'I queued for half an hour just to get leeks and potatoes. They've got less food on their shelves than we have.' I take out the vegetables and hang the bag behind the kitchen door. 'At least I brought you back the latest gossip.'

Dorothy sniffs. 'I suspect you're making all this up.'

'The local paper goes to press on Tuesday. What's the betting it'll be there on the front page? Shall I order us a copy in advance in case they're sold out?'

'The less interested we appear to be, the better. Let the spotlight fall on someone else, for once.'

'I think, as long as he's in Cookham, Stanley's going to remain the centre of attention. What defeats me is why two sophisticated women would descend to fighting over someone who is married. What do they expect to gain? It's not as if the winner gets the spoils.'

'I dare say if you've shared an up-in-heaven moment with another human being, it remains with you.'

'I wouldn't know.' She's giving me that hard stare. 'What I mean is…'

'Yes, dear, I know what you mean.'

VI

When I look in on Stanley, three days later, it takes so long for him to come down and let me in that if it wasn't for the curtain twitching at the window, I might have assumed the house was empty. He's in his pyjamas, but he's kept his vest on underneath. He stands there in the passage, his hair standing up on end and his toes curling on the lino. There are dark rings underneath his eyes.

The house, like all the others Stanley's lived in, has a derelict, unwelcome air about it. Through an open doorway off the corridor I glimpse a room that's facing front and doubling as a bedroom/studio. A table by the window is piled high with art materials. There is a metal Army bed against the wall with Stanley's blue and gold checked dressing gown thrown over it, a bible on a bedside table and an open fire, unlit. Next to the door are several unpacked crates.

'Has Charlotte gone then?'

'Both of them have gone,' he says, but he looks past me down the path to make sure no-one's lurking in the undergrowth. He holds the door back and then locks it after me.

'I brought a lettuce from the garden.'

'Thank you.' He unwraps it from the newspaper and puts it in the sink. He fills the kettle and then leaves it on the draining board.

'I heard about the fight.'

He looks pained. 'They were arguing, that's all.'

'From what I heard, it was a little more than that.'

He rubs his eyes. 'It's Daphne. She insists on seeing me. She won't accept it's over.'

'Charlotte's still the one you're having joyful moments with at present, then?' I wonder whether to suggest he lights a taper underneath the kettle.

He sits down. 'She wanted us to have a child.'

'Who? Charlotte?' He nods. 'What did Graham say to that?'

'I don't know if she told him.'

'He'd have had to know at some point,'

Stanley shrugs. 'It didn't happen anyway.'

'How did you manage to persuade them both to leave?'

'I threatened I would go to court if Daphne kept on stalking me like this. It's not so bad with Charlotte; she moved down to London to be near me for a bit when I left Glasgow, but she's back now.'

So it's some time since he left Port Glasgow. I feel piqued that Stanley hasn't bothered keeping me abreast of what is going on. But at least we can talk to one another now, if not like friends at least like fellow human beings.

'You ought to be grateful that because you're married, neither of them could lay claim to you. I reckon I've done you a favour, Stanley. What have you arranged with her?'

'She says she'll leave me on my own if that's what I prefer.'

'And is it?'

'Yes. I need them all to go away. I don't want anybody anymore.'

'Not even Hilda?'

'Hilda? Yes, of course I want her. Hilda is the only person I feel peaceful with. We love each other. Hilda trusts my visions.'

Instantly whatever goodwill has grown up between the two of us evaporates. Whilst Hilda is the only person I'm prepared to share the stage with when it comes to

Stanley's muses, I still feel a level of resentment when he throws her the bouquet I never wanted anyway. Or did I?

He pulls down his sleeves, then rolls them up again. He's scratching at the skin above his wrists.

'What is it, Stanley. Is there something on your mind?'

He finds a bit of loose skin on his thumb and nibbles at it. 'I need you to give me that divorce, Patricia.'

'Oh for God's sake, Stanley. On what grounds?'

'Non-consummation of the marriage.'

I can feel my knees begin to buckle. I sink down into a chair.

'Why bother getting a divorce if you don't want to marry either of the women you've been having an affair with?'

Stanley clasps his hands together. 'I've decided that I want to marry Hilda and for me to do that I have to persuade her that I never really left her.'

'That's ridiculous. Of course you left her.'

'An essential part of me remained hers. That's what matters to her.'

'Hilda doesn't want you, Stanley. She's in love with God.'

'I'm helping her to get to him.' He arcs one arm over his head and runs his fingers through his hair. 'I'm down there in the oozing froth and scummy waters at the bottom of her love.'

'Oh, grow up, Stanley. You can't keep on waltzing in and out of marriage on a whim, you know. As I reminded you the last time you brought up the subject, marriage is a sacrament.'

'That's why I need to marry Hilda. It's what God wants.'

'That's what you said when you went down on your knees to me. It's not as if I asked you to.'

'You're saying no, then? You intend to contest the divorce.'

'Not only that; I'd win.' All thoughts of getting through this situation on diplomacy have disappeared. 'You're not the only one in a position to throw mud and make it stick. Forget it, Stanley.'

Part Eight
Retribution

I

'Would you believe it! Now he's managed to get shot of Daphne Charlton and the other woman, Stanley has convinced himself he wants to marry Hilda!'

Dorothy was bound to get wind of what Stanley had in mind so I'd decided I would get in first with my objections. I did not want Stanley turning up and putting his side of the argument before I'd had a chance to put mine.

She was in the studio when I got back. I waited until six o'clock and took her up a whisky. She was scraping down her palette, putting any excess paint into a crucible to mix into a neutral grey which is the hall mark of her painting.

'Well why shouldn't he?' she says.

'For one thing, Hilda has already said no. She'll refuse to marry him again.' I put the whisky on the bench and Dodo takes a swig out of the glass. 'He wants to sue me for non-consummation of the marriage.'

She looks up over the glass. At least his action demonstrates to Dorothy that although I might have got into bed with Stanley what took place there stopped short of full intercourse. If he had only made it plainer, Dorothy might not have left me when she did.

She puts the glass down. 'Hilda would refuse to marry him if she thought your relationship conflicted with the one he'd had with her. If you can reassure her that was not the case, there isn't any reason why they can't get back together.'

'Let him sue me for non-consummation of the marriage!'

Dodo spreads her hands out in a *why not* gesture.

'Do you really want the lurid details of our marriage broadcast to the world at large?'

'I doubt the world at large would be that interested,' she says, shortly.

'You don't know the way they twist things. You weren't there when old man Gilbert had his heart attack. The newspapers as good as said I'd lured him to the lake that day and then pretended I was drowning so that he would feel obliged to come and rescue me.'

'It was a quarter of a century ago. I doubt that anyone except you still remembers it. What's news today will serve to light the fire tomorrow.' Dorothy begins to clean the palette with white spirit. It's a smell that seems to sum up our whole life together. Like somebody brought up on a farm whose nostrils twitch each time they smell damp straw, the scent of oil and turpentine has worked its way into the bloodstream. I could no more live without it than I could live without air.

'What is it you're afraid of... really?' She has stopped what she was doing and is fixing me. 'Well?'

'People can be cruel.'

She shrugs. 'We've always known that.'

'They can be especially cruel to people like us.'

'Lesbians, you mean?'

'I wish you wouldn't use that term. It's....'

'Clinical?'

'Unsympathetic.'

She gives me her *so that's it* look. 'You're scared that if Stanley sues you for non-consummation of the marriage, everyone will know that you're a lesbian?'

She throws the rag into the box next to the work bench and goes over to the window. There's a sound out in the garden and I wonder for one awful moment if it's Stanley who's thought up another reason to divorce me and can't wait to tell me what it is. And then I hear rain pattering against the glass.

'What is it about being married, other than its function as a smoke-screen, that appeals to you?' says Dorothy.

I'm glad I had the foresight, when I brought the whisky up, to bring my cigarettes as well. I take one from the packet.

'I suppose I like the structure of it. It gives a relationship parameters. As Stanley Spencer's wife I have a status. People may not like me or approve of me, but they are forced to recognise me.'

'I see.'

I draw on the cigarette and turn my head away, so I'm not blowing smoke in her direction. 'Do you?'

'Yes, I think so. You like to be grounded.'

'I doubt Stanley could make anyone feel grounded. It's a label, that's all. If you'd been a man, I would have married you.'

'Assuming that I'd asked you,' she says.

I look round for something I can tip the ash into. 'Why wouldn't you?'

'For one thing, you're impossible to live with.'

Is she joking? 'Well you didn't have to go on living with me.'

'I did leave, if you remember.'

'You thought I was having an affair with Stanley.'

'You were married to him. You could hardly call it an affair. To sleep with him would have been normal in the circumstances.'

'Normal'. I laugh. 'Oh yes.'

Dorothy is looking at me as if I've just proved her point. 'Until you can own up to what you are, Patricia, and until you can be true to that self, how can you be true to anybody else? All Stanley's done is bring into relief a situation that was always going to become an issue in your life at some point.'

'I can't be as brave as you are, Dorothy.'

She tilts her head back so the lids are almost covering her eyes. 'You might find cowardice more costly in the end and no less painful. Pour me out another whisky, would you.' She holds out her glass.

I pour another inch into her beaker. Whisky isn't rationed, thank God, but the price of it is going through the ceiling. Arkwright has installed a hand-pump in the store to pull pints. For a few weeks Dorothy and I drank beer instead but then we heard a rumour he was making it himself out of potatoes.

She sips slowly from the glass as if she's choosing her words carefully and testing each one before she releases it.

'The trouble is, you see, that underneath it all, Patricia, you're a very ordinary person. You ought to have married someone like a plumber or a lorry driver who got drunk on Friday nights and beat you. You would have had half-a-dozen children who were also unexceptional. After a quarter of a century you would be prematurely old, your children would have left home and you would have been condemned by those parameters you put such store by to a miserable old age followed in due course by death.'

'I never realised what an opportunity I'd sacrificed when I threw in my lot with you.' I look for somewhere I can stub the cigarette out.

Dorothy grunts. 'Throw that pack of cigarettes across here.'

'You don't smoke.'

'I do tonight.'

'Smoking's bad for your bronchitis.'

She snorts. 'Spoken like a housewife.'

'If we carry on like this we'll have a real fight.'

'Well perhaps it's time we did.'

I throw the pack of cigarettes across to her. She starts to take one out, then puts it back again. 'You're right, it's bad for my bronchitis.' She goes over to the only chair and sits. She leans back with her eyes closed. In the artificial light her skin looks blue. The minutes pass. I'm wondering if she's dropped off to sleep. And then I see she's gazing at me underneath the lids.

'Might your reluctance to grant Stanley a divorce have also been affected by that article in last week's supplement, suggesting that his name could be put forward for a knighthood?'

I draw breath. 'Of course not.'

I had wondered when I read the article, what Dorothy would say if she caught sight of it.

'You wouldn't relish the idea of being *Lady Spencer* just a teeny bit?' says Dorothy. 'That amethyst and diamond necklace Stanley bought for you at Aspreys would pale into insignificance beside the perks a title would bring with it.' She's still toying with the cigarette pack.

'Obviously, there'd be advantages.' I watch her, guardedly. I need another cigarette out of the packet.

'So you've thought about it?' she says, mildly.

'I would qualify for Stanley's pension, for example. If we were divorced and he remarried Hilda, she would get the title and the pension.' Dorothy's face isn't giving anything away. 'It would be nice to have a pension, wouldn't it?'

'It would be lovely, but I'd rather not have someone else's.'

'Don't you think we've earned it?'

'No, I don't. If Stanley got a pension, it would be in recognition of his services to art. You've made it clear you don't have much regard for Stanley's work and therefore it seems wrong to gain from it.' She turns the cigarette pack in her fingers. 'What about the ceremony at the palace? Will you be there with him to collect his gong?'

'I doubt the King would want to meet him on his own. I'd need to make sure that he'd changed his underpants and didn't wear that awful hat he goes out painting in.'

'I see you've got it all sussed out.' She gives a long sigh. '*Lady Spencer*. Well, well…' She gets up. 'I think I'll turn in.'

'Don't you want some supper?'

She picks up her whisky glass and holds it to the light. There's still an inch of whisky in the bottom. 'No, thanks. This will serve me as a nightcap. I feel rather tired.'

II

Since then, there's been no further conversation on the subject. Dorothy behaves the same: she's courteous and distant. She pretends there hasn't been a shift in our relationship but obviously there has. Occasionally, she comes into my room at night, makes love to me and goes away again. She's rougher that she was before. I'm often left with bruises on my arms and inner thighs. She doesn't ask me if I want her to make love to me; it's something that she takes for granted.

Once it's over, I try not to cling to her. I know that she'll reject me if I do. What I need most is to be held and cosseted and reassured of her affection, so this is what she's withholding from me. What she gives is just enough to show me what I've lost.

If it had not been for the knighthood, I was on the point of giving in. Before he caught me off-guard by demanding it, I'd almost come to the decision by myself that a divorce would be a sensible decision. I'd expected Stanley to resist and yes, I had been hurt by his apparent readiness to let me go. But that aside, to have come all this way, to have endured so much and then to give up at the very moment when my star went into the ascendancy... no, I decided, *that* I couldn't do. I wondered why, since Dorothy already knew about the knighthood, she had not said anything before, but no doubt she'd been wondering the same about me.

Trying to pretend it had no bearing on the issue had been a miss-calculation. Stanley might be vague about my motives for remaining married to him. So was I. But Dorothy was not. Was I excited by the thought of being *Lady Spencer*? You bet.

All I had to do was gently go on putting obstacles in Stanley's way until the idea of divorce lost its allure. It wasn't likely Hilda would go back to him, whatever happened; Stanley was contaminated goods and as for Dorothy, the interlude with Dora Gibbons would have been enough to show her she had nowhere else to go. We'd been together all this time. I didn't think that Dorothy would leave me now, though I remembered thinking something rather similar of Hilda days before she had walked out on Stanley.

III

When I'm notified by Stanley's lawyer that he is petitioning for the annulment of our marriage, it feels as if someone has just punched me in the stomach. I'd assumed the threats I threw at Stanley would have been enough of a deterrent. It's the first time he has openly defied me.

Where's the man who begged me on his knees to marry him, who swore that I was his Supreme Muse? I'd curse Stanley for his fickleness, but Stanley isn't fickle. He's the same in all ways other than in his relationship to me. I feel rejected, tearful, angry and bewildered. For the first time I can understand how Hilda must have felt when Stanley left her.

'You had better get yourself a lawyer if you're going to contest it,' Dorothy says, blandly.

Dodo knows I can't afford a lawyer and she isn't likely to contribute anything in terms of money or advice. She is affecting to have lost all interest in what she refers to as my 'marital affairs'.

I drop enough hints about what I'll do if Stanley tries to push through a divorce, that in the end his lawyer recommends a legal separation, to spare Stanley's reputation rather than my own. Over the past year his work has begun attracting more attention, partly due to a concerted effort on the part of friends and partly to an exhibition at The National Gallery of two of Stanley's paintings of the shipyard in Port Glasgow. It seems Jas was right - the tide is turning in his favour - though it's hard to know what came first, rumours of the knighthood or the upturn in his fortunes.

I tell Dorothy what Stanley's lawyers have negotiated and she shrugs. A legal separation doesn't count for much in her book. Most of my allowance will go straight into the lawyer's pocket.

There's a reproduction in *The Times* a few months later, of a picture Stanley's showing in his latest exhibition. It's called *Dinner on the Ferry Hotel Lawn* and it shows me and Dorothy on one side of the table, Daphne and her rival Charlotte Murray on the other. Though the table's laid with silver cutlery and serviettes, there is no sign of food.

'I'm glad I wasn't present at that feast,' Dorothy says wryly. 'Stanley could at least have put some bread rolls on the table. Still,' she adds, 'it's more a comment on what we gave him than what he gave us, I expect.'

IV

We don't see much of Stanley in the weeks that follow. Once you start engaging lawyers, there no longer seems to be much point in talking to each other. It's discouraged by the very people who say they are acting for you, but who stand to gain most from a breakdown in communication.

The privations of the war and the harsh winter following it, have left Dorothy's already ravaged constitution struggling to remain afloat. That March, just as we think the worst is over, there's more snow and Dorothy is laid low by another lung infection. There's a slight improvement in the weather during April, but towards the end of that month temperatures fall back to freezing and her cough returns.

She is insistent that she doesn't need a doctor. He's been known to give his services for free to several families in the village but he either thinks we're better off than we appear or that we're less deserving. Dorothy would not accept his charity in any case.

The winter we first moved here, when she was so ill, I did a bit of research in the library and discovered there are thirty thousand cases of tuberculosis every year. They call it the poor man's disease. Her fear is that if Dr Sandford thinks she has tuberculosis, he'll be duty-bound to pass the information on to the authorities. She could be carted off to hospital by force. That wouldn't only wipe out any savings we had but would wipe her out as well, she says. She's never been an ideal patient. She insists that since tuberculosis isn't curable, there isn't much point in a doctor being brought in to confirm you've got it.

One day, when her cough is so bad I have no choice but to call him, I move her things into my room once he's gone and tell her I'll sleep on the sofa downstairs. It's a measure of how ill she is that for once she accepts that if she's goes on sleeping in the studio she will end up in hospital or worse. I manage to persuade her to remain in bed the first day.

'I can bring you up a tray,' I say.

'Please don't, Patricia. I hate having meals in bed. The crumbs get everywhere.'

'I'll change the sheets.'

'There's no need. When I'm hungry I'll come down.'

She leans back and a moment later, she's dropped off to sleep. Her head is sliding off the pillow but I don't dare pump it up for fear of waking her.

She's still asleep when I come back an hour later. I can't see her breathing and there's no expression on her face. She could be dead for all the indications to the contrary. I touch her cheek. There's no response and then I see her eye-lids flicker. Her eyes open and she stares at me a moment before closing them again and sinking back into whatever dream she's having. Everything she does these days has the effect of making me feel more excluded. I've lost Stanley and increasingly I sense that I've lost Dorothy as well.

Although I've got her back into my bed, I feel obliged to leave her on her own in there so that it doesn't look as if I've engineered the move for motives other than her health. However, as all my belongings are in what is now her bedroom, I am popping in and out a dozen times a day.

I gradually extend my visits, parking myself on the bed to talk to her or bringing up the mail if there is anything addressed to her. We're careful not to mention the divorce or anything concerning Stanley. Dorothy shows every sign of having perfectly adapted to our new relationship whilst I am at a loss to know if what we have now qualifies as a relationship at all.

Once when she's still asleep at 6 o'clock, I take her in a whisky. It's still on the bedside table when I go back half an hour later. Dorothy is sleeping soundly.

I take off my skirt and blouse and creep in next to her. There is a magazine beside the bed and I pretend I'm reading it. As if I'm not aware of what I'm doing, I begin to trace lines idly up and down her forearm with my finger-tips, withdrawing my hand every now and then to turn the page.

There's an alertness in her now that tells me she's awake and looking at me, but I go on reading with my left hand slowly moving up and down her arm. She clears her throat. I glance down.

'You're awake.' I put the magazine aside. 'You slept a long time. You must have been tired.' I slither down the bed so that we're lying side by side and facing one another. I am inches from her ear. Once, when she said she wasn't in the mood, I managed to seduce her just by nibbling at her ear-lobe, but as I am shifting my head closer Dorothy gets up onto her elbow and throws back the cover.

'Are you getting up?'

'I have something to finish in the studio.'

'Can't you stay quarter of an hour? You've been working non-stop for the past three weeks.'

'I need the daylight.'

'It's already after 6 o'clock. I think you've missed it.'

There's a pause. She reaches over, lifting up the bit of blanket covering me, to see what I'm wearing. 'What's this all about?' she says.

'I thought I'd creep in next to you. Just being friendly. We don't seem to spend much time together. Properly, I mean.'

'We made love last week.'

'No we didn't, Dorothy. We had sex.'

'Would you rather that we didn't?'

'I would rather that you didn't treat me like a whore.'

'I treat you like a whore because that's what you are. A whore is somebody who sells themselves. The only question is the price.'

'I don't know why you bother making love to me at all, if you despise me.'

She looks down at me. 'There's nothing wrong with whores, as long as they accept it's what they are.'

'In that case, maybe next time you could pay me. You won't mind if I get something out of it. God knows there hasn't been a lot of pleasure in it, recently. Perhaps it's time we put the whole thing on a business footing.'

'You think I would pay to sleep with you?' she sneers.

There is no going back now. We are on the brink. The only thing I care about is getting my revenge.

'I don't see why not. Stanley did.'

I go to slide away from her, but in a deft move Dorothy has pinned my left arm to the mattress. She secures my free hand, holding it above my head in one of hers and giving me a sharp slap with the other.

I'm shocked. Dorothy has never laid a hand on me before. There is a hardness in the way she's looking at me now that frightens me. She throws the pillows on the floor, so that I'm lying flat. I'm suffocating underneath the weight of her. My mouth's the only bit of me that I can move.

'Don't!'

'Don't what?'

'Don't do that. You're hurting me.'

'I want to hurt you.'

'Please. This isn't like you, Dorothy.'

'Shut up! If you want paying, you can earn it.'

She tears off the shift I'm wearing, forcing her knee inbetween my legs and with her free hand she starts groping me. We usually pleasure one another, taking it in turns to bring each other to a climax. This is horrible, but there is something thrilling in the strangeness of it. It's like making love with somebody you've only just met. She's behaving like a man. She doesn't care what I want. This is all about her.

I'm not sure that either of us gets much satisfaction from it. By the end I'm crying, not so much because she's hurt me as because I think it's what's expected. Dorothy wants me to be humiliated and all right, I can put up with that if afterwards things are all right between us. I would rather that we didn't have to go through this again and I suspect that she would but at least it's cleared the air. When she's got dressed, she picks my shift up from the ground. It's shredded.

'Looks like we shall need to do a bit of shopping.' She stands with the torn shift in her hand and looks at me. Now is the moment when I might expect a cuddle or at least a 'Thank you.'

'Better get yourself dressed,' she says.

We don't talk about what's happened. That night she moves back into the studio. The next time we make love it's more the way it used to be, although the spectre of that afternoon still hovers in the air between us. Now that I know Dorothy is capable of violence, I am careful to avoid a situation that might lead to it. Since we first lived together, our relationship has never been as volatile as this. I wonder briefly whether to tell Stanley I'll let him divorce me after all. I'm looking at a future without either of them. I thought it was Stanley who could not endure to be alone, whereas I now know that it's me.

V

One Sunday, as we're sitting down to breakfast in our dressing-gowns, the doorbell rings. We glance at one another.

'Who on earth can that be on a Sunday?' Dorothy gets up. I hear the front door open.

'Stanley!' she says. 'You look awful.' It must be the first time we've seen Stanley in a month. 'You'd better come inside,' she says.

On Sundays we have breakfast in the living-room so that we can spread out the papers on the table. Stanley follows her inside. She gestures him towards the chair next to the fire. It's raining outside and when Stanley sits down there is water dripping off his coat onto the carpet. He looks dizzy with exhaustion.

'Hilda's had a breakdown,' he says. 'She woke everybody up last night and told them they must barricade themselves inside the house. She thinks that Mrs Harter's out to murder her and both the girls.'

I glance at Dorothy. 'I thought that she and Hilda were the best of friends.'

When Stanley registers my presence he looks fixedly at me, as if I've resurrected memories from a previous existence and he's having to collate them. 'They were,' he says, finally. He wraps the two flaps of the mackintosh across his knees.

I pour a cup of tea and hand it to him. The cup judders in the saucer. Stanley lowers it onto his lap.

'Where have they taken Hilda?'

'Banstead. It's a lunatic asylum.'

For a moment neither of us speaks. We've both become a trifle blasé in the face of the catastrophes that have befallen Stanley since we met him, but this falls into a different category.

'Have you seen her?' I say.

'Yes.' He watches as a rivulet of water slowly drips onto the floor and puts his foot out heedlessly to cover up the puddle. 'It was terrible,' he whispers. 'At the hospital they didn't want to let me see her. They thought Hilda might attack me.'

'And what happened? Did she?' I persist.

He looks insulted: 'Hilda is my soul-mate. Why would she attack me?'

Dorothy gives Stanley's knee a pat. 'Why don't you take your raincoat off?' He doesn't answer. 'Stanley, drink your tea. You need something inside you.'

Stanley shakes his head: 'She's not mad. Hilda talks to God. It's what she's always done. I told them that, but they're insisting that if God is telling her to fight the nurses, either she is mad or He is.'

'Maybe someone from the Christian Science Movement could be asked to intercede for her?' says Dorothy unwisely.

'I can intercede for her,' says Stanley.

'But if God's the only person she will listen to….'

'He talks to me as well. I often pass on messages.'

'It's just that, if I understand correctly, he's told Hilda Mrs Harter's out to murder them.'

'She probably misunderstood. The message isn't always clear.'

'It makes you wonder which of them should be incarcerated,' I say, after Stanley's gone. There's no response from Dorothy. Like me, she may be thinking that it's sad and rather touching that, although we are estranged, it's us who Stanley sought out in extremis rather than his friends in London.

I am wondering if, in light of what's now happened, I should offer Stanley a divorce for Hilda's sake. I don't feel much of a connection with her but I wouldn't want to think that I'm the cause of Hilda being sectioned.

On the other hand, the word 'divorce' has not been mentioned recently and I am loath to bring the subject up again. I tell myself that a divorce at this stage could be damaging to Stanley's prospects of a knighthood and particularly if he then got married to a woman who is clinically insane.

He's spending three days every week with Hilda at the hospital. From Cookham it's a round trip of eight hours and he has to change trains three times between here and Banstead. Hilda loves sweets so he takes her chocolates every time he goes. In a perverse way, once he's got into the rhythm, he seems happier than he's been for a long time.

When I meet him after one of his excursions to the hospital, he tells me Hilda's doing splendidly.

'What do you talk about when you're together?'

'Sometimes we read through the letters we've sent one another, or we talk about the latest messages from God. We're closer than we've ever been in some ways. She gave me a letter to deliver to the King the other day.'

'And did you?'

'Well I tried, but she had written *Mrs Perkins* on the envelope. The man I spoke to at the Palace said there wasn't anyone of that name there.'

He shakes his head ingenuously. I hope Stanley gets his knighthood before the authorities decide to section him as well.

'Why is he doing this?' I say to Dorothy.

'He loves her,' Dorothy says simply.

VI

Six months later, just as she's about to be discharged from the asylum, we learn Hilda has been diagnosed with cancer. It's a measure of her disillusionment with Christian Science that she's ready to submit to a mastectomy, instead of leaving the decision in the hands of God. The surgeon, primed of Stanley's situation, takes a painting and agrees to waive his fees.

Whilst she's in hospital, and afterwards when she's recuperating, Stanley barely leaves her bedside. I don't know what irritates me more, the depth of his devotion or the fact that it's no longer aimed at me.

I'm torn between the need to make a gesture that will demonstrate to Stanley's friends that I am not the demon they imagine me to be, and a reluctance to agree to a divorce just at the moment when I've most to gain from being married to him. Once we were divorced, I doubt that he would bother to remain in touch with us. Since he turned up that night at Moor Thatch he's been totally preoccupied with Hilda. These days, if I want to know how Stanley is, I have to ask.

I'm walking down the High Street on my way to pick up some provisions from the General Store one morning, when I recognise the person trudging down the road towards me with a bunch of kindling underneath his arm, as Stanley. I'm appalled. He looks years older than he did the last time we met. He is hollow-eyed and his hair's gone completely grey.

'I've not been sleeping well,' he says. 'And what with looking after Hilda, I'm not getting much work done. Tooth's asked for a replacement for two paintings he sold last week.'

'That's good, isn't it? Your work has found an audience. At least it solves your money problems.'

He nods. 'Maybe.' But he doesn't look convinced.

We're standing opposite The Copper Kettle. 'How about a cup of tea?' I steer him over and we sit down at a corner table. I mouth *tea* to Ida. Her eyes pass from me to Stanley and she nods.

'Is it the travelling back and forwards that's exhausting you?' I say.

'It's everything,' says Stanley and for once I know exactly what he means.

The tea arrives. He wraps his hands around the cup.

'How are the girls?' I ask. He blinks as if he has forgotten he has children.

'They're all right,' he says, at last.

'They do spend some time with their mother, then?'

'Of course. They're often there.'

I wonder if I ought to order him a sandwich but I have the feeling he'd forget to eat it.

'Only Unity seemed pretty disenchanted with the situation when we last met.'

'It's not Hilda's fault she can't look after them,' says Stanley, wearily.

'No, I appreciate that. How was Hilda when you saw her?'

'We talked for an hour and a half.'

'She didn't find that tiring? After all, she's had a major operation.'

'It was me who did the talking,' Stanley says,

No change there, then. 'When do you think she'll be discharged?'

'They reckon she'll be out by Christmas,' he says, brightening up a little.

'And what are your plans then?'

He shrugs. 'It depends on Hilda.' He puts down the cup and clasps his hands together, rubbing one thumb back and forth across the other.

I breathe in and give the air a chance to circulate inside my lungs before expelling it. I have the feeling I'll regret what I'm about to say, but suddenly I can't endure the limbo we are in a moment longer. I lean forward, cupping my hand over his. 'Do you still want to marry Hilda, Stanley?'

'Yes, of course I do.' He says it without any expectation in his voice.

'It's just that, Hilda being ill and all that, maybe we could come to an arrangement.' Anything, I think, to dent the stalemate we're all locked in. Once I've acted, Dorothy will have to, even if that action is to leave me altogether. Nothing could be much worse than the present situation.

He nods vaguely. I'm not sure he's understood me. He's already cataloguing all the things he's saving to tell Hilda in the morning.

'If you really want to marry Hilda, I might be prepared to give ground, Stanley,' I say, pressing home the message.

I was not expecting him to weep with gratitude but I'd expected something in the way of a response. He goes on staring at the wall. He's in a world in which the only other living soul is Hilda.

'Stanley?' He's not listening to me. He's beyond all that. And so, it would appear, is Hilda.

VII

'I've told Stanley I'll divorce him.'

Dorothy is reading with her legs up on the pouffe. I leaf through the letters I've just picked up off the mat and put the bills in one pile and the fliers in another. I pick out a letter from Lefevre's which I'm hoping might contain a cheque for two still lifes of Dorothy's that sold in their last mixed show.

She continues looking at me for a moment and then runs her index finger down the page to find her place and goes back to her book.

'I thought you would be pleased.' I rummage in the bureau drawer to find the paper knife and slit open the envelope. She puts her book down on her lap. 'It's what you wanted, isn't it?' I say.

'I wanted you to want it.'

'All right, now I want it.' There is nothing in the letter other than a list of future exhibitions, but at least we're on it.

'You know what you would be giving up?' says Dorothy.

I laugh. 'You mean the curtsy I hoped I might get from Mrs Arkwright next time I went in for some of her spring greens.'

'You won't get any credit either. It's not just about posterity.'

'If you go on like this, you'll talk me out of it.'

'I think that by tomorrow you'll have talked yourself out of it.'

'You must think me very shallow,' I say. I think Dorothy and Stanley must be vying with each other to see which of them can show the least enthusiasm. Knowing Dorothy, I wasn't expecting a round of applause but a pat on the back would have been nice. 'What's odd is that when I told Stanley I was willing to divorce him, I got the impression that he didn't care.'

'He has more pressing things to think about. His wife's in hospital because of you.'

'Don't you think Daphne Charlton and that other woman, Charlotte what's-her-name ought to bear some responsibility?'

'We know that Stanley wouldn't have looked twice at them if Hilda had still been his wife, or if you'd been a proper one. Her life's been stolen from her. It's no wonder the poor woman's ill.'

'If Hilda's ill because he left her, what could be more pressing than me giving him the opportunity to get her back? He could at least have thanked me for the offer.'

Dorothy looks up over her glasses. 'You would rather not be seen as the hyena circling the encampment. Is that what the gesture's aimed at?'

'Hilda isn't that ill.'

'She has cancer.'

'Stanley says they've cured it. She'll be out of hospital by Christmas.'

'Good. That's excellent.' She shifts her feet onto the floor and shuffles on her slippers. 'With luck they'll be able to begin the New Year where they left it fifteen years ago.'

'And what about us?'

'What about us?'

'Can we start the New Year where we left it fifteen years ago? I hate this half and half relationship. I don't know where I stand.'

'No,' she looks at me, thoughtfully. 'I'm not sure sometimes where you stand.' She puts her head on one side in an attitude of mock bewilderment. 'You're not agreeing to give Stanley a divorce because you recognise that in the circumstances it would be the decent thing to do. You would have granted him one earlier if that had been the case. So let me ask, why are you doing it?'

I stick my chin out. 'If you must know, Dorothy, I'm doing it because it's what you said you wanted. And you're very good at sulking till you get your own way.'

'Ah.'

'In fact these days you're very good at sulking anyway. No matter what I do, it doesn't seem to make much difference.' I draw breath. That's done it. Now I'll have to go down on my knees and say I'm sorry. Then I think, why should I?

'Maybe you should question why it doesn't seem to make a difference.'

'If I'm doing what you want, I can't see that it matters why I'm doing it?'

'It matters that you're honest where your motives are concerned.'

'All right. If I agreed to a divorce I'd want to know that we would be together afterwards.'

'And if I couldn't give you that assurance?'

'Then I wouldn't do it.'

'But you see, that proves my point. Self-interest is the lynch pin of your moral compass.'

'Screw you, Dorothy.' I throw the letter from Lefevre's on the pile of fliers to be thrown out. It skims off onto the floor. 'When you're a lonely and embittered old dyke living on your own with just a neighbour's cat for company, I shall be *Lady Spencer*. I shan't have to go down on my knees to anyone.'

'You don't have to go down on your knees now.'

'I've spent half a lifetime on my knees in front of you. Go back to Dora Gibbons. See if I care.'

'Dora Gibbons?' Dorothy adjusts her glasses. 'What a quaint thought.' She lets out a laugh that turns into a cough. She gets up and goes over to the door, still chortling. 'Dora Gibbons. That's a good one.'

She leans on the door-post for a moment. Getting to her feet has stirred the mucus up inside her lungs. She starts to speak, but suddenly the cough takes hold.

She gulps in air. Once she starts coughing, she can't stop. She grips the door-post for support and fumbles for a handkerchief. I watch. Is this a ploy to capture my attention? It's what I'd do in the circumstances, but it's not like Dorothy.

I'd normally be guiding her towards a chair and rushing off into the kitchen for a glass of water, but I'm rooted to the spot. I've never had a chance to stand back when she's having an attack and watch. My interest is forensic. For the first time I have no desire to intervene. I'd quite like to pull up a chair so that I can observe what's happening in comfort.

She subsides against the wall. The air inside her lungs is harsh and gravelly. She drops her handkerchief and grapples for it, then gives up, exhausted, and starts sliding down the wall until she's on the carpet and her legs are splayed in front of her.

Her face is grey. If she were to expire there on the floor infront of me, would that be my fault? Our eyes meet. There is surprise in hers, but it's quite mild and as

I'm watching it's already fading into resignation. When she takes in air, I hear it whirring like a motor running down inside her lungs. The sound reminds me of the V2s flying over in the War whilst underneath we waited for the engine to cut out and for the plane to drop out of the sky. Her eyes close.

'Dorothy?'

VIII

When Doctor Sandford saw her he insisted he would need to call an ambulance. By that time Dorothy was barely conscious but I saw the terror in her eyes. She shook her head and tried to speak.

'She doesn't want to go,' I said.

'She must,' said Dr Sandford, picking up his Gladstone bag and packing up the stethoscope. 'Your friend was lucky to survive the last attack. The next time she might be less fortunate.'

He'd not addressed a single word to Dorothy, except to mutter 'Well what have we here,' when he arrived and even that was not a question that required an answer since it was apparent that what he had was a half dead woman on his hands.

He pats his knees and gets up. 'Do you have a telephone?' He takes a notebook from his pocket.

Dorothy looks over at me and her eyes lock onto mine. I read the message in them. For the first time in her life, she is acknowledging that her fate lies in my hands.

'Thank you,' I say, 'but we'll manage. Dorothy hates hospitals. She'd rather die than be admitted to one.'

Dr Sandford's eyes pass briefly from my face down to the dress I'm wearing and then back to Dorothy and I know what he's thinking. He shrugs. 'It's your choice, of course.'

'No,' I say, 'it's her choice.'

'I have to make it clear it's contrary to my advice.'

'I understand that.'

He leans forward. 'Maybe we could have a word in private.'

'I would rather you said anything you have to say in front of Dorothy.'

He looks between us and then shakes his head. I have the feeling Dr Sandford's washed his hands of us.

He doesn't put much store by women when it comes to making sensible decisions. As the village doctor I expect he's heard the rumours. When he came the first time, I saw his eyes darting round the walls and taking in the paintings. Like most men he's wondering why a woman who is reasonably presentable would throw her lot in with another woman and especially one like this who will be lucky to survive the weekend.

He prescribes a mix of kaolin and morphine, which I'll need to pick up from the pharmacy. He'd previously recommended *slops:* steamed fish, raw eggs, beef tea and fresh air, preferably in a different climate. I'd heard dandelion leaf sandwiches were beneficial. He'd smiled patronisingly. At least he'd stopped short of suggesting that we take the *train bleu* to the South of France.

The wealthy in the village have their medicines wrapped in white paper sealed with wax, delivered by the doctor's errand boy, so it seems Dr Sandford's got the measure of us.

Whilst she's convalescing, our roles are defined. When Dorothy jokes that she'll take the kaolin and morphine with her glass of whisky in the evening, I tell her she'll have it when I say so.

I rig up a bench across the bed so she can draw and do some water colours, but the studio is out of bounds. A thimbleful of whisky in the evenings is her one treat if she's good. We play cards and I read to her from books I've brought back from the Lending Library. I get hold of one that's only just been published which I know she'll be excited by.

She scans the title page and puts it on the bedside table without bothering to open it.

'There are six people in the queue for that one. I had to agree to take it back next week.'

'I dare say I'll get round to it before then.'

'I thought you'd be desperate to get your hands on it. Seems everybody else is.'

She picks up the book again and turns it over. 'It's his brother Julian who heads up the Eugenics faction.'

I know vaguely what that is. They're saying stupid people reproduce more rapidly than those with higher IQ's. I'd have thought that was self-evident but like most issues, this one's complicated. It's the poor and unemployed who they say are hereditarily defective and need to be sterilised to stop them having children.

'But there are three million unemployed,' says Dorothy. 'They can't all be genetically unfit!'

What is upsetting her is that some writers who she liked before, including Shaw and Chesterton, have given their support to the idea. When Dorothy found out about it, she went round the house collecting up whatever she could find of theirs into a sack and told me to get rid of it.

She could have put the books straight in the dustbin so I gathered she was not so disenchanted that she wanted to destroy them. When I took them to the library I told Miss Barrett she was welcome to distribute them as she saw fit. The problem now is that she'll no doubt put them on a shelf inside the entrance selling at 1d and they'll be the first thing Dorothy sees when she's well enough to make the trip into the library by herself.

'I'll take it back then, shall I?' I say, thinking that if it's that controversial I might have a look at it myself first. *Brave New World* is an intriguing title.

'Leave it with me for the moment,' she says.

When I pick the book up two or three days later, I see that she's reached page 96. She's hooked. She has strong views but quality will always win out. You won't find a third rate reproduction of *The Laughing Cavalier* on her wall.

Thinking of those cheap cards that you looked for every time you bought a pack of cigarettes, I have a sudden memory of Fleur Laycock staring at the card between her fingers for a second and then glancing up and saying 'And are you that way inclined?'

I feel an unexpected wave of grief. I thought our paths were bound to cross again at some point, but they haven't. I was not invited to another soirée and I couldn't have gone even if I had been. So Fleur Laycock has become another of those tantalising *might-have-beens* that one's past life is littered with.

A few days later, when I'm taking Dorothy her breakfast tray, I find she's dressed. I put the tray down on the dresser. 'What's this?'

'It's me getting up.' She sits down on the bed to put her socks on. She's still coughing but I tell myself that once she starts to chafe at the restrictions, it's a sign she's getting better.

I go down onto my knees and put the socks on for her, rolling them to slot over her toes and smoothing them over the bridge. I hold the foot inside my hands a moment.

'What's this all in aid of?' she says.

'It's me going down onto my knees in front of you for what is absolutely the last time.'

'I'm glad to hear it. You look like a supplicant.'

I smooth the other sock onto her foot and get up. 'What are you doing that you can't do in your dressing gown?'

'I'm going for a walk and then I'm going to spend half an hour in the studio. I need to work out what I want to do in there tomorrow.'

'One cough and you're out of there.'

'You've had the windows open for the past six weeks. The only smells in there come from the farmyard down the road.

'How are you feeling?'

'Fine.'

'You're sure you're strong enough to get up?'

'If I spend another hour looking at these four walls, I'll go crazy.'

I pick up the tray. 'I'll take this downstairs to the kitchen then. We might as well have lunch together.'

'Good.' She takes the lid off the plate and sniffs the contents. 'Macaroni cheese. Mmm.'

For the past three months, Moor Thatch has been our world. I haven't bothered keeping track of Stanley or events outside. Then something happens to remind us that the outside world is still there, whether we acknowledge it or not, and sometimes we have no choice in the matter.

Part Nine

Transfiguration

I

'She's dead!' I stand clutching the receiver. I can't breathe. I know now what it's like for Dorothy when she has one of her attacks.

The telephone call doesn't come from Stanley but from Jas Wood. Dorothy is hovering behind me. She leans over and unwraps my fingers from the mouthpiece.

'Sit down.' she says. 'Take a deep breath.'

When I do, it comes out as a gasp. I clutch her arm. She puts back the receiver, wedging her hand underneath my elbow, steering me towards the parlour.

'Hilda's dead,' I say. 'He says that Hilda's dead.'

'I heard you. It's all right. We'll deal with it.'

She pushes me into a chair and sits down on the arm. I hold my hand out mutely and she takes it, rubbing her thumb up and down my palm until I quieten down. A part of me is thinking *But it's only Hilda. Why am I reacting like this*? I begin to cry. 'I'm frightened, Dorothy.'

She presses me against her. 'It's a shock. It wasn't what we were expecting.'

She seems unsurprised by my reaction, although it seems inexplicable to me. We sit there, rocking back and forwards.

'I don't understand,' I say. 'I didn't think she was that ill.'

'It's often difficult to tell with cancer.'

'When we last saw Stanley, he said she was doing splendidly.'

'He could have been referring to the conversations they were having rather than the state of Hilda's health.'

'I can't believe it. Hilda gone!' I feel myself unravelling again. 'I don't know what to do.'

'Calm down. You don't have to do anything at present. In a sense you don't have to do anything at all. I don't imagine Hilda's family will want us there.'

'Is it my fault she's dead?'

'Of course not.'

'You told me it was. You said I was to blame for all of it.'

She sighs. 'I was upset. I wanted to encourage you to take responsibility for your part in the breakdown of the marriage, but it's not your fault she's dead.'

'I didn't even like her much,' I whisper. 'I don't know why I feel so...bereft.'

'She functioned as a buffer between you and Stanley. You knew you would never have to get too close to him whilst she was there.'

I look at her. Is that it? 'Could I have a whisky, Dorothy?'

'It isn't good to drink when you're in shock.' She glances at the clock. 'Well, all right. I could do with one myself.'

She fetches beakers from the kitchen and pours out two measures. 'I think this time we might have it neat.'

She hands me mine. We sip in silence for a moment. 'What will Stanley do without her?' I say. 'Hilda's always been there for him.'

'There's no need to worry on that score.' She rests her glass of whisky on the chair arm. 'Hilda, now she's dead, will play a bigger role in Stanley's life than she did when she was alive. Who telephoned you?'

'Jas Wood. Richard Carline called him yesterday. His mother's desperate. Hilda is the third child she's lost.' I take small sips from the beaker. 'Should I write to her?'

'You'd better, as a courtesy, but not yet. You won't be the person she'll be turning to for consolation. Did Jas say how Stanley's taking it?'

'He blames himself because he wasn't there when she *passed over*; those are Stanley's words, not Jas'.'

'Probably she felt obliged to wait until he wasn't in the room, for fear of interrupting him.'

'Jas said that. He thought Hilda's timing was impeccable.'

'Poor Stanley.'

Our eyes meet. The thought is there in both our minds that I might have been mourning Dorothy, not Hilda, at this moment and I wonder whether anybody would have offered sympathy or even understood what that might mean for me.

If I had not called Dr Sandford when I did, I doubt that Dorothy would have survived. She knows it, too. That she's alive, is down to me. She is alive and Hilda's dead. It seems to represent a turning point in our relationship.

I'm wondering if, in her own way, Hilda was a catalyst for the upheaval that came afterwards and now she's gone she's taken the upheaval with her. It's as if her death has opened up a valve inside us and the anger we've been harbouring since Stanley came into our lives has found an outlet. Certainly the space we're in feels emptier. The only people occupying it are me and Dorothy and for the first time in a long time there is nothing to disturb the intimacy of the moment.

'Dorothy?' I hold my hand out.

'Yes, dear?'

'Do you think we could lie down somewhere for half an hour?'

She looks at my hand as if I'm offering her something that she needs to think about before accepting. Then she takes it.

We spend what's left of the afternoon in bed, curled up companionably in each other's arms. In Paris we would often spend our afternoons like this: for warmth, or comfort, or because it was a place of safety. We lie like two spoons with her knees tucked into the gap behind my own. We haven't made love - in the circumstances that would have seemed inappropriate - but I know that tonight we'll both be sleeping in the same bed. We doze intermittently. The next time I wake up it's getting dark outside and rain is pattering on the windows. We've been lying there for hours.

I go back over what's happened from the moment I picked up the phone. I'm glad it wasn't Richard Carline who passed on the news. Perhaps Jas volunteered to be the one. On the occasions when we've run into each other since the wedding, he's been courteous but distant. If he's disappointed in me he is careful not to let it show.

'Do you think Jas Wood is a friend?' I say.

'To whom?'

'Well I suppose that's what I'm asking. He was Stanley's friend first.'

'He was best man at your wedding.'

'He was Stanley's best man. You were my best woman. I'd still like to think that you were my friend first and foremost and not Stanley's. Certainly not Jas'.'

'What's your point?'

I roll onto my back. 'That maybe Jas is not impartial.'

Dorothy hurrumphs: 'I don't think I've met anyone who qualifies as that.'

'Did you know he'd proposed to Hilda once, before she was engaged to Stanley?'

Dorothy looks quizzical. I'm not the only one who's found the notion hard to come to terms with. I remember going to the funeral of someone I thought I knew intimately and discovering so much I didn't know about them from the eulogy that I'd begun to question whether I had inadvertently walked in on someone else's service.

'Hilda turned him down, of course,' I say, unnecessarily. 'It makes you wonder, though.'

'He can't do anything for her so I'm sure he will do his best to prop up Stanley, which is not to say he'll take sides. He'll just think, and so do I, that having made your bed, Patricia, you're obliged to lie in it, at least till Stanley's had time to recover. You can hardly go ahead with the divorce whilst he's in mourning. Still, whatever way you look at it you're better off than he is. Stanley's lost his soul-mate and his muse. You've lost an ex-wife. In most people's minds that would be something of a coup.'

It's when she starts to tease me that I know she's coming back to me at last. She wouldn't do it, otherwise. This is her way of saying she's forgiven me.

II

I'm not invited to attend the funeral. Apparently the Carlines made it clear, through Jas, that they would rather I was not there. That's all right. I'd rather not be there as well, though I feel miffed at being publicly excluded. As the current wife I'm surely owed some recognition.

When he turns up on our doorstep two weeks later, Stanley's not the broken wreck consumed by grief that I had been expecting. He seems almost cheerful, as if he has also been released from something. Since she died, he's written Hilda fifty letters and begun a painting of her, an *Apotheosis*, he says, showing her ascending up into the clouds on Hampstead Heath. He plans to put it on the altar in his *Church of Me*. The project's been on-going for the past two decades, so as Dorothy remarks, Hilda might still have bit of a wait before she actually ascends.

'How are you coping, Stanley?' she asks. 'Is the family looking after you?'

'The family?'

'Hilda's family. They didn't want us to attend the funeral or we'd have been there. We felt we ought to respect their wishes.'

Judging by his blank expression, Stanley wasn't asked for his opinion. It's quite possible he didn't even notice that we weren't there. He seems agitated but not in a *going crazy* sort of way, more as if he's preoccupied with something that excites him more than Hilda's funeral and can't wait to get on with it.

'I hope she didn't suffer too much at the end,' says Dorothy. 'These things are never easy.'

Stanley ponders. 'Hilda won't have minded suffering. She saw it as a rite of passage. God had told her she was not to worry; he was waiting for her.'

'I suppose it helps if one's expected,' Dorothy observes. 'I'll get the tea.'

'I'll do it,' I say, quickly.

'No, dear, you stay here and talk to Stanley.' Dorothy gets up deliberately and motions me into the chair she has vacated. We exchange a glance. Hers is unreadable.

It's obvious that whoever has been looking after Stanley, hasn't done it very well. There is a dank smell, redolent of river water, clinging to him and he hasn't shaved for several days. He peers short-sightedly into the middle distance from behind the steel-rimmed spectacles.

'How are you managing then, Stanley?' I say. 'You spent so much time with Hilda at the end, you must be missing her.'

'I am. But we still talk to one another. Actually we get on rather better now. It's easier for her to see things from my point of view.' He gives a coy laugh and I'm not sure for a moment if he's joking. And then it occurs to me that although what he says is often laughable, I've never heard him crack a joke. Of course, in present circumstances one would not expect it.

'I just wish I'd had an opportunity to marry her again before she died,' he whispers, almost to himself.

I wonder whether he recalls our conversation. I decide there's no point in reminding him about it now that it's too late to make a difference. 'That was never really on the cards,' I say. 'In any case, from what she told you about her relationship with God, there wouldn't have been room for both of you.'

He shrugs. Out in the kitchen Dorothy is making rather more of a performance than is strictly necessary to put three cups and a plate of biscuits on a tray.

'What are your plans, then, Stanley?' I say.

'I've decided to move back to Cookham,' he says, adding 'After all, the village is my home.'

I hesitate. Whilst the idea of Stanley settling back in Cookham is no longer one that troubles me, I hope he isn't planning to move out of Cliveden View and into Lindworth. It's unoccupied at present because I've decided that it's time to sell it. Stanley might not need the money any longer, but we do. The house is far too big for Stanley anyway.

'I thought you'd want to be in London? All your friends are there and you'd be near the girls.'

'But all my up-in-heaven moments happen when I'm here.'

'You told me you'd had one on Hampstead Heath. And isn't that where Hilda's taking off from?'

Dorothy comes in and puts the tray down on the coffee table.

'I don't want to be in London without Hilda,' Stanley says. 'It wouldn't be the same.'

'From what you've said, in her case geography's not that important.'

'But it is to me.' He clasps his hands in front of him. 'I need to focus on my visionary work. The chapel is my magnum opus.'

'Stanley you've been looking for a patron for your chapel ever since I've known you.'

'I've been working on the paintings all that time. I know exactly where they're going.'

'Do you really think you'll find someone to build a church for you and then allow you to put what you like in it?'

'The Behrends did.'

'Their chapel was a War Memorial to someone in their family. They might have given you free rein to decorate it as you chose but it was never meant as a memorial to you.'

'It is me,' Stanley says. 'Without me it would not exist.'

'Well isn't that enough, then? Do you need a chapel of your own?'

'I want to dedicate it to the women in my life,' says Stanley. 'You and Hilda, Elsie, Daphne…Charlotte.'

I still feature on the list, then. I suppose that's something, although then another thought occurs to me.

'Which paintings do you plan to show there?' I ask warily.

He gives a bright smile. '*The Beatitudes*. I had the chapel in mind when I painted them.'

The teacup judders in my fingers. I replace it in the saucer. 'Stanley, you can't possibly be contemplating showing those appalling pictures. You'd be prosecuted.'

'When they're all together it'll make sense,' he says. 'They're a hymn to love. They show how we can use sex as a way to God.'

'They're pornographic.'

'You don't understand.'

'If I don't understand, what makes you think that anybody else will? Elsie is a married woman now. What do you think her Ken will make of it?'

'He'll understand.'

'I promise you he won't. And I forbid you to show anything you've done of me.' I take a deep breath. 'I know you're in mourning, Stanley, and I sympathise. I absolutely understand that you want some kind of memorial to Hilda, but the chapel's simply not appropriate.'

He looks at Dorothy. She clears her throat. 'It's hardly something you need argue over now,' she says.

'Why don't we wait till Stanley's found a patron. Once the Chapel's built you can discuss what goes in it.'

What Dorothy is saying is that no-one in their right mind would be likely to finance the building of a chapel dedicated to the carnal fantasies of Stanley Spencer. The idea is ludicrous. She throws a warning glance in my direction and I nod. 'All right.'

'I'll find someone to foot the bill,' says Stanley gaily. 'You'll see.'

'He seems to be bearing up,' says Dorothy. She's standing at the sink. 'At least he isn't moping.'

'Dorothy, if anybody got to see those paintings, I'd be mortified. I think the final months he spent with Hilda must have severed Stanley's last links with the real world.'

'You said Eddie Marsh agreed with you. He thinks too much of Stanley to allow him to destroy his reputation at the very moment when his work is gaining public recognition.'

'But you know what Stanley's like when he gets an idea into his head. He's utterly convinced he's right; it's everybody else who's got it wrong.'

'Well who knows, maybe history will prove him right.' She rinses out the last cup. 'Hang the tea towel on the radiator, would you, dear. Then it'll dry in time for supper.'

She still has her back to me. I drape the tea towel on the cast-iron radiator. There's a view of Torquay Harbour on it, brought back from our trip to Cornwall. It's the only souvenir I have. The picture's almost faded off the linen.

'I've decided to sell Lindworth by the way,'

There is a pause, then Dorothy pulls out the plug and we watch as the sudsy water spirals down into the drains. 'Have you told Stanley?'

'Not yet.'

'What if Lindworth's where he'd planned to stay when he comes back to Cookham?'

'There's no reason why he would. He's never really lived there and he's more or less established now at Cliveden View.'

'From what I've heard, that house should be condemned.'

'We know that comfort isn't a priority with Stanley. Anyway, there are a dozen places he can rent if he decides he doesn't want to go on living there.'

'What made you think of selling Lindworth?'

'I don't want us to be forced to spend another winter here. I thought we might go to Le Touquet for a week or two in January when it's cheaper. Or we might spend Christmas there.'

I watch as Dorothy smooths out the creases from the tea towel I've just hung over the radiator. 'This year will be Stanley's first one without Hilda.'

'I'm not sure he'd want to spend it at Moor Thatch in any case. He's still got Annie, or there's Gilbert. They're his family.'

'So are you, officially.'

'He's not as helpless as he seems.' The fact is, that with Hilda gone I had expected Stanley to be more reliant on me than he seems to be. I had been readying myself to gently keep him at arm's length, but it seems none of that is necessary. 'Stanley's always had a knack of getting friends to rally round.'

'We don't need to consider him, then. That's good.'

'Own up, you would like to go somewhere a little warmer, wouldn't you?'

'Indeed, although one could just spend November through to March in bed.'

'You wouldn't get much painting done.'

'Aye, there's the rub.' She idly takes a packet from the shelf and turns it upside down. The latest rumour is that Marks and Spencer have begun to stamp a *use-before* date on some products. Mrs Arkwright has pooh-pooed the notion. She says you can tell if something's off by sniffing it; why would you need a *use-by* date? But at the moment it's a bit like having a new shade of lip-stick. Having searched the underside, she puts it back onto the shelf.

'A change of scenery would be quite welcome anyway,' I say. 'It's not as if there's anything to keep us here.'

'Apart from Stanley.'

'Would you rather I took Stanley to Le Touquet?' I say, teasingly.

'I think, for someone who sees Cookham as God's paradise on earth, Le Touquet would be tantamount to the *Inferno*.'

'I can't see them taking to him either.'

'There you could be wrong. He's an eccentric English genius. The French would love him. Have you spoken to the agents about putting Lindworth on the market?'

'No, I thought I'd better talk to you first.'

She waves me away. 'Don't bring me into the discussion. This is between you and Stanley.'

'I can tell him you agree with me, though, can I?'

'I don't think I'd go as far as that.'

'There are times, Dorothy, when you can be infuriating.'

'Yes, dear. So can you.'

III

Persuading Stanley that we needed to get rid of Lindworth, wasn't going to be easy. I remembered how distraught he'd been when I suggested renting it. Imagine my surprise and horror, therefore, when I told him what the sale might be expected to bring in and having thought about it, he said all right, if he couldn't find a patron for his *Church of Me*, he'd use the cash to build the thing himself.

'You think he means it?' Dorothy, as usual, refuses to accept that we have a potential crisis on our hands.

'He's mad enough. I thought he'd dig his heels in over Lindworth, but he sees the prospect of the money as a gift from God. What better way to spend it than on the construction of his blessed Chapel. I can't risk it.' So much for Le Touquet, I think. We'll have no choice but to spend another winter here now.

'So you won't put Lindworth on the market, after all? Why not let Stanley have it, then?'

'He's not the most reliable of tenants. Let him buy it, if he wants to.'

'You're suggesting that he might buy back his own house?'

'Why not? He's not poor. He doesn't have to trail round Cookham looking like an old tramp, pushing Shirin's pram with all his paints and canvasses piled up in it as if he doesn't have two halfpennies to rub together. And he's harping on about his bloody Chapel and what's going into it, to everyone he meets.'

'He has a dream. At least you're part of it. You'd like to be remembered as the great man's inspiration, wouldn't you?'

'Not if I'm credited with *The Beatitudes*. I'll find another path to immortality.'

IV

I would have ample time to find another path or, as it turned out, to accept there wasn't one. By then there was another monarch on the throne.

The death of George V1 a month into the New Year, shocked the Nation. It seemed hardly any time had passed since we'd been burying his father. Five days earlier we'd watched the Pathé newsreel of him waving off the Princess on a tour of Africa. 'He looks as if he ought to be tucked up in bed with a hot water bottle and a poultice on his chest,' said Dorothy.

He'd never wanted to be King. I would have given my eye-teeth to wear that crown although I'd read that it weighed the equivalent of two full bags of flour and unless it was positioned four-square on your head you had no chance of fielding it if it began to slide.

The months before the Coronation of Elizabeth are taken up with preparations for the great day. Coronation fever grips the country. Children at the village school pin cut-outs of the Royal procession on the walls of every classroom.

I wish I was still a seven-year-old able to indulge in it all unashamedly. I secretly still pasted cut-outs in my scrap-book, though when Dodo caught me at it with some paste I'd mixed up in her favourite mug, she merely commented that she hoped I would not leave any in the bottom. As she turned away she gave me a good-natured pat, the sort you'd give a dog.

A decade and a half before, it had been the new cash register that Sergeant-Major Arkright couldn't wait to get his hands on. Now he's managed to acquire a television set. It stands against the back wall of their parlour like a sentry. I'm not sure I'd want one permanently in the corner of the room. I'd feel that I was being spied on.

So far nobody had seen it switched on. When we do, all you can see are faces in a snow-storm with a static that suggests wires on the inside are short-circuiting. The word's gone round that a few loyal customers might be invited in to watch the Coronation as it happens.

'As it happens, Dorothy. Imagine that!'

I had forgotten Dorothy preferred to have her history packaged.

'We can see it in the cinema next week,' she says, but this time I am not prepared to wait until the moment's past before I can experience it.

'I want to be part of history, Dorothy, not looking at it afterwards.'

'You sound like poor Felicia,' she says, but I know in that moment that Felicia has carved herself a place on Dorothy's own war memorial and you don't get your name on that by waiting till the war is over.

When I ask the Sergeant-Major outright what you'd need to do to get an invitation, his leer is the answer I'm expecting. I presumed that he was getting something different from Miss Barrett the librarian, since she was in her early sixties. She was in a good position to procure a copy of that play by Beckett, *Waiting for Somebody Un-pronounce-able* that everyone was gossiping about. I knew there was a queue for that. But I did not think Sergeant-Major Arkwright would be on it. Certainly he hadn't anything to gain by letting Dorothy into his back room.

In the end I manage to get us an invitation by suggesting I will make a cake sufficient to provide a slice for everybody present.

Though the War is over, nobody seems better off. When rationing was introduced it meant that everybody got a share of what there was, officially, although as always Sergeant-Major Arkwright favoured certain customers. I might still have been one of them but I could not pretend I found that man attractive, even for an extra ounce of suet.

Needless to say when I go into the shop to buy the things I need, the Sergeant-Major won't let me have more than my allowance and I have to pay the going rate. It would have served them right if I had bulked out the ingredients with saw-dust.

V

On the morning of the Coronation, the streets leading from the War Memorial are hung with bunting. On the News we hear that Edmund Hilary and Sherpa Tenzing have climbed to the summit of Mount Everest. I envy him that moment, standing where no other human being has stood, looking out over the world.

In Arkwright's store, the back room has been rigged out like a cinema with chairs in rows before the tiny screen. We are directed to the back row, crammed between George Hatch and his wife who've walked over from the farm and with five rows of chairs infront of us, all occupied. The Arkwright's daughter and her family have travelled in from Reading so of course they have priority.

The Sergeant-Major is in uniform, directing operations from the front. You'd never know the War was over. Mrs Arkwright hands round lemonade and crackers topped with anchovies.

'We would have seen as much if we'd stood in the back yard of Moor Thatch and trained binoculars on Pall Mall,' Dorothy observes. But once the service starts and Sergeant-Major Arkwright has turned up the sound, a heady atmosphere of expectation ripples down the rows and mingles with the faint smell of manure coming from George Hatch's jacket and the scent of beer and smoked fish from the front of shop.

A dozen of the village children sit cross-legged infront and wave the little paper flags they have been given. We can see their outlines silhouetted on the screen as if they're in the crowd.

It's raining but the people in their mackintoshes, some of whom have been there all night, wave and yell and there is nothing I can do to stop the lump that's forming in my throat.

'It makes you feel proud to be British,' I say.

'What does?' Dorothy says gruffly. 'The colossal waste of money? The class system it entrenches? The idea of all that pomp and ceremony which was out of date five hundred years ago, still going on? No wonder countries in the Commonwealth are pushing for their independence.' But she squeezes my hand nonetheless.

It's when the Queen of Tonga passes in an open carriage in defiance of the downpour, smiling enthusiastically and waving to the crowd as if she's at a football match, her saturated silk gown clinging to a body that refuses to pay credence to the boundaries of postwar austerity, that everyone goes wild and even Dorothy lets out a gruff 'Hurrah'. This is a woman after everybody's heart.

'That's someone you could share a pint of beer with in the pub,' says Dorothy.

My cake fills up that awkward interval when the official business of the day is over but you feel obliged to stay and thank the hosts before you go. I'd spent a long time trying to make something that reflected the occasion but I'd added too much carrot as a sweetener and used mashed potato to bulk out the flour, so although it looked attractive with a cochineal crown on the top, nobody wanted seconds. What remained, stood in the middle of the table, a raised section of the crown split into fragments.

It's as we are coming out onto the pavement that I catch a glimpse of somebody I haven't seen for ages. Elsie. She is looking very pretty in a fetching blue dress with a cardigan slung carelessly across her shoulders and she has a young man with her who is feeding her small spoonfuls from a tub of ice cream. Is this Ken? It doesn't look like him.

I'd heard they'd moved to Caversham where Ken was working as a driver. She must come into the village regularly since her family live here, but until now our paths had not crossed.

I'd like to tell her that I never meant her any harm, that I wish we had said goodbye on better terms and that I'm pleased she's obviously so happy in her life. I call out: 'Elsie!' and she jerks her head round. Her eyes scan the crowd. I wave and call again. She sees me but instead of waving back, she frowns. She murmurs something to the young man next to her and he laughs.

Then I realise that it isn't Elsie. It looks like her and the way she tilts her head and gives her hair a little toss, is very similar. But it's not her. And it occurs to me that this girl is too young to be her anyway.

I glance at Dorothy. She's giving me an odd look as if she is waiting for me to catch up. She sees the blank expression on my face and pats my hand.

'Come on, old girl. It's been a long day. Let's make tracks.' As we link arms, I see a woman farther up the High Street, standing with a middle-aged man and a boy of maybe twelve or thirteen outside 'Griggs', the ironmongers. The look the woman's giving me is hostile. The man follows the direction of her gaze and nods.

I don't feel I can walk away without acknowledging her. I half raise my hand and curl the fingers. She does not raise hers.

I lean into the arm that Dorothy has offered me. She tucks her hand around mine and we carry on along the High Street.

As we're walking back across the common I think what an odd day it's been. We've just celebrated the beginning of an era but it feels more like the end of one.

VI

'Remember you've still got your hat on. Don't forget to take it off before you're shown into the room. In fact, perhaps you ought to give it to me now. I'll fold it up and put it in my hand-bag.'

'No thanks. I would rather keep it on until we get there,' he says, stubbornly.

'I don't know why we had to take the bus. I would have thought on this occasion that you might have splashed out on a taxi.'

'I like buses.'

We stop in the Strand. More people crowd on, shuffling down the aisle. The silk dress I am wearing is already crumpled and my perfume's mingling with the sweat from half a dozen bodies crammed into the same space. I feel agitated and although one reason for me coming was to make sure Stanley stayed calm, I'm the one in need of calming.

'You know not to speak to her until she speaks to you. She might not want to have a conversation. There'll be other people in the queue. They might be running late.'

'Don't fuss, Patricia.'

'I'm just trying to impress on you that there are certain rules of etiquette which need to be observed.'

'I'll tell her about Mrs Perkins if she mentions Hilda.'

'She won't mention Hilda. She won't have a clue who Mrs Perkins is. Just go in there and kneel down. Don't say anything.'

He leans across me to the window and begins to trace his index-finger through the grime. There is a thin screech of his nail across the glass. I wince.

'Don't do that, Stanley. You'll get dirt under your finger-nails.'

He sighs. 'You didn't have to come.'

'Of course I had to come. I wanted to make sure you didn't let yourself down.'

'Jas said you'd insist on being there because you want your picture in the paper. You want everyone to know you're Lady Spencer.'

'Well, what if I do. You owe me that much.' It seems I was right in thinking Jas was Stanley's friend, not mine.

I feel oddly disappointed. I thought being *Lady Spencer* meant that everyone would treat me differently, but it's just one more thing to criticise. I don't care. Once I've got the title, I can please myself.

'We'll need to get you a new carrier of some sort for your paints and easel when you're painting outside.'

'I'm all right with Shirin's pram. I can fit everything in there and put the hood up when it rains.'

'That's not the point. Think of the headlines in the press. *'Sir Stanley Spencer wheels his pram through Cookham.'* Do you want to be a laughing stock?'

'I don't mind.'

'Well you ought to mind. You've got a reputation to maintain now.'

'Don't you mean that you have.' Stanley looks at me and for a moment I think he's decided that he'll tell the Queen he doesn't want a knighthood after all. I've almost come to the decision I don't want one either, if we have to go through this to get it.

Stanley's sitting with his hands clasped in between his knees, his lips pursed sullenly. I must be careful. I don't want him to get up and take off in the opposite direction.

I give him a reassuring pat and leave my hand bunched lightly over his. 'Not long now,' I say. He sighs.

I turn to look out the window and that's when I see her, walking alongside the omnibus and keeping pace with it. She's wearing billowing silk trousers that are all the rage now, although not for somebody of her age. The bobbed hair-cut is the same. She's with a young man who's at least ten years her junior. She has her arms wrapped firmly around one of his and she is leaning into him, her head lodged in between his neck and shoulder. He has floppy hair and pale ascetic features and responds to everything she says with trilling laughter.

The bus halts at traffic lights and they stride on. We overtake them seconds later and then they outstrip us once more, as if we're engaging in a complicated *pas-de-deux*. I keep her in my line of sight and, maybe sensing that my eyes are on her, she turns suddenly and looks straight at me. Our eyes lock together for a second and I think she's recognised me. Then she turns away. She whispers something to the young man and they carry on their way.

The bus conductor makes his way along the centre aisle until he gets to Stanley.

'Where to, mate?' He taps him on the shoulder.

Stanley riffles through his change. 'The Palace,' he says, handing him a shilling piece. 'Two singles.'

VII

She looks up as I come in. I stand in the doorway for a moment.

'Why are you staring at me?'

'I was looking to see whether there was anything about you that was different.'

'Tell me when you've made your mind up.'

She continues looking at me for a moment and then goes back to her crossword. I sink down onto the sofa. My feet ache and the new shoes I bought have cut into my heel. I ease them off. I wonder whether I can ask her for a foot massage. I sit there wiggling my toes.

'You don't want to know how it went?'

She mutters underneath her breath and pencils in a word. 'How did it go? Did Stanley wear his hat?'

'Of course. But I reminded him to take it off before he went in.'

'That's a shame. He could have doffed it to Her Majesty. I'm sure she would have been enchanted.'

'Coming from your background, Dorothy, I would have thought you might have more respect for royalty.'

'I've plenty of respect for them. It must be hard work to bring down the blade on fourteen shoulders at a time.'

'Fifteen.'

'And how did Stanley take it?'

'If he'd known what it entailed, I think he might have turned it down.'

'At least now he can run a slate up at the framers.'

'So can we, I hope. It means he can renew his membership of The Academy as well. They won't dare turn his pictures down now.'

'Weren't you worried about what he might want to exhibit.'

'Once he's come to terms with what it means to be Sir Stanley Spencer, hopefully he'll be more circumspect about what he exhibits.'

'I think what you've got to come to terms with is that Stanley never had a problem with his pictures. You're the one who had a problem with them.'

'I was not the only one.'

'But you had most to lose if they were shown in public, which they will be finally. You need to take a long-term view, Patricia. One way or another, Stanley's voice is going to be heard.'

'I can at least make sure that my voice is heard, too.'

'How will you do that?'

'I shall write my memoirs. Stanley has gone back to writing his. The publishers are more inclined to let him have his way now. More's the pity.' I let out a husky little laugh. 'I might have no choice but to offer my side of the story.'

Dorothy folds up the paper carefully and puts it on the table. 'Your side of the story. Yes, well that would be of interest to the tabloids, I imagine. *Lady Spencer tells all*. Are there going to be other characters, apart from you, in this scenario?'

'There'll obviously be Stanley.'

She nods. 'Anybody else?'

I hesitate. 'You.'

'Might I ask how you'll explain my presence? As your sister, maybe?'

'Maybe.'

She looks at the ceiling with her head on one side. 'It's one thing to introduce me as your sister on the few occasions when I go outside the door. But once these things are written down they're open to investigation and if they're disproved it calls your general credibility into account. There are the exhibitions we've had, for example.'

'What about them?'

'It would not be hard for someone dedicated to the task to find out that you weren't the artist. For a quarter of a century you have been claiming authorship of paintings that you didn't do. It's not exactly forgery since I was party to it, but the people who have bought those paintings would be justified in feeling cheated. Do you want a reputation as a con-artist and lesbian who married one of England's best-loved artists, took over his assets, most of which she subsequently sold and then refused to give him a divorce because she fancied being *Lady Spencer* and the pension came in useful. Think about it, Pet, and then perhaps you'll put the kettle on. I'm parched.'

VIII

'I'll have a packet of dried egg and three ounces of your cured ham, Mrs Arkwright.' Dorothy and I have sometimes had to make do with the '*maka*' she produces – mutton dressed as bacon, but it takes a leap of the imagination and though bacon is beyond me, I feel '*maka*' is beneath me now.

I take a jar of fish paste and a tin of corned beef from the shelves whilst Mrs Arkwright's slicing off the ham. She keeps her head bent but she raises her eyes every now and then to glance at me. We've never had much in the way of conversation when I've gone into the shop, but I had thought she might have made some comment on last week's events. It was in all the papers, after all.

'I see you have some raspberries.' Those are certainly from somebody's allotment; they're all different sizes and the stalks are still attached to some of them. 'Are they the first this season?'

'That's right, Mrs Spencer,' she says, and we stand there looking at them for a moment. 'Will you have some?'

'Why not? Dorothy loves raspberries. Maybe you could pick me out a punnet.'

There are several people in the queue behind me. I don't look round, but I wait until the shop bell's pinged twice more and then say, casually. 'It's *Lady Spencer* now. Perhaps you've heard.'

She looks at me under those thick brows. Cookham is so inbred, half of those who live here don't know if their cousins are their uncles or their mothers are their aunts. Her only claim to fame is that she had a walk-on part in Stanley's *Resurrection*.

'*Lady Spencer*, is it?' she says. She looks hard at me and then her eyes move to the people in the queue behind me. 'I'll be with you in a minute, Mrs Pritchard, once I'm done with Lady Spencer.'

There's a titter and the colour rises in my cheeks.

'Will that be all, then?' She begins to tally up the items. This must be the only General Store in England now that doesn't have a proper cash till. Mrs Arkwright sold it second hand to Remington's, the garage in the High Street that provided Stanley with his one and only car. They took that back eventually, too.

'Give me a minute,' I say and I tap my fingers on my mouth. I'll make them pay for laughing at me. 'Yes, ten Capstan, please.' My eyes pass longingly over the jars of barley sugar twists and sherbet lemons but we've used up our sweet ration for the week.

There is a shuffling in the queue behind me and the shop bell pings again. 'That's everything for now, I think. Perhaps you'd add the bill to my account.'

She pauses, glancing at the raspberries and then back at me. 'You want it on the slate?' she says. Why can't she call it an 'account' like anybody else?

Although I know she's come to an arrangement with a lot of customers, sometimes exchanging eggs for cabbages (or raspberries) from their allotment, all we have to bargain with is parsley and a lettuce every now and then.

'If you could be so kind. I'll settle with you next time I come in.' I lift the shopping basket off the counter.

'Don't forget your raspberries, Lady Spencer.'

I turn back and scoop them off the counter. 'Thank you.'

I am halfway to the door when I see who is waiting in the queue.

'Jas!'

His eyes flicker and move sideways to the women standing either side of us. I have the feeling he would rather I had not acknowledged him.

'Patricia,' he says.

'Are you waiting in the queue for something?'

'I came in to buy some ham. I'm having lunch with Stanley.'

'And he's sent you out to buy it?' I laugh.

'There was nothing in the house.' He looks embarrassed. 'Nothing.'

His eyes linger briefly on the overflowing wicker basket I am carrying. I glance at the two women standing next to us, who've turned around so they can better overhear the conversation. 'Can we go outside, Jas. There's no need to queue. I'll give you what you need for lunch from what I've bought.' I tilt my head towards the women and he nods.

We step outside onto the pavement. Jas is wearing a loose, open-necked shirt and blazer. Stanley's hung on to his old brown suit and black tie and refuses point blank to replace it.

'You know what he's like, Jas. He lives hand to mouth. He gets up when he feels like it, eats when he's hungry, sometimes goes to bed with all his clothes on or goes out in his pyjamas...'

'He's not well, Patricia. Cliveden View is isolated. It has no hot water and no telephone. He ought not to be living there.'

'The last time I saw Stanley, he said he was perfectly content in Cliveden View.'

'That's not the point.'

'You can't help someone if they're not prepared to let you help them, Jas. I know that Cliveden View is primitive but that's what Stanley's used to. All his life he's lived in houses like that.'

'But he wasn't ill before.'

'He's just run down.'

'I think it's more than that. Since Hilda died he's let things slide.'

'You think I haven't tried to make him lead a better sort of life? It's not as if he can't afford it now. He's better off than I am. I go round there most weeks and he has a woman from the village who comes in to do for him.'

'But if he felt ill in the night or if he had a fall, no one would hear him.'

Dear Jas, I think. If he'd been a woman Stanley might have married him instead of me. 'I'll call in on him. How long will you be here?'

'Just for the day. I'm going back this evening.'

I nod. 'I'll pop in and make sure he's all right.'

I realise that in fact it must be two weeks since I last ran into Stanley. You would think that living so close we'd be bumping into one another all the time. We're friendly when we do meet. There's no animosity between us. It's as if the things we held against each other cancelled one another out but what was left did not amount to very much. Occasionally, if I see him coming down the road towards me with the pram, I do a detour. It's not Stanley I'm avoiding, it's the pram.

'And how have you been?' Jas says, almost as an afterthought.

'Oh, you know. We get by.'

'Has it made any difference, being *Lady Spencer*?' He's not mocking me, although I see his lip twitch. He'll have witnessed the exchange with Mrs Arkwright.

'I suppose it makes it easier to ask for credit.'

'Things still tight?'

'I sometimes think that Dudley's set on starving me into submission.'

'Still, you've got the pension to look forward to.'

I catch his eye but there's no malice in. He takes out his pocket watch. 'I'd better get back. Stanley's waiting.'

'Here, take this.' I reach into the basket for the ham and then on second thoughts I hand the raspberries over, too. 'I'm so pleased I ran into you.' I lean across and peck him on the cheek.

He hesitates. 'Goodbye…' *Please don't*, I think. 'Goodbye, Patricia.'

IX

Meeting Jas like that, especially in the village shop, which is like being on-stage at the theatre, has unsettled me. For ten days afterwards I don't go out at all. I'm not sure I can cope with Stanley in my present state, so although I'd said I would call on him, I don't.

It's some weeks later when I see him shuffling ahead of me across the common. I can understand why Jas was so concerned. I run to catch him up and he peers at me through the round-rimmed spectacles as if he's not sure who I am.

'Patricia', he says, finally.

'I heard Jas had come down to see you. I ran into him in Arkwright's.' I step back. There is an atmosphere about him like you find in houses when they've been shut up for too long and no air has circulated through the rooms. 'How are you, Stanley?'

He thinks for a moment. 'Not good. That toad at the R.A – Munnings – tried to have me prosecuted for obscenity. As if it wasn't bad enough to have the Inland Revenue pursuing me, without him putting in his oar.'

'You've got that sorted out now, surely, the dispute over your taxes?'

He nods. 'Dudley put me onto an accountant.'

'Good. You'll need one now you're doing so well.'

Stanley runs his fingers through his hair. His new-found status as a famous artist hasn't made much of an impact on him. As he's aged you would expect that *little boy* look to have metamorphosed into something else. He still looks like a schoolboy except now his hair is grey and the expression on his face, although still curious, is tinged with resignation.

He bends down and kicks a pebble underneath the front wheels of the pram to stop it taking off. It's what he would have done when it had Unity and Shirin in it, only now it's filled with paints and canvasses. I can see his pyjama collar sticking out from underneath his shirt.

'I meant your health when I asked how you were. Jas told me you'd been ill.'

He lifts the pram hood to protect the contents from the drizzle.

'I'm all right. They want to move me out of Cliveden View, though. They say it's not feasible for me to be without hot water, gas or electricity and no one within shouting distance. I shall probably go back to Fernlea. It at least has a piano.'

'You can hardly summon help with a piano.'

'Oh, you'd be surprised.' He curls one hand around the handle of the pram and starts to push it back and forwards vacantly, forgetting that the stone under the wheels is getting in the way.

'So you're still painting?'

'Yes, of course I am. The paintings keep me company. I find I don't want to be parted from them.

They're like children. I'm much happier when I have only got myself to satisfy. It's such a bother having to consider someone else.'

He kicks the stone away. The pram rolls forward and he lunges for the handle. 'How about you?'

'Dorothy and I are planning to go somewhere warmer for the winter. I'm afraid she won't survive another one here.'

'That's what you said last year.'

'She survived because we did go somewhere else.'

He gives a bland smile: 'It's the devil to be old.'

'We're not…' The light is shining in his eyes and I can see myself reflected there. 'Well, yes, perhaps we are.'

He nods. We lapse back into silence. It seems there is nothing else to talk about. He steps back, pulling the pram after him and raises one hand. 'Tally ho, then.'

I watch as he walks away across the common, the wheels rattling on the stones. A swarm of rooks flies up into the air and circles him. As he turns down the path towards the copse, he lifts one hand in what could be a farewell wave or possibly a blessing on whatever he is accidentally crushing underneath the wheels.

Epilogue
Cliveden
1959

The room is stark. There are no pictures on the walls and just a vase of half-dead roses to relieve the sterile whiteness of the decor. Stanley is in bed, the blanket pulled up to his chin, his fingers curled over the top, the index fingers making patterns in the air as if conducting. Or perhaps he thinks he's drawing. He hums intermittently, but as the sound fades I can hear his breathing and it's scratchy and laborious.

I pull up a chair. A nurse comes in and stands beside the bed. She looks at him, picks up his chart and makes a mark on it and then goes out without acknowledging me. When I look at him again, I see that Stanley's eyes are open, but they have that milky quality. I'm not sure whether he can see me.

'Is that you, P?'

'Yes.' I go to kiss him and then squeeze his shoulder with my hand instead. The bones are sharp under the striped pyjama top.

'I'm still here, then?'

'Looks like it.' I take off my jacket.

'Ah well, no rush.' His hand crawls across the blanket. I sit with mine clasped together in my lap.

'I didn't know if you'd be in the mood for visitors so I thought I'd turn up and if you weren't I'd go away again.'

'No, no. It's nice to see you. Dorothy's not with you, then?'

'We didn't want to crowd you. Matron said you get tired easily. You had a deputation yesterday, I gather, from the League of Brewers.'

'Yes, I did a *Crucifixion* for a school they sponsor; set in Cookham, naturally. I got the idea when the Council started laying mains drains. There were all these interesting piles of rubble in the street.'

'I thought you were tee-total. Why take a commission from the League of Brewers*?*' I could use a drink now, I think. And a cigarette.

'They offered me a free hand.' He is peering at me. He's not got his glasses on and I know that he can't see much without them. 'You don't look well,' he says.

'I've been suffering from anaemia.'

'You're still in Cookham, then?'

'We didn't have the wherewithal to move.'

'I would have given you the money if you'd asked. Why didn't you? You always have before.'

'Dorothy wouldn't let me. She didn't want to be responsible for you defaulting on your obligations to the tax authorities again.'

'That's thoughtful of her.'

'I said now it hardly mattered. You could always sell another painting. I heard one of yours had sold for £700,000. You could afford to buy up half of Paris.'

'Heavens, all that money for a painting. Which one was it, do you know?'

'*Dog Worship,* where the greyhound cocks its leg against a tombstone.'

'You weren't very keen on that one, were you?'

'No, I wasn't.' I look around. 'There isn't much to look at in here, is there?'

'No, but then I sleep a lot. I dream I'm back in Cookham.' He sinks down into the pillows. 'Last night I was lying on the grass beside the stream next to a colony of flying ants.' He tails off, but his bottom lip is quivering, so I know there's more to come. 'I watched them climb the grass stalks one by one and fly off. Some fell back and had to start again.' He swallows and I hear a faint click in his throat. 'It struck me that they had to reach a certain height before they could take off.' His eyes move round to me. 'I wonder if that's what it's like for us.'

'I don't know.'

The lids close over his eyes like curtains. 'Not long till I find out.'

'Are you looking forward to your up-in-heaven moment?'

'Seeing Hilda will be nice. We've got a lot of catching up to do.'

'Try not to dominate the conversation when you get there, Stanley. You were never very good at listening.'

'Nonsense. I was always happy to consider someone else's point of view. It's just that mine was usually better.'

'You're not worried that some of the things you did might count against you at the end?'

'What things?' He gazes at me with a look of innocent inquiry.

'*The Beatitudes*, for instance?'

'*The Beatitudes* were an expression of God's love.'

'No, Stanley. They were an expression of your own frustrated lust. You'd hoped to land both me and Hilda and you ended up with neither of us. You were like a dog on heat.'

'There's nothing wrong with dogs on heat.'

'But don't you think there's something questionable about a forty-seven year old man on heat.'

'God understands, Patricia. That's the way he made us.'

'He might understand but an important question, possibly, is whether critics of the future will.'

'Have you come here to bully me?'

'You don't think now you've got a knighthood that it's something you should take into account?'

'You're saying they might change their minds? They wouldn't do that, surely.'

'Stanley, even your close friends had trouble with the work you did during your years with me. Those paintings weren't the peak of your achievement.'

He sighs: 'If you don't mind, I think I would like to rest now.'

'I've been talking to John Rothenstein. There's nobody more sympathetic to your work than him. The Rothensteins supported you for months when you were homeless.'

'Thanks to you.'

'We needed Lindworth to raise money, Stanley. You agreed. You didn't have to go to London looking like a derelict and begging friends to rally round you. There were other possibilities.'

'*Christ in the Wilderness* came out of those months.'

'Those are not the pictures I'm objecting to. It's *The Beatitudes* and what you call the *Scrapbook Drawings*. I think you should keep that work back, Stanley. In fact, I think it should be destroyed.'

His eyes fly open. 'No!'

'The drawings are obscene. There's one of you and Pa with huge erections and your trousers round your ankles and another with a crowd of women clutching at a huge pole sticking up between your legs. What's anybody meant to make of that?'

'The one conclusion that I've come to in my life, Patricia, is that we can only reach God by rejoicing in our natures. Animals do what they want and nobody objects. We need to follow their example.' He groans.

'Shall I get the nurse?' He nods. I call out and the nurse appears. She takes his pulse and makes a face.

'I'll give him an injection.'

'Could we have five minutes first?' I lean across the bed and get a sudden whiff of Stanley's breath. I draw back and then put my face up next to his. 'We need to talk about this Stanley.'

'Not now,' says the nurse. 'The poor man needs to sleep.'

'I've done another drawing for you, Matron,' Stanley murmurs, scrabbling at the sheet. 'It's in the bedside cabinet.'

'I'll get it later,' she says.

'No, now. It's important. I want you to have it.'

She sighs, putting the syringe aside and rummaging inside the bedside cabinet. She lays the drawing on the blanket without bothering to look at it and picks up the syringe. I look away as she pumps Stanley's arm to find a vein and gives him the injection.

'There we are.'

A smile comes over Stanley's face. 'You did that beautifully,' he says. 'Thank you.' I watch as his features settle. 'You know, this is probably the most exciting thing that's ever happened to me,' he says as he drifts off.

'Wait, don't go to sleep yet, Stanley. We were talking.'

He stares over my right shoulder to a corner of the room. 'Ah, look at that.'

'What is it?

'By the door. Six Angels. They've been sent to offer me a hand.' He gives a blissful smile and seconds later he has drifted off to sleep again. The nurse gets up and takes the empty syringe in the saucer over to the sink. She writes on Stanley's file and loops it back over the bed rail.

'Don't forget your drawing,' I say as she turns towards the door.

She comes back to the bed and picks it up. As she goes out, she drops it in the waste-bin. I look quickly back at Stanley but his eyes are closed.

His lips move as if something in the space behind them can't get out. 'Nobody,' he says, and sighs.

'What's the matter, Stanley. Are your lips dry?' There's a swab next to the bed. I dip it in the water jug and press it to his lips. He mutters: 'Nobody.'

'Nobody what?'

He blinks a few times and then sinks back. 'Nobody will ever love you.......' He frowns.

'Nobody will ever love me? Stanley, that's unfair.' But then it strikes me that it could be someone else he's talking to. There is a pause. His tongue is struggling to get the words out.

'Nobody will ever love you as much as I did...'

'Maybe you could let the family know,' the nurse says. 'I doubt he'll last through the night.'

I whisper: 'Are you certain he can't hear you?'

'Oh no. He'll be well away.'

I pause and stretch my hand towards him, but my fingers curl up. The nurse leaves the room. I gather up my handbag and stand for a moment by the bed. 'I'm going, Stanley,' I say, just in case he's listening. 'I hope you feel better in the morning.' There is no response. I pat the sheet next to his hand and turn away.

As I go past the waste-bin I bend down and take the drawing out. It's creased across the centre and I smooth it out against my leg. When I glance back at him, his eyes are open but they're gazing past me.

'I'll look after this,' I say. 'I'll take good care of it.' I slip the drawing in my bag and stand there for a moment, not sure if it's me he's looking at or something else. His skin is luminescent. There's a faint glow round his head as if his face is lit up by a low watt light bulb from within.

I blow a kiss. 'Safe journey,' I say, as I close the door behind me. 'Pass on my regards to Hilda when you see her.'

END

Acknowledgements

Many people – friends, colleagues and other writers - have contributed towards this book, either directly or by way of encouragement. I owe them all a debt of gratitude. 'Pippa', to whom the book is dedicated, gave invaluable advice after reading the first draft. Laurie Robertson, my agent at Peters Fraser & Dunlop, has been unstinting in her enthusiasm and went far beyond the call of duty in reading, editing and suggesting improvements to subsequent drafts. The cover painting 'Homage to Stanley Spencer', the discovery of which was such an unexpected stroke of serendipity, was painted by a former tutor of mine at Edinburgh College of Art, a protegé of Stanley Spencer's. The image was kindly leant by his son Andrew Clarke. It's been an added bonus to have that direct link with the past.

Few, except perhaps his wife Hilda, would have suggested Stanley Spencer was an easy man to live with. His obsession with his muse, Patricia Preece, like everything else in his life, was totally consuming. Patricia's dependence upon Dorothy, her long time lover, was similarly all-embracing. Hilda loved Stanley who loved Patricia who loved Dorothy. For more than a decade they fought and sashayed their way heedlessly towards the edge of the abyss.

I have based my reconstruction of those years on letters, diaries and biographies of Stanley Spencer, plus a memoir written by Patricia Preece. The women's lives are not well documented although Dorothy, like Hilda was a gifted artist in her own right.

Of the four, Patricia, with no obvious talents other than her looks, has not been kindly judged by history. I've made her the narrator, not because she was the most deserving but because I wanted her to have a voice, even if she damned herself with it. 'The Lovers and the Dustman' is her story.

***

Printed in Great Britain
by Amazon